PRAISE FOR THE
FRANCES DOUGHTY
MYSTERY SERIES

'If Jane Austen had lived a few decades longer, and
spent her twilight years writing detective stories,
they might have read something like this one.'

Sharon Bolton, bestselling author of the Lacey Flint series

'I feel that I am walking down the street in
Frances' company and seeing the people
and houses around me with clarity.'

Jennifer S. Palmer, Mystery Women

'Every novelist needs her USP: Stratmann's
is her intimate knowledge of both pharmacy
and true-life Victorian crime.'

Shots Magazine

'The atmosphere and picture of Victorian
London is vivid and beautifully portrayed.'

www.crimesquad.com

'Vivid details and convincing period dialogue
bring to life Victorian England during the early
days of the women's suffrage movement, which

increasingly appeals to Frances even as she strives
for acceptance from the male-dominated society of
the time. Historical mystery fans will be hooked.'

Publishers Weekly

'[Frances'] adventures as a detective, and the slowly
unravelling evidence of multiple crimes in a murky
Victorian setting, make for a gripping read.'

Historical Novel Review

'The historical background is impeccable.'

Mystery People

A FRANCES DOUGHTY MYSTERY

MURDER
AT THE
BAYSWATER
BICYCLE
CLUB

LINDA STRATMANN

The
Mystery
Press

This book is dedicated to my husband Gary, who learned to ride a penny-farthing just for me, and Edwin J. Knight, who taught him how.

First published 2018

The Mystery Press, an imprint of The History Press
The Mill, Brimscombe Port
Stroud, Gloucestershire, GL5 2QG
www.thehistorypress.co.uk

© Linda Stratmann, 2018

The right of Linda Stratmann to be identified as the Author
of this work has been asserted in accordance with the
Copyright, Designs and Patents Act 1988.

British Library Cataloguing in Publication Data.
A catalogue record for this book is available from the British Library.

ISBN 978 0 7509 8440 9

Typesetting and origination by The History Press
Printed and bound by CPI Group (UK) Ltd

PREFACE

Summer 1881

Morton Vance was riding for his life, and he knew it. The worst of his predicament was that he couldn't be sure exactly who wanted to kill him, or even how many of them there might be. He had found himself in the miserable and terrifying position of being able to trust no one, even, and in fact most especially, his fellow members of the Bayswater Bicycle Club.

What had started out as a pleasant and healthful exercise on a tranquil afternoon had led him into a nightmare. He had stumbled across the unthinkable, the unimaginable. It had taken time for his mind to accept what he had seen, to recognise that it was a horrible truth, and not a cruel prank or a delusion. Now he could not erase the sight from his mind. All he knew was that he had to get away as fast as possible.

More than ever he was thankful for the smooth and efficient performance of his new mount, the Excelsior, with its hollow front forks, sprung saddle, robust rubber tyres and 50-inch front wheel, so much better than the old boneshaker on which he had first learned to ride. As his feet pounded at the pedals, wheels throwing up little puffs of dust like smoke almost as if they were on fire, he wondered with grim irony if he was breaking a record, or achieving a personal best at least. He was certainly breaking the law, but that couldn't be helped. For once he actually hoped he might meet a constable on the road who would want to pull him up for furious driving. A stiff fine was the least of his worries.

He was riding south down Old Oak Common Lane, and would normally have turned right into East Acton, but that was now the one place he had to avoid at all costs. He rode on, with broad open fields on either side, his path flanked by ditches and hedgerows, and the long culvert covering the flow of the old Stamford Brook, passing the occasional low stone cottage and sensing from time to time the hot reek of a pigsty. The worst threats here were the dry rutted road that could without warning cause a spill over the handlebars, and a possible encounter with Sam Linnett the pig keeper, who hated all bicyclists and never lost the opportunity of taking his horse-whip to a passing wheelman. Vance fixed his determination on one task; all he had to do was reach the Uxbridge Road and the well-populated route into Hammersmith and he would be safe.

In the warm quiet of the summer's day, with barely a breeze to cool him, he began to hear what he had most dreaded, a whisper of sound behind, a narrow gauger on packed earth, the faint crunch of dry mud under rubber and metallic singing of turning cranks. He risked a rapid glance over his shoulder, and as he feared it was another bicycle, still too far away for him to recognise the rider, only that he was in the Bayswater club uniform; but whoever he was, he was pedalling fast and gaining.

Vance redoubled his efforts, but he was tiring, and the other man was better, fresher, long legs pumping strongly. He knew that he must be nearing a sharp curve in the road up ahead, and looked for the white marker post that acted as a warning sign, telling bicyclists that it was time to check their speed, but either he had failed to see it in his panic, or it was missing, and now, to add to his woes, he was unsure of exactly where he was and what he should do. It was a risk, but he kept going.

Moments later he saw the overhanging branches that signalled the curve in the road only yards away, and was obliged to put some back pressure on the pedals, to slow as much as he dared so as to avoid a spill. At least he knew his pursuer would have to do the same.

When he saw the new danger ahead it was far too late to avoid it. He tried to slow further, as safely as he could, knowing that too sudden a stop would only propel him forwards, parting him from the machine. He would then be offered the choice of all men who came a cropper from such a height, a broken skull or a flattened nose. The handlebars rocked in his grip as the heavy front wheel juddered and twisted, but his palms were sweating and he had still not come to a halt before he lost control. He made a last desperate swerving skid before the inevitable collision. It was side on, but more than enough to violently dislodge him, and he crashed out of the saddle and onto the rocky path, his stockinged shins cracking against the handlebars, his shoulder driving into the baked mud and collapsing with the unmistakable sound of fracturing bones, a thump on the side of his head following for good measure.

At last he came to rest, the dented frame of his prized Excelsior lying across him, its steel backbone warm like a living thing. Dazed and nauseous, his chest heaving for breath, he gazed up at the bright sun, knowing that this was his last pain-free moment before his shocked body began to register its injuries.

The other rider, perhaps more skilled, and having more time to react, must have avoided a crash, for he heard no sound of violent contact. Instead, there was a brief grinding of rubber on earth, signalling a sudden stop. A few moments later Vance heard footsteps coming towards him. Sweat dripped into his eyes, but despite the heat he began to shiver. A figure stood over him, a black silhouette against the clear bright sky. All hope of help vanished. He thought of his parents; he thought of Miss Jepson and the things he had meant to say to her and never had, and now never would. The figure did not speak. He was holding something, a staff or a cudgel, and raised it up purposefully over the fallen man. Vance closed his eyes.

CHAPTER ONE

Summer 1882

'Good afternoon, Miss Doughty.'

On a clear and sunny afternoon, Miss Frances Doughty, often hailed in the popular press as London's premier lady detective, was taking the air in Hyde Park, when as if by chance, she met a middle-aged gentleman of respectable demeanour.

As every government agent knows, if secrecy is essential there is no better place to hide oneself than in a teeming and diverse crowd of persons all earnestly devoted to their own individual business. The great undulating space of parkland, dotted here and there with clumps of craggy trees, was crossed by many paths along which groups of strolling visitors were strung like beads on silk, inhaling the grassy perfume, admiring clusters of flowering shrubs and whispering words of scandal, intrigue or romance. The more drably clad males of the species were accompanied and outshone by their ladies, who greeted the sun in brightly coloured dresses and straw bonnets garnished with ribbons. If the park was a little scant of shady woodland in which to linger, this was more than compensated for by small forests of parasols. There were solitary figures, too, artists with their sketchbooks and pencils trying to capture the refinements of nature, and idle youths lying on the cool thick grass and contemplating nothing at all.

At that hour of the day all the public gates were open, and far more persons were eager to enter the park than were prepared to depart. It was time for the fashionables to make themselves known, and promenade around the carriage drive in the kind of elegant equipages that most Londoners could only inhabit in their dreams. So profuse were they that vehicles slowed with every new arrival and occasionally even stopped altogether, giving the strolling crowds the chance to pause and speculate on which noble personages might be within. There were other carriages, too, a little brighter and smarter, the horses coiffed to perfection, which, it was believed, were occupied not by the higher ranked ladies of society but by the female gentility of quite another world, who attracted many curious eyes. Their smiles, at least, were offered gratis.

The early morning bathers had long departed the grey waters of the Serpentine, and their places had been taken by boats, both of the narrow variety propelled by diligent oarsmen and the miniature wooden sailing vessels of children, adding laughter and ripples to the atmosphere. Later that evening, as the sun declined and the hour of dinner approached, the park would be quiet, almost deserted, the carriages gone, the horses gone, the hire boats drawn up onto the banks of the Serpentine like beached dolphins, and new inhabitants would arrive, those for whom the turf was the only soft place where they might lay their heads, and others whose only thoughts were of mischief.

That afternoon, however, a lady and a gentleman who had important business to discuss without anyone taking particular notice, might well use Hyde Park for a secret meeting.

Frances took the gentleman's arm, and after strolling for a few moments they found a bench and sat side by side, looking for all the world like a modestly clad niece enjoying the pretty scene with her favourite uncle. In all their meetings, Frances had never learned his name, or even asked for it, but he was a pleasant looking silver-haired man approaching sixty, who inspired both confidence and respect.

'I trust you are well?' he asked. There was a note of caution in his voice, and the creases around his eyes deepened with concern. It was more than just the usual polite enquiry.

Frances' reply was strong and confident, yet calm. She knew that she often sounded and looked more confident than she felt, but her profession required it, and the deception had become easier with time. 'I am, thank you, very well indeed.'

'Last year we had some fears for your health.'

'As did I, and my friends, but I am fully restored now,' she assured him. 'There were some terrible times, tragedies, actions on my part that I regret, and always will, and I still mourn those who are lost, but life continues, as it must. I continue.'

His expression eased and he nodded approvingly. 'I am glad to hear it, because we have a new mission for you, and I wanted to be sure you could undertake it. It is,' and he permitted himself a pause, 'a little different from what you have been asked to do before. You may refuse it if you wish.'

'Tell me,' said Frances. 'I am ready.'

A cluster of young women walked past, deep in conversation, stabbing the air with little trills of laughter. The gentleman was silent until they were out of earshot. 'In two weeks' time, the Bayswater Bicycle Club will be holding its annual summer meeting. There will be a large gathering of spectators, races, displays, sales of goods, a band, prize-giving, light luncheon and afternoon tea. You will attend.'

'That sounds very pleasant. Where will the event be held?'

'At Goldsmith's Cricket Ground, East Acton. The club's chief patron is Sir Hugo Daffin, a long-time enthusiast of the wheel who lives in Springfield Lodge nearby. The club members use rooms in his house for meetings and social events, and those who are unable to keep their bicycles at home in town can store them in his coach house together with the machines that are owned by the club and kept for hire to the public.'

'And what must I do?'

He gave her a searching look softened by a slight smile. 'As little as possible. Observe. Listen. Take great care not to draw attention to yourself. If you notice anything that strikes you as unusual, or suspicious, make a note of it. Remember, but write nothing down. As ever on these occasions, if your true intentions are suspected we will not admit to having sent you. And at the first hint of danger, you must leave at once.'

Frances absorbed this, but had to admit that there was little enough to absorb. 'Can you tell me nothing more? For what am I looking or listening?'

The gentleman considered this question for a while, and she guessed that he was debating with himself how much he might safely tell her. At length he spoke again. 'We believe that the club is being used by unscrupulous and traitorous persons to carry secret messages and stolen documents to anti-government agents. The bicycle is a fast and silent mode of transport unimpeded by the usual vagaries of horses or weight of traffic. The club structure and current enthusiasm for the bicycle, the many informal and recreational journeys taken at all hours of the day, and even at night, are the perfect concealment for this activity. We don't know who is organising this, it could be anyone, not necessarily even a member of the club, perhaps a relation or an associate, but the club is somehow at the centre of it. We know this because of a message intercepted by one of our agents, but the messenger himself could not or would not tell us any more except that he had been paid for his services in the usual way. We kept a watch on him, but he managed to elude us and we have not been able to trace his whereabouts.'

Frances was thoughtful. 'I seem to recall reading that a member of the club was murdered last year.'

'Yes, the club secretary Morton Vance. He was killed by a pig farmer who had a grudge against bicyclists.'

'Do you think there was a connection between the murder and the traitorous activities?'

'Naturally we considered it, but on the whole, we think not. The farmer, Sam Linnett, was an illiterate brute, and a thoroughly untrustworthy type. Not a man one could rely upon to keep secrets. A criminal agency wishing to conceal its activities would not employ him for choice, and there is no evidence that he was paid for what he did. As for Vance, we have made careful enquiries and discovered nothing against him. A member of a respectable family, he had no unsavoury associates, and left a modest estate all accounted for by his salary and a small inheritance.'

'I see,' said Frances. The murder and subsequent trial had been fully reported in the *Bayswater Chronicle*, and she resolved to refresh her memory on the subject when she returned home.

'We have sent a male agent to join the club, and participate in its activities,' the gentleman continued, 'but it would be useful to have a lady present as she might learn something from conversation that a man might not. But don't be deceived – the people concerned may appear reputable, but they will be ruthless and dangerous. For that reason you must not go alone. Take a small party of friends, and it must be composed of people you trust above all others. They, too, must be subject to the same rules as yourself. Quiet observation, no more. Reveal to them only that you are watching for criminal behaviour, although I understand that your associate Miss Smith knows more of your affairs than most. You must confide your true purpose to no one else.'

Frances was surprised. 'Not even the police?'

His gaze hardened. 'Most especially not the police, as we hope our mission will proceed without anyone suspecting what is occurring. If they should need to be informed, it is we who will take that decision, and not you.'

Frances sensed a difficulty. 'These events attract a substantial crowd. What if I encounter someone who knows me, and guesses that I am there for work and not recreation? That is a possibility.'

'We have every confidence that you will be able to deal with that eventuality.'

There was no point in contradicting him. 'I suppose even a detective can enjoy a day of leisure. Very well, the first person I shall consult is a good friend who took up bicycling last spring, and is a member of the club. He assures everyone who he meets that it is the finest sport in the world. Often at some length – and in very great detail.'

The gentleman smiled. 'Yes, we know. Mr Cedric Garton. He is your introduction to bicycling.'

'Ah, now I see why you have offered this task to me.' Frances' mind inevitably drifted to a story she had read not long ago, a penny publication called *Miss Dauntless Rides to Victory*, by W. Grove, in which the valiant heroine had leaped onto a bicycle on which she had pursued and captured a criminal. Miss Dauntless was an invention of the writer, a lady detective who dared do all a man might do and far more. Some of Frances' clients assumed that this fictional Amazon was a thinly disguised portrait of herself, and she was obliged to disabuse them of that belief very firmly. She might have been annoyed with Mr Grove, except for what had transpired at their one and only meeting. He had then been rather dashingly and mysteriously arrayed in a long black cloak and Venetian mask, and had proceeded to save her from certain death. So relieved was he to find that she was unhurt that he had then clasped her warmly in his arms, a familiarity which under the circumstances it would have been churlish for her to refuse. Frances could still recall the pleasing aroma of his Gentleman's Premium Ivory Cleansing Soap. She wondered where he was now, and what he might be doing.

'Miss Doughty?'

Frances realised that she had been daydreaming. 'I'm sorry. I was thinking … I was thinking … er … do I need to learn to ride a bicycle?'

To her surprise the gentleman laughed gently. 'Oh, dear me no. The bicycle is not for the female sex. Well, not unless they are persons of a certain kind – in a circus and therefore improperly dressed – or possibly French. Ladies, and older gentlemen, married gentlemen who do not wish to risk life and limb, prefer the tricycle, or indeed the 'sociable', that is a machine which permits two persons to ride side by side.'

'Well that sounds very pleasant. I should like to see that.'

'Then you accept the mission?'

'I do.'

The gentleman had a folded newspaper under his arm, which he handed to Frances. 'You will find the information you need in there.'

Frances took the newspaper. She knew better than to unfold it in public. There was an envelope lying between the pages and she would open it and study the contents when she was alone.

On the other side of the Serpentine music began to play, a lively tune emanating from the bandstand that nestled amongst the trees of Kensington Gardens.

'I must leave you now,' said the gentleman, rising to his feet and taking a packet of cheroots from his pocket. 'I have one more word of advice. If you should meet a man called Gideon, he is your friend.' He stuck a match and lit the cheroot. 'We have never met. This conversation never happened.' He walked away.

CHAPTER TWO

Dainty ladies who valued their pale complexions might have taken a cab home, but Frances, whose overly tall angular figure could never be thought dainty, liked the sunlight, and enjoyed a walk in fine weather. When her father, William Doughty, had been alive, and she had been little more than an unpaid servant in his chemist's shop on Westbourne Grove, his extreme parsimony had required Frances to walk almost everywhere, and even now that she could afford to travel by cab, she often chose not to. Long walks cleared her mind, as well as exercising her body. A mystery that might have puzzled her as she sat by her own fireside could sometimes be brought to a clear and obvious solution as she walked. The worries and frustrations of daily life were eased by her brisk vigorous stride, and she would arrive home refreshed rather than weary.

After the gloom and distress of last autumn and winter, the warm weather had brought Frances a kind of rebirth. Weeks of suffering that might have crushed another person had only served to prove to her that she could endure terrible trials and they would not weaken her; in fact, in a way that she did not fully understand, she felt stronger than before.

In the spring she had at last shed the grey demi-mourning she had worn in memory of her father and older brother, and found new shades of quiet blue and subtle violet, restrained yet pleasing. Her mirror showed her a new woman, one who, while still very young, had a world of experience behind her eyes, and was eager for more. Not only had she healed and flourished, there lay in the deepest recesses of her mind another thought, a tantalising possibility that she could be better still, in ways that she was yet to discover.

The detective business was doing well. Frances tried to avoid fame and drama, although she was not always successful in this, especially since her natural curiosity and instinct to solve a puzzle prompted her to pursue enquiries even when unasked. Her clients, who included some of the most respectable denizens of Bayswater, valued her industry and discretion. She was careful, however, never to allow her portrait to appear in any publication. Her government missions made it imperative that her face was not widely known.

Frances had not encountered any cases of serious crime for some months. Small thefts, missing persons and pets, suspicious behaviour connected with love and marriage, disputes with neighbours; these were the humdrum events by which she earned her daily bread. Swiftly dealt with, usually without unhappy traces remaining. Sadly, one could rarely draw a line under felonies; catastrophes whose spreading stain of loss and shame reached determinedly into the future. Her work had left her with few enemies. Those criminals she had brought to justice had received the penalty of the law; others whom she merely suspected but whose guilt could not be proved had fled to new lives.

There was one remaining anxiety; the evil and malodorous criminal known as the Filleter due to his sharp knife and lack of restraint in using it. It was Frances who had apprehended him during the widespread terror in the autumn of 1881 caused by the horrible murders of the Bayswater Face-slasher, indeed for some time he had been suspected of actually being that shadowy figure. The Filleter had been confined at Paddington Green Police Station, but before he could be charged, a destructive storm had swept through London, and the station roof had collapsed into the cells. The prisoner, his body horribly crushed, was taken to hospital where he lay close to death for some weeks before his foul associates came to remove him. Months later, he remained too broken to prowl the streets, and in any case, Bayswater had become a little too dangerous for his liking. He was now, so Frances had been informed, conducting his nefarious business south of the Thames, where he controlled a youthful gang of criminals. If he held her responsible for his infirmity, and meant to exact his revenge, he would have agents who would know where to find her, and might be waiting their moment.

As Frances approached the exit from Hyde Park on that delightful afternoon she found the Italian water gardens more alluring than ever, and paused to admire them. The white marble urns gleamed in the sunlight, and the delicious spray of the fountains cooled the air. She had once been told that this beauty had been created by love, a gift to the Queen from Prince Albert, her adored and adoring consort. Frances, wondering if the Queen herself had stood on this very spot and found peace and pleasure, could not help but reflect on the Queen's married happiness and how tragically it had been cut short. Was it better to be so beloved only to be left cruelly alone, or never to have found love at all?

Frances dismissed those difficult musings from her mind and walked on; all her wits would be needed when crossing the teeming thoroughfare of Bayswater Road. Safe at last in the shadow of the lofty white villas that faced the park, she devoted her thoughts to those she would ask to accompany her on her new mission. Happily, she had no difficulty in identifying her most trusted allies.

Sarah Smith had once been the Doughtys' maid-of-all-work, when the family had lived in apartments above the chemist's business on Westbourne Grove. More than that, however, she had been the closest female companion of Frances' childhood, her friend, her support in times of trouble, and the nearest she had ever known to a sister. When Frances launched her career as a detective Sarah had proved to be both an invaluable assistant and strong right arm. She was the only one of Frances' associates who was aware of the occasional government missions, and often felt concerned that she had not yet been asked to play a part, if only to ensure her friend's safety. Brought up by the East London dockside as the only girl in a family of nine siblings, Sarah was forthright and practical, stood no nonsense from anyone, male or female, and seemed to fear nothing. Her brother Jeb, a boxer known as the Wapping Walloper, had been heard to say that if Sarah had ever gone into the ring, there were many men she might have left the worse for wear.

Cedric Garton was Frances' near neighbour and friend, who lived in a beautifully decorated apartment with his faithful and attentive manservant, Joseph. Cedric had been born in Italy, where his family was engaged in the export of wine, but after visiting London for the inquest on his brother, a Bayswater art dealer, he had been obliged to remain to deal with the complicated issues that had arisen from that loss. Cedric liked to adopt the air of a languidly idle aesthete, which concealed a fine brain and a strong active physique. Bicycles were his new passion.

Tom Smith had once been the Doughty chemist shop's delivery boy, and was said to be Sarah's cousin. Frances had long suspected that the family relationship was far closer, and most probably the reason behind Sarah's glowering contempt for most men, whom she liked to instruct, sometimes quite forcefully, on the correct way to treat women. Sarah would have been fourteen when he was born, the same as Tom's present age, and as he grew to young manhood the resemblance between their facial features became increasingly obvious. An enterprising youth, Tom spent every waking moment considering how to make money, and had built up a thriving business, a message and delivery service known as 'Tom Smith's Men', with nothing but hard work, dedication and careful conservation of his resources. He had a clear ambition in life, to own property, become very rich and marry Miss Pearl Montague, the niece of the chemist shop's new owner. No member of Miss Montague's family, least of all the enchanting maiden, suspected that she was the object of Tom's silent and respectfully distant adoration. Tom, and anyone who knew him well, had no doubts that in time all his ambitions would be realised.

'Ratty' was the nickname of a fifteen-year-old boy who had spent much of his early life without a home following a family tragedy that had deprived him of his parents. He was Tom Smith's best agent, and since meeting Frances had developed ambitions to become a detective. He currently assisted her enquiries, managing his own group of boys whose eyes and ears were all over Bayswater. Fast on his feet, Ratty knew West London as if he had an unrolled map in his head. His courage and initiative were beyond question.

For some months, Sarah had been walking out with Professor Pounder, the proprietor of a high-class sporting academy that taught the gentlemanly art of pugilism. Cedric exercised there, and regarded his instructor with considerable respect. Sarah had begun teaching female-only classes, demonstrating to Bayswater ladies how to exercise themselves for health and take care of their safety, preferably with a concealed weapon. It was there that Frances had learned the art of the Indian club, a practice of rhythmic manipulation that helped her strength and dexterity and brought peace to her mind in times of trouble. The Professor was tall, athletic, good-looking, calm and quietly spoken. His devotion to Sarah was tangible in a way that did not need to be expressed. Although Frances had not known him for long she could recognise that he was utterly dependable when any kind of danger was present. She also knew that for a man to earn Sarah's trust he had to be truly exceptional.

Before plunging into the long terraces of Bayswater proper, Frances studied the traffic of cabs, carriages and delivery carts, and the surging mass of shiny-flanked labouring horses. In amongst them, daring and darting, were young men on bicycles. Now she thought about it, the bicycle was starting to appear on the London streets with increasing regularity. Barely four or five years ago one almost never saw a high-wheeled bicycle in town. It was a youthful novelty, and so fraught with risk that it was seen almost entirely as a countryside touring vehicle. The earlier invention, the velocipede, often referred to as a 'boneshaker' with, she had been assured, very good reason, was by comparison a heavier but slower and safer vehicle, whose wheels were more similar in size. Difficult to steer and a desperately uncomfortable ride on all but the smoothest of surfaces, it had nevertheless earned many dedicated adherents, principally for want of something better.

The velocipede, according to Cedric Garton, could never be the ultimate in wheeled rider-propelled vehicles. It had only ever been a promise of what might be possible in future. That future, Cedric had enthused, with all the verve of a recent convert, had come to its full flowering in the high-wheeler. It was fast, it was light, it was elegant, it was a beautiful design that brought pleasure to the senses and would last forever. There was the small matter of the danger of catching one's legs in the handlebars when taking a header on a sudden stop – a not infrequent occurrence – but great minds were working on that difficulty, and in the meantime one could always drape one's legs over the bars when running downhill.

The secret of the bicycle's speed was the enormous front wheel, which quite dwarfed the trailing wheel, and could reach heights of sixty inches, the choice depending on the leg length of the rider. The recent innovation of tubular steel for many of its parts had resulted in a machine that was both strong and light, and skimmed along with ease.

Despite Cedric's predictions, Frances could not imagine that bicycles could ever be truly useful in town, where riders balancing high on a slender wheel would have to try and steer a safe path between horse-drawn carriages, omnibuses and careless pedestrians. A stray dog, a stone or a nervous horse was all that was needed to cause a dreadful accident, and there had been several of late, resulting in grave injuries and even the deaths of both pedestrians and riders. It was unsurprising that from time to time bicyclists avoided muddy, crowded roads by taking to the pavement, much to the annoyance of those on foot. Newspapers were frequently bombarded with irate letters from citizens who declared bicycles to be a menace, and urged that they should be banned altogether. Occasionally frustrated waggoners would deliberately drive into bicyclists and knock them down.

On reaching Westbourne Grove, the vibrant heart of fashionable Bayswater and West London's leading shopping promenade, Frances left a message for Tom and Ratty at the office of Tom Smith's Men, and continued to Westbourne Park Road, where she left a similar message for Cedric Garton before taking the short walk to her home. Sarah had not yet returned, but was expected back for supper. Professor Pounder's whereabouts would not be hard to discover since he lived in the ground floor apartment of the same house in which Frances and Sarah occupied the first floor. The Professor often joined the ladies for supper, although there were also evenings when Frances was left alone with her thoughts and her reading and Sarah and her beau kept company.

The top floor of the house was home to a spinster lady who was engaged in works of charity, but she had recently announced her intention of quitting London at the end of the month, and going to those parts of the country where she felt her energies could be better applied. The landlady, Mrs Embleton, was already looking for a new tenant. Frances could not help wondering if Mrs Embleton might be concerned that prospective tenants would be anxious about sharing an apartment house with a private detective and a professor of pugilism, a house, moreover, which had once been the scene of a violent death for which one of the occupants had been responsible. Mrs Embleton, although a kind and understanding lady, had seen a great deal of upset both in the house and immediately outside it since Frances had taken lodgings there, and more than once it had been touch and go as to whether the troublesome tenant might be asked to leave. Although Frances took great care never to be late with the rent, and had once been of service to Mrs Embleton in a small matter of some stolen washing, for which she had made no charge, she still felt her situation to be precarious.

Frances had therefore decided to put a suggestion to her landlady that Tom Smith and Ratty should take the upper lodgings. They had been living in cramped circumstances in a corner of their office space on Westbourne Grove, but the rapid and profitable expansion of their business had made this situation increasingly difficult. Tom was always looking for talented and hardworking boys to employ, and he often found them living on the street in miserable and unhealthy conditions. He offered them regular paid work, somewhere warm and safe to lay their heads, as much day-old bread as they could manage, and copious libations of hot tea. Now that their ablest lieutenant Dunnock had reached the advanced age of thirteen, he was considered mature enough to supervise the more junior agents in the absence of the main men. Tom and Ratty at last felt able to enjoy their success by luxuriating in their very own bachelor apartment, and were eager to move in.

Although Frances had been advised that the murder of a member of the Bayswater Bicycle Club in the previous year was not thought to be connected with the subject of her mission, she could not help but reflect on it, while reminding herself that this was one occasion when she did need to keep her curiosity in check. If she was to attend a race meeting, however, she ought first to find out all she could about the club, its members and its history. Frances was a close reader of the *Bayswater Chronicle*, copies of which she saved for reference, and determined that once she was home she would search her collection for the trial report. Still more than the murder of the unfortunate wheelman, however, there was something else on her mind, an insistent provoking little idea that no matter how hard she tried, she could not control.

In her own cool and quiet parlour she might have opened the large brown envelope she had been handed by the silver-haired gentleman she had officially never met at a meeting that had never happened, or brought out her editions of the *Bayswater Chronicle*, but instead she made a nice pot of tea and sat down to consult her copy of the penny story *Miss Dauntless Rides to Victory* by W. Grove. She had not misremembered it – that annoyingly impossible Miss Dauntless really had sprung valiantly onto a high-wheeler and not a velocipede, and bowled along the road like a champion racer in pursuit of her quarry. Unfortunately, the engraving on the front cover did not offer any clues as to how the redoubtable heroine had actually achieved this feat, as it only showed the top half of the lady's unnecessarily buxom figure, and left the rest to the imagination. Now that Frances thought about it, from a practical point of view any woman who attempted to straddle such a vehicle would be unable to do so with any measure of decency or safety when encumbered by long heavy skirts and petticoats.

That conclusion ought to have been the end of any thoughts Frances might have entertained of learning to ride a bicycle, yet she remained unwilling to abandon the idea. She had noticed that Mr Grove's stories sometimes seemed to hold messages for her. Sarah had suggested that they were really thinly disguised love notes, but Frances was sure that they were something more. Before Mr Grove had appeared before her in his rather fetching cloak and mask, he had written a story in which Miss Dauntless was romanced by a man clad in exactly that way. It was as if he was preparing her to recognise and trust him. Was this story of Miss Dauntless and the bicycle a suggestion that she should learn to ride? Or was it simply a challenge to her determination, energy and ingenuity, to see if she could overcome the obstacles? If so, it was a challenge Frances felt she would like to accept.

CHAPTER THREE

Frances finished her tea and opened the envelope she had received in confidence. It contained a map of East Acton and the surrounding area, the last quarterly newsletter of the Bayswater Bicycle Club, and a notice of the arrangements for the annual meeting. There was to be a special parade of new vehicles, a competition for the best turned-out bicycle, and a busy programme of races over varying distances and for all classes of riders. This included a contest reserved for professional wheelmen, a competition for boys, novices' races, and a tricycle race for ladies. The prizes took the form of medals and cups generously donated by the club patron, Sir Hugo Daffin. The most sporting wheelman of the year, an award voted for by the committee, would have his name engraved on the Morton Vance memorial cup.

Frances frowned as she read that name, and then began to search back through her copies of the *Bayswater Chronicle* of 1881, which were stored in a neat pile on her dressing table. Since starting to keep her weekly issues for reference, she had accumulated some two years' supply, a measure that had saved her many a visit to the newspaper offices on Westbourne Grove. Her growing library also included street directories, maps and timetables. She might have been anxious that the collection would eventually outgrow the space allocated in her bedroom, but since she owned few personal luxuries, that eventuality was still some way in the future.

Recalling that the trial of the young bicyclist's killer had taken place at the Old Bailey during last year's autumn session, she located the report without difficulty. Sam Linnett, aged forty-eight, a pig farmer of Old Oak Common Lane, East Acton, had been tried for the murder of twenty-seven-year-old Morton

Vance, commercial clerk and secretary of the Bayswater Bicycle Club, who had been found battered to death the previous August.

Linnett, said the prosecution, was notorious for making unprovoked attacks on passing bicyclists, by cutting at them with a horsewhip or throwing stones. He had twice been arrested and appeared before the magistrates at Hammersmith Police Court, who had fined him for these offences. He was also in the habit of cutting staves from the hedgerows and leaving them lying in the path near the entrance to his farm, although there were no witnesses to him doing so. A horse, the learned gentleman pointed out for the benefit of the non-bicycling members of the jury, might pick its way neatly over such an obstruction, but a high-wheeler could be so unsettled, bouncing off the rough wood on its hard rubber tyres, that it would propel its rider violently to the ground, resulting in serious injury or even death. The court would hear from members of the Bayswater club who would testify that they had learned to be wary of Sam Linnett. Since the lane was the principal way between East Acton and the Uxbridge Road it was hard to avoid using it altogether. The club members had very sensibly placed a white-painted marker post as a warning to all riders that the farm entrance, which when approached from the north was partly concealed by a curve in the lane and overhanging hedgerows, was imminent. When wheelmen saw the marker post they knew to slow down and look out for potential danger, hoping not to encounter the irate pig-man. Some actually dismounted and walked past the farm entrance, wheeling their machines along, so as to be less vulnerable to attack, and any staves found lying in the road were picked up and thrown into the ditch.

That fatal afternoon, Morton Vance had been riding south down Old Oak Common Lane when he had collided with Sam Linnett's high-sided livestock cart, which had been turning into the farmyard, creating an impassable barrier across the width of the narrow roadway. The accident, if that was what it was, had resulted in broken bones; however, according to the prosecution, Sam Linnett had then descended from his cart, picked up a discarded stave and murdered Morton Vance with two hard blows to the skull, after which he had calmly proceeded about his business as if nothing had happened.

The jurymen, wrote the *Chronicle's* reporter, had looked on the accused with ill-concealed disgust. Sam Linnett had entered the dock in his stained workaday clothes, which in the warm, crowded and airless court exuded an eyewatering and stomach-turning reminder of his occupation. What appeared to be a permanent scowl was fixed to his face, although, said the *Chronicle*, it could not be determined whether this was evidence of how he felt about his unenviable position, or his everyday expression, revealing the monstrous character of the man.

Sam Linnett's defence counsel did his best for his unprepossessing client, explaining that there were mitigating circumstances that had caused the farmer's antagonism to bicyclists. A year earlier Linnett's only son Jack, then aged sixteen, had been driving the pig cart when his horse had shied and bolted on encountering a passing bicycle. The cart had overturned, and crushed the boy's leg. Although he had not lost the limb, he was now crippled for life. The defence gave a moving description of the fond father's overwhelming grief at this tragedy, asserting that since then Linnett had become excited to the point of insanity, and possibly even beyond, at the mere sight of a bicycle. It was this misfortune that had led him to make the attacks with whip and stones, and lay the staves, all of which offences he freely admitted. Linnett had given up laying staves after being warned about it by the police, and he had not made any attacks after being fined. He still shook his fist when he saw a bicyclist go past, but that was wholly understandable and could hardly be counted as a crime. This did not mean that Linnett had killed Morton Vance, an act he strongly denied. He had no quarrel with Vance as a man. The rider who had caused young Jack's calamity was not even a member of the Bayswater Bicycle Club. It was well known that he was a Mr Babbit of the Oakwood Bicycle Club, who, although he was not obliged to do so, had actually admitted some liability and paid the farmer a sum of money in compensation.

Sam Linnett, said the defence, made no secret of the fact that on the day of the fatality Morton Vance had collided with his cart; however, the accident had been entirely Vance's fault. His client utterly denied that he had deliberately used his cart to obstruct the roadway. The young bicyclist, he stated, had been riding down the lane at a dangerous speed and would have been able to stop and avoid a collision had he been proceeding at a sensible pace. The young man was lying in the road, very much alive, when Linnett had last seen him. He had no duty of care over Vance, and therefore had no compunction in leaving him where he lay, assuming that his associates would shortly come and assist him. The speed of the bicycle had led him to believe that Vance was racing, and that another man would arrive very soon. He didn't see another bicycle but then there was a slight bend in the road and some overhanging hedgerows just north of the farm, which would have hidden an approaching bicycle from his view.

Yes, Sam Linnett had abandoned a seriously injured man lying in the road, that much he admitted, but he had not killed Morton Vance. Another person, possibly a fellow bicyclist, must have arrived soon afterwards and committed the murder. The jurymen, according to the *Chronicle*, had narrowed their eyes sceptically at this unconvincing explanation.

There were several witnesses for the prosecution. Members of the bicycle club testified describing previous acts of violence towards bicyclists by Sam Linnett. Morton Vance, they said, was an excellent young man, a hard-working club secretary, who had not had a falling out with anyone. Particularly distressed in the witness box was fellow bicyclist Henry Ross-Fielder, who had discovered the body of his friend. There had been no doubt in his mind that Vance had already breathed his last and was beyond any help. He had known better than to appeal to the Linnetts for assistance in removing the body and had ridden to East Acton as fast as he could to get a carrier.

A surgeon, a Mr Jepson of Acton Town, who had examined the body, confirmed that Vance had died from blows to the head inflicted by some hard object. The collision with the cart would not have caused those injuries or been fatal. A stave found lying in the roadway was stained with blood, and hair resembling Vance's was sticking to it. He had no doubt that this was the murder weapon. He had also examined Linnett's pig cart and there were marks on it that looked as if they had been made by a recent collision with another vehicle. The bicycle, which was painted dark blue, was damaged, and he had found flakes of the same coloured paint on the pig cart.

Jack Linnett was called to give evidence and there were gasps of surprise and sighs of pity for the fine-looking youth who limped to the witness box on a twisted leg. His working clothes were rough but clean and well mended, and he did not bring the odour of the farmyard into the court with him. Many of the onlookers, including the *Chronicle's* correspondent, found it hard to believe that this was the true offspring of the surly degenerate in the dock. The young man's evidence, given quietly and with due respect to the court, was oddly unhelpful to either side. He said that he had not witnessed the accident, but recalled his father bringing the cart home on the day of the murder. Sam Linnett had mentioned only that a bicyclist had been racing down the lane and collided with the cart, but he had made no further comment, and had simply gone about his work and eaten his dinner as usual.

Even without the reporter's embellishments, Frances could imagine how well the pig-man's defence had been received in court. While the accused deserved some sympathy for his son's circumstances, and had in all probability acted in the heat of the moment, nevertheless he had a record of assaulting men who had had nothing to do with the accident involving his son and had unashamedly admitted his disgracefully callous behaviour towards a badly injured man.

The jury had taken several hours to reach a verdict and finally declared Sam Linnett guilty of murder, with a recommendation to mercy. That mercy had been denied, and Sam Linnett had gone to the gallows.

CHAPTER FOUR

There was one name in the trial record that was familiar to Frances, since she was sure she had seen it in the newspapers quite recently. She looked back through her copies of the *Chronicle* and found the trial of Robert Coote, unemployed, aged twenty-five. Some two months ago, Coote had been found guilty of aggravated assault causing actual bodily harm in a public place against the Reverend Duncan Ross-Fielder of Holland Park and resisting arrest, resulting in minor injuries to Police Constable Gordon. Although the Christian names differed and the clerical victim of the assault could not therefore have been the same man who found the body of Morton Vance, the unusual surname and the Holland Park location, not far from East Acton, suggested to Frances that the two were related.

Unusually, Coote had asked for permission to make a statement to the court. On learning of this request, his counsel had asked for time to consult with his client in private, and this had delayed the hearing by several minutes. When counsel and prisoner returned to the courtroom it was apparent from the strained manner of both men that there had been a heated exchange of words. Observers inferred that Coote's own defence had strongly advised him against making the statement. In the event, the court had denied the request. The nature of the statement remained a mystery, although it was rumoured that the prisoner was intending to make accusations against his victim that could not be substantiated, and counsel must have felt that this would hinder rather than assist his case. For the remainder of the trial, Coote stood silently in the dock, his mouth twitching with the words he wanted to be heard.

There were several witnesses to the crime. Coote had been seen lurking in the street near to Ross-Fielder's home for at least an hour before the assault. He had not attempted to beg from anyone else, but on seeing the reverend gentleman he had approached him with urgent demands for money. When this request was refused in the mildest of terms, he had then launched an unprovoked attack. The respected clergyman, aged fifty-three, had been punched, pushed to the ground and kicked violently. Several witnesses had cried out for help, and Constable Gordon, who had come running to the reverend's aid, had also been assaulted. A second policeman had been required to secure the struggling, abusive prisoner and remove him to the police station.

Coote, said the prosecution, had never previously met or been employed by Ross-Fielder, although he had recently been annoying him with a spate of barely literate letters asking for money. It was thought that he had made the clergyman a target of his demands because his victim was a man of honour, well known in West London for his service on a number of charitable bodies, and who gave alms by private donation.

The defence could only say in mitigation that his client was in straitened financial circumstances having lost his employment as a parcel carrier through no fault of his own. He was also distressed by the recent death of his widowed mother. He had come to court alone, and had no friends or family to assist and support him. Coote had freely admitted that he had written to the clergyman asking for money, and on receiving no reply had approached him in the street to beg assistance. When the reverend had instead directed him to an appropriate charity, he had been upset, and had simply lost his temper.

Had the incident occurred between two drinkers in a beer house, Coote might have been consigned to prison for six months, but violence towards both a clergyman and a policeman were more than the judge could stomach, and with many harsh words he sentenced Coote to eighteen months with hard labour.

As Frances waited and made her plans, her associates gathered. First to arrive was Sarah, who, once she knew what was proposed, quickly arranged a hearty supper of bread and butter with cold meat, cheese, pickles, hardboiled eggs and tomatoes, and sent the maid out to fetch strawberry tarts. Professor Pounder, who was next, was immediately deputed to bring bottled beer and cordials.

Cedric Garton arrived in lively form, freshly shaved and cologned, dressed in the newest and most fashionable gentleman's apparel with a flower in his buttonhole and eagerly enquiring why he had been summoned by Bayswater's finest detective. Tom and Ratty soon followed. Everyone assembled around the parlour table, piled their plates with food, helped themselves to their chosen beverages, and gazed at Frances expectantly.

'I have been asked to undertake a mission,' said Frances, nibbling the edge of a crusty slice with care, so as not to interfere with her address, 'and it is a very simple one, but one which may potentially have some danger attached to it. I have therefore been advised that for safety I should be accompanied by those people I trust most.' She looked about her and smiled. 'And here you all are, my dearest friends and associates, those who I know to be brave and clever and honest. My task will be undertaken while spending a delightful day out in East Acton for the annual summer race meeting of the Bayswater Bicycle Club.'

'My word!' exclaimed Cedric, almost dropping a neatly constructed sandwich of cold chicken. 'Well that won't be hard for me, as I am to attend that event myself. I am entered for the two-mile handicap, and the competition for the best turned-out machine. But what is your mission? Are you permitted to reveal the identity of the client?'

Frances had given a great deal of thought to how much she could reveal. 'All I am allowed to say is that my task is simply to observe my surroundings and take note of anything that might strike me as unusual. That may seem very simple, but it requires unceasing vigilance, and I am instructed to be very careful to do nothing adventurous that might attract attention.

'Mr Garton, your advice would be extremely valuable. I would like to learn all you know about the club and its members. It would be a very great help if you made a list of the gentlemen's names with notes of anything you know about them. You can include their friends and family too, if you have any information. But please, and this is very important, you must not ask any questions. If you make special enquiries of your own you might reveal too much in the wrong quarters.'

Cedric gazed at her enquiringly. 'And now I am more than a little concerned; not for myself, but for you. What, exactly, are the wrong quarters?'

'That, unfortunately, is the one thing I don't know, which explains the potential for danger. We can't tell who our friends and enemies are.' Apart, she thought, from the mysterious Gideon mentioned by the gentleman with silver hair. 'We must trust each other, of course, but we trust no one else. So you must assemble that list from memory alone.'

'You are stretching the capacity of my poor brain again,' sighed Cedric, smoothing his already smooth blond hair, 'but of course, for you, dear lady, as always I will do my best.'

'So there'll be dangerous types there?' asked Sarah, with an anticipatory glint in her eye.

'Possibly.'

Sarah cracked her knuckles. 'We can deal with them.'

Professor Pounder said nothing but he glanced at Sarah, and his expression spoke for him.

'But suspicious persons are not to be approached,' warned Frances. 'That rule is for us all. Should there be any hint of actual danger I am under strict instructions to leave at once.'

Cedric nodded approvingly. 'We'll keep you safe, have no fear!'

'That nasty Filleter won't be there, I hope?' said Sarah, wrinkling her nose with disgust.

'I doubt it,' said Frances. 'Even if he could be, and I understand that nowadays he is unable to walk unaided, he is a crude individual and this is a different matter altogether.'

'That filthy fellow would be spotted at once and thrown out of any sporting event,' declared Cedric. 'His picture was in all the illustrated papers last autumn, and I for one have made it my business to study his image and look out for him. I can promise you he has not been in Bayswater again, for which we can all be thankful.'

'But he will have agents,' said Frances, 'and they will be no better than he.' She glanced enquiringly at Tom and Ratty, who exchanged looks. Tom shook his head and swallowed a mouthful of cheese and pickle. 'Nah. We ain't seen 'im. An' if 'e's got men, we ain't seen 'em, either.'

'I find it hard to believe that any of the club members are involved in crime,' Cedric continued. 'They all seem such decent sorts.'

'How many members are there?'

'About a dozen or so I think. We meet up once a week for a club ride, and there are race meetings in clement weather and the most delightful social events in the winter.'

'Tell me about the patron, Sir Hugo Daffin.'

Cedric wielded a napkin with dexterity. 'Oh, he's a splendid fellow, must be sixty-five if he's a day, but he still rides around the village on his bicycle. We have suggested that he might be better advised to take up the tricycle but he'll have none of it. It's thought he must have been on two wheels since the days of the dandy-horse. He lives at Springfield Lodge in East Acton and the club uses his rooms to meet, and he has visiting wheelmen to stay when they are touring. He's dedicated to improving the lot of bicyclists and is forever patenting new inventions.'

'What kind of inventions?' asked Frances, scenting the possibility of work that might make the inventor the target of thieves.

'In the last few months he has been testing stabilising wheels for older gentlemen or novices who are nervous of riding high bicycles. And he has announced his intention of devising a more comfortable saddle.'

'Has his industry brought him much success?'

Cedric gave a little sigh of regret. 'To be truthful, no. I don't think he has found a manufacturer willing to risk his capital.'

There was a gentle cough from Professor Pounder, who, despite his height and breadth was so quiet that his presence in any location often went unnoticed. 'When we attend this meeting, what are we to look out for?'

'A good question,' Frances replied. 'I haven't been told that myself, but I think I can understand why. If my attention is directed in one particular way then I might miss something I am not anticipating. But here are my suggestions. Look for secret conversations, and things changing hands; behaviour that seems to be out of the common way. People at the event who just don't appear to be part of it, who look as though they might be there on business of their own. Anything you see or overhear that seems suspicious, remember it, and tell me. But write nothing down. The event will be held on a cricket field, so there will be a great deal of ground to cover. Tom, Ratty, I want you to keep your eyes sharp for useful information. Keep moving and looking about you. And please, don't get into trouble.'

Tom and Ratty exchanged looks again. It was always a little worrying when they did that, but Frances knew that any enquiry as to the reason would not prove informative.

'It would be best if we didn't all arrive as one party, which could seem unusual. There should be two groups. Mr Garton and I will travel up together with Ratty. Sarah, you can travel with Professor Pounder and Tom. We will look like families out for the day.' Frances consulted a directory issued by the London omnibus companies. 'There is no direct train to East Acton, and the green Bayswater omnibus to Acton does not make an early enough start, so we will make the journey by cab. The two parties must not appear to know each other, and will only communicate when it will not look like a pre-arranged meeting. If other persons introduce us, only then can we talk. Otherwise, Tom and Ratty, you will carry messages by word of mouth only, taking care that no one notices what you are doing. And Sarah and I have our hand signs, too.'

Sarah grinned and signalled agreement. She and Frances had made a study of sign language ever since taking a case involving a school for deaf children. It was an amusing diversion of an evening, and often useful.

''Ow much do these bicycles cost, then?' asked Tom, who was studying an advertisement in the club magazine.

'That depends,' said Cedric. 'A second-hand velocipede for a novice to learn on can be got for a pound or two. But a high-grade bicycle can be £20 or more.'

'An' 'ow fast c'n they go?'

'Velocipedes are heavier, with a much smaller front wheel, so only about seven miles per hour, eight at a pinch, depending on the road. High-wheelers can actually go ten, twelve miles per hour or even more with a strong rider.'

'And a nice fine for furious driving, if they do,' Frances reminded him.

'Gotter catch 'em first,' said Tom with a grin. Frances knew that Tom had been handing Sarah his business profits to invest, with the intention of buying property when he was old enough, but she could see the way his thoughts were tending; a fleet of bicycles with strong active boys taking messages and parcels about London far faster than any pedestrian or cab. Some firms would pay a premium price for such a service.

'You take care,' said Sarah sternly. 'There was a butcher's boy knocked off his bicycle and killed the other day when a horse shied. He was your age, too. Nasty business.'

Frances turned to Cedric. 'Did you ever meet Morton Vance?' The question took the others by surprise and she pushed her copy of the *Bayswater Chronicle* with the report of the trial of Sam Linnett across the table so they could see it. They all studied it intently.

Cedric shook his head. 'No, that was before I joined the club. Horrid business. I heard all about it from the members, of course. Vance was very well thought of. That Linnett must have been a savage type. His son is a good sort, though.'

'You know him?' said Frances, surprised.

'I've met him, yes. Numerous times. In a strange kind of way losing his father did him a good turn. He never wanted to be a pig farmer but didn't have much choice. The father deliberately kept him ignorant and useless for any better kind of work, so he could keep him on as a labourer. After the trial the pigs were sold off, the farm closed down, and the boy did what he had always wanted to do, got himself apprenticed to a blacksmith called Hicks in East Acton. He repairs bicycles and helps Daffin with his work, so you often see him around the lodge.'

Frances remained astonished. 'Isn't that awkward for the members, given his history? Do they not regard him as a sprig of his father? Does he bear no grudge against bicyclists?'

'You would think so on both sides, but no. The boy is quiet, intelligent and hard working. Nothing like the sire. He's sure to be at the races, helping to keep the machines in good trim.'

'It will be very interesting to meet him,' said Frances. She studied the club newsletter. 'It says here that the club rooms are open in the summer from four in the afternoon until seven on weekdays, nine a.m. to seven p.m. on Saturday, and from noon to seven on Sunday. So, I think it might be an idea if I made a preliminary visit quite soon, just to look about and get an impression of the place. Would you be willing to accompany me?'

'Certainly,' said Cedric. 'Whatever day you wish. The weather is fine, and we can have quite a jolly little outing.'

The meeting was done. Sarah cleared away the remains of the supper and she and Professor Pounder went down to the kitchen for a private talk over the dishes, while Tom and Ratty hurried away on fresh business. Frances was quietly thoughtful as she saw Cedric Garton to the door.

He paused in front of the hall mirror to check his grooming. 'You have something on your mind, dear lady. Are you permitted to tell?'

'You know me too well. Yes, there is another very particular thing you can assist me with, but I didn't want to mention it until we were alone.'

'Oh, mention away! My pleasure, as always.'

Frances took a deep breath. 'I want you to teach me how to ride a bicycle.'

CHAPTER FIVE

At four o'clock the following afternoon, a cab which had followed a circuitous route from Bayswater through Notting Hill and Holland Park and along the Uxbridge Road, brought Cedric Garton and his young companion to East Acton and the gates of Springfield Lodge. Mr Garton was jauntily dressed in the bicycle club uniform, which comprised a short coat and knee britches of dark grey, light grey stockings, black shoes well-shined, a flannel shirt with collar and cuffs of celluloid to avoid the ravages of excessive perspiration, and a light grey polo cap with a handkerchief attached to the back by dress hooks to protect the back of the neck from the sun. The cap was embellished with the Bayswater Bicycle Club badge, depicting a spring of water and the letters BBC entwined.

His companion, a tall slender youth, was conventionally dressed, yet despite this, appeared to be more self-conscious about his appearance. In particular he made regular adjustments to the position of his hat, which was perched awkwardly on his head and looked ready to fall off at the slightest provocation, an eventuality he took very seriously indeed.

There were two previous occasions on which Frances had, in her role as a detective, adopted male attire. She had been masquerading as a newspaper correspondent in her late brother's suit of clothes when she had first met Cedric Garton, an event that often stimulated a misty-eyed reminiscence in that gentleman. For her second impersonation she had purchased a better-fitting suit, and Cedric had instructed her how to stand and walk so as to avoid being discovered as a female. Frances had found that if she spoke as little as possible, and did not display the smoothness of her face too closely or under a revealing light, she could carry off the deception rather well. She was aware, however, that women who dressed as men often did so for a criminal purpose and found themselves in court accused of theft or fraud, and it would cause serious harm to her reputation if she were found out. The private cab kept her safe from risk of exposure and enabled useful conversation.

'I shall introduce you today as my cousin Frank Williamson,' said Cedric. 'That will avoid any difficulty later on when you attend the race meeting under your *nom de guerre*, and the resemblance is noticed. You will then simply be Frank's sister, and that will explain everything. This afternoon, however, you will be taken for a handsome boy.'

'That is the best plan,' agreed Frances, pushing stray strands of hair under her hat.

'And what will Frank's charming sister be called?'

'Rose,' said Frances, almost without thinking, her mind still dwelling on her recent reunion with her mother Rosetta. Having been estranged for so many years it was curious to think that she had a mother at all, but the process of growing close had been and continued to be one that gave both of them great comfort and pleasure.

'And whichever sex you may choose to be on any such visit, you must address me as Cedric. In fact,' he paused and gave her a serious yet affectionate look, 'I would be honoured if Miss Doughty was to call me Cedric also, and if I might be permitted to address her as Frances. We are practically cousins in reality after all!'

Frances smiled her agreement. 'Of course!'

'Since we last spoke I have been working my poor brain half to death with the list you have asked for, but it is almost done and I promise to deliver it to you this evening. In the meantime, I will endeavour to answer any questions you might have.'

It was Frances' first venture into that part of Middlesex. Her map, which she had studied carefully, told her what she could not see, that just north of the dwellings and old inns that lined the Uxbridge Road there was a bleak row of brick yards and clay pits and beyond those an expanse of farmland, bordered to the west by Old Oak Common Lane, which was almost unpopulated at its southern end. At its furthest northern extreme, the lane was flanked with cottages, and curved east to meet the open public common of Wormwood Scrubs with its military exercise field and rifle range. Just south of the common was a prison, which had been in the process of enlargement by the hard labour of its own convicts for some years.

The cab turned north up the narrow lane, rattling and lurching over the uneven track, and for a while there were no more houses to be seen. Frances knew that before reaching the turn into East Acton they would pass the spot where Morton Vance had met his end at the hands of Sam Linnett, and she stared out of the window, but given the anonymous long green hedgerows, it was hard to make it out. 'Can you point out the location of Morton Vance's murder?' she asked.

'I don't really know this path very well, I've only ever ridden it once or twice, but I think that's the old pig farm, coming up on our right,' said Cedric, helpfully.

They were past it too quickly for a good look. Frances only saw the ungated entrance to a farmyard, and then it was behind them. Not very far ahead the cab turned left into East Acton Lane, a village street with a smoother surface to its roads. This was a quiet place of well-behaved people who took pride in their surroundings. On their right was a stud farm and orchards, to the left the sprawling estate known as The Grange. Large handsome houses stood contentedly in their own grounds and there were smaller but equally well-kept cottages. A little further on, just where the roadway divided in two with a long central green between its branches, was a long stone wall clearly announcing that a private estate was within, and an opening ahead that must surely lead into a carriage drive.

'Is this the place?' Frances asked.

'It is indeed,' said Cedric. Frances was expecting the cab to turn into the carriage drive, but to her surprise Cedric asked the driver to stop short of the entrance in the village street. She wondered for a moment if there had been a mistake, but then reminded herself that her companion was a frequent visitor.

The masquerade proper had begun, and the first part was when Cedric, deeming it unnecessary to help his boyish cousin Frank descend from the cab, obliged Frances to make her own trousered way down the steps. Cedric paid the driver and the cab drew away, leaving them standing in the deserted street. 'And now the fun will begin!' said Cedric, striding away. Frances followed.

Springfield Lodge was not at all what Frances had imagined. The perimeter wall was so ancient and ivied it looked like the entrance to a mythical castle where one might expect to find the occupants in an enchanted slumber. The gates, however, were open; indeed, they appeared to have been wedged in that position for some years, the curls of ironwork being so brown with rust that they looked like plant stems with roughened bark growing out of the soil. The house, which must have been young when there were kings called George on the throne, was comprised of two storeys of aged and weathered stone, bounded by well-worn paths dotted with weeds. In front of it was a circular carriage drive bordered by some miserably neglected trees, surrounding a ragged patch of grass.

It wasn't until they had passed through the gates that Frances saw the answer to the mystery of the cab.

Perambulating slowly around the drive balanced precariously atop a high-wheeler was a gentleman of advanced years and broad burly frame. He was having some difficulty in grasping the handlebars, which were hidden from his view by the protrusion of his stomach. As he laboured to turn the cranks and steer the machine along the path, he grunted and puffed with effort, his face bright red and glistening with perspiration. The rider wore the club uniform, with the same colours and badge as Cedric, although he preferred an elderly top hat to the polo cap, and sported a monocle. The picture was completed by a wildly flowing mane of grey hair, exuberantly lengthy beard and an expression of steely determination.

Limping along beside him was a youth of about eighteen, in working clothes, offering anxious guidance and prepared at any moment to save the rider from harm. Although of slender build, there was a wiry strength to him especially about the shoulders, and his sleeves, which were rolled to the elbow, revealed strong tanned forearms.

The bicycle, Frances noticed, had been provided with an extra set of wheels, each no more than four inches across, and attached by a metal rod to the centre of the back wheel. The intention of this novel device was presumably to prevent the machine tipping over, although the effect actually being produced was to restrict the speed, especially when the attachments ground into the earth, which they did often, thus making the ride harder.

'Good afternoon, Sir Hugo!' said Cedric, as if the sight was the most natural thing in the world. Frances now understood that the carriage drive must often be used in such a manner, and it was not therefore a place where a cabdriver would be advised to take his horse. Sir Hugo, too breathless to talk, nodded a greeting. 'How is it going, Linnett?' added Cedric.

Young Jack Linnett dared not take his eyes off the rider. 'Not as well as we might like, sir.'

Sir Hugo wobbled dangerously, but struggled on and managed to make it as far as a small tree, where he flung his arms around its slender trunk and clung on. Linnett hurried up to help and was able to assist his exhausted master from the machine before man, tree and bicycle collapsed in one heap together. The fact that Sir Hugo did not seem to be alarmed by this outcome to his ride suggested to Frances that it was a frequent occurrence. 'I think the side wheels might be made larger, what do you think, Jack?' he gasped, labouring to regain his breath.

'We might try that, sir,' said Jack obligingly, though he didn't sound convinced that this would be an improvement.

'So, what do we have here?' asked Sir Hugo, brushing himself down, roughly. 'A new votary to the art of the wheel?'

He adjusted his monocle and stared intently at Frances, who looked at her feet.

'My cousin Frank,' said Cedric heartily. 'A bashful lad, I'm afraid; we can hardly ever get a word out of him. But he would like to try it.'

'No better way of making a man out of a boy!' exclaimed Sir Hugo, beaming with delight. 'Go to it. He's a good height. There's a fifty-two incher might suit him. Take a few turns around the drive and then put him on the road. We'll have him in the novices' race if he's game.'

'I'll make a wheelman of him in no time,' said Cedric.

'That's what I like to hear.' Sir Hugo clapped his young assistant on the shoulder. 'Come on, Jack, work to be done!' He marched away pushing his unwieldy machine, with Jack limping along by his side.

'He has a workshop where he devises all his inventions,' Cedric explained. 'I think it used to be the gardener's cottage. He spends more time in there than he does in the house.'

Frances glanced around. 'I assume there is no gardening done around here now.'

'Not for many a year, no. There used to be a wonderful kitchen garden once,' he added, nodding to a weather-beaten door in the perimeter wall, 'but it's a veritable jungle nowadays. The place is badly neglected, but still sound.'

'Sir Hugo has no family?'

'None that I know of. But he's taken young Jack Linnett under his wing recently. You'd think they were grandfather and grandson sometimes. But let's get you on a bicycle, if you still think it's a good idea?'

Frances was having second thoughts but dared not say so. 'I'm here now, so I had better try. After all,' she said, making an effort to sound confident, 'what is the worst that can happen?'

'Ah, well, as long as I'm here to catch you when you fall off, you should be safe enough!' said Cedric cheerily. Frances was not encouraged.

CHAPTER SIX

They followed the path around the side of the building, which sat squarely with venerable dignity despite its crumbling edges, and located the entrance to an old coach house, its double doors wide open and held apart by stones.

Inside was a row of racks fashioned from bent steel rods occupied for the main part by narrow-gauge high-wheelers, but at the far end and facing the doors were two larger vehicles, a tricycle and the double-seater machine known as a sociable. Both the tricycle and the sociable sported two high wheels, one on either side, the tricycle having a single small front wheel and the sociable a small wheel both at the front and rear. Instead of pedals there was a treadle arrangement, so the feet rotated around an oddly shaped crank to turn the wheels. The seats were flat with a low back, which looked a great deal more comfortable than the hard leather wedge on which solo gentlemen bicyclists were expected to balance.

In one corner was an assortment of poles of the kind used to mark out tracks for racing, and coils of rope were hung from a series of hooks on the wall. On the opposite side was a rail from which hung a selection of rain capes and woollen wraps, and beside it was a desk at which there sat a short, round bespectacled young man in club uniform in conversation with two other members.

'Some of these machines belong to clubmen, others, including the tricycle and sociable, are available for daily hire,' Cedric explained. He started to examine the bicycles. 'Different sizes as you see. The longer the man's leg the larger the wheel.'

'I hope no one means to measure me,' whispered Frances anxiously.

'That would be awkward, but I fancy Sir Hugo estimated rightly, the fifty-two inch is for you.' Cedric extracted a machine from the rack.

'Good afternoon,' said the bespectacled young man appearing by his side, plump hands clasped together in a gesture that suggested anxiety to please.

'Ah, Toop, just the fellow. My cousin Frank is all eagerness to enter the world of the wheel and I thought to start him off with this one. Frank, this is Mr Toop, our club secretary. Always busy, always here to help any fellow bicyclist.'

Frances, inspecting her feet once more, thought it would be rude to enquire what size wheel Mr Toop rode. She could barely imagine him keeping his balance on such a tall, narrow machine, on which he might resemble a rubber ball balanced on a stick, bobbing and bouncing this way and that. In the next moment she felt sorry for him. It was not his fault he lacked inches in height, although he ought not to have compensated by adding more about his waist than was good for him.

'Delighted to meet a new wheelman in the making,' smiled Toop. 'This is an excellent choice. Take care now, and you'll be a champion, yet!'

Frances merely smiled at her feet.

'He's a bashful chap,' explained Cedric. 'I thought, teach him bicycling and it will improve his confidence no end!'

'It will, it will,' agreed Toop. 'Two shillings the afternoon, that one, and if the young gentleman should wish to buy it then we can come to an arrangement with a small weekly payment.'

Frances patted her pockets and realised to her embarrassment that her money was in her reticule, which she had necessarily left at home, but Cedric smiled and came up with the fee. Mr Toop returned to his desk, put the money in a cash tin and made a note in a ledger. The other club members had now moved away from the desk and were selecting their own machines.

Cedric took charge of the bicycle and wheeled it outside onto the path, one hand grasping a handlebar, the other on the curved steel back, but after a few moments he stopped and said, 'You had better get used to the weight of it. Here.'

Frances approached and took hold of the bicycle, unsure of precisely how she should prevent it from falling over. The immediate answer to that question was that she couldn't, and it was alarming to discover just how dangerously unstable the machine was. She marvelled that anyone without the skills of an acrobat could ever master it. As soon as Cedric released it into her grip it started to fall away from her. She managed with an effort to pull it upright and, of course, it then began to tilt towards her, and for a moment she thought she would find herself lying on the ground underneath it. Cedric remained on hand in case she needed assistance, but allowed her to get the feel of the machine for herself. Finally, Frances was able to persuade the bicycle to remain vertical and felt ready to wheel it to the front drive, an achievement in itself, as once it was in motion it developed a determined new will of its own, and seemed to be constantly trying to get away from her. At last, and by an eccentric rather than a straight route, they reached the driveway where they paused.

'Well done,' said Cedric. 'Now, before you try and mount, just a lesson in the construction of this fine machine.' He gestured like a connoisseur of art describing his favourite classical sculpture. 'Notice its elegant simplicity, the solid firmness of the tyre surrounding the delicate spokes. This long curved part we call the backbone. Then there are the front forks, leading to the cranks, and pedals. The front wheel drives it; the back wheel is only for balance. Your feet go on the pedals, and one turn of the cranks means one turn of the wheel. The bigger the wheel, the further it goes. The handlebars – hold on tight, best not to let go – they control the direction. And it's a bit of a bother if you fall off head-first, so try not to do that.'

'How do I get on?' asked Frances, since the saddle was shoulder height.

Cedric pointed. 'See here – there's a little step jutting out just to the left of the back wheel. You start by standing behind the bicycle, reaching out and holding onto the handlebars, then you put one foot on the step and start it moving along by pushing against the ground with your other foot. Once it's well and truly going, you straighten the leg that's on the step, and give a good pull to bring yourself up into the saddle. After that you have to be quite smart about getting your feet onto the pedals, as it will go over if it isn't moving fast enough. It's the moving that keeps it upright.'

'And how does it stop? I assume Sir Hugo's method is not the most usual – or is it?'

'Sir Hugo is not unique, but have no fear, I will demonstrate. Some bicycles have brakes to slow them down, but for a beginner they can be more trouble then they're worth, so I selected one without.'

Frances looked at the machine with some dismay while Cedric smiled encouragingly. 'I have no doubt you can achieve it. But let me show you first.'

He took the handlebars from Frances and positioned himself behind the bicycle, and then, placing his left foot on the little step, he began pushing along hard with his right. It was not the most graceful movement, especially viewed from the rear, but it did get the machine moving along, and after a few moments Cedric was able to raise himself up into the saddle and find first one and then the other pedal with his feet. Frances began to run alongside him, holding her hat onto her head in case it flew off to reveal her long hair. 'You'll find,' said Cedric, a little breathlessly, 'that when you turn the crank with the right foot the wheel wants to go left and when you turn it with the left, the wheel wants to go right. You use the handlebars to adjust the direction.'

Frances thought it looked like an uneasy contest between man and bicycle, as if the man could only ride the machine if it allowed him to, like a lion tamer performing a show with an animal that he could not fully trust and which might turn and bite him at any moment.

'When you want to get off,' puffed Cedric, 'it's like getting on, only the other way about. Slow down gradually, using a little backward pressure on the pedals, but not too much so it falls over; just wait till you can get your foot down onto the step again and then hop off.' It was a little uncertain, but Cedric managed it, and he gave a smile of triumph. 'There! The first few times I did it I just fell off. You probably will too. We all do.'

'I think I see,' said Frances, wishing she had bandaged her elbows and knees before setting out. She was just contemplating the prospect with some concern, and wondering if she ought after all to forget what had been a foolish idea and go home, when one of the other members of the club walked past wheeling a gleaming new machine. A tall, handsome, athletically built fellow with wavy hair and a marvellous moustache, he made a brisk salute to Cedric, vaulted smoothly and effortlessly into the saddle and rode away.

'Rufus Goring, club captain,' said Cedric. 'Now, are you ready? Or perhaps you might prefer not?'

'I'll do it,' said Frances.

'All right. Tuck your trouser bottoms into your socks first. I'll walk along beside you.'

Frances adopted the awkward position as demonstrated, and uttered a silent prayer, convinced that she was on her way to broken bones and severe embarrassment. Then she began to push. And it was not quite as difficult as she had thought. The machine began to bowl along, and then, with a great effort, she drove off hard with her left foot, and pulled herself into the saddle. There were a few moments of panic as her feet sought the pedals, and the machine wobbled violently and threatened to tip over, but then, almost by chance, first her right foot and then her left found their places, and gasping with relief, she began to turn the cranks. It was only then that she became fully aware of just how high above the ground she was, and between that and the struggle to keep the machine going ahead, she began to perspire in alarm. 'How do I turn the corner?' she exclaimed.

'Use the handlebars!' called Cedric, trotting along beside her. 'Not too much. Smoothly. Don't pull! You're doing well. Keep going.'

Frances, thankful for the hours of walking that had given strength to her long legs and exercises with Indian clubs that enabled her to direct the handlebars, rode on, doing her best to steer carefully around the curve of the carriage drive. The bicycle was, despite Cedric's claims, a large, ungainly, heavy beast that constantly fought against Frances' best efforts at control. A number of times the wayward machine threatened to career off the drive into the trees, and once this was corrected, it decided rebelliously to try veering off in the other direction into the long grass, but each time she managed to persuade it to do as she asked, and eventually she began to feel more comfortable and was able to make the small adjustments necessary to follow the centre of the path. The saddle, creaking on its springs, was an uncomfortable ridge of hard leather where she might not have wanted it, but she supposed that she could get used to it.

Gradually she became more accustomed to the ride, and began to find the rhythm of the pedals, the grind of metal and the crunch of dry earth under the tyres almost calming. The sensation was like nothing else she had ever experienced; she was facing directly into the world ahead, with nothing before her; it was as if she was floating in the air like a cloud, or flying like a bird. She risked glancing about her, and saw Cedric trotting by her side, grinning broadly.

'What do you think?' he asked.

This was it, Frances realised, the freedom that men talked about, riding the steel beast that needed little stabling and no feed, such a simple machine but one that held the promise of the open road, the delights of the countryside, clean fresh air to invigorate the body, and, most importantly, independent travel. So, ladies couldn't ride the high-wheeler, could they? Miss Dauntless could and now Miss Doughty could, too.

'It's wonderful!' she declared.

Chapter Seven

As Frances continued her unpredictable ride around the circular carriage drive, she found that every moment in which she was able to advance without actually falling off the bicycle served to increase her confidence. She felt sure that with sufficient practice she could manage to tame it, and create a willing servant out of a creature that was currently planning mutiny.

She had still to achieve the art of dismounting, an exercise that was a hard blow to her new-found assurance. On her first attempt she was unable to find the step with her foot, and the machine tilted over. She would have crashed to the ground if Cedric had not moved up and caught her, supporting the bicycle so it did not fall on top of her. 'You were almost there,' he said, as she paused to get her breath back.

She could see that he was waiting for her to say she would like to end the lesson for the day but something, she hardly knew what, made her go on. She nodded. 'Thank you, I think I know what I did wrong.' She took hold of the bicycle, pushed off again and mounted, moving off with an alarming display of instability that nearly sent her into the trees before she managed to gain control. A second failure to dismount safely only added to her determination, and once again Cedric was there to save her from injury. This time, no sooner had she got her feet to the ground than she dragged the recalcitrant machine upright again and propelled it forward for another try. On her third attempt she finally found the little step, and dismounted without assistance.

'Oh bravo, Frank, well done!' exclaimed Cedric. 'I'll swear you are a wheelman born and bred. Might I perhaps suggest that that is sufficient for the first lesson?'

'Just a little longer,' she said. 'I want to be sure that I can do it.'

'Very well.'

Frances repeated the mounting and dismounting twice more without accident, upon which Cedric clapped her on the shoulder in brotherly fashion, and they both laughed with happiness and relief.

Frances was allowing herself a brief rest when a thought occurred to her. She had brought the map of East Acton with her and now she took it from her pocket and unfolded it. Having already noted the site of the murder of Morton Vance, she knew that it was a short walk or an even quicker bicycle ride away. 'As I am here, I want to go and look at the place where Morton Vance was killed,' she said.

Cedric was clearly surprised by this announcement. 'Oh? Have you been asked to investigate that? Surely not? Or is this just your curiosity getting the better of you?' He tilted a warning eyebrow. 'It has been known.'

'I admit it is the latter. I can never keep away from cases of murder however hard I try, and I thought – as we are so near – I would like to see for myself where it happened.'

Cedric grinned. 'Wait here, I'll get my bicycle and we'll ride there together. It's a bumpy track, not nearly as forgiving as the driveway, and you'll need someone with you.'

He was back soon, with a shiny new machine of which he was clearly extremely proud and regaled Frances in some detail on the subject of patented adjustable ball bearings before taking the lead on their ride. 'I won't go too fast, stay close, and I'll call out first if I mean to stop.'

They rode out through the gnarled brown gates and turned east, travelling along East Acton Lane in the direction of Old Oak Common Lane. Although it was worrying to be elevated to some seven feet or more in height while perched on top of a barely controllable machine, Frances found that her position also enabled her to appreciate her surroundings in a way that a carriage ride could never allow. She could see over walls into the flower gardens of the manor houses, past cottages to open fields of wheat ripe for harvest, and into orchards where rows of trees promised an abundance of autumn fruit. Every view was a new and unexpected pleasure, with the notable exception of the waving expanse of tall faded weeds in what had once been Sir Hugo's kitchen garden.

'There's a sharp right up ahead,' called Cedric, 'just after this row of cottages. We'll be passing over the culvert of Stamford Brook; that's the old waterway, it was covered over when they made it part of the drainage system, so take extra care as that's a difficult ride; you'll need more weight on the pedals to get over the bump, then we turn south down the lane. After that it's just a mile or so to the farm entrance.'

Frances had to concentrate far harder than before to steer her bicycle over the uneven track. It was some time before she dared look around her again and was rewarded with a wonderful view over a hedgerow and across open fields. It was near enough a year after the death of Morton Vance and she thought the weather had then been much as it was now, a bright and sunny August after a cool wet July.

'Slow down!' called Cedric.

They both gradually slowed. Cedric dismounted and Frances followed suit. As they wheeled their machines forward all was quiet apart from the sound of rubber on earth and the creak of rotating cranks. 'See there,' said Cedric. He was pointing to a wooden stake painted white driven into the edge of the ditch on the left. 'The club had that put in specially to warn members against the approach to a blind corner.'

'Was that there when Morton Vance was killed?'

'Good question. It ought to have been. I was told that when it was first put in old Linnett used to uproot it and throw it away, but the members kept putting in a new one. He stopped doing it after the police spoke to him. But I understand that it wasn't there on that day so maybe he had started up his old tricks again.'

'And the entrance to the farm is near? It certainly can't be seen from here.'

'Yes. Just around the corner. It's not used for pigs any more. I think pig farming is going out of fashion in the area, there used to be several farms but there's only the one left now, a mile or two further north, near Wormwood Scrubs. Linnett only rented his.'

Frances wheeled her bicycle forward. The hedgerows were thickly grown, but she thought the new occupant of the farm must have given them enough of a trim for vehicles to go past unimpeded. 'I wonder if the hedgerows were like this last year?'

'I don't think Linnett ever cut them. He wasn't about to trouble himself for passing bicyclists; in fact, he enjoyed contributing to a nuisance. Anything he could do to hinder the wheelmen, he did. The club members had to trim the hedges back just to be able to ride past.'

As they moved forward, they found the bend in the lane, too small to trouble a mapmaker, which concealed the farm entrance. Here the road was marked by wheel prints leading through an open gateway into a yard surrounded by low out-buildings, a ramshackle cottage, stables and sagging barns. 'It doesn't look occupied. Does anyone live here now?'

'No, I think it's just used for storage.'

'I can see how a cart turning into the yard would have been hidden from a rider's view until he was quite close. If a bicyclist had been travelling south and going too fast he wouldn't have had time to stop.' Frances moved past the gateway to where the road became a straighter run, then turned and looked back. 'Yes, coming up from the south the view isn't impeded.' She gave the question some thought. 'Can we try an experiment? I will stand just here where the cart must have been. Could you move away out of sight and then ride slowly towards the farm entrance? I want to see how much time you have to stop.'

Cedric obliged and wheeled his bicycle out of view. 'Starting now,' he called, and Frances watched for his approach. Moments later, Cedric came riding around the corner, pedalling slowly and cautiously. He had just a few feet in which to stop, and was able to do so, quickly hopping off one side of the machine.

'Thank you,' said Frances. 'So, if Morton Vance had been going carefully there wouldn't have been a collision at all, or at the worst a very minor one. And he must have known the dangers.'

'All the members knew them, yes.'

'So it follows that if he had wanted to race another rider this would have been the very last place he would have chosen.'

'I would say so. Undoubtedly.'

Frances wheeled her bicycle into the farmyard, which despite its lack of pigs still caught at the nostrils with the sour reek of manure. Wooden fencing created a large pigpen enclosing two troughs and a low house built of stone, the surface of the ground like a choppy sea of dried mud. Now pig-free it was being used to store farming equipment. Nearby, a high-sided two-wheel cart was tilted forward, resting on its shafts.

'Ah!' said Frances.

'What have you seen?' asked Cedric, following her into the farmyard.

'This,' said Frances, pointing to the cart. 'I'm wondering if it's the same one Morton Vance collided with.' She rolled her bicycle forward. 'What size bicycle did Morton Vance ride?'

'I'm afraid I don't know.'

'Where is it now?'

'I really can't say. Maybe it was returned to his parents after the trial. It was badly damaged, that I do know.'

The pig cart, for all that it had obviously seen years of hard use, was a substantial vehicle, with a long outer framework of steel rods around thick planks, and tall heavy wheels. When laden with pigs it would have been slow moving and a formidable barrier. It was certainly not something that any man on a bicycle would want to collide with at speed if he could possibly help it. It was clear from the size of the vehicle that when turning into the farmyard there would be several moments when it entirely blocked the roadway to all traffic.

Frances examined the cart more closely, running her fingers over its surface. Long dry cracks in the wood spoke of age and natural wear, but there were also deep scratches carved into the planks that were only on its left side. She brought her bicycle closer and found that the scratches matched fairly well with the position of the handlebars. Further down was an indentation that could only have been made by collision with a projecting pedal. The cart had been painted when new although its colour was so long faded that it was impossible to tell what it had once been. There were other smears along its side that looked like tyre rubber, and tiny shreds of dark blue paint. 'This must be the cart,' she said. 'The position of the marks show that a bicycle going south down the lane ran into it.' She turned to Cedric. 'Imagine that you are Morton Vance, going fast down the road. You see this blocking your way. You can't go around it and you have no time to stop. What would you do?'

Cedric contemplated this hazardous situation. 'Bad business. But I don't see why he would have been going fast. Everyone knew not to do it. Vance even wrote about it in the magazine. And remember, we only have old Linnett's word for it that Vance was racing. He was probably lying.'

'But just imagine that for whatever reason you are going too fast, and you suddenly see this cart ahead of you. What then? What do you do?'

Cedric's expression showed her that this was not a pleasant thought. 'Well, there's not a lot of choice – I mean there's going to be an awful crash whatever I do – but I suppose if I had to ride into something, I'd try and see if I could go into the hedge. Sooner that than this thing.'

'So you'd swerve to one side?'

'Yes.'

'And even then there might not be enough time to do that, but a side-on collision would be better than head-first I suppose?'

'I'd say so. If Vance had been going at a sensible speed, he might still have run into the cart, or gone into the hedge, but then he'd have got away with a few bruises and scratches. We've all ridden off the road from time to time.'

'Take a look at this,' said Frances. She brought her bicycle close to the cart and matched the deep indentation with the pedal and the gouge with the handlebars. 'I suspect that Mr Vance had a slightly smaller wheel, but the proportions are about right. This is hard wood. That's a lot more damage than can be accounted for by a collision at low speed. Have any other members of the club ever collided with the cart?'

'No. I'm sure they would have said so if they had.'

'What about Mr Babbit of the Oakwood club? It was he who was involved in the accident that injured Jack Linnett. I found a report in the newspaper but it didn't give any details, only that the horse shied. Did Mr Babbit collide with the cart?'

'No, I was told that the animal bolted after he had ridden past it, and then the cart went into the ditch and overturned. Babbit wasn't injured at all.'

'So as far as we know the only bicyclist to have collided with the cart was Morton Vance?'

'Yes.'

There was a long silence then Cedric examined the marks and compared them with the bicycle. 'Do you know, I don't like to say it, but the evidence is there. Vance really was going too fast.'

'Then Sam Linnett was telling the truth.'

'On that point at least, I have to admit he was.' Cedric frowned. 'But he was lying about everything else.'

'Was he?'

'Of course he was. I mean, who else would have wanted to kill Vance?'

Frances had no answer to that question, but realised that she would very much like to discover it.

CHAPTER EIGHT

Frances returned home with a bruised elbow, a scraped knee that would require a repair to her trousers, and an aching shoulder. She had fallen off the bicycle three times in all, and she didn't care. Twice when learning to dismount, she had been caught by Cedric, and thus avoided injury, but on her return from the abandoned pig farm overconfidence had led her to go too fast and outpace him, and she had overturned while taking a sharp left into East Acton Lane. The small amount of pain she brushed aside, it was worth it for the excitement and exhilaration. The experience was far more, she realised, than just about riding a bicycle. She had done what men thought she could not do, or even if they thought she could, what they had decreed she ought not to. Their opinion was based on no other reason than that she was a woman, as if it was somehow self-evident that her sex rendered her incapable of those mental and physical achievements they deemed to be beyond her capabilities. These were not bad men, she had to remind herself, or even thoughtless men. They just had no imagination and could not conceive of a world that was other than the way they had been taught it was and would always be. Frances Doughty had proved them wrong.

While Frances had no especial desire to be a man, she had come to appreciate how the simple device of wearing trousers allowed a freedom of movement that was denied to her when encumbered with long heavy skirts and layers of petticoats. Trousers were such a practical garment she wished they would become a permissible part of everyday female attire. She felt sure that most of the things that women were constantly being told they could not do, would be perfectly possible if society was a little more accepting in the matter of dress. Why was it, she wondered, that the supposedly weaker sex were obliged to spend their days being weighed down as effectively as convicts in leg irons, by garments far heavier than those worn by men, that prevented them moving as athletically as they were surely able to? She had once, when acting as a detective, been obliged to climb over a fence and what a bother that had been in her long skirt.

It was ironic, she realised, that if trousers ever did become acceptable wear for women who were not on the music hall stage, even if only for those engaged in sporting activities, she would as a result find it far harder to carry out her deception. As things now stood, the mere fact of wearing a man's suit announced her, at least at first glance, to be a man, and it was only as a man that she could hope to ride a bicycle.

Frances had seen posters advertising circuses in which women in colourful costumes that revealed the shape of their limbs to ogling men, were able to mount and ride the high-wheeler. But these were understood to be females of a certain kind, having nothing in common with ladies. Now that she had mastered the bicycle, she determined to discover how she might ride it in public, safely, without offending popular taste or risking arrest for indecency. It was a subject she could broach with those doyennes of the female suffrage movement and devoted companions, Miss Gilbert and Miss John, who had taken an interest in the new movement of dress reform for women, and would be sure to have some interesting suggestions.

Frances had just completed a sponge wash and change of clothes when Sarah arrived home, but she was still simmering with the memory of her ride.

'What have you been up to?' demanded Sarah, suspiciously. 'I can see it from your face.'

'I have been enjoying my little excursion with Mr Garton.'

'Oh?' Sarah gave Frances a look that would have cracked granite. 'It's more than that, though. You've not been – I mean,

I thought you weren't likely to – not with him anyhow – isn't he one of those inverted types?'

'I was inverted three times today, and I should like to try it again,' said Frances. She laughed at Sarah's astonished expression. 'We were bicycling, that is all,' she said reassuringly. 'I fell off, but that's quite usual, so it's nothing to worry about.'

'What, dressed like that?'

'I wore the suit. And do you know what I discovered? Women can ride bicycles just as well as men, it's only their clothes that stop them.'

'And common sense, too,' growled Sarah.

'I just wanted to try it for myself,' Frances explained. 'If I'm to go to the race meeting and talk with all those devotees I thought I should at least understand why they love bicycles so much. And now I do understand. It's more than just having the newest ball bearings and taking pride in the size of one's wheel. It's about being free to go where you want and when. It's something all women should be able to do.'

Sarah looked dubious.

'I learned to mount and dismount, and steer. I rode around the carriage drive at Springfield Lodge, and once I felt I had the measure of the machine, I rode out onto Old Oak Common Lane and visited the place where Mr Vance was killed.'

'Did you learn anything?' asked Sarah, putting supper plates on the table.

'Yes, I did. The inquest report stated that the flakes of paint from Vance's bicycle were found on the left-hand side of the cart. I had a look in the farmyard, and there is a cart there, a high-sided one for the transport of livestock. I'm sure it's the same one. If it was turning into the farm entrance then it would have blocked most of the roadway, and there would have been no opportunity for a fast-moving bicyclist to stop in time to avoid a collision. A man moving slowly, as the club members were all advised to do, would have been safe. The paint-marks demonstrate very clearly that Vance must have been travelling south when he struck the cart. If he had been going north he would have seen the cart well in time to stop, but from the south his view was impeded.'

Frances pushed aside the dishes, unfolded the map of East Acton on the table, and pointed out the location of the murder. Sarah stopped her work and came to stare at the map.

'The road bends slightly just before the farm entrance, which is partly obscured by hedgerows, but the club members knew this very well, and they also knew about the threat posed by Sam Linnett. The club had put a white-painted marker post by the side of the road as a warning to slow down or dismount and walk. If Vance was racing another bicyclist, as was suggested, then that makes two men who were doing something that was far from sensible. But where is the other man? No one has come forward and said that he and Vance had decided to race down the lane.'

Sarah stuck out her lower lip. 'What about the man who found the body? Could he have been the racer? He might have been, and lied about it.'

'If so, he never admitted it. He was Henry Ross-Fielder, the club's vice-captain. He said that he was taking a gentle ride to enjoy the fine weather.' Frances found the newspaper account of the trial. 'Yes, here it is, he lives in Holland Park and said he was bicycling along the Vale towards East Acton, then he went north up Old Oak Common Lane, when he found the body.' Frances studied the map to establish Ross-Fielder's route. 'If he's telling the truth he can't have been the racer. He was going the wrong way.'

Sarah re-read the report and stabbed a finger at the newspaper. 'Look at those injuries. Vance hit the ground hard, there's no doubt about it. A strong young man doesn't get all them broken bones from a little spill.'

'No, and the marks on the cart do suggest a heavy collision, so we have to conclude that he was going too fast. That much at least supports Sam Linnett's story. But why? Why do something so foolish? There must be safer places to race.'

'Might have been a betting matter,' said Sarah. 'Men do all sorts of silly things they shouldn't just for a bet.'

'That's very true,' said Frances. 'And if he was racing for a bet, I suppose the other rider would have been ashamed to admit it, since the foolishness led to a man's death.'

She studied the report again. 'The last person to see Vance at Springfield Lodge was Mr Toop, who saw him take his bicycle out. I have met Mr Toop and I don't think he is a racing man. So Vance stored his machine in the coach house there, and took it out about an hour before he was found. But where did he ride? Why did no one see him, or report having seen him? And an hour later why was he riding south away from East Acton where he should have been going if he wanted to replace his machine?'

'What are you thinking?'

'I'm thinking that there may be more to the murder of Morton Vance than is generally supposed.'

'Man's been hanged for it,' Sarah reminded her.

'Yes,' sighed Frances. 'I know.' She took out her notebook and began to write down all the things that puzzled her and what she might need to find out.

'You've not been asked to look into that,' said Sarah, setting out the plates again. 'And supposing Sam Linnett did get hanged for a murder he didn't do? You can't unhang him.'

'No, but a murderer has gone free, a man who allowed another to suffer for his crime, and he should be brought to justice.'

'He'll be dangerous, mind.'

'I have no doubt of that. I do understand, of course, that I have not been engaged to find Morton Vance's murderer, but at the same time it is possible that that crime is in some way connected with the criminal activities, which I have been asked to look out for.'

'Well, I'm only glad your friends will be there to watch over you. Cold pie and eggs?'

'Yes please,' said Frances absently, staring at her list. Sarah grunted and went to fetch supper. The meal was almost silent, as Frances made notes, eating what was put on the plate before her without paying a great deal of attention to it.

The only sounds for some time were Frances' busy pencil, and Sarah scraping out the pickle jar.

After a long pause, Sarah coughed. 'The thing is, Pounder and me we want to get married.'

Frances nearly snapped the pencil lead. 'Well, that's wonderful!' she said, when she had recovered her composure. 'When will the wedding be?'

'We thought next month.'

'And afterwards, will you both be living in the ground floor apartment?'

'We want to, yes, but I remember when we took this place we were told that we weren't to have animals and children in the house.'

Frances smiled. 'And I assume that you are not planning to adopt pets. Very well, I shall write to the owner and ask if the rule can be removed. After all, the only other tenants are myself, and hopefully Tom and Ratty soon, so we will be very like a family.'

Sarah nodded but she was clearly pleased by the prospect.

A thought struck Frances. 'Sarah – you're not —?'

'Don't know yet,' said Sarah, and went to make tea.

With Sarah and Tom under one roof, Frances reflected, it would be a family in more ways than one. Sarah had never revealed the identity of Tom's father. It was a memory she had buried, and it was understandable that she would not want to relive the terror, shame and betrayal that her robustly nurturing family had helped her to survive. Now that Sarah was no longer a frightened girl but a stout brawny woman, Frances could only hope that the man was well out of her associate's revengeful reach.

Frances completed her notes and once she and Sarah were settled over tea she decided not to press her companion for further details of her wedding plans, which she doubted would be forthcoming, but turned instead to another issue.

'One thing about today's adventure, it has made me think very seriously about how women's clothes stop them from doing things they are perfectly capable of doing. I am sure Miss Gilbert and Miss John would have something to say about it.'

'Oh, they're are all for dress reform, as they call it, and I can see their point. But it's not something you could walk down the street in and not be made a laughing stock. Wasn't there this American woman, Bloomer? Made a right spectacle of herself she did.'

'I am sorry to say it was not a flattering garment,' said Frances, who had been shown pictures of the lady, 'but she did try to address the problem we all face. My argument is this; what ladies may do in their own home, or even in convocations of like-minded friends, is one thing, but in public we are meant to squeeze our bodies until we can hardly breathe, and go about in something that would do duty for a theatre curtain. And if we dare to choose something that is good for our health, and does not restrict our movement, we are ridiculed. It is only male prejudice that states what women can and cannot do, and this is maintained by the practice of encasing us in highly impractical clothing. No one, male or female, could ride a bicycle in long skirts. The bicyclists I have seen wear knee britches and stockings.'

'Well I might see you in that yet. Didn't Miss Gilbert and Miss John go to some sort of exhibition on new clothes for women?'

'They did, yes, some months ago. They sent me an advertisement but I was engaged that day. Let me look for it.'

Frances searched through her papers and since they were carefully arranged she soon retrieved a handbill announcing an exhibition of 'Hygienic Wearing Apparel for women and children' which had taken place the previous March, a display from which men were to be absolutely excluded. The leaflet was not illustrated but it promised those ladies who attended the sight of beautifully embroidered dresses in the Greek style, garments that removed all temptation for tight lacing, which would impede the delicate classical flow of the draperies.

'I recall Miss Gilbert saying that she wanted to dress in the Greek fashion while Miss John declared that she would adopt the trouser,' said Frances.

'I suppose they know their own business,' said Sarah, with the implication in her tone that for Frances the selection of either garment for daily wear would be a serious mistake.

There was another style described in the leaflet, however, a novel kind of skirt, which was divided in two sections, each enclosing one leg, in order to give greater freedom of movement in activities such as boating and tennis. The upper part of the costume was said to resemble the *polonaise*, which had recently come back into fashion, an overdress, cut long over the waist and hips, the effect being to make the new skirt indistinguishable from the usual kind in general wear.

Frances knew that every time she went out dressed as a man she was taking a risk, but this invention was a step in the right direction, a garment that would provide her with greater freedom of movement without the possibility of being arrested for indecency or insulted in the street. She made a note of the name of the maker and determined to pay her a visit without delay.

CHAPTER NINE

That evening Cedric arrived at Frances' apartments bearing a bottle of port wine and a nice Stilton cheese as a gift for his dear cousin Frank, and a set of written notes for Frances.

It was the perfect complement to her modest supper. She had been reading quietly alone, since Sarah and the Professor were out teaching at the sporting academy, and tempted by the unexpected treat she soon provided plates, cutlery and glasses. Her home had no drinking vessels suitable for port but Cedric said that in such an extremity sherry glasses might serve the purpose, if one could ignore the incorrect shape.

'Now I don't pretend to know all the club members well,' Cedric admitted, sipping his port. 'They do seem to be decent fellows but then, as you know,' he pressed the fingertips of one hand lightly to the region of his heart, 'I am as an innocent babe in such things.'

Frances took a cautious taste of the sweet drink, which she found rather good, and read through the notes in Cedric's elegant handwriting. She had been musing on the type of person who might indulge in the activities mentioned by the silver-haired gentleman she had met in Hyde Park, and in particular who might be willing to undertake the abominable treachery of selling secrets of the British government to another country. It was very possible that those who actually carried the messages had no idea what it was they were delivering; after all, much of her own work for the government involved the transmission of papers she was trusted not to open, and Tom and Ratty sometimes carried urgent sealed letters for commercial companies. Carriers had only to be paid for their trouble like any messenger, perhaps with a suitable bonus to ensure speed and silence.

The person who directed the actions of this little army was another matter. He knew himself to be a traitor, endangering the safety and prosperity of the country of his birth, and did so with no sense of guilt or regret. If he had ever had a conscience about his actions, it had died long ago, or he could not have continued. Perhaps he gave no thought to the consequences of what he did, the harm that might be inflicted on Britain and its people. A murderer could kill just one person, and be filled with remorse. A traitor might be responsible for the death of thousands, and care nothing.

Frances had met several murderers and was well aware of the common motives that induced people to commit that dreadful crime. Treason was something with which she was unfamiliar, but the more she thought about it the more she came to the conclusion that there was only one possible reason for someone to betray the Queen's own country, and that was the most sordid reason of all – money. From what Cedric had said, his fellow bicyclists were drawn from the respectable middle ranks of society, young single professional gentlemen. Was there one, perhaps, who had a special need for money? A man who had hidden debts, unusual expenses, or was the victim of blackmail? Or was he simply greedy for the things money could buy?

Her commercially minded friends, Chas and Barstie, directors of the Bayswater Design and Advertising Co. Ltd on Westbourne Grove, had always told her that ultimately all things came down to money. Frances felt that some things at least were down to love, but in this case she thought they were right. If Frances had been pursuing one of her usual cases she would have consulted those gentlemen, who always knew or had the means to discover the financial secrets of Bayswater. On this occasion, however, the constraints of her mission prevented her from using that avenue of enquiry. Both men were, in any case, occupied with their own affairs.

Barstie, who had recently commenced what promised to be a long betrothal, was a little more optimistic since his future father-in-law had finally agreed to set a date for the wedding. It was still some way off but at least he had a page on the calendar that he could stare at wistfully. Chas was in hearty mood, since he had just become engaged to a young lady who was as charming as she was beautiful. She was the daughter of a highly important businessman from Sicily and was often referred to as a princess, though what country she might be princess of was unclear. Still, her father was very rich, and happy to accept an English son-in-law, which he felt gave his family a touch of refinement.

Frances began her questioning at the top of Cedric's list. 'Tell me more about Sir Hugo Daffin. Now that I have seen Springfield Lodge all I can say is that while the land must be worth something the house is terribly neglected and sorely in need of attention. Is he one of those gentlemen whose entire fortune is in an estate he cannot afford to maintain? Is he anxious to make a profit from his inventions?'

Cedric, having discovered to his dismay that Frances did not own a cheese scoop, cut some neat cubes of Stilton, arranged them on plates for them both, and ate his by spearing them with a small fork. 'As to his monetary worth, I can't say, but Sir Hugo loves the old lodge just the way it is, and appears to be blind to its defects.'

'You told me he had no family. Has he never married? Does he have heirs?'

'I don't know. I have never heard of anyone, not even cousins. The household at the lodge consists of just three persons – Sir Hugo, his housekeeper Mrs Pirrie and the manservant Waterfield, who is seventy-five if a day, perhaps older. Both servants have been with him for many years, and take excellent care of him. Jack Linnett doesn't live there; he lodges with the blacksmith, Tom Hicks, in the village. But you'll meet Mrs Pirrie, I expect. She bakes cakes for the race meetings and helps to serve luncheons and teas on the day. A good soul, she is devoted to Sir Hugo.'

Frances nodded and returned to the notes. 'The club captain, Rufus Goring. He lives in Bayswater and is a founder member of the Bayswater Bicycle Club.'

'Ah, yes, of course you saw him earlier today. He is reputed to be the handsomest man in West London, and who shall deny it? It is said that ladies have been known to faint dead away at the mere sight of his moustache, and for myself, I can hardly blame them. In fact,' Cedric gave a mischievous grin, 'I think my young cousin Frank was more than a little taken with that delightful appendage, if the truth be known.'

Frances refused to be drawn into making a comment. 'What are the duties of the captain?'

'He directs the weekly rides. When we go out, we travel in single file for safety, and he rides at the head of the line, looking out for any difficulties. He carries a bugle and a whistle and signals us when to stop and start. And of course, he has to be an all-round good fellow, too. Experienced rider and trustworthy.'

'Is he?'

'I believe so. Solid man by all accounts. His father is something on the stock exchange and Goring is likely to go that way.'

'Then he is rich, I suppose?'

Cedric nibbled cheese and grinned again, accompanied by a suggestive flutter of the eyebrows. 'Rich as any man in his position, I believe. Owns several bicycles, if that is anything to judge by.'

'Do you judge a man by the number of bicycles he has?'

'It's certainly a question one should always ask. Goring keeps the usual ones at home for practice spins along the leafy boulevards of Bayswater, but his lightweight racing machines are in East Acton. He is a strong, sound rider with a good many prizes to his name. But,' sighed Cedric, 'we fear that his days as a bicyclist may be numbered.'

'Why is that?'

'It is well known that he is highly interested in Miss Adela Farrow, only daughter of General Farrow. I know this because

Miss Farrow's brother George is a keen bicyclist and a member of our club. Just recently he intimated that Goring may be selling off his bicycles and going in for a sociable instead. A sure sign of an impending engagement.'

Frances felt a slight prickle of disappointment, but quickly pushed it aside. She had to admit to herself that she had not been unimpressed by Mr Goring's good looks, but knew that even had she been clad in her best gown and taken the trouble to trim her bonnet such a man would not have given her a moment's glance.

'Now young Farrow is a splendid example of the power of the bicycle to improve a man. Last spring he was sent down from university for wild behaviour. Quite how he transgressed I have never found out, and I suspect that no one ever will, but I believe he was a grave disappointment to his father, who is rather strict. But since he took an interest in the wheel, he has steadied himself wonderfully and has a whole host of respectable new friends. His father is very pleased with him.'

'Does Mr Farrow have an occupation?'

'No profession as yet; he lives off an allowance, as do many young men when they have rich fathers. Not a great exerciser of the brain, but the General is prepared to be generous if his son behaves himself and looks about for something. I'm sure that in time he'll be found a suitable post that isn't too arduous.'

Frances addressed herself to the list once more. 'Henry Ross-Fielder, of Holland Park, he is the club vice-captain, and I believe the man who discovered the body of the unfortunate Mr Vance?'

'Yes, that was a nasty shock. Ross-Fielder is quite a sensitive fellow and he and Vance had been on good terms for some years. Finding his friend dead in such unpleasant circumstances was something from which he may never recover. As you might deduce, the vice-captain's duty is to bring up the rear of the line when we go out, to ensure that no one falls behind. He is also club treasurer.'

'Does the club have substantial finances to look after?'

'Quite modest, I believe. The members pay a fee, and there is income from race meetings and hiring out machines. Expenditure is on prizes and the club magazine, and then there are social events held during the winter months.'

'Even so, a man who has been put in charge of money should always be trusted not to treat it as his own.'

'He is. Father is a respected clergyman, though Ross-Fielder doesn't intend to go into the Church, he has a brother who is taking on that filial duty and who feels for some reason that bicycle riding is incompatible with piety. Ross-Fielder is studying to be an accountant. The only slight blot on the family happiness is his father being attacked in the street by a beggar recently. I suppose you know all about that.'

'I do. Does he talk about it?'

'Only to say that his father was badly bruised and shaken but is himself again.'

Frances nodded and read on. 'Now I met Mr Aaron Toop, the club secretary, on my visit this morning. He too is a Bayswater man. If I have learned nothing else about bicycling, I now appreciate that length of leg is an important factor in success, so I assume that he is not a champion racer?'

'No, but he is still very eager to ride when he can show off his machine. You'll recognise his when you see it, smaller front wheel, of course, and all the latest features that money can buy. Best quality ebony handles, nickel-plated cyclometer, double-lever spoon brake. He likes to make a good impression. Keeps his machine in East Acton and takes it out to polish it, but doesn't ride it in races in case it gets damaged.'

'But can he afford it? Are such embellishments expensive?'

'Oh yes. Toop's father owns an engineering company. Toop's on the board of directors, and will be in charge one day no doubt. He's an organising kind of man, bustles about, here there and everywhere, always very busy, makes himself useful. He may strike you as thinking a lot of himself, but he is also a good friend to his fellow man, always ready to help others.'

'This next name on your list sounds familiar; James Jepson. That is the surname of the surgeon who gave evidence at the trial of Sam Linnett.'

'Yes, he's the son, a medical student up at Barts. Father has a practice in Acton. And there's a pretty sister called Maud, who likes to attend the races. Quite a few of the fellows find her interesting. I don't myself, that is not the kind of beauty I admire, but she's a nice enough girl for those who like that sort of thing.'

'And there are some names here I don't know – Paul Iliffe, another Bayswater resident. You say he is the club's champion rider and a professional wheelman.'

'Yes, he enters competitions all over the country. Anyone who competes for money is deemed to be a professional and is not allowed to ride in amateur races. He's another man with several machines, some of them prizes. There'll be a special race for professionals at the meeting, the main rivalry being between Iliffe and Babbit of the Oakwood Bicycle Club. Very keenly anticipated. I wouldn't mind predicting there'll be heavy bets laid on it.'

'Is there a lot of betting on bicycle races?'

'Oh there's bound to be some, usually private wagers between gentlemen, although I believe there are a few sharp customers running illegal betting books who have taken notice of the possibilities of the wheel world recently, and strayed from the racecourse where they belong.'

'How does Mr Iliffe make his income when he isn't on a bicycle?'

'He gives lessons to amateurs, and publishes a magazine. *Wheelmen of England.*'

'No "Wheelwomen"?' asked Frances teasingly.

Cedric smiled over his port. 'Ah, no. Although there is a magazine for tricyclists of whom many are ladies. We will see more ladies on wheels in future I am sure, and they are always very well represented in the crowd at gentlemen's races. In fact, Iliffe talks about opening a new sports ground, just for bicycle races. Most of the London ones have tracks that are very poor.

Hard gravel surfaces, dangerous corners, spectators wandering back and forth across the course without looking where they are going. Iliffe wants to improve on that.'

'That would be an extremely expensive undertaking.'

'It would. I don't expect him to succeed very soon.'

'What about his rival, Mr Babbit? Where does he live and what does he do?'

'Babbit lives in Hammersmith, and has a small post in a City office. So small it is hardly visible and he never talks about it. The two are not at all friendly by the way. They have never yet come to blows, but if looks could kill, one or the other would be dead long ago.'

'Is that the same Mr Babbit who caused the accident that injured Jack Linnett?

'It is.'

'Is there any ill will between Babbit and Linnett? I could understand it if there was.'

'I've never noticed it. But then the two rarely see each other. I rather think Linnett has put all that behind him. He's not one to bear a grudge.'

'I assume Linnett doesn't ride a bicycle?'

'No, well there's yet to be a machine made for a man with one leg shorter than the other.'

Frances returned to the list of names. 'Phineas Vance? Is he related to Morton Vance?'

'Yes, he's the older brother. He was once very devoted to bicycling but his heart went out of it after his brother's death, and he gave it up. He was vice-captain last year, before Ross-Fielder succeeded him. He still comes to social events to meet up with his friends. Oh, and there's a younger sister, Sybil. Strange girl. Rather excitable. She took her brother's death very hard, and Phineas still has to keep an eye on her. There was a time we thought she and Goring might make a match, but it wasn't to be.'

'Is the Vance family very prominent? Perhaps I ought to ask how may bicycles they have?'

'None, at present, I believe. They are not prominent; the father was a senior clerk, and the sons have followed that profession. Respectable, but not substantial. Then you'll see two more names on the list, Miles and Fletcher, both friends of mine. I suggested they try bicycling and they joined a few weeks ago. And there's a new fellow only just joined; can't remember his name; I haven't met him yet.'

Frances said nothing but wondered if the new member was the mysterious Gideon.

Chapter Ten

Cedric addressed himself further to cheese and port, and Frances did the same while completing her notes. 'I assume,' said Cedric, after a meaningful pause, 'that there is a good reason why you are not telling me more precisely what it is you are looking for.'

'Those are my orders, I'm afraid. All I can say is that there is a clever criminal who may be connected in some way with the club, or is merely using its amenities. Perhaps there is more than one. But whoever it is has no conscience and acts only for the money he will make.'

Cedric nodded. 'Understood. Ah, and now I see the reason for your interest in the financial position of the members.'

'That is correct. I was looking for a criminal, not a husband.'

'No reason why you shouldn't look for both,' he said with a smile, 'although I shall make a close study of any man who catches your eye to ensure that he is worthy of you. You may rely upon me for that.'

'I am not sure I will ever marry,' said Frances, realising that much as she craved love, even if she was to find it, it would be very hard for her, after engaging in a career as a detective, to settle to a quiet humdrum domestic life. Contentment and fulfillment as a woman would come at a heavy price, and she was not sure it was a sacrifice she was prepared to make. Cedric looked sympathetic, but as a man of great sense, who understood women better than most, he always knew when to abandon a subject.

Frances used the lull in conversation to unfold her map and lay it across the table. 'I have been examining the map of East Acton and two questions arise. Where was Morton Vance going when he was killed, and where had he come from? According to information given at the trial of Sam Linnett he lived in lodgings in Acton, only half a mile from where his bicycle was stored. But unusually, on that day, he was late for the club ride. He had been working that morning and was delayed at the office. Do you know where he worked?'

'Yes, he and his brother shared an office in Churchfield Street, Acton.' Cedric pointed it out. 'It's still less than a mile from Springfield Lodge.'

'I assume he would have walked from there to East Acton and collected his bicycle. But where did he go then?'

'The murder took place not long before last year's summer race meeting, so he was probably getting some practice, strengthening himself. He wasn't a great racer, but he had entered some of the handicaps. From East Acton he could have taken a nice little ride west up to Friar's Place, then across the railway bridge, and up Wales Farm Road and that would take him to the top of Old Oak Common Lane. Then he would turn south, back to East Acton and get there in time for tea with his friends.'

'That's not a long ride,' said Frances, following the route on the map with her finger.

'No, about half an hour.'

'If Mr Toop was right when he gave evidence as to what time Vance took the bicycle out, and Ross-Fielder was right about when he found the body, which was still warm, either Vance took a rather longer route, or he stopped for a time on the shorter way.'

Cedric nodded thoughtfully. 'If he was practising for a race he could well have taken a longer ride. There is a good one, here – you go further west through Acton then north up Horn Lane. That also goes up to the top of Old Oak Common Lane. It's about an hour.'

'That sounds more likely. But no one seems to have remembered seeing him on the way. At least no one who was called to testify at the trial.'

'Of course, bicyclists are not a rare sight around there. All the men, not only from the Bayswater but the other clubs, would have been out practising for the races. There was more than one club ride and a few men went out alone.'

'If a man had been going too fast where there were houses and passers-by, would that have been noticed and remembered?'

'Very likely, yes. Angry letters to the *Times* asking for the menace to be banned from the roads. People demanding that bicyclists pay the same tax as carriages. Any police who saw it would have reported it.'

'But there are very few dwellings along Old Oak Common Lane. And there was no policeman in the area at the time of the incident. Once Vance rode south again, he should have turned west onto East Acton Lane to put his bicycle back in the coach house at the lodge. That turning is north of Sam Linnett's farm, so he would never have needed to go that far down the lane.'

'I agree.'

'Instead of which he continued riding south, past the turning, as fast as he was able, away from safety and towards a known danger – Sam Linnett.'

'Since you put it that way – yes.'

'How can we explain that? Do you really think he was racing someone down the lane? And if he was, who was the man he was racing? Surely in the interests of discovering the truth someone would have admitted to it? Or would he have been too ashamed? I thought the club members were decent men and would have owned up, but no one did.'

Cedric leaned back in his chair and gave the question serious thought. 'I don't think Vance was racing. I never met him, but I have read his contributions to the club magazine, and he struck me as a very steady and sensible fellow who would never have done such a thing.'

'You would never dream of racing down that lane, not even for a wager?'

'No,' said Cedric, emphatically. 'I value my life and limbs too much. And Joseph is hysterical enough every time I go out for a club ride.'

'So, tell me, what would make you ride as fast as you could into possible danger?'

He mused on this for a while. 'Some urgent, deadly affair. A vital message to deliver. Or some terrible threat, a danger behind me far worse than a violent pig-man.' Cedric paused. 'I think I can see what you are hinting at. Sam Linnett claimed that he had left Vance lying in the road, hurt but alive, and someone else came up afterwards and committed the murder. Is that possible? You don't think Linnett was innocent, do you?'

'I don't know. Only I feel that there is more to the murder of Morton Vance than was revealed at the trial.'

Cedric shook his head. 'Bad business hanging a man, even a horrid brute like Linnett. Not a mistake that can be put right.'

They were both in a serious mood as the port bottle was closed up and the remaining cheese wrapped carefully and placed in the larder.

'Mr Garton – Cedric,' said Frances, 'when your cousin Frank's bruises have eased a little he would like to pay another visit to East Acton before the race meeting. I want to see if I can find any clues as to what sent Morton Vance on that last desperate ride. According to the evidence at the trial he was his normal cheerful self when he took his bicycle out. An hour later he was not. I want to know why.'

CHAPTER ELEVEN

Despite the scratches and bruises, the very real risks of more serious injury and the muscle strains she had suffered in places where she would never have suspected she even had muscles, Frances found herself eager to ride the bicycle again. How she wished that she could ride openly as a woman and not in disguise. Was this really an activity to be confined solely to the circus? How she would shock people if she tried it in the respectable avenues of Bayswater! If Frances had had no concerns for her reputation she might have been tempted to try it, but being found improperly dressed in public would not assist her claim to run a respectable business. There were enough men who believed that a woman detective must be a creature of loose morals, even without a public scandal.

A tricycle was all very fine, and might even be suitable for town use, as it was slow enough not to alarm horses, but Frances had no stable for it, nowhere to keep such a large machine. If she purchased one for country excursions, would she be permitted to keep it at Springfield Lodge? Did the club even accept women members? In any case, now she had tasted the heady delights and dazzling freedom that could only be afforded by the high-wheeler, Frances knew that she would not be content with a tricycle until such time as age and infirmity dictated it necessary. After all, she reminded herself, Sir Hugo Daffin was sixty-five and he still rode a bicycle.

Curious to learn more, Frances paid a visit to the Bayswater public reading rooms, where she studied a selection of periodicals devoted to the new recreation of bicycling. She found that it was possible for a woman to ride the smaller wheeled velocipede, but only at the cost of drawing up her skirts to expose her lower limbs, something Frances did not feel ready to do. She also discovered that someone had once adapted a high-wheeler so that ladies in long heavy skirts could ride side-saddle, although in practice this was slow and awkward, the machine proving to be even less stable than the male version. The device, after a brief status as a novelty, had not proved popular. Something, she felt, should be done to give women the independence they could achieve by riding a bicycle, without abandoning either decency or respect, but she didn't know what it might be.

There was an interesting advance in store for the bicyclist, since an American inventor, a Mr Edison, who was reputed to be a very clever man, was about to patent a bicycle powered by electricity, the mechanism being enclosed in the hollow backbone. Several articles were devoted to the possible military use of the bicycle, suggesting that troops could employ them to move in silent speed and less tiringly than on foot. It was proposed that a volunteer corps of bicyclists should be formed, whose chief function would be to convey intelligence, a scheme that had already been discussed by the War Office. The main practical drawback was the potential for falls on the kind of rough terrain encountered by armies, a difficulty that had not yet been solved.

On the day before her second bicycling expedition Frances received a small gift from Cedric, a new invention, a pair of gentlemen's trouser fasteners, loops of springy steel that men could use to clip around their trousers at the ankle to stop them flapping as they rode. It was such a small thing yet it offered another freedom, the ability to ride a bicycle safely without resorting to knee britches and stockings. Men, she realised, with a sigh of frustration, had given yet another freedom to men. It was obvious that if women were to achieve what they desired they would have to do it for themselves. No wonder the daring Miss Dauntless performed the apparent madnesses she did, she was only taking what should have been hers.

When Cedric and his young cousin Frank next visited East Acton, Springfield Lodge was alive with activity. Many of the members had arrived to take out their machines for exercise or repair, and Jack Linnett was on hand to advise and assist. There was talk of the current good weather and if it would hold, as the month was predicted to end wet and cool, and farmers were hurrying to get the harvests in. Speculation was lively as to the outcome of the duel between Iliffe and Babbit, the only question being by how much Iliffe would triumph. Sir Hugo was striding about cheerfully, looking on at the busy scene and polishing his monocle with gusto. Toop hurried up with some papers, which he showed to Sir Hugo, the order of the proposed races for the forthcoming meeting, which was duly approved. The only unhappy face in the entire crowd was that of a tall young man with an over long neck and underdeveloped moustache, who was examining his bicycle and shaking his head in dismay.

'That's Ross-Fielder,' said Cedric. 'I hope there is nothing the matter with his machine.'

'Can you find out?' asked Frances, quietly.

Cedric nodded and sauntered up to Ross-Fielder, who was bending down beside the bicycle, staring intently at the front wheel. 'Something the matter, old chap?'

'Yes, it's bad,' sighed Ross-Fielder. 'Very bad. Look at this.'

Cedric squatted down and examined the problem. 'Two of the spokes are broken,' he said. 'Well, not to worry, Jack is here and they can be replaced easily enough.'

'No, you don't see it,' insisted Ross-Fielder, miserably. 'They haven't broken. They've been cut through. See how clean and sharp the ends are. I rode out yesterday and everything was in order, so it's happened since then.'

Toop hurried up. 'Your machine is damaged?' he exclaimed. 'Oh, bad luck!'

'It's not bad luck,' moaned Ross-Fielder, 'it's been done on purpose! Look at the spokes. Someone has taken a wire cutter to them.'

'Oh surely not. Who would do that?' Toop bent and examined the damage, then abruptly straightened up. 'Oh, damme, Ross-Fielder, you're right!' A sudden thought struck him and he gave a little yelp of alarm, and dashed into the coach house.

'This is a bad business,' said Cedric. 'Toop is right to be concerned, we had better check all the others before any one else goes out.' He beckoned to Frances. 'Frank, come with me.' Frances, who had been standing a little back, hurried to his side and bent to look at the wheel. Now that it had been pointed out she could see that the spokes were cleanly cut.

'What is this?' asked Sir Hugo approaching them, and Cedric left it to Ross-Fielder to explain. 'How this saddens me!' sighed Sir Hugo, grunting as he straightened up after examining the damage. 'The ignorance of people who cannot see a good thing without destroying it.'

By now, Jack Linnett as well as the other wheelmen still present had realised that something was amiss and gathered about Sir Hugo for instructions. 'I am sorry to tell you,' said Sir Hugo, heavily, 'that some vandal has made an attack on Mr Ross-Fielder's machine, severing two of the spokes.' There was an immediate burst of incredulity but he raised his hands for silence. 'There is no mistake. The spokes are not broken, they have been cut through. We know nothing of the machines that have already gone out and can only hope that if there is any damage it is of a similar minor nature, which will enable our men to return unhurt. In the meantime, all the remaining machines must be brought out of the coach house and examined with great care before anyone rides them. For myself, I will go and check the workshop and hope that all is undisturbed there.'

There was immediate assent to carrying out this task as swiftly as possible, and Sir Hugo walked away shaking his head.

There were enough members still present to bring out the machines onto the pathway and look at them in daylight. Frances managed to occupy herself and avoid any awkwardness by working with Cedric. Sir Hugo soon returned to say that the workshop was still safely locked. Ultimately the exercise resulted in a delay of only about twenty minutes, and the verdict was that the only machine that had suffered any damage was Ross-Fielder's.

'I'll have to stay and check it over very thoroughly before I ride it again,' said that gentleman unhappily. 'Who knows what hidden mischief there is? Better safe than sorry.'

'Really this makes no sense at all,' said Cedric to Frances as they took their bicycles out. 'If anyone was going to be attacked in that way it would probably be Goring or Iliffe, as they are the ones most likely to win the best prizes. And why cut the spokes? The only thing that has achieved is to prevent Ross-Fielder from going out today but of all the things that could have been done it's the most easily mended.'

'What if he hadn't noticed the damage before he set out?' asked Frances.

'With only two spokes gone, he would have sensed some instability in the wheel before he had gone very far, and turned back. No real harm.'

'It might just have been chance that it was his machine,' said Frances. 'Some person who hates bicyclists. There are enough of them. And if they didn't know any better they might have thought it was more serious damage than it actually was.'

'From what the other fellows were saying there have been no strangers seen about the place. Only club members and one or two men who have hired machines before and are well known.'

Frances felt that she would have liked to interview all those who had been present that afternoon, since she thought that if she did so she would be able to solve the mystery, but no one had mentioned consulting a detective. The club members, in all probability, would assume that there had simply been an intruder they had failed to notice, and pay better attention to the safety of their machines in future. If the nuisance persisted the police would be called, and if the threat became serious, Cedric might propose that Miss Frances Doughty should be engaged.

'How easy is it to tell the difference between individual machines?' she asked.

'Very easy for the regular rider. There are different designs, colours, manufacturers. All kinds of special features. Lamps, oil cans, some even have brakes, though you know my opinion on those.'

'But to the non-enthusiast who might not know them apart? If he wanted to tell one man's bicycle from another's? How would he do that?'

'Oh, I see what you mean. Many members have their initials engraved on the backbone, or have a tourist's bag behind the saddle with their name stamped on the leather.'

'Does Ross-Fielder's machine have such markings?'

'Yes, he bought a new tourist's bag the other day; he showed it to us. He had HRF stamped on it. Toop was positively jealous and went out and bought one just like it, only his had to be the best cowhide and cost an extra five shillings.'

'So it is possible that the person who damaged Ross-Fielder's machine might have known that it was his, and made him a specific target?'

'I suppose so.'

'You wouldn't remember if his bicycle was stored near the door, or far from it?'

'Hmmm. Not really. I don't think it was the nearest one.'

'So other men's machines were overlooked in order to damage that one?'

'Oh, I see what you mean. Yes.'

'Can you think of anyone who might have wanted to take action against Ross-Fielder?'

'No, I can't. He's a most inoffensive type.'

'No one with the same initials or a similar looking machine?'

'No.'

'What about the man who attacked Ross-Fielder's father? Robert Coote. I know he's in prison, but he might have associates.' Even as she spoke, Frances thought back to her reading of the trial. Coote, it had been said, was an orphan, and he had been brought to court unsupported by any family or friends. It was a curious mystery, but she had no further ideas to offer. Perhaps she would find out more later.

Cedric Garton and his cousin Frank rode west through the village of East Acton, then turned south, past the smithy, a small school, and the outbuildings of Manor Farm. They were soon in the outskirts of Acton proper, turning to head west again, past some enclosed lands, the little railway station, and bumping over the bridge that crossed the North and South Western junction line. The streets were narrow with houses and shops ranged tightly against each other on either side, and there was enough horse traffic to ensure that anyone on a bicycle needed to proceed with caution. The riders took care to slow down when passing any horses, and the animals were only a little unsettled, suggesting that they were beginning to get accustomed to bicycles even if they didn't precisely approve of them.

Circling around a walled estate they turned north up Horn Lane. This moderately well peopled route bought them to the bridge crossing the Great Western Railway line, and Willesden Lane.

Here they stopped briefly to consult a map. 'Do any of the club members live along this route?' asked Frances.

'I don't believe so.' After some study it was agreed that the route most probably taken by Morton Vance on the day of his death did not take him near to the homes or places of work of any fellow members of the BBC.

They remounted and rode on, reaching at last the northern end of Old Oak Common Lane. It was a slow ride from there as Frances was still not skilled enough over the rough pathway, having to take especial care to avoid ditches on one side and the culvert of Stamford Brook on the other, with the added dangers of cast-iron access plates for the drains. It was as they turned into the narrow path over the common that they began to see unusual activity. A number of uniformed men were walking in a line, spreading out, looking in ditches and hedgerows, exploring clumps of trees and prodding suspicious looking bushes with sticks.

'Well here's a thing!' said Cedric. 'I wonder what's afoot?'

The dark drab uniforms suggested at first that these were policemen but Frances noticed that they wore peaked caps instead of helmets, and thick key-chains were attached to their belts. 'Those aren't police,' she said. 'They're prison officers. They must be from Wormwood Scrubs.'

One of the men approached them, looking rather hot and worried, and signalled that he wanted to speak. They slowed and dismounted.

'Have you seen anyone behaving suspiciously, sir?' asked the man.

'No, my cousin and I were just taking the fresh air on this fine day,' said Cedric heartily. 'What should we be on the look-out for?'

'Prisoner escaped from the Scrubs,' said the man. 'Violent type, too, so I suggest you take care. If you see a young man with a shaven head, and wearing a suit with broad arrows on it, don't approach him. Stay well clear, remember where you saw him, and tell us or the police at once.'

'We will,' said Cedric. The guard passed a hand over his sweating brow and trudged away.

Frances and Cedric mounted their bicycles and continued on their way. 'Poor fellows,' said Cedric. 'I mean the prisoners. It's bad enough to shut them away for their crimes, but they work them like slaves, too. Can't blame a man for making a break for it.'

They rode south cautiously, looking about them, but saw nothing to alert their attention. 'Is this a frequent occurrence?' asked Frances. 'Was there a prison escape when Morton Vance was killed? I don't recall seeing anything in the newspapers.'

'I'm sure it would have been mentioned at the trial. This is the first such incident I have heard of since I joined the club.'

Police officers had come to swell the numbers of prison guards, and the men were fanning out across the fields, which had been recently shorn of their wheat and were dotted with bundles of hay, but there was no sign of a desperate figure leaping out of the hedgerows or outbuildings or from behind a hay bale, and making a sudden run. The two riders reached the turn into East Acton Lane without further incident, and headed back to the lodge. The first thing they saw was the police.

Frances, aware that it might go badly for her if she was discovered to be a female dressed as a male, gave a little gasp and hesitated, then decided to brave it out. 'I'll do the talking,' said Cedric as they dismounted and rolled the bicycles back to the coach house. A sergeant was talking to Ross-Fielder who was looking distraught, and Sir Hugo and Mr Toop were standing nearby with serious expressions.

A constable approached Cedric. 'Good afternoon sir? Might I have your name?'

'Cedric Garton, I am a member of the club and this is my cousin, Frank Williamson. I am teaching him to ride.'

'Have you been in the area of Wormwood Scrubs at all today?'

'We were there just now, and saw a number of police and prison officers looking for an escaped convict. I'm sorry to say that we saw nothing that could help you. Is the man still at large?'

'I'm afraid so. We're asking all members of the public to look out for him, but not to approach him if he is seen. Just notify the police at once.'

'We'll be sure to do that,' said Cedric. 'I do hope he is found soon.'

'Thank you, sir,' said the constable and re-joined the sergeant, who closed his notebook and bid Ross-Fielder farewell. Cedric and Frances took their bicycles back to the coach house. Once alone there Frances said, 'I am not a great believer in coincidences. That is, they may happen occasionally but I do not like it when they occur too often. It is very strange that we have an escaped convict and damage to Ross-Fielder's bicycle on the same day.'

'You have such a devious mind, Frank, I commend you for it.'

Frances thought it over and shook her head. 'Even so, it makes no sense to me. If the escaped man came here, he would surely have been seen in such distinctive clothing. And why damage a bicycle? Why not steal one and make his escape? He could have put on one of those capes as a disguise.' Frances examined the row of capes at the back of the coach house, but all the hooks were occupied.

Ross-Fielder came in, sighing, accompanied by Toop. 'I will hire a bicycle to go home, I have not finished checking over mine, but I need to go and see father at once.'

'Take whichever one you like,' said Toop. 'No charge. It's really the least we can do.'

Ross-Fielder went to fetch a bicycle, while Toop noted the hire of the machine in his ledger.

'Very bad business, his machine being attacked like that,' said Cedric. 'Upsetting. But I am sure it can be mended without any trouble.'

'Oh yes, young Linnett can see to it, and it will be as good as new in no time,' said Toop. 'No, the circumstance that particularly distresses our friend is the identity of the escaped criminal. It's Coote, the same reprobate who attacked his father; that is why he is hurrying home, to be with him. The police have already advised the Reverend Ross-Fielder of possible danger, but understandably the son wishes to fly to his side to reassure himself that all is well.'

'Oh my word!' exclaimed Cedric. 'Do you think it could have been Coote who damaged the bicycle?'

'Well now, I hadn't thought of that. The coach house has been open since this morning with men going back and forth, and one can't keep an eye open for all possibilities. I know we have not seen a man in convict's uniform, but he might have had a friend who could have lent him some clothes. Oh dear, oh dear.' Toop took a large silk handkerchief from his pocket and passed it across his forehead.

'If it is he, then I doubt he'll be back,' said Cedric. 'He'll want to get away as far and as fast as he can.'

Frances tugged at Cedric's sleeve and whispered.

'Ah, yes,' said Cedric. 'That's a thought. Are there any machines missing?'

'You think he might have stolen one?' gasped Toop. 'Yes, of course, so he might. Oh how terrible for this to happen now! I shall have to check and see. But, of course, we won't know for certain until all the members are back.' Toop groaned and hurried away.

'What does the noted detective say?' asked Cedric.

Frances considered this. 'It's like opening a box of puzzles and being told that I am not to try and solve any of them.'

'And now I am worried,' said Cedric.

CHAPTER TWELVE

During the next few days, as Frances prepared for her visit to the race meeting of the Bayswater Bicycle Club, she made a further study of the circumstances of Morton Vance's murder. She had often observed that some newspaper reports were better than others. The time available, the column space, the skill of the correspondent, and the vagaries of shorthand all led to slightly differing accounts of the same event. Vital information included in one description could be entirely omitted from another. Additionally, she had found that small details might only be mentioned once, at the inquest, or the subsequent committal proceedings, or the trial, so for the fullest possible picture she needed to gather all available information from all sources, and put them together like the pieces of a jigsaw puzzle.

Her main concern was to discover whether another member of the club could have been riding down Old Oak Common Lane at the same time as Morton Vance. None of the witnesses could be precise about any of the timings, except that a lady who had been tending her garden at the very northern end of Old Oak Common Lane had told the inquest that she had seen a bicyclist who resembled Morton Vance pass her by, going south, and it had then been a little after five o'clock. He had been going at a leisurely speed, and gave no signs of anxiety. A few minutes later she had returned indoors to prepare for visitors, and it was for that reason she had glanced at her mantel clock, which she knew to tell the correct time. The clock showed ten minutes past five. She had not seen another bicyclist.

Frances, having ridden the route, knew that if that rider had been Morton Vance he would have reached the place where he was murdered about five minutes after being seen, assuming that he had not paused on the way.

Henry Ross-Fielder had told the inquest that he could not recall exactly what time he had left his home in Holland Park for his ride, but he thought it would have been after five o'clock. He had not been intending to go to East Acton at all, but take a circular route that did not go through the village, and return home. When he had found the body, no one else was in sight. He had stopped to see if there was any assistance he could give, but it had taken him very little time to realise that there was no hope for Vance, and he had ridden as hard as he could to arrive in East Acton, where he arrived just as the clock of St Dunstan's Church was striking the half hour.

It followed, thought Frances, that Morton Vance must have been killed between five o'clock and half past, and most probably during the fifteen minutes between ten past and twenty-five past the hour.

Frances turned to other accounts of where the club members had been that afternoon. They had assembled at Springfield Lodge at half past three, and after a brief meeting set off in line for the club ride at about a quarter to four. The only members who were not with them on that run were Ross-Fielder, Morton Vance who, they were told, had been delayed at his office, and Mr Toop, who had remained at the lodge in charge of the coach house. Phineas Vance had said that he didn't think his brother would be joining them for the ride so they didn't wait, and had gone without him. In the event, Morton Vance had arrived at the coach house unexpectedly at about a quarter past four and taken his bicycle out, saying that he expected to be back within the hour. This, thought Frances, fitted well with the sighting of the rider thought to be Vance at the top of Old Oak Common Lane shortly after five.

The club riders had returned to the lodge at about five o'clock. After putting their bicycles away, they had gone indoors to wash their faces and enjoy a light tea, which was prepared for them by Mrs Pirrie. There were two exceptions to this. Mr Toop, whose mother was unwell, had left to visit her as soon as the others returned, and the club's professional racer, Paul Iliffe, saying he needed to make some adjustments to his bicycle, had volunteered to look after the coach house in his place. Mrs Pirrie had sent Waterfield out to him with a cup of tea and sandwiches. She hadn't made a note of the time, but it would have been about the same time as the other young men sat down to their tea, perhaps ten or at most fifteen minutes past five o'clock.

Waterfield confirmed that he had taken tea and a plate to Iliffe and had a brief conversation with him before returning indoors. Not long afterwards, Ross-Fielder had ridden up to the lodge, found Iliffe in the coach house, and given the alarm.

All the club members who had been on the weekly ride were therefore in the lodge having tea at the time of Vance's murder, apart from Iliffe, who had been in the coach house where he was seen by both Waterfield and Ross-Fielder. Toop had told the inquest that he could not recall whether or not he had mentioned to Iliffe that while they were on their ride Morton Vance had arrived and taken his bicycle out, but on the whole he thought that in his eagerness to get home he might have forgotten.

It seemed likely, thought Frances, that all the club members apart from Toop had assumed that Vance was not out riding at all. Even if someone had known, it was unlikely that he would have set out on purpose to intercept him, since no one could possibly have known precisely where he would be at any moment, and an individual's absence would have been noticed. If Vance had encountered another rider, either a bicyclist or a horseman, it was most probably pure chance. She wondered briefly if there had been some prior agreement between Vance and another man to rendezvous in secret, and Vance's supposed lateness had simply been a device to allow time for the meeting, a meeting that had ended with a race, or even a flight, down Old Oak Common Lane. Whoever that unknown pursuer was, he could not have been a member of the club. There was insufficient time for Iliffe to leave the coach house unattended and go out to meet Vance, Toop was not a racing man, and all the other members were together having their tea.

Chapter Thirteen

During the days that followed there was no further news of the escaped convict Coote. The newspapers carried reports of the incident, recalling the circumstances of his crime and conviction, and offered words of sympathy for the Reverend Ross-Fielder. He replied graciously that he had already forgiven his attacker, and declined to make any further comment.

Interviews with those who resided near to the prison revealed only mystification. No one claimed to have seen the escaped man, neither had anyone loaned any form of transport to a stranger. Coote had simply disappeared.

Cedric informed Frances that a careful survey by the members of the Bayswater Bicycle Club had confirmed that no machines had been stolen from the Springfield Lodge coach house, from which he assumed that if Coote had been there he must have left on foot. The prevailing point of view in the club was that the damage to Ross-Fielder's machine was nothing to do with the escaped convict.

There was one other fact that Frances needed to check with Cedric – Mr Toop's excuse for leaving the coach house early on the day of Morton Vance's murder. All that Cedric could say was that he could quite believe this since Toop's mother had passed away some four months ago after a long illness.

The newspapers included one paragraph that Frances found extremely disturbing.

The betrothal has been announced of Mr Timothy Wheelock, to Leonora, eldest daughter of Henry Marsden the well-known Bayswater solicitor. Mr Wheelock has recently completed his articles and after taking the Law Society examinations has been admitted to practise as a solicitor. He has also become a junior partner of his future father-in-law's practice, which will be formally changing its name to Marsden and Wheelock. Mr Wheelock is 25 and Miss Marsden 16. The wedding will take place next spring.

Frances' concerns were all for the unfortunate Miss Marsden, almost certainly an innocent pawn in a very calculated game. Timothy Wheelock had been the confidential clerk of her former solicitor Mr Rawsthorne, who was currently serving a prison sentence for the embezzlement of his clients' funds, including those of her own father. On the death of William Doughty, Frances, his only surviving child, had been expecting to inherit the chemist's business on Westbourne Grove, however, it was not to be. Rawsthorne, who William had trusted and counted as a personal friend of many years standing, had brazenly informed Frances that her fortune was gone. He had blamed the situation on her father's previously unsuspected habit of gambling on the stock exchange, which had proved disastrous. She had always believed Rawsthorne to be an honest guardian of the family finances, and it had never occurred to her that he was telling her anything other than the facts. It was only recently, and through information supplied by Wheelock that she had discovered the horrible truth.

It had been a devastating blow to lose her inheritance, but it was the circumstance that had set her life on its present course. The business had been sold to pay debts and she had been left with almost nothing. Faced with the options of accepting the charity of an uncle, making a grim loveless marriage, or becoming a professional detective, she had made the hardest choice and had never regretted it. In a curious way the disaster had been the making of her. Rawsthorne's descent into disgrace and bankruptcy had given her no pleasure, but she did feel a great sense of satisfaction in knowing that all she currently possessed she had earned herself.

Wheelock was a thoroughly unpleasant young man who sailed so close to illegal practice and blackmail that he was frequently in danger of falling over the edge, yet always found himself able to escape what would have been a well-deserved fate. The secret of his advancement was the careful preservation of information that he could use against others. He did not care for Frances but neither did he dislike her, and regarded her with wary respect. It was due to her that he had avoided being charged with the murder of his former wife, and to his way of thinking he was in her debt. Frances usually tried to have nothing to do with him, but their fortunes collided with uncomfortable frequency.

The only man who repelled her more than Wheelock, apart from the horrible Filleter of course, was solicitor Henry Marsden, who lost no opportunity of sneering at and belittling her activities as a detective. Wheelock and Marsden were well suited, a partnership made not in Heaven but a quite different place.

And Marsden's daughter, Leonora? Frances had never met the young lady, although there had been rumours that she was unlikely, due to some fault in her appearance, ever to be presented in society. Mr Wheelock was a man incapable of any tender emotion. His first marriage had been a calculated attempt to obtain possession of an elderly lady's fortune, and Frances did not think the second one was likely to have been contracted for any more romantic reasons. She only hoped that since the unfortunate Miss Marsden was a valuable connection, she would be treated with kindness, or at least without cruelty. The first Mrs Wheelock, Frances recalled, had been kept quiet and compliant with sherry. Marsden would almost certainly live to rue the day he had ever allowed Timothy Wheelock into his life. Frances knew, although Mr Marsden did not, that his future son-in-law held papers in a bank vault that could be brought out and used to destroy him at the right moment. When that moment would be, she did not know, but Mr Wheelock would calculate it down to the exact second.

There was worse news in the post. Frances received a letter from the owner of the house in which she lodged. She thought she had worded her request very politely, asking that he reconsider his rule that children should not be allowed to live in the house, and had anticipated a favourable reply, but this was not to be. He would not change his mind. If Miss Doughty wished to purchase the house – and here he mentioned a figure far beyond her means – then as the owner she could make whatever rules she pleased, but not until then. If Sarah and Professor Pounder were to marry and raise a family, then they would have to find other accommodation.

In the days before the race meeting Frances and Sarah were both busy interviewing new clients for the detective agency, and pursuing their own cases. Since the secret mission would occupy the whole of one day, it was important to try and conclude as much business as possible beforehand. The summer, Frances noticed, was the time of year for inadvisable romances, and she often had to deal with irate parents whose sons and daughters had been carried away by balmy weather and sunlight. Tom and Ratty were expert at finding lost pets or missing children, as well as drunken persons who had strayed far from home. Sarah's speciality was defending women from selfish and profligate husbands, and settling disputes between neighbours that often descended into violence. She had recently started a campaign against a carrier who ill-treated his horses. This led Frances to wonder what the streets of the metropolis would be like if horse transport became a thing of the past, apart, necessarily, from the carrying of heavy loads and drawing omnibuses, and the roads were otherwise populated entirely by bicycles and tricycles, carrying people to their destinations. Quieter, certainly, and cleaner, with better air. Would she miss the constant noise of harness, hooves and the turn of carriage wheels? What would happen to the unneeded horses and how would coachmen and carriage-makers fare? She had no answers.

Sarah had said nothing more about her wedding plans, but she seemed content. On the evenings when both she and

Frances were at home they sat companionably in the parlour, and practised speaking in signs. They were not as proficient as deaf children, but by confining their studies to the most used words and the alphabet they found it a valuable skill, and given the circumstances of their forthcoming mission, felt that a little practice would not come amiss.

There was one other important preparation Frances had made for her visit to the race meeting, the construction of her new divided skirt and *polonaise*, which were by far the most expensive and elegant garments she had ever purchased. Once the costume, in a beautiful shade of muted violet, was complete, she put it on and took some turns in front of a mirror. She found the ensemble both elegant and practical. She had instructed her dressmaker that she required the costume for the purposes of playing lawn tennis, and therefore lightness was essential. The skirts, in a fabric appropriate to the summer months, had been carefully cut to give the impression of fullness yet required far less volume and weight of material than was usual. In walking she was not nearly so encumbered as she had been before, and could therefore move more freely and with greater energy, yet nothing in the new fashion offended any notions of decency. Whether it was possible to ride a bicycle in such an ensemble she rather doubted, because the two parts of the skirt were still wider and heavier than the legs of trousers, but it would be a great boon if she ever had to climb another fence, especially if she used the trouser fasteners to hold some of the fabric at bay. After some experimenting she saw that it was a definite improvement. With that in mind, she put the trouser fasteners in her reticule. A lady detective never knew when she might need them.

Chapter Fourteen

The day of the Bayswater Bicycle Club's annual summer race meeting promised to be fine and dry, and there was a good breeze to help cool the riders. Since Cedric had attended a similar meeting in the previous spring, he was able to tell Frances during the journey there what she might expect. Goldsmith's Cricket Ground was to be open to the public from late morning, and a substantial turnout was anticipated since all amateur riders were eligible to enter the competitions, and their families and friends and all other interested spectators were welcome to attend. The hours before luncheon were mainly devoted to social interaction, taking advantage of numerous opportunities to purchase refreshments and anything bicycle related, the provision of lessons by experienced wheelmen for those eager to learn, promenades of new machines, the contest for the best turned-out bicycle, and some of the minor races. The more demanding competitions were to begin after luncheon at two o'clock and continue throughout the afternoon with a necessary break for tea, culminating in a grand prize-giving.

A sixpenny ticket purchased from the club or at the gate would ensure entry to all the amenities but a more expensive ticket, which Cedric had already secured for them all, included luncheon and tea. 'We are promised that this will be even bigger and better attended than the last meeting,' said Cedric, as they boarded the cab. He handed Frances a copy of the club programme. Ratty, who rarely had the opportunity to travel by that mode of transport, found a comfortable place in one corner, and stared out of the window in wrapt fascination. 'The leading manufacturers of wheeled machines will be there to tell us all about their innovations,' Cedric continued. 'The races will be very thrilling. Ladies will find it a perfect feast of manly beauty. There will be single young gentlemen of athletic proportions as far as the eye can see.'

'C'n I go ridin'?' asked Ratty.

'Of course you can,' said Cedric.

Ratty squirmed in excited anticipation.

'The meeting last summer was due to take place very soon after the murder of Mr Vance,' reflected Frances. 'Or was it cancelled out of respect?'

'No, his parents insisted that the club should not cancel it, and it was agreed to hold the event in his honour. I understand there were many affecting tributes, collections for charities to be donated in Vance's name, and the inauguration of a special cup for the most sporting wheelman. It will be awarded for the first time today and we anticipate that Goring will receive the accolade.'

Frances studied the race list. 'There is a ladies' tricycle race,' she said. 'If I was not otherwise occupied I might almost think to enter it. I'm sure I could give a good account of myself.'

'The ladies are very keen on that competition,' said Cedric. 'Quite as much as the men – in fact, probably more so as it is their only race.'

'Then there ought to be more,' said Frances severely. 'The only real attempt to enable ladies to ride bicycles was by devising great awkward machines to accommodate heavy skirts that were of no practical use, when from my observation the trouser has already been invented. Can men not see what is before their eyes?'

'Usually, no,' said Cedric, sadly.

'Miss John has declared that she will abandon ladies' garments altogether in favour of the trouser.'

'Has she? In public? I am not quite sure the world is ready for that.'

Ratty sniggered.

'Perhaps it is not, but I hope one day it will be. It is only common sense. I think that all men should be made to wear female clothing for at least one day and then they will see how cumbrous it is.'

Cedric's eyes opened wide and he was silent for several minutes.

Arriving in East Acton, they passed by the entrance to Springfield Lodge and saw BBC members taking their bicycles out and wheeling them towards the cricket ground, which was very close by.

Theirs was not the only cab drawing up in front of the entrance to the ground, although other arrivals were travelling in by bicycle and tricycle, and there were couples treadling in on sociables. Frances commented on how convenient the sociable must be for friends and married people, and Cedric said, 'Oh yes, apart from the drawback that one must have a coach house to keep it in, because of the size, you know. Not a racing vehicle, of course. But they are becoming more popular all the time. It is said that in time they will replace the hansom, which has rather upset cabdrivers.'

Cedric handed Frances down from the cab, a gallantry he had had to avoid doing when she had been in male attire, and Ratty jumped down, all eagerness, as if he was on springs. 'I shall fetch my bicycle from the coach house and rejoin you very shortly,' said Cedric. 'The club machines are to go into a tent on the field, and there will be lessons given gratis. We are hoping to gain many new members. It will be so jolly!' He hurried away.

As Frances, accompanied by Ratty, showed their tickets at the gate, and entered the large open space of the cricket ground, she saw not so much the prospect of jollity but a great number of opportunities for committing crime. Anyone with sixpence, old, young, male, female, could enter the grounds and wander at will about the field. Most visitors were in pairs or groups, but there were a few individual men, and while many were doubtless there to sample the new pastime, Frances felt sure that a significant number had no interest in bicycling and were bent only on mischief. How many of the youths who paid their fee for the afternoon were out to make a profit from thieving, or meeting with criminal contacts, and passing messages and stolen items unsuspected? Was the club involved, or were its members simply the innocent providers of an opportunity for exchange?

'What do you see?' she asked Ratty.

He grinned. 'Lotta things. Buyin', sellin', pickpocketin', all sorts.'

'Well, just for once you must look but do nothing. Once Mr Garton returns, walk about the field, and report back to me when you can.'

Frances tried to get a measure of how the field was laid out. It was an irregular shape, which she knew from her map to be roughly rectangular. At one end was a handsome little whitewashed pavilion with the flags of the East Acton cricket club and the Bayswater Bicycle Club quivering in the breeze. A veranda at the front of the house was provided with tables and chairs. One could enter the pavilion by a set of central wooden stairs but there were also rows of deeper steps on either side, occupied by chairs for spectators. Other onlookers were catered for by a single row of bench seating forming an oval around the field, but there was also a substantial amount of space for those who preferred to stand.

The main grassy area of the playing field had been marked out with a double row of poles and ropes for use as a bicycle track, with gaps here and there for access, although this also gave onlookers the choice of crossing the track to watch the races from inside the course. Only the central area of the field was covered with a protective tarpaulin and roped around presumably to dissuade visitors from walking on it. Surrounding the track and outside the bench seating were a variety of tents, stalls and enclosures.

A tent had been erected in one corner of the field, to which club's wheelmen were bringing their mounts, and there was a signboard advertising free quarter hour lessons for beginners, and afternoon hire of bicycles at reduced fees. The Bayswater men were evident in their uniforms, but once they had their caps on, Frances found that from a distance they all looked rather alike, apart from Mr Toop, whose rotund figure marked him out. She wondered if one of them was the special agent sent by the silver-haired gentleman to join the club, possibly the mysterious Gideon he had mentioned.

Another tent formed a repository for accommodating the bicycles of visiting contestants, and there was also a larger roped-off area for the spectators' machines, perfect places, thought Frances, for the exchange of news and messages with people from outside the club. An enclosure had been provided in the name of Hicks, the East Acton blacksmith, offering small repairs on the spot, with Jack Linnett and another apprentice on hand. Frances had no doubt that there would be a constant flow of custom there.

Several merchants were displaying a wide selection of used bicycles for sale. They also offered velocipedes, a design that had surely had its day, but one that had given birth to the swifter, lighter, more elegant bicycle.

Cedric returned to the field with his bicycle and wheeled it over to the club tent, then he came to join Frances and Ratty. Sarah and Professor Pounder had just arrived and began walking together, arm-in-arm, looking very comfortable. Their glances about the field appeared to be no more than the natural interest of visitors, but Frances knew that they were watching carefully. A small hand sign from Sarah told her that all was well. Tom, who was rather small for his age, began moving about the field showing an innocent childlike interest in anything and everything, smart enough to be engaging, but never going so far as to invite suspicion.

Ratty, who was much the taller of the two boys, could pass as an older youth, just the sort of lad who looked ready to enter the world of the wheel, and he hurried away to get a closer look at the bicycles for hire. Frances watched him go with an almost sisterly pride. She recalled her first meeting with him; a ragged urchin, unable to read or write, with a strong natural intelligence and an ingrained terror of authority. The support of Frances and Cedric had given him confidence and an education. The scars of his younger life would never fully heal, but they would not now prevent him making a good future for himself. He had even started working as a private informant to the police force.

'Ah, the wheelman's paradise!' said Cedric, taking a deep breath to inhale the grassy scent. 'All one could wish for is here, and there are novelties impossible to imagine until one has actually seen them.' He offered Frances his arm, she took it, and together they began to tour the field.

All around the perimeter, tradesmen were busy setting up stalls displaying every addition to the bicycle that industry and ingenuity could create. Moving casually from each one to the next Frances was fascinated by the sheer number of ways in which manufacturers were anticipating and catering to the needs of the enthusiast. There were special paints and enamels to protect machines against the weather, devices for lighting one's way in the dark, carrying bags that fitted neatly and unobtrusively behind the saddle and claimed to hold everything the touring man might require, and tins of concentrated meat lozenges, a single one of which was said to be as nourishing as a meal. Individual parts of both bicycles and tricycles were laid out on trestles, displayed like the sections of a disarticulated skeleton. Here were wheels, tyres, forks, spokes, oil cans, bells, ball bearings, cranks, pedals, treadles, and saddles. The amateur with less money to spend could purchase the 'bicycle cabinet', a boxed collection of parts that he could take home together with a set of instructions for making his own bicycle. There was everything the rider might wish to wear – suits, stockings, jockey caps, polo caps and rubber rain capes. Understandably there was also a selection of liniments and rubbing oils to anoint sore muscles and heal sprains.

Non-bicyclists could purchase sweetmeats and bottles of aerated waters in a wide variety of flavours, and, in anticipation of a large female attendance, there was a selection of refreshing colognes to cool the skin in hot weather. Frances reminded herself that wherever conversation, money and products were being exchanged, so could other less commendable things.

More bicyclists were arriving in substantial numbers, displaying a variety of club uniforms mostly in sombre colours, although there were some that stood out in vibrant blue and light brown ornamented with silver and gold braid. The spectators who strolled around the field were dressed as for a summer outing, although the scene was less of an ostentatious fashion parade than Hyde Park, and in Frances' opinion, none the worse for it.

From time to time Tom or Ratty passed by Sarah and Pounder and after a few moments came close to Frances. A brief nod suggested that there was nothing to report.

The turn about the field brought Frances and Cedric in front of the pavilion. Some apron-clad ladies had emerged from the building and were busy laying the veranda tables with cloths, china and cutlery, ready for the sandwich and salad luncheons and the scone and cake teas that were to follow. Might those ladies be the purveyors of secrets as well, wondered Frances? Ladies could be spies just as well as men, perhaps better, she thought, because they were less likely to be suspected, and conversations that men dismissed contemptuously as gossip and did not bother to attend to could have a serious purpose.

To one side of the pavilion there was a small dais with a set of steps leading up to a platform, and on a table beside it, under the watchful eye of an attendant, was a modest collection of silver cups and medals in a locked glass case. A small group of men, already perspiring in heavy bandsmen's uniforms and carrying brass instruments, drums and music stands, were matching in line to a place near the dais, and began to arrange a convenient situation from which to entertain the crowds. A placard painted in maroon and gold, the same colours as their uniforms, announced them to be the Acton Brass Ensemble.

Opposite the pavilion was a large signboard painted black, with slots where boards marked with numbers could be

inserted to show the scores of cricket matches. Since it would
not be required that day, a Bayswater man was busily unfurling
a club banner with the intention of draping it from the board.
Frances, who was continuing to survey the field, suddenly saw
a flicker of impulsive movement out of the corner of her eye,
and glanced back to see that the clubman had abandoned the
banner and was striding away from another man. From the
jerky determined gestures of his arms he looked angry. Even
at a distance Frances felt sure that the clubman was Rufus
Goring. The other man, plainly dressed and rather shorter with
a bull neck, gesticulated and said something, but after a quick
look about him, decided not to go in pursuit. A moment later,
however, Goring turned about, and it was obvious that hard
words were being said. He gestured towards the entrance to
the grounds in an insistent manner, and it was clear that he was
ordering the man to leave.

They were too far away for Frances to overhear what was
being said or gather a great deal from facial expressions, and
it would have been too obvious for her to move closer. The
attitudes of the speakers left her in little doubt, however.
Goring was outraged by the presence of the smaller man, who
remained obdurate and unmoved.

Frances signed to Sarah, who was far closer to the confrontation, and she and Pounder surreptitiously moved into earshot,
while Ratty lurked nearby. Once again, Goring turned his back
on the unwelcome visitor, and, obviously eager to place a good
distance between himself and the other man, strode rapidly
to the club's bicycle tent where Ross-Fielder was in charge.
A conversation ensued and Ross-Fielder glanced at the object
of Goring's annoyance, who remained in the vicinity of the
scoreboard, looking unconcerned. Ross-Fielder nodded and
sent another club member to take over the duty of unfurling
the banner. Whoever it was seemed not to be worth approaching and performed the task unimpeded.

'What man is that?' asked Frances, 'the one who was talking
to Mr Goring just now.'

'Hmm,' said Cedric. 'I have seen him about before – I think he's the same fellow who made a nuisance of himself at the last race meeting. He's a bookmaker. I expect there's nothing much happening on the turf today, which is why he is here. His business is legal at the racetrack but this doesn't count, as he well knows, since this is not Ascot and we are not horses.'

Tom, enterprising as ever, had found himself an occupation handing out advertising leaflets for a bicycle manufacturer, and as he passed Cedric he said, 'I know 'im. That's Archie 'Opper. Runs a bettin' book. Track, street, any place 'e can. If I had ter place a bet on anythin' I'd say 'e'd just offered money to that bicyclist to lose a race.'

'Whatever his scheme, Mr Goring was having none of it and has warned his fellow club members,' said Frances. As she glanced that way again, a strongly built youth on a battered velocipede rode up to Hopper and the two began to talk in a manner that suggested private business. The youth looked as down-at-heel as his machine, in rough serviceable clothes that had been made for a smaller person, perhaps himself when younger, or another boy. Although he towered over Hopper, there was no doubt that the older man was in charge.

'Who is that other person?' asked Frances.

'That's Peters, 'is number one bully. Good for anythin' bad that one.' Tom scurried away.

Their business done, Peters nodded to Hopper and rode away, circling around the field, taking very little notice of the convenience or safety of those on foot. As he passed near to Frances she saw hard features almost bereft of sensibility, arms thick with muscle, meaty hands with dirty bruised knuckles.

Hopper remained on the field, meandering alone, but not going far, his eyes flickering about watchfully. Here was a man who cared nothing as to how he was turned out or what face he put to the world. He had an ill-natured look and his clothes seemed to be of the general kind that went to all places in all seasons. Every so often he ducked behind the scoreboard, which Frances guessed was his place of business.

'We can trust Pounder to keep an eye on Mr Hopper and do the necessary if he tries it again,' said Cedric. 'I have no doubt he is running an illegal book on the afternoon, and was hoping to profit from some skulduggery. The committee would never stand for that. The trick, of course, is to catch him at it.' He looked thoughtful. 'What about Pounder and that Peters fellow in the ring – bare knuckles for choice. Now that would be a match. Both big and strong but I know who's the cleverer man. Five guineas on Pounder.'

Some of the bicyclists were taking the opportunity to warm their muscles with a short ride around the course. It was also a chance for gentlemen supporters to wave them on and ladies to admire the flexing of male calves that resembled in shape and hardness those of a classical statue. 'Ah, now there's Iliffe,' said Cedric, pointing out a tall broad-shouldered man rotating first one arm then the other in slow and determined callisthenic exercises. Frances judged him to be in his late twenties, and he had the sturdy assured air that came with experience and knowledge of his art. 'Our professional wheelman. We expect him to win well today.'

'This is the race against his great rival, Mr Babbit?'

'Oh yes, there is some excitement on the boil about that.'

'Have they raced against each other before?'

'They have, several times, and are very well matched. The honours are even, I believe, although Iliffe's adherents think he has the edge, and he has only ever lost to Babbit through bad luck.'

A lady, accompanied by a young bicyclist in Bayswater uniform, walked up to Iliffe, the man smiling broadly, the lady with a softer, rather coy expression. She wore a pink gown with matching bonnet and pretty white lace mittens.

'Ah, they are the Jepsons, brother and sister,' said Cedric. 'Miss Jepson is very much admired for her attractive features and good temper. She has no sweetheart that we know of, but it is thought that she has a fondness for Mr Iliffe and that he returns that feeling.'

'Do you think there will be an engagement?' asked Frances.

'One day, perhaps, but not while Iliffe pursues his bicycling career.' Cedric paused and glanced across at the entrance to the ground. Frances followed his gaze and saw that a group of uniformed wheelmen had arrived, their coats and knee britches in brown with rust-coloured stockings. 'I see that Babbit has come with his friends from the Oakwood Club. Let us see what transpires.'

'Why, what usually transpires?'

'Oh a little drama, if we are fortunate. They usually stay at opposite ends of the field and fire barbs of hatred at each other with their eyes, but sometimes they move closer and utter growls like wild beasts. They should really go on the stage.'

Mr Babbit was of similar age and build to Iliffe. Both were powerful and long in the leg. Both were surrounded by an atmosphere of self-confidence. Iliffe, however, looked to be the quieter man, while Babbit had an unattractive swagger in his walk. He led the little party of Oakwood men as if his friends were merely acolytes there to attend him.

Babbit smiled when he saw Iliffe, as if already anticipating victory. He smiled still more broadly on seeing Miss Jepson, although the nature of the smile was not dissimilar. He paused and ran a forefinger over his moustache, first one way then the other. It was a glossy beast, much pomaded and turned up at either end, not quite of the order of the handsome Mr Goring's appendage, but still very impressive.

The Jepsons had also noticed the new arrival, and looked concerned. Iliffe merely shrugged and spoke reassuringly to Miss Jepson, then, in a gallant manner, took her hand and brought its lacy covering close to his lips. As he did so, he inhaled and smiled, as if imbibing a delicious perfume.

Babbit saw this gesture as he was clearly intended to, and his eyes narrowed with displeasure. Iliffe ignored him, and directed his conversation almost entirely to the young lady, although he also exchanged some light-hearted words with her brother, who did not appear displeased at the attention paid to his sister by the celebrated wheelman. At last the Jepsons bid farewell to the champion, the young man going to get his bicycle, and Miss Jepson indicating that she had seen some lady friends and would join their party to accompany them to the pavilion. Iliffe reluctantly took his leave with a respectful salute, and made his way to the bicycle enclosure, while Miss Jepson began to walk towards her friends, who waved at her in greeting.

It was a matter of moments for Babbit to dart forward and intercept Miss Jepson. He bowed, doffed his cap, and offered her his arm. She hesitated, looking confused as to what she ought to do. Frances could understand the lady's difficulty. The interloper was being polite and courteous, but at the same time he was a bitter rival of the man she clearly admired.

All might have gone without incident if Iliffe had not observed Babbit's attentions to Miss Jepson, but at that moment he happened to look around, and his face convulsed with rage. He turned on his heel and strode back. 'Babbit, you are here to meet my challenge on the course and not to annoy the ladies!'

'There is no annoyance given or received, if you would only observe, but I suppose I cannot expect an ill-educated oaf like you to recognise polite behaviour!' snapped Babbit.

'Oh my word,' declared Cedric. 'This has gone up a notch or two.'

'Miss Jepson,' said Iliffe, turning to the young lady, 'please take my arm and I will conduct you away from this impudent fellow and to your friends.'

'Nonsense!' exclaimed Babbit. 'I made the first offer, and it has not been refused.'

'But neither has it been accepted.'

Miss Jepson, in evident distress, placed a white mittened hand to her face. 'Please, both of you, settle your differences but do not make me your plaything!' She walked away alone, and one of her female friends ran up to offer comfort and accompany her to join the little group of sympathetic ladies.

Babbit and Iliffe squared up to each other like pugilists coming up to the mark. Their raised voices had attracted considerable attention, and a crowd was beginning to gather, although those gentlemen visitors who were accompanied by ladies were starting to ensure that their female companions were conducted to a safer if less interesting distance.

Mr Toop, his forehead glistening with nervous perspiration, hurried up. 'Please, I beg of you gentlemen, this is no way to conduct yourselves! There are ladies present! If you cannot shake hands and agree to be friends then at least part without rancour. There will be time enough today for you to prove yourselves by the wheel.'

Fortunately this was sufficient to end the confrontation, and the two adversaries, after fierce glares, turned their backs on each other and walked away. Toop uttered a sigh of relief. 'So it is more than just a sporting rivalry,' said Frances.

'It seems so,' said Cedric. 'Unless Babbit has been paying attention to Miss Jepson solely in order to spite Iliffe, which would be a disgraceful way to behave.'

'I can see one person who is delighted by the confrontation,' said Frances, noticing that Mr Hopper, who was leaning against the scoreboard, was chuckling to himself. 'That argument will be sure to increase interest in the race. Is there much prize money to be won?'

'There is, since it is the only professional race at the meeting. There are five men entered, and a pot of fifty guineas, half of which goes to the winner. These are the celebrities of the wheel world, much lauded and admired. Bicycle makers give them machines gratis so they can be seen riding them. They have a thousand little ways of making a fortune from their expertise, but of course it can only be a short career, and they must have another string to their bow. The amateurs race for medals, their names engraved on the club cups, and a mention in the *Wheel World*, which in my opinion is enough glory for any man.'

'How is Mr Iliffe progressing with his second string?'

'The sports ground? I have heard he is casting about for investors, and his name should enable him to attract them. He certainly needs an assured income if he is to make an offer to Miss Jepson. But that is all in the future. In the meantime, Mr Hopper is probably the man making the most money out of the meeting. I am sure he is infringing any number of laws, but he is very careful not to be seen doing so.'

This, thought Frances, was the type of individual Sir Hugo Daffin would doubtlessly want watched and escorted away at the first sign of dubious behaviour, but as she glanced about the field she found that she was unable to see the club's prominent patron, and that, she thought, was more than a little strange.

CHAPTER FIFTEEN

'When will Sir Hugo be here?' she asked.

Cedric looked around. 'He ought to be here already.'

Frances silently berated herself. She had been so concerned with seeing what was there that she had given no thought to what was not there but should be.

'At the spring race meeting, what time did Sir Hugo arrive, and what did he do?'

'Oh, he was here from the start, well before the official opening. He inspected the stalls, supervised the layout of the course, consulted with members, that sort of thing. Then he made a speech, declaring the event open. Said what a wonderful day we had in store. The usual kind of speech, really.'

'What time was that?'

'Eleven o'clock. Then there were some races for boys and novices and ladies. And a parade of new bicycles and tricycles.'

'He watched all of those?'

'Yes, he did.'

Frances glanced at her programme and her pocket watch. 'Opening speech, eleven a.m. There's still time. Even so …' Ratty was inspecting the traveller's bags on a nearby stall, and she went to look, with Cedric following.

'Very well made,' said Cedric, picking up one of the bags, 'light and strong. How does it fasten?' The stallholder obligingly provided a demonstration, and while this was under way Frances spoke quietly to Ratty.

'I don't see Sir Hugo Daffin about. Gentleman with long grey hair and beard who wears a monocle. Don't ask anyone, but you and Tom must both look about you and if you see him, report back to me.' Ratty nodded and set about it.

'Perhaps Jack Linnett will know something?' Frances suggested, when Cedric had made his purchase.

'I'll ask him,' said Cedric. 'It's a natural enough question.' They linked arms and strolled over to the smithy enclosure, where Jack Linnett was in charge of a tidy array of spare parts and tools that might be needed for the small repairs that could be carried out on the field.

'Good morning, Linnett!' said Cedric. 'A busy day ahead, I expect.'

'Yes, sir, I hope so. I like to keep all the machines running well.'

'This is my cousin, Miss Williamson, who is very eager to see me race.' Jack made a deferential nod. 'Sir Hugo not about?'

'No, sir, I haven't seen him this morning.'

'Really? He's usually in the thick of things. Is he well? Not had another of his falls, I hope?'

'Oh no, sir. We were working till eight last night and he was very well then.'

'Ah, yes, of course, the new invention. The extra wheels. How are they progressing?'

Jack looked pessimistic. 'To be honest, sir, I'm not sure we can make them work the way we would want them to.'

'Perhaps that is what is occupying him now,' said Cedric, as he and Frances strolled away. 'Getting his bicycle ready for the parade of new machines.'

'I hope so, but I have been asked to look out for anything unusual and I would like this matter explained. If Jack hasn't seen Sir Hugo since last night, who will have seen him this morning?'

'The housekeeper, Mrs Pirrie, I expect, and the manservant, Waterfield.'

'Very well, let us talk to Mrs Pirrie first and see what we can learn.'

They walked to the pavilion, where a lady in her middle years, arrayed in a colourful summer gown overlaid by a large white apron and tightly curled hair controlled by a white cap, was overseeing the arrangements for serving refreshments.

'Good morning, Mrs Pirrie,' said Cedric jovially. 'Why you are looking so very charming today! What a fine gown! How well the colour matches your eyes!'

Mrs Pirrie tried to look unmoved by the compliment but failed to do so by a wide margin. 'I just thought as it was such a lovely day I would get into the spirit so to speak.'

'Allow me to introduce my cousin, Miss Rose Williamson. She has never attended a race meeting before and is all agog to see the excitement.'

'I am very pleased to make your acquaintance, Miss Williamson. I do hope you will enjoy one of our salad lunches and our teas. We have sandwiches, and cakes and scones, and Bakewell tart, all my own making.'

'Mrs Pirrie does bake the best cakes,' added Cedric. 'Her refreshments always restore us beautifully after a club ride.'

'I look forward to that very much,' said Frances. 'It must be hard work for you, with so many to provide for.'

'Oh, I don't mind that, and I'm not on my own – Mrs Hicks and her sister are giving me a hand.'

'My cousin is especially eager to be introduced to Sir Hugo,' Cedric continued. 'Is he about?'

'Not at present,' said Mrs Pirrie, 'but he should be here shortly. He went up to London on business this morning, but he said he would be back in time to make the opening speech.'

Cedric looked at his watch. 'Then we can expect him very soon. It must be important business to take him away from here at such a time.'

'I am sure it is, but of course I know nothing of it.'

'I trust he was in his usual excellent health this morning?'

'I didn't see him before he left, but he was very well and cheerful last night. He asked me just to put out some bread and cheese and hardboiled eggs for his breakfast, and make the coffee for him to warm up, as he knew I would be busy with the teas and lunches this morning.'

'Ah, that was thoughtful of him. Has Mr Waterfield gone to London with Sir Hugo, or is he here?'

'No, Mr Waterfield has been given a day's holiday to go and see his sister.'

Mrs Pirrie glanced across the field and her expression suddenly darkened. Frances followed her gaze, but it was hard to identify what had caused her disquiet. 'You appear to be disturbed by something,' said Frances. 'May we assist you in any way?'

The housekeeper was noticeably reluctant to respond. At last she said, 'It's not my place to say it, but there are some here who in my opinion need to mind their manners. Not that I'm naming any names. And the rest of the family so respectable, too! That's all I will say on that subject.'

Cedric nodded. 'I think I know to whom you refer.'

'Well I hope she doesn't try her wiles on you, Mr Garton.'

'I have no fear, Mrs Pirrie, I am immune to persons of that kind.'

Frances, now aware that it was a female who had earned Mrs Pirrie's displeasure, looked about and soon guessed the identity of the less than reputable visitor.

A buxom young woman was parading around the field unaccompanied. She wore a summer costume in bright pink, with abundant rows of yellow flounces, and a bonnet trimmed with a profusion of yellow ribbons and clusters of pink rosebuds. The ribbons were worn long, forming a cascade that fluttered in the breeze like beckoning fingers. From the manner of her walk it was clear that she knew all too well that she had the power to attract male attention. At the same time, her eyes were looking about keenly, as if there was a specific person she wanted to see.

Taking their leave of Mrs Pirrie, and promising faithfully to return and enjoy a slice of cake, Frances and Cedric strolled on their way.

'Could that young person be troublesome?' asked Frances.

'Possibly, although she should not concern us. She is Clara Hicks, the blacksmith's daughter. I have heard a whisper that young Jack Linnett finds her interesting but she has no regard for him, because he is merely an apprentice. I am sorry if that is true, but he is young and looks no further than a face and figure and a fine bonnet. I hope in time he will find a more worthy object for his affections. The mother and aunt, who are here assisting Mrs Pirrie, are respectable and industrious people and the father is a good hard-working family man. He does a great deal of business repairing bicycles for the club, but thereby of course many single young men well above the daughter's station in life will call at the smithy, and I fear she entertains hopes that one day she will secure such a man as her husband.'

'Is there any real prospect of that?' asked Frances, concerned that Miss Hicks might find herself in a very unfortunate position if she was not in that position already, and discover that the entire membership of the Bayswater Bicycle Club was unwilling to admit any responsibility towards her.

'None at all, I would say. Oh it's not so much her low rank; there are young ladies whose faces and manners, charm and wit, can advance them in society, but – and I am sorry to have to say this – she is known to display certain freedoms of behaviour of the kind that a young gentleman might find diverting in a friend, but would not prize in a wife.'

'Perhaps if she accepted Jack he might steady her,' said Frances, hopefully, although she feared that that might only happen if the wayward girl discovered that she was in urgent need of a husband and was not able to make a better match.

Walking on, Frances was amused to see that Ratty had been trying his hand at riding a bicycle and had hired one for the afternoon. He was taking to it extremely well, displaying a natural athleticism and sense of balance. He rode up and dismounted with some style. 'Tom 'n me, we've looked all over fer Sir Yugo an' we ain't seen 'im. Not nowhere on the field or roun' the back or in the pavilion. People 'spect 'im ter be 'ere an' all, they're startin' ter ask about 'im.'

Ratty remounted the bicycle and rode away. Frances saw Mr Toop moving about the field anxiously talking to club members and visitors, and guessed that he too must be looking for Sir Hugo. Toop, after a brief conversation with Jack Linnett, shook his head, and then went to the club tent.

'It's nearly time to start and Sir Hugo is still not returned,' said Frances.

A young man in club uniform hurried up to speak to Cedric, his naturally pale features reddened by the sun and an anxious expression in deep-set grey eyes. 'Ah, Garton, there you are. I was just asking Linnett about Sir Hugo and he told me you had been asking, too. Where can he be?'

Cedric quickly introduced Frances to the youth who was George Farrow, son of the General. 'Yes, my cousin was so looking forward to meeting him, but I have been told that he has had to go to London on business.'

'Really?' said Farrow, with a yelp of dismay. 'Today? When is he expected back?'

'No one seems to know.'

'That is very strange. Sir Hugo is due to have a meeting with my father immediately after he delivers the speech opening the event. I don't know the subject of the meeting, but I gathered that it was of some importance.' He sighed dejectedly. 'I suppose I have to go and tell father. He will be very displeased.'

With unwillingness in every step, he crossed the field to where a gentleman of mature years with a military bearing stood with his watch in his hand, surveying his surroundings. As he did so the clock on St Dunstan's church struck eleven.

Chapter Sixteen

rances turned to Cedric. 'As you know, I have been asked to look out for and make a note of anything unusual. I think we would both say that Sir Hugo not being here to open the competition qualifies perfectly for that description.'

'I suppose it does,' Cedric admitted. 'We would all expect him to be here. He's never happier than when he is surrounded by bicycles and bicyclists, and the summer competition is the highlight of his year.'

'So only something of extreme importance would have induced him to be anywhere else this morning?'

'Yes. An emergency, some business that could not wait.'

'It was a planned absence, as we know, although an emergency or extra business could have arisen while he was away. According to Mrs Pirrie, he intended to go to London, but he has been very secretive about his reasons, so much so that I am not even confident it is true. Not only that but I can find no one who has seen him since last night. I feel extremely anxious about that.'

'Anxious? You mean for his safety?'

'Well, I hardly like to say it, but in my experience people who go mysteriously missing … Cedric, you know the cases I have undertaken —'

He looked solemn. 'Ah. I see. Yes. They are usually found deceased.'

'They are.'

'But would you say he is actually missing? He might just have been delayed.'

For a moment Frances wondered if she was being over-anxious, but concluded that even if she was it was better than lack of caution. 'We don't know where he has gone; we don't know who he intended to see and why; we don't know when he left or how he travelled. All we know is that he has not returned. To me, that means he is missing.'

Cedric nodded. 'He has not told Jack what he is about, which suggests personal business rather than anything to do with his work on the bicycles. A solicitor perhaps? Maybe he is signing a will? That would explain the early start, to get into London in time for the office to open, transact any business and then return in time to enjoy the race meeting.'

'Which is due to start now. He ought to be here making his speech. And the longer he is not here the more worried I am.'

Frances saw Mr Toop having a word with the bandsmen, who obligingly took up their instruments, selected a sheet of music and prepared to play. 'I think Mr Toop is hoping to delay the start until Sir Hugo arrives.' She linked her arm in Cedric's. 'Come, let us go for a stroll. The weather is fine and I doubt we will miss anything of significance here.'

'Of course.' They moved off. 'Where are we strolling to?'

'We are going to look for Sir Hugo Daffin.'

'Really? So you know where to look?'

'No, but when a man cannot be found, the obvious place to start looking is the place where he was last seen. We are going to Springfield Lodge. We might find a clue there.'

Cedric stopped. 'Forgive me if I am wrong, but don't I recall you saying that you were under strict orders to do nothing except observe?'

'That is true, but I don't believe I was ordered not to take a pleasant walk in the sunshine with a friend. And, of course, while my cousin Frank has viewed the lodge, I have not. It is natural curiosity, that is all.'

Tom came past with a fresh bundle of leaflets, and Frances asked him to tell Sarah that she was taking a walk to view the lodge. He nodded and dashed away. Sarah looked quizzical at the news, and Frances signed that she was looking for Sir Hugo. Since Sarah's reaction was not one of alarm followed by an order to immediately desist, Frances felt confident to press on.

Leaving the cricket ground, which was permitted as they
still retained their tickets, Frances and Cedric passed onto East
Acton Lane, where cabs were still drawing up and discharg-
ing occupants, and bicycles and tricycles were flowing in. Apart
from the visitors there was no other traffic.

'It's such a quiet little hamlet in the ordinary way,' said
Cedric. 'That is one reason we like it. We don't have to ride
through town to get here and risk falling under the wheels of
a cab. And the cost of taking a bicycle on a train is outrageous.'

As they walked, the noise of the crowds retreated until they
became a part of the air, like the sound of a distant breeze.
Then came the loud booming of a big drum, as the Acton Brass
Ensemble struck up its own variety of music, and started pumping popular melodies into the air in a bold burst of energy.

'They played for the spring races, too,' noted Cedric, in a
voice that lacked enthusiasm. 'Not easily forgotten.'

They arrived at the gates of the lodge, which, without the
presence of Sir Hugo and the club members, looked as if it had
been long abandoned and left to dissolve into a ruin in its own
good time.

Frances went up to the front door and tried the handle, but
it was locked. 'I suppose with Mrs Pirrie and Mr Waterfield
away the house has been secured,' she said. 'Is there another
way in?'

'There is a side entrance that leads to the kitchen and basement, but when the club is in residence it's usually open and
the members use it freely. There is a connecting passage to the
hall and the library where we meet.'

They walked around the perimeter path but the side
entrance, too, was locked up, as were the double doors into a
drawing room. Frances peered through the windows but on
the shadowy side of the house hardly any light pierced the
interior. All was dull and quiet, and there was no movement
within. 'Let's try the coach house and the cottage,' she said.

The coach house doors, which had been open on her previous visits, were now closed and fastened with two padlocks.

Frances examined the locks but all was secure. She pressed an ear to the door but could detect no sound from within. 'I think they added the second padlock after that business with Ross-Fielder's bicycle,' said Cedric. 'I hope you don't mean to break in,' he added nervously.

'I usually employ Sarah for breaking down doors,' said Frances, 'but only in emergencies. I shall send for her if required.' They walked on, still with the distant squeals of cornets and the groans of euphonium and tuba in their ears, punctuated by the deep thud of side and bass drums. The cottage workshop was also closed up and padlocked. Frances tried to peer through the window, but it was mostly occluded by a curtain. All she could see inside was darkness.

'I don't think anyone is here,' said Cedric. 'And if Sir Hugo was still at home, I think this is where he would be.'

Frances continued around the exterior of the lodge, reaching the entrance to the disused kitchen garden. She pushed at the door, and while it was clearly unlocked, it seemed reluctant to open. 'Can we go in?' she asked.

Cedric tried the door, which continued to resist any attempts to move it. 'I doubt that this has been opened for a very long time,' he said. He was about to walk away but Frances did not like to give up, and pushed again harder. Cedric came back and assisted her, until at last the door, its base wrapped in clinging weeds, opened with a grinding screech, wrenching long, thickly growing stems from their roots.

Frances gazed into what must once have been a well-cultivated garden, but if there had been rows of lettuces and asparagus once, they were no more. A meadow of tall coarse grass had choked the life from what had once been a pleasure and an ornament to a gentleman's table. A gardener's shed must have leaned against the wall, but its weathered planks were now half collapsed into the ground, and its appearance suggested that it had long been in that position. Some broken seed trays were piled beside it, together with a few rusted and useless tools, many of which had long parted company with their handles, and there was a heavily dented spade whose wooden shaft had snapped clean through.

'How little effort it would take to make this good again,' said Frances. She was about to go, but took one last look around; something was puzzling her, and then she realised what it was. 'When we rode past, I could see over the wall, I could see the tops of the weeds. But look here. The weeds that are just inside the door – yes they are well grown, but not nearly as well grown as those in the centre.'

'I see what you mean. The door has been used – but not very recently, surely?'

'No, not for some time.' Frances took a few steps forward, the thick grass catching at the hems of her skirts. She picked up a hoe, whose gnarled metal head promptly dropped off, and used the shaft to explore the ground.

The search turned up only a few dropped copper coins, but as she persevered, moving around the heap of dry wood that that had once been a shed, she saw something else. Lying on the ground with weeds growing vigorously through the spokes of its wheels was a velocipede.

'Look at this!'

Cedric came forward and stared at the machine.

'Do you recognise it?'

'No, I don't. No one in the club uses them. We are all devotees of the high-wheeler.'

Frances examined the fallen machine. 'Is it damaged or useable? How long do you think it has been here? Many months I would say.'

'Yes, I agree.' Cedric pulled the machine upright and examined it. There were dry dead weeds marking out its shape where it had lain. 'No damage, just the usual wear. Give it a clean and it would be quite rideable.'

There was a small leather bag strapped behind the seat but it was gaping open and empty. Frances found some scratches on one handlebar, and cleaned away dust and dirt with a handful of grass to reveal some roughly incised letters. 'EDW,' she said. 'Does that mean anything to you?'

'No. The initials of the owner, perhaps? But I don't know anyone that would fit.'

Frances looked about her again. The small area of less overgrown soil, which, now she looked back on it, precisely matched where the door opened inwards; the abandoned velocipede; the open bag; the dented spade with the snapped handle. 'Whatever happened here it wasn't recent.'

'Nothing bad, I hope,' said Cedric.

'Who can say? Well, all I can do is keep my eyes and ears open for clues.'

The Acton Brass Ensemble, which had paused, briefly, broke into a strident marching tune, with much vigorous thumping of the drum. It seemed to be coming from another country, another time, while all that existed in the abandoned garden stood still and quiet.

Frances walked back to the path, brushing dried grass from her hands and shaking it from the hems of her skirts, and looked about her once more. The door to the kitchen garden was in a shaded area, not in clear sight of either the roadway, the carriage drive or any entrance to the house. It was not a secret place but it was secluded.

'Shall we return?' asked Cedric.

'I'd like to take just one last look,' said Frances, reluctant to tear herself away before she could be certain she had seen all she could. She began to retrace her steps around the house, peering more closely through the windows into gloomy rooms filled with antiquated furniture, rubbing at grimy glass to get a clearer view, and testing door handles again, none of which granted her entry.

The band finally blared into silence, leaving a breathless shimmer in the air. The only sound was the distant chatter of crowds and their own footfall, until another slighter noise broke in. Frances paused. 'Did you hear that?'

They both listened, and detected a faint scratching. 'It's coming from the cottage,' said Cedric. 'I hope they don't have rats.'

Frances hurried to the cottage and made a great effort to look through the window, but the curtain had been drawn across, protecting the secrets within. There was a small sliver of a gap just above her eyeline, and she stood on tiptoe. All she could see was the surface of a workbench, with some unidentifiable shapes of tools and metal parts. She pressed closer, trying to block the external light and accustom her eyes to the inner gloom. The noise came again, almost like a tapping now, and not at all the kind of sound a rat would make.

'A machine of some kind, maybe; Sir Hugo's latest invention?' she mused. 'Cedric, let me have a step up so I can see better.'

'But wouldn't it be easier if I —'

Frances took the trouser fasteners from her reticule and put them on. 'There! I came prepared.'

'You are a wondrous girl,' he said. 'You have destroyed my argument entirely.' Cedric linked his hands as if assisting Frances to mount a horse, and she raised herself up to get a better view, grasping the window ledge. The cottage was only one storey, and sufficiently low that she was almost on a level with the eaves. She saw that the roof, that might once have been thatched, judging from the dry tufts that remained, had been mended over the years with slates, which were now much broken, their deficiencies partly covered by a sheet of rubber held down by nails.

From this new vantage Frances could now look down into the shadows of the cottage, and saw what at first she took to be a pile of clothing but then with a gasp recognised the shape of a man lying on the floor. 'There's a body in here!'

'Oh Lord, no! Is it Sir Hugo?'

'I don't know – he's in club uniform, I think. It's hard to see.'

'Shall we fetch help?'

'Not yet. For all I know this is a dummy figure Sir Hugo is using to test inventions.'

'I'll help you down and take a look. If we think it is Sir Hugo we will have to break the lock and fetch assistance.'

Frances knew full well that she had already far overstepped the bounds of her instructions but felt justified to continue if there was a possibility of a life in danger. And she did so want to see how she would manage this adventure in her new divided skirt. 'No, stay there, I can see where I can get in.' She climbed onto the window ledge, balancing awkwardly on her toes and holding onto the edge of the eaves with one hand, and began to pull away the rubber sheeting. Fortunately, it came away easily, the nails popping from their holes. Reaching forward she grasped an exposed wooden roof beam and pulled herself up, first with one hand and then both.

'What are you doing?' called Cedric. 'Frances, be careful!'

'There's a hole in the roof. I think I can get in that way.' Frances wriggled onto the roof, which had very little elevation, bracing her feet on the upper lintel of the window and then the eaves. At last she was able to put her feet through the gap that had appeared, pushing any extraneous skirt material aside, and then, holding onto the beam, she eased herself through, slipping into the building, and, after hanging by her hands for a moment, dropped the short distance to the floor. Outside she heard Cedric's scrambling efforts to follow her.

She knelt by the figure on the floor half expecting it to be a thing of wood and cloth, but to her astonishment it was a warm living man, not Sir Hugo, but someone taller and of far more slender build. He gasped and moaned as she touched him, and as her eyes grew used to the dim room she saw that he had a sack over his head, and there was a rag bound tightly over his mouth to prevent speech. His hands were tied behind his back and his ankles were also secured, and she discovered with some alarm that he had been trussed not with cord, but some kind of wire, wound very tightly, the bonds cutting into his flesh. She couldn't be sure how long he had been there, but she knew he had to be freed as soon as possible if some permanent damage was not to result. As he struggled, using his whole body to writhe, she realised that it was this movement, causing the rough ends of the wire to scrape and tap against the floor, that had made the slight noises they had heard.

'Who is it?' called Cedric, dropping to the floor beside her.

'I don't know. Look around. We need something to cut the wire.'

'No! Wait, before we do anything that might be unwise. I mean, for all we know this fellow could be the most horrid villain. Perhaps he was caught committing a crime and has been put here to keep him from escaping while the police are being brought to take him away.'

'Possibly,' said Frances, although another thought was forming. 'But I think I know who he might be, and I want to question him.' The room was understandably musty, and there was the harsh smell of a workshop; metal, oil, rubber, grease, but she had detected as she bent over the man a quite different aroma, one that was altogether more familiar to her, that of Gentleman's Premium Ivory Cleansing Soap, gentler and more masculine than Cedric's favoured cologne.

Cedric grunted. 'Very well. But we must be careful. If he starts any rough business, or calls for his associates, you must let me deal with him.' He knelt beside the figure. 'You, fellow. Now listen to me. We will take away the gag so you can answer questions, but if you shout out it will be the worse for you, do you understand?'

The figure nodded, and Cedric, with noticeable reluctance, untied the knotted rag.

'What is your name?' asked Frances.

The unknown man blew the sacking from his mouth. 'Gideon,' he croaked.

Frances turned to Cedric. 'Untie him. You'll need something to cut the wire. Be very careful. Don't hurt him.'

'Are you sure?' Cedric demanded.

'Yes, I am quite sure. Please, no more delay.'

'Then you know him?'

'I suppose I do, in a way. And he is a friend. That much I am certain of.'

Cedric shrugged and looked about for the tool he needed. Frances helped the man sit up and pulled the sack from his head. Dark straight hair, worn long, tumbled over his face. 'You're Mr Grove,' she whispered, and he nodded.

'Ah, just the thing,' said Cedric, returning with a wire cutter and making short work of the metal twined about Grove's wrists and ankles.

'Thank you,' said Grove. He rubbed life back into his fingers and flexed them cautiously, then ran his hands through his hair, pushed it back from his face and looked up.

Frances took a step back and clasped a hand to her mouth. Cedric stared. 'I say – isn't that – isn't he —?'

Mr W. Grove, author of the Miss Dauntless stories, also known as government agent Gideon, gave a rueful smile. 'The Filleter, yes. And I can see I have a great deal of explaining to do.'

CHAPTER SEVENTEEN

rances could only look on in astonished silence. The man before her was, or had once been, the Filleter, of that she was certain. The resemblance could not be denied; the aquiline face and piercing dark eyes held no doubts for her, but that individual had been dirty and repellent, with blackened teeth, filthy hair, and a softly sneering, threatening voice. Mr Grove was an altogether different man, clean and tidy in his person, any slight disarray in his appearance solely due to the ordeal he had recently suffered. Most importantly, he showed no evidence of ever having been crushed almost to death in a roof fall. 'I think I understand,' she said at last.

'We can't trust this fellow just because he has had a bath!' exclaimed Cedric. 'He's a known assassin! Frances, get some rope or wire, we need to tie him up and fetch the police! Don't worry, I'll protect you! And you, sir, stay exactly where you are, don't move, or you will have to deal with me! I have been trained by Professor Pounder himself!' He adopted a pugilistic stance.

Frances placed a firm hand on Cedric's arm. 'We must trust him,' she said steadily. 'Please believe me. This is Mr Grove. I told you about him. He saved my life once.'

'And now you have saved mine,' said Grove. 'For which I heartily thank you.'

Cedric hesitated, and Grove risked standing up, although he kept a wary eye on Cedric as he did so. As the Filleter he had adopted a crouching posture, but now he stood straight, wincing a little. Recovering his club cap from the floor, he eased it on to his head with some care. There was blood on his wrists and cuffs where the wire had cut into his skin, but the stout bicycling socks had prevented similar damage to his ankles. 'I think the only reason you found me alive is that the men who trapped me here are intending to return and question me later, and I have little doubt as to how that would have ended. But let us go.' He glanced at the door. 'How did you get in?'

'We climbed through the roof,' said Frances.

Grove smiled. 'Naturally you did. Then we will leave the same way. If my captors return to check that the building is undisturbed they will see it apparently secure.'

'Who captured you?' asked Frances.

'I wish I knew. The memory may come back to me.' He made a quick scan of the interior. 'You don't see any books bound in red leather by any chance? Sir Hugo's notebooks. He does keep them in here.'

'They're not here now,' said Cedric sternly. 'I saw them once, they were on the workbench.'

'As I feared, stolen,' said Grove. He patted his pockets and frowned. 'And that's not all that was taken.' He set a stool in place under the hole in the roof, and prepared to climb out. 'Is Sir Hugo safe?'

'We don't know,' said Frances. 'He didn't appear at the race meeting and we were concerned and came here to look for him. He had told his housekeeper that he intended to go London on business this morning, and would be back by eleven. It is past that now.'

'That is very worrying indeed,' said Grove. 'He is in grave danger and we must try and find him. There are messengers I can send to London to report what we know, but I must stay here and do what I can.' He climbed up onto the stool and peered through the hole in the roof. 'All clear, but we must be quick!' With great agility he pulled himself up onto the roof then leaned down. 'Miss Doughty, give me your hand and I will assist you.'

Frances had no hesitation. She reached up and took his hand, which for all its slenderness was very strong, and, blessing the day that she had adopted the divided skirt, stepped nimbly up onto the stool, and was able to wriggle through the gap in the roof. Cedric followed, and by helping each other, all were able to reach the ground safely. As a last act, before descending from the roof, Grove folded the rubber sheet back over the gap in the tiles, and pushed the nails back in place with his fist, so their method of exit was not obvious.

'Have you looked in the coach house?'

'It's padlocked, I'm afraid,' said Frances. 'The whole house is locked up. We did look in the old kitchen garden, and there was an abandoned velocipede there, with initials scratched on it, EDW. It's been there for some time. Does that mean anything?'

'I'm afraid not.'

'There was no sign that anyone has been there recently.'

Grove nodded. 'The coach house, then. A padlock will not present any difficulty.' They followed him along the path. 'Incidentally, I must congratulate you on your costume, Miss Doughty. Both practical and charming.'

Frances hardly knew what to say, and murmured a modest thank you. She suddenly realised that she was still wearing the trouser fasteners and hastily removed them and put them in her reticule. Cedric still bore an expression of extreme distrust. He was not, fortunately, one of those men who felt that he ought to be the leader of any group, but he continued to regard Grove with suspicion, and the other's immediate assumption of leadership did not assist that situation.

Frances knew that she could not tell Cedric about Grove/ Gideon's true status, that he was undoubtedly a government agent; that would be for the man himself to disclose, and she was happy for him to take the lead since he clearly knew more about the mission than she did.

At the coach house Grove produced a tiny lock-pick from his cuff and made short work of the padlocks. Opening the double doors, they found the machines gone, which was to be expected as they had all been taken to the field, and the secretary's desk was bare. Frances looked in the desk drawers and found only an older notebook, a record of hire for the previous year. Out of curiosity, she examined the pages to see if any machines had been hired out on the day of Morton Vance's murder, and found the record blank.

'How did you come to be in the workshop?' she asked Grove, as the coach house was re-locked.

'I was looking for Sir Hugo, as I wanted to warn him to be on his guard. I heard a voice inviting me in, and thought it was his. I was attacked from behind as I entered. I should have been more careful. It was a serious mistake and I can promise you it won't happen again.'

Cedric coughed gently. 'Frances, my dear, I seem to recall you telling me that you were instructed by whoever it was who hired you for this mission to go home at the first hint of any danger. Now it strikes me that there has been more than just a hint. So I propose that I should now go and hire a cab and take you home.'

Frances hesitated. 'I'm not sure I want to leave just yet,' she said. 'And as for danger – didn't they mean danger to me?'

'Any danger at all, I would have thought,' said Cedric earnestly. 'Please let me take you home. If anything happened to you I would never forgive myself.'

'It's a matter of interpretation,' said Frances, stubbornly. 'And we still haven't found Sir Hugo. Three of us will search for him better than one. Mr Grove, I assume the locked doors of the lodge will be no obstacle to you?'

'None at all,' said Grove. They walked on, and Cedric, sighing with frustration but clearly unwilling to abandon Frances, brought up the rear.

Frances had the slightly heady feeling of being in an unreal situation, as if she was wandering in a strange dream, or taking part in a play where she was obliged to act out a role that was not herself. How could she be talking so calmly to this man, rather a tall man she happened to notice, and quite handsome in an unusual kind of way, who had been both her bold saviour and the one person she had always wanted to avoid? At least the fact that Mr Grove did not have the Filleter's characteristic stench of the dung heap, and his teeth appeared to be both sound and white, was a great help in her acceptance of his true identity.

She decided that she would find it easier to keep her equilibrium if she tried not to look at him and devoted all her attention to the current emergency. All the same there were too many memories of their last encounter, both good and bad, and they were hard to suppress altogether.

As she had expected, Grove had no difficulty in opening the side door of Springfield Lodge, and they entered the house, finding a set of stairs down to the basement kitchen and a narrow corridor. The kitchen door was open, showing that it was empty. It was well kept and tidy, but only modestly stocked with foodstuffs. The room yielded no further information and they passed along the passage, which opened into a large hallway.

'Not all of the rooms in the house are in use,' said Cedric. 'About half of them, I think. Sir Hugo uses the breakfast room for all his meals, and then there is the drawing room where the club members meet and we have tea after the club rides.' He pointed to two doors on the other side of the hall, both of which were glazed. They peered inside, but both rooms looked unoccupied. The drawing room was comfortable in the way that an old cracked and familiar chair was comfortable, cosy with faded draperies and antiquated lamps.

In the breakfast room was a long plain table with a set of old dining chairs and a sideboard. One of the chairs was out of place, set back from the table, as if recently vacated by someone who had not troubled to put it back in line with its fellows. On the table was an unused plate, and a tray covered with a cloth. Frances drew back the cloth to reveal a half loaf of bread, a round of cheese, and two hardboiled eggs. 'This is Sir Hugo's breakfast,' said Frances. 'Mrs Pirrie told me she had put it out for him so he could eat before he went to London, but she also said that she had made a pan of coffee and left it ready for him to warm. There is neither pan nor cup to be seen either here or in the kitchen. And his breakfast is uneaten. I don't know if Sir Hugo ever meant to go to London but even if he planned to, I don't think he did.'

The remaining ground-floor rooms held only old furniture covered in dustsheets, and yielded no more clues. The little party progressed up a wide set of carpeted stairs. Frances noticed that Cedric was still keeping a wary eye on Mr Grove, and knew it was for her sake. She had endured a great deal in the last two years, and he was a kind friend who had always been there to help and support her. To see her ally herself with a man he was only familiar with as a wanted murderer must have been disturbing to say the least.

They arrived at a long landing with a series of solid closed doors. 'These rooms are always kept available for visiting members of the Bicycle Touring Club,' said Cedric, 'but if there are any members staying here at present they will be at the race meeting.'

Grove turned to Frances and spoke softly. 'Please stand back. Unless, of course, you have a gun.'

'Really,' muttered Cedric, 'whatever would Frances be doing with a gun?'

Frances had once held the Filleter captive with a gun she had borrowed from Miss John, enabling Sarah to pin him to the ground with her knee and tie him up with a Women's Suffrage ribbon. She suspected that Grove was gently teasing her, and smiled. 'I don't have one,' she said.

He nodded. 'A pity, they have stolen mine. Well, let me go first. Mr Garton, please be on hand if there are any surprises.' Without pausing to see Cedric's response, Grove very quietly opened the first door, peering in cautiously to establish that it was unoccupied before entering. Once he knew it was safe, he beckoned the others, and they followed. It was a plainly furnished bedroom with the usual amenities, and a travelling bag and a set of pyjamas showed that it was currently being used by a gentleman visitor. They made a brief search, but there was nothing to discover. One by one the rooms were examined in this manner. All were unlocked and provided no useful information except for the last, which was locked.

Grove listened at the door. 'Can you hear anything?' asked Cedric.

Grove shook his head. 'All the same, why should this one be locked and not the others?' He produced his lock-pick and after few seconds a soft click told them they could enter. 'And now we must all be very careful.' He turned the handle slowly and it gave noiselessly, without resistance. He pushed the door open just enough to look inside, and gave a sharp intake of breath. Carefully, he swung the door open, until it was certain that no one could be lurking behind it, then he entered the room.

It was a simply furnished gentleman's bedroom. Stretched across the bed, fully clothed, his face deathly pale, mouth agape, was Sir Hugo Daffin.

CHAPTER EIGHTEEN

Once they were all inside, Grove closed the door and pushed the back of a chair under the handle to prevent unwanted entry should anyone be hiding in the house, then he crossed to the windows and threw back the curtains, letting daylight flood into the room.

Frances ran over to the motionless figure on the bed, convinced that she would find him dead and cold, but to her surprise Sir Hugo's hands were merely cool. He was breathing, and seemed not to be in any distress, but the rise and fall of his chest was barely visible.

Frances burrowed her fingers under the flowing beard to unfasten Sir Hugo's collar, which was tight around the fleshy neck. 'Open the windows, he needs air!'

Grove complied.

'Is he ill or asleep?' asked Cedric.

She shook the unconscious man gently, then when he did not respond, more firmly. 'Sir Hugo!' she said, very close to his ear, then gave the back of his hand a hard pinch. It was impossible to rouse him. 'This is no natural sleep. Cedric, look about the room for any bottles that might tell us what he has taken.' Cedric obligingly began to search the nightstand, a little dressing table and a wardrobe. 'Do you know if he took any medicines?'

'No. Of course, if he did suffer from an indisposition he might not have told us. He liked to think of himself as very robust for his age. Jepson might know.'

Grove came to examine the unconscious man. 'Laudanum?'

Frances leaned towards the unconscious man's mouth and sniffed carefully. 'No, or I would be able to smell it. It's very distinctive.' She sniffed again. 'But I can tell that he has drunk coffee.' She pulled back one heavy eyelid. A glance at the constricted pupil told all she needed to know. 'He has been drugged. Morphine, in all probability.' She glanced around. 'Cedric, have you found anything?'

'No. An impressive collection of liniment, antiseptics and bandages, but nothing for internal use. He wouldn't have swallowed any of this, would he?'

Frances shook her head. 'If he had, the symptoms would have been quite different.'

Grove placed his hand on Sir Hugo's wrist. 'His pulse is very feeble, and his breathing so shallow it is hardly there. Can you help him?'

'If he was conscious I would give him an emetic, but he is much too far gone for that. He should be taken to a doctor at once, and we must try to keep him alive until then. Let us rub his hands and feet, to stimulate the circulation.'

'Jepson's the nearest,' said Cedric. 'He'll be on the cricket field to watch his son racing, and I think he is Sir Hugo's physician. Shall I fetch him?'

'Can we trust him?' asked Frances, starting to rub the unconscious man's hands. She was painfully aware that a doctor, the very person most likely to have a supply of morphine, could well have been responsible for Sir Hugo's condition. It was a dilemma but a decision that only Grove could make.

'I know nothing against him,' said Cedric. 'There's another doctor in Acton; Barraclough. But we don't even know if he is at home.'

Grove was removing Sir Hugo's shoes and stockings. 'I suggest we risk Jepson. Any delay could well prove fatal. Garton, you know Jepson better than I. Could you fetch him here and order a cab? And please do it without attracting attention or letting anyone know what you are about.'

Cedric looked a little stunned at being given orders in that way, but recognised the importance of swift action. 'Very well. Frances, will you come with me?'

'I need to stay here,' said Frances, busily massaging the patient's chilled hands. 'Go! Quickly.'

Cedric gave a glance of grave mistrust at Grove, who was vigorously rubbing Sir Hugo's feet, and hurried away.

There was a strange silence in the air as they both worked to help revive the unconscious man. When Mr Grove had been in his disguise as the horrid Filleter Frances had usually had something to say. Now she had to search for words. 'I don't know how the morphine came here, but it has a bitter taste,' she said at last. 'I think I can guess how it was given to him. If the coffee was set out last night for him to warm this morning, there was a long period of time when many people, both club members and visitors, were in the lodge, and anyone could have added morphine to the pan. And whoever did it has since destroyed the evidence. But who would have done this and why?'

'The same persons who stole his notebooks. If that was all they needed they might well have killed him outright. As it is, they must want to know more as they have kept him alive in order to extract information. Even now they are taking part in the race meeting, and will return as soon as it is over to spirit him away. But I also think that whoever gave him the drug was probably not a doctor, and certainly not Sir Hugo's doctor. It was a miscalculation of dose that has brought him close to death.'

'But what information could they want?' asked Frances, relieved to have directed the conversation to the mission in hand. 'Surely not the secret of his invention of the extra wheels. I have seen them in action and they did not look at all promising.'

'Was he working on anything else?'

'He did talk about inventing a more comfortable saddle, I believe, but I am not sure if he had made a start on it.'

'We would all want that,' said Grove, and she could tell from his voice that he was smiling, 'but I doubt that anyone would be prepared to endanger the life of an elderly gentleman for it.'

'The only other thing that I have been able to discover is that Sir Hugo had arranged a meeting with General Farrow to take place after he had made his opening address.'

'Farrow?' said Grove. 'Now that is interesting. Farrow has recently been looking at the possible military application of bicycles. He has been asked to report to a government commission on the subject. I wonder if Sir Hugo intended to discuss a new idea of his that could have importance in that area.'

'I read an article in a periodical about the military possibilities of bicycles,' Frances told him. 'It was proposed that there should be whole battalions of men travelling entirely by bicycle. The only difficulty was moving over rough terrain, which could cause a spill. I had understood that Sir Hugo's extra wheels were intended to assist older or less experienced riders, but perhaps they might have another purpose.'

'But you thought they looked unpromising.'

'They didn't seem to be working as he might have hoped, but they might go better with a younger man. And perhaps he has improved them since. Maybe that was what his planned trip this morning was about; obtaining some materials he could not find nearer home – something he could use when demonstrating his invention to General Farrow?'

Grove considered the position. 'Whoever has done this has succeeded in three things – they have Sir Hugo's notes, they prevented him carrying out whatever it was he intended to do in London and also prevented him discussing his work with General Farrow. They have left him alive because the one thing they don't have is the secret of the invention itself, which he might not have committed to paper, or has carefully hidden, and which they must believe has the potential to be valuable to a foreign power.'

They worked on in silence a little more, Frances finding herself impatient for Cedric's return, and wondering how easy it would be for him to find Jepson without alerting anyone else.

She looked at Sir Hugo's face to see if there was any change in his condition. Could it be that his cheeks were gaining a little colour? 'Is Gideon your real name?' she asked.

There was a long pause, so much so that she glanced at Grove, who was looking thoughtful.

'Or can't I be trusted to know that?' she asked.

'I think you can, although here I prefer to go by the name of Grove. But yes. I had better tell you all. My full name is Gideon Horatio Alexander Locke. I am the third son of Admiral Sir Alexander Locke. I was educated at Eton and Oxford, and I then went into government service. Although as yet I am only a humble foot soldier in that particular regiment.'

'Nevertheless, what you do is extremely dangerous.'

'It is. Almost as dangerous as Eton. To complete my history, I am currently twenty-seven years of age, and a bachelor.'

Frances wondered why he should have provided such intimate detail. 'You should really stop writing the Miss Dauntless stories.'

'Why is that? Don't you like them?'

'Oh, they are entertaining, I grant you that, but some of my clients think I am Miss Dauntless. They think I can do all that she does.'

'You could do all she does and more,' he said quietly.

Frances felt her face grow warm. 'Why "the Filleter"?'

'Oh, he was only one of my disguises. The least comfortable one. But he could go where others could not and be accepted in circles where I could not go.'

'You smelt as if you had rolled in a dung heap,' she said severely.

'I am sorry to say that there was a good reason for that.'

'And you followed me about … why? Not to threaten me, as I once thought.'

'No. To be on hand if you needed assistance. I used more than one guise. Most of the time you didn't see me. My one regret is that I was absent from London on a mission and therefore unable to foil that attack on you outside your own house. But you dealt with it most admirably yourself.'

'I took no pleasure in it.'

'I would not have expected you to.'

'So last year, when you were the Filleter, and you were under arrest and being held in the cells at Paddington Green Police Station, and there was that dreadful storm – the story I was told by the police about your being badly injured in a roof fall – that was just a ruse to get you away?'

'The roof came down, that much was true, but the worst of the damage was to an empty cell. I had told the Scotland Yard men who I was and once they checked my credentials they knew they had to release me, but they needed a good reason to do so in order to avoid suspicion. They couldn't just report me as having escaped. The storm came along at just the right moment. Even Inspector Sharrock didn't know about the deception. I have to say I was tempted to dispose of the Filleter altogether, but he's far too useful.'

'You once told me – that is, the Filleter told me – that you had killed people.'

'That is true. I have. My work sometimes demands it. But you know that yourself, now.'

There was another period of silence.

'What will you do when we have Sir Hugo safely away?' Frances asked.

'I will return to the field, but for your own safety we must maintain the pretence that we have not met. I suggest you inform Miss Smith of our conversation. I wouldn't care to have her arrest me again. Once your friend has knelt on a man he can never forget it.'

'But your enemies, whoever they are, they will know you are free. Won't they attack you again?'

'It's a risk, but I will be in a crowd, and this time, I promise, I will keep my wits about me.'

'You still have no memory of who struck you?'

'I'm sorry to say I don't. It may return. I hope it does. I should like to meet him again on more equal ground.'

'Do you have a headache? You don't appear to be dizzy.'

'There is a slight bump, but that is all. The skin is not broken. I was wearing the club cap at the time, which is well padded, and that saved me from any worse effects.'

Frances frowned. She hoped that the injury was trivial, since if it was not there was nothing a doctor could do. 'Cedric wants to send me home but I don't want to go. You're not going to try and send me home?'

'I wouldn't dare.'

There were footsteps on the stairs and Cedric hurried in. 'Mr Jepson is here, and I have a cab waiting with instructions to take a man to his surgery in Acton. I have told Jepson we think it is an accidental poisoning and he is keeping quiet out of respect for Sir Hugo.'

Surgeon Jepson, who followed Cedric into the room, was a slightly stout gentleman of middle years, bespectacled, and with the confident manner of an experienced medical man. He gave a little gasp of concern on seeing Sir Hugo, then at once took the patient's pulse, lifted a heavy eyelid, and completed the examination with a stethoscope which he brought out of an inner pocket. 'And you found him like this only minutes ago?'

'Yes,' said Cedric. 'We were concerned when he wasn't at the race meeting.'

'You did the right thing; he'll have to be removed to my surgery at once. Gentlemen, between the three of us I think we can lift him and bring him downstairs.'

It was an awkward but necessary co-operation as the surgeon, Cedric and Grove together carried Sir Hugo downstairs to the waiting cab.

'Cedric, could you go with him, and let me know any news?' asked Frances.

Cedric paused for only a moment before he agreed. 'Please take care,' he begged. He leaped into the cab beside Jepson and the patient, and the vehicle rattled away at a good pace.

'Now there is something a bicycle cannot do,' said Frances. 'Or even a sociable.' She tried to imagine how a sociable could transport a sick man; it was not an easy proposition. Perhaps there was still plenty of opportunity for horses, after all. 'And now, Mr Grove, you must come back inside and I will clean the wounds on your wrists and take a look at that bump on your head.'

'Oh, they are nothing,' said Grove, about to pull the lodge door closed. To his surprise she blocked the doorway and faced him with cold determination.

'My dear brother Frederick suffered an injury in a fall which he said was nothing. But it wasn't. His blood was poisoned. I nursed him until he died. Now you are to go back into the house and have those cuts dressed, and I will not take no for an answer.'

For a few moments he gazed at her with an unreadable expression, then he obeyed without a murmur.

CHAPTER NINETEEN

Once inside the house Frances was the unbending model of decorum. She ordered Mr Grove to be seated in the breakfast room while she fetched what was needed from Sir Hugo's bedroom. A brief examination of the bump on his head suggested that he had probably been fortunate, and no action was needed. Next, seated beside him at the long table she cleaned and dressed the cuts on his wrists, a process to which he submitted meekly. Since he wore cyclists' celluloid cuffs Frances was able to remove all external traces of blood, so he could conceal the injury and avoid searching questions. Her ministrations were carried out in silence, and she directed her attention to the work. Only once did she glance up at him and saw him gazing at her watchfully. She quickly lowered her eyes again.

'There, it is done,' she said at last.

He rose to his feet. 'Thank you. I hope not to put you to such trouble again, although I can't guarantee it.'

Once the medical materials were returned to their proper place the house was closed up. Grove hurried back to the field, and Frances, after a short interval, followed. She was extremely anxious while she waited for Cedric's return, as she was far from confident that Sir Hugo would recover, but took the opportunity to send the necessary information to Sarah. Even from across the expanse of field she could see her assistant's shocked expression as Tom passed on the message.

There was a certain amount of unrest amongst the crowds as it was now well past eleven o'clock and the opening speech had not been made. Every time the band stopped playing there was a hum of cheerful anticipation, to be followed by a groan of disappointment as it embarked on another melody.

Finally, Mr Toop, looking overheated and unhappy, mounted the dais and signalled to the band with a fretful wave to cease, which, after a few more bold thumps on the drum, it did. The impatient crowd realised that the event was at last about to start and began to move towards him. Toop took up a speaking trumpet.

'Ladies, gentlemen – may I beg your attention please!'

Conversation gradually hushed. 'Now I know that in the past we have been honoured at our meetings to have the opening speech delivered by Sir Hugo Daffin, a gentleman whom we all hold in the highest esteem. I have just been advised that this morning Sir Hugo has been detained in London on important business, and he will therefore be delayed in joining us. We anticipate, however, that he will be here in time to watch the afternoon races and award the prizes. However, we must proceed, and I am delighted to say that our distinguished visitor General Farrow has agreed to formally open the event. Please give your warmest welcome to General Farrow!'

There was enthusiastic applause and Toop left the dais with some relief.

Frances could not help glancing about, trying her best to look like an innocent observer simply appreciating the scene, but she really wanted to know where Mr Grove was. Given the number of gentlemen present all in club uniform it was not an easy task, but at last she saw him, over at the bicycle enclosure. Was there, she wondered, someone on the field who would be astonished and alarmed to see him? There was safety in numbers but all the same he was taking a risk.

General Farrow mounted the steps to the platform. He was a solid looking man of about fifty, straight if not tall, with close cut hair going grey. He took up the speaking trumpet, and after a glance, put it down again, as if disdaining its assistance. The crowds listened attentively. 'Thank you, Mr Toop, the honour is all mine,' he said in a voice that would have carried to the furthest extent of a field of battle. 'As I look about me and see so many fine examples of British manhood, all devoted to the health and vigour that has made our country great, I see our future and I know it will be a good one. The bicycle is the supreme form of road travel. Fast and modern, making all that went before it obsolete. Our county's greatness rests on two wheels, and it is safe in the hands of its young men. Today we can look forward to a display of strength and expertise that can leave no one in any doubt of this. It is my great pleasure and privilege therefore to declare the annual summer race meeting of the Bayswater Bicycle Club open!'

There was enthusiastic cheering, and Farrow, with a short bow stepped down. Mr Toop ascended the platform once more, and took up the speaking trumpet.

'Thank you General, for a truly inspiring speech. And now a word to the contestants. Those of you who have not yet collected your race numbers, please go to the table on my left, where these will be issued.' He indicated a table that had been set up nearby piled with numbered sheets of paper, and manned by a club member. 'The first event will commence in a few minutes and will be a parade of the most novel and interesting new machines, ridden by members of the Bayswater Bicycle Club and representatives of the manufacturers. 'I now hand you over to my good friend Mr Phineas Vance.' A gentleman in conventional clothes joined Toop on the platform and was given the speaking trumpet. Slightly built and aged about thirty, with short light brown whiskers, there was an air of melancholy about Phineas Vance as he surveyed the field. A fresh sadness creased his face, the knowledge perhaps that however hard he looked, his brother Morton would not be there, and never could be.

The race entrants had formed a queue to obtain their numbers. Frances realised that since the uniforms made it hard to distinguish one man from another when riding at speed, it made sound sense for each rider to have a card attached to the back of his coat if the placings of a race were in dispute. She saw Mr Grove in line being given the number six.

A parade of machines had emerged from the visitors' enclosure and was being pedalled up to the course. 'Ladies and gentlemen,' said Vance in a clear but gentle voice, 'may I draw your attention now to the splendid spectacle before you. You will be seeing the finest in bicycles and tricycles, some of which are novel new designs that will make the experience of travelling more comfortable than ever before. Our leading manufacturers of machines, parts, and everything the bicycling gentleman or tricyling lady might require, have brought their newest creations and are eager to show them to you.'

Frances decided to watch, partly out of natural curiosity, partly in the vain hope that someone might have invented a bicycle a lady could ride, but mainly because she thought it would offer some clue as to the direction in which inventors were thinking, and suggest what it was Sir Hugo might have devised that a foreign power would covet enough to steal.

'First,' said Phineas Vance, as the parade began with what looked like a conventional high-wheeler, 'we have Mr James Jepson, demonstrating the Coventry Roadster, with the new Salisbury improved noiseless hub lamp. Suitable for use in all weathers; this lamp cannot be detached by the vibration of the machine. Those of you who have lost your lamps in the dark will know the value of this device.'

Jepson was granted polite applause, and Miss Hicks waved a pink and yellow handkerchief as he passed by, which he acknowledged with the slightest of nods. He was followed by another man on a bicycle.

'And now we have Mr Rook riding a Number One Viaduct, fitted with the very latest in saddles,' continued Vance. 'This invention is so secret that no one but Mr Rook is allowed to ride it, but I am given to understand that with a little more development it will be available to us all. All I am permitted to say is that it has been constructed by a special patented process on the pneumatic principle, affording a most pleasant and comfortable ride.' Mr Rook paraded past with a blissful smile.

The next device was like nothing Frances had ever seen before, a tricycle ridden by George Farrow, but in a standing position. 'This next machine ridden by Mr Farrow is the Rucker tricycle. As you know, in the standard tricycle the rider is seated and moves the treadles by the extension of the legs. In the Rucker model, however, there is no seat; the rider stands above the treadles and the motion is more similar to walking, thus producing greater power with less fatigue. The manufacturers claim that this is an improvement not just for an age, but for all time. This is the tricycle of the future, and you have seen it here today!' Miss Hicks greeted young Farrow with a wave, but unlike Jepson he took care not to notice her.

Frances might have thought that that was the strangest invention she would see that day, but still stranger was to follow.

'And now, Mr Ross-Fielder riding the patented American Star bicycle. No, ladies and gentleman, he is not riding it the wrong way about, this machine really does have a front wheel smaller than the back. It is operated by treadles not pedals, and is guaranteed to prevent the danger of tipping forward, the fear of which prevents nervous gentlemen attempting to ride. This arrangement also enables the same machine to be ridden by gentlemen of different sizes. I have been told that an enterprising American is already experimenting with fitting out this model so it may be powered by steam. Is this the bicycle of the future? Time will tell.' Ross-Fielder, not looking entirely happy with his mount, nevertheless rode it well and so determined was his concentration that one might have excused him for not noticing Miss Hicks.

'The last item in this exciting parade is the new family sociable, a special adaptation of the Premier machine, driven by Mr Goring and Miss Farrow. It seats two persons in the front, but at the rear is a bench suitable for luggage. A perfect arrangement for friends who wish to take a holiday, or even dare I say it, married persons on a day's outing who might like to seat smaller persons behind them.' There was a titter from the audience at this suggestion. 'Despite the size of the machine, it is very light and easily directed, and a pleasant ride may be achieved without fatigue.'

Mr Goring and Miss Farrow made a handsome couple. The lady was very young indeed, a dainty creature arrayed in pale blue silk, carrying a tiny parasol, her hair an arrangement of golden curls so perfect that they might have been carved from marble and gilded, nestling in a frilled bonnet fastened by a pearl pin. She was clearly more interested in the impression she was creating than making any great effort to drive the sociable. Her tiny feet barely touched the pedals, not that it made much difference, given Mr Goring's powerful limbs. Miss Hicks gave a fitful flutter of her handkerchief as they passed by, but it was clear that she knew that her rival had conquered that particular field.

After a circuit of the course, the machines headed back to the visitors' enclosure.

'And now, ladies and gentleman,' announced Vance, 'the first competition of the day will commence in ten minutes. A prize will be awarded for the best turned-out machine of any kind.'

Mr Vance left the dais and was joined by two ladies, one of an age to be his mother, the younger tall and proud, with long auburn hair and fierce blue eyes. She took his arm and held it tightly, and he pressed her hand. As the sociable carrying Mr Goring and Miss Farrow moved away she glared at it, with an expression of purest hatred.

At last, Cedric was back, and joined Frances at the perimeter of the course. To her relief he appeared to be the bearer of good news. 'Sir Hugo is safely delivered,' he said. 'Jepson looked him over and thought he would recover, but in view of his age he will need rest and care. Jepson agreed with your diagnosis, by the way. Morphine. He is anxious to avoid any suggestion of attempted *felo de se* in such a respected gentleman. It is no secret that Sir Hugo used an embrocation for his back, but he may have obtained morphine by some means or other, and men without medical knowledge have been known to overdose themselves by mistake. Jepson absolutely denies providing Sir Hugo with morphine, and I am obliged to believe him. He will stay with his patient for the time being, and his wife will help with a little tender nursing. He suggested that because of the risk of Sir Hugo over-taxing his strength, he should not be permitted to leave until this evening, when he can return home, and Mrs Pirrie and Waterfield will be available to look after him, and I agreed.'

'That is a considerable relief. All that has happened in your absence is the opening speech made by General Farrow and the parade of new machines. Mr Vance described them. The ladies with him, are they his mother and sister?'

'They are. The girl is a fascinating creature, but one never quite knows what she might do next.' He glanced about. 'Is our new friend here?'

'Yes. He is number six.'

'And you're quite sure you can trust him?'

'Remember, it was he who saved me from the Face-slasher. Why should I not trust him?'

'Ah, yes, the dashing gentleman in the mask, he with the enticingly scented soap you asked me so earnestly to identify. I thought I recognised it. He certainly knows how to creep about in disguise. Well, one word of advice, you must take very great care not to fall in love with him. Or is my warning already too late?'

'We did have an interesting conversation,' said Frances, quickly deflecting both Cedric's thoughts and her own from that difficult subject. She explained the theory about Sir Hugo's invention and why he had been stopped both from perfecting it and discussing it with General Farrow.

'I can't say I was impressed by what I saw of those side wheels,' said Cedric, 'but you are right, he might have found the secret of improving them and making them a valuable commodity. There's many a manufacturer who could profit from such a thing. Let me get my race number and then we can think further. You're sure you won't go home?'

'Cedric, you can't take me home if you are to compete.'

'My dear Frances,' he exclaimed earnestly, 'I will gladly miss all competitions to ensure your safety.'

'Very well,' she said soothingly, 'let us agree on this. You can take me home once you have completed your afternoon race. But aren't you due to enter the competition for the best turned-out machine? It will start in a few minutes, and you don't have your number yet.'

Cedric agreed with some reluctance and went to get his number. In truth, although Frances was touched by Cedric's obvious concern, and his prudent insistence that she should go home, she realised that she didn't want to leave at all.

Mr Vance announced the parade, and proceeded to read out the names of the competitors, who wheeled their machines to the course with proud smiles. These were machines coated in the finest new enamels, every metal part polished to a mirror-like shine, the rotating spokes twinkling as they turned. The diminutive star of the display was Mr Toop, balancing atop his elegant little bicycle, which sported every addition that could possibly be attached to it whether it was needed or not. There was the new front wheel spoon brake, gleaming hub lamps, miniature front lamps, cyclometer, cowhide bag, and polished ebony handles. The rotund rider looked supremely pleased with himself as he pedalled sedately around the track. He had taken the requirement for embellishment to even greater extremes since he had included himself in the description, adding a fresh flower, a cream coloured rosebud, to his buttonhole and combing his hair flat in a slick of pomade.

Toop, Frances reflected, was the epitome of the little man of no great presence who sought to make himself larger though purchases. If taken too far the result could be more comical than impressive. Cedric, who was now sporting a number twenty-eight on his back, could not outshine Mr Toop in the matter of excess, but was easily his superior in the question of tasteful restraint, and Frances waved to him as he pedalled past.

The first real race of the day was between six ladies on tricycles, and while it could not be denied that they put a great deal of effort into it, it was clear to Frances that the machine could never rival the bicycle for ease and velocity. Not only was it heavier, but the position of the treadles in front of the rider could never allow her to put enough pressure on them as she might have done with the pedals of a bicycle. The new Rucker model would overcome that difficulty, but even so, the wearing of long heavy skirts remained a serious obstacle to attaining any great speed. The benefit of tricycles was that they combined healthful exercise with safety and mobility, but only as long as they were used for country excursions. Their size, which required a stable to keep them, as well as the cost, also meant that tricycle use was restricted to ladies of some means.

Frances was musing on this subject when she heard a familiar voice at her side. 'Well, well, Miss Doughty, as I live and breathe! What brings you here?'

She turned around and to her astonishment and dismay saw the ruddy features of Inspector Sharrock of Paddington Green.

Chapter Twenty

Frances took a deep breath before she replied. 'A lady may take an excursion and amuse herself, may she not?'

'Ah,' he said, with a knowing grin. 'I understand. Detective work. Well I only hope you're not running about after murderers again. I can't think how many times I have spoken to you about that, but you never listen.'

'Inspector,' she said quietly, 'I wish only to observe the races as anyone might do. For that purpose, I am not Frances Doughty today, I am Rose Williamson, Mr Garton's cousin.'

'Of course you are,' he said, with an exaggerated wink. 'Just don't get into any trouble.'

'I have no intention of getting into any trouble.'

'You never do, and then next moment you go out searching for it.' He looked around him. 'Do you know Sir Hugo Daffin? Old gent, monocle, usually makes all the announcements. Is he about?'

'The club secretary Mr Toop has just told us that Sir Hugo is delayed in London on business, but is expected to return soon.'

'Ah,' said Sharrock. 'I wonder what that was about?' He narrowed his eyes and gave her a searching look. 'Do you know?'

'I'm afraid I don't. Were you supposed to have a meeting with him?'

'No, only I am here at his request. He asked for an officer to come and give a talk about bicycle safety. We had some leaflets made, but I shouldn't think they'll do much good.' He nodded to where young Constable Mayberry, who regularly assisted him in his work, was handing out papers. 'To be honest with you, I don't think the words "safety" and "bicycle" have much business being together. Dangerous machines. The sooner they are given up and those who feel they have to ride about on wheels turn to tricycles, the better. I still wouldn't have them on the city streets, though. Horses will never stand for them. But even on country roads these dare-all young men need to be reminded how to behave. A bicycle is a carriage in law, and is subject to the same rules of the road. You don't see carriages driving on the pavement and neither is that any place for a bicycle.'

'I'm sure the members of the Bayswater and other clubs will be very pleased to have that made clear to them,' said Frances. 'Perhaps you might also remind carriage drivers and carriers not to make unprovoked assaults on bicyclists, since that seems to be a common sport nowadays.'

Sharrock's expression showed that he accepted her point. 'If they do then I promise you they will be met with the full force of the law. Can't have the streets of the metropolis turned into a Roman circus now, can we?'

Frances hoped that the intrusion of the police would not affect her mission, but now she thought about it, it could be a good thing, since their presence on the field might deter Mr Grove's attackers from making another attempt.

Mr Toop had noticed the new arrivals, and after making sure that his prized machine was carefully put away, he hurried up to the Inspector. Frances decided to remain nearby, affecting a keen interest in the preparations for the boys' race, but staying within earshot.

'Inspector,' said Toop, breathlessly, 'I do hope the police are here to tell us that the escaped convict has been recaptured. We have all been very alarmed, especially since it seems he must have entered the coach house at Springfield Lodge where our machines are stored without being noticed and actually,' Toop paused and made little gasping noises before he could go on, 'actually caused damage to a bicycle by cutting the spokes. I am only thankful it was no worse.'

Sharrock did not appear to find an outrage committed upon a bicycle quite as serious as did Toop. 'I am sorry to say that as far as I have been informed the convict Coote is still at large. If you have reported the damage to the Acton police I am sure they can be relied upon to look into it. But in my experience these convicts only want one thing – to get as far away as they can as quickly as they can, so I doubt that you need to be concerned. No, I am here at the request of Sir Hugo Daffin to give a talk on bicycles and the law, and how to ride safely.'

'Oh!' said Toop. 'I'm afraid he hadn't mentioned that to me; of course, he has been so very busy of late. But it is a splendid idea, and I am sure we can all benefit from it. Do you ride, Inspector?'

'I do not,' said Sharrock, firmly. The words 'and never will' remained unspoken, but still hung in the air.

Toop was undeterred. 'I understand that many police forces in the country districts have taken to the wheel with great advantage.'

'Well, I can see the usefulness there,' said Sharrock reluctantly, 'although they still need to be careful around horses.'

'Of course, of course. When do you wish to make your speech?'

Sharrock looked at his watch. 'Whenever it will do most good.'

'Splendid! Just before the afternoon races, I think. There will be a good crowd then. I'll advise the committee. And I will see to it that you and your constable are given luncheon at the club's expense.' Toop hurried away.

Sharrock looked a little brighter at the prospect of luncheon, and Frances took the opportunity to question him. 'Inspector, it does seem strange to me that the convict was able to make his escape and disappear so easily. Would he not make a distinctive figure in his uniform? Or does he have friends in the area who can hide him and help him get away?'

'Yes, and no,' said Sharrock. 'I am not looking into that business, it's a matter for the Hammersmith police, but if I was to hazard a guess I would say that the ease of the escape suggests that the man had inside help.'

'Inside? In the prison? You mean one of the guards?'

'Oh yes, it has been known. You only need one wrong'un who'd turn a blind eye and leave an old suit of clothes and some food lying about.'

'For money, I suppose.'

'Well, it would have to be. They don't get paid enough. Like the police.'

'But Coote had no money.'

'No, but he might have had criminal associates. They might have owed him a favour so he would do them one in return. It's a funny world.'

'Do you know if anyone visited him in prison?'

Sharrock smiled. 'I am sure the Hammersmith police are looking into that very question even as we speak.'

'Mr Toop just mentioned that one of the bicycles stored in the coach house at Springfield Lodge was damaged. I'm not sure if you are aware of this, but it was the bicycle belonging to Mr Ross-Fielder, the son of the reverend gentlemen who was attacked by Coote. Can that be a coincidence?'

Sharrock's eyebrows went up. 'So is that why Mr Toop thinks it was Coote who did it?'

'It does seem strange that it was that specific bicycle that was singled out from all the others. It had Mr Ross-Fielder's initials on the travel bag.' Sharrock looked at her suspiciously. 'I know about this because my good friend Mr Garton is a member of the club.'

Sharrock was considering this information when a sergeant in the uniform of the county police appeared, clearly wanting a word with the Inspector. Frances left them to talk. The boys' race was about to begin, and she saw that Ratty had decided to enter. A small assemblage of eager youths all aged about twelve to fifteen on a variety of bicycles had lined up ready, and at a signal, mounted their machines and set off at a pounding rate. Frances kept her eyes on the race, but made sure to listen to the conversation behind her. It was extraordinary, she thought, that as long as she did not obviously appear to be paying attention to what was being said, men were often quite happy to conduct their conversations within her hearing, assuming no doubt that these serious matters were not something she would find interesting. Sharrock, who knew Frances too well, was aware that she would be listening, and despite his overt and often repeated objections to her meddling in police affairs, knew that this frequently resulted in an arrest for which she was happy to give him credit.

'Sergeant Hambling, sir, Acton police, just to inform you that we are here to issue handbills regarding the escaped convict Coote.' Hambling was accompanied by several constables, who were busy distributing papers to all the visitors.

'Still no sign of him, I take it?'

'None, sir.'

Sharrock took a handbill. 'I'm here to give a speech about bicycle safety so I shall make sure to advise everyone to read these carefully and keep a sharp lookout.'

'Thank you, sir.' The sergeant paused. 'I happened to notice that Archie Hopper is about. I just saw him duck behind the scoreboard. He's well known to the police in these parts. Slippery type. I've had words with him before, but I might do so again. We're fairly sure he runs an off-course betting book. In fact, Coote used to be one of his messengers.'

'Is that so?'

'Oh yes, that's what makes him so hard to pin down. He's got half a dozen of them at least; some are boy runners, and the older ones are on velocipedes. We've questioned him about Coote but he claims to know nothing of course.'

'Do you think it was Hopper who helped Coote to escape?'

'We're keeping an open mind on that. I don't think Coote was so valuable to him that he would have done. After all, messengers are easy enough to come by, and if what I heard is true, there was bad blood between them in the end.'

'Bad blood, you say?'

'Yes, Hopper knew that one of his messengers was cheating him, and thought it was Coote, so he told him he wasn't wanted. Then it turned out that it was another of his men, Cowdray, who was the cheat; the man absconded with a pile of cash. Coote never had a good word for Hopper after that, so we don't think he would have gone to him for help.'

'He might have blackmailed him if he knew enough about the business,' said Sharrock. 'Did he write to him from prison? Did Hopper visit him?'

'No, I think the only visits were from the Reverend Ross-Fielder.'

'What? The injured man?'

'In a spirit of Christian forgiveness.'

'Well that was very good of him. All the same, he is the last man who would have wanted Coote to break out of prison, so I think we can rule him out as a suspect.'

'That's very true, sir.' The sergeant went about his business.

The young riders were bowling about the course in an alarming manner, both fast and reckless. Ratty, having only just ridden a bicycle for the first time that day, could not hope to compete with the more experienced riders but he did well, and managed to finish the course, which was more than some were able to. Frances cheered him as he rode to the finishing flag.

'I suppose you overheard that?' said Sharrock.

'Of course,' said Frances, waving at Ratty. 'And it does lead me to believe that if Mr Coote was at one time working as a messenger for Mr Hopper, it could well be that he knew how to ride a bicycle, or at very least a velocipede.'

'That's possible, yes.'

'In fact, I was told that velocipedes are sometimes used to train beginners who might be nervous, to give them confidence before they attempt the high-wheeler.'

'So, what are you saying?'

'I'm saying that even if Mr Coote had never ridden a high-wheeler his experience with the velocipede might have given him enough practice to do so. And if he had somehow managed to enter the coach house unobserved, he could have stolen a machine to make his escape faster. Instead of which he chose to cut the spokes on Mr Ross-Fielder's bicycle.'

'Yes, that does seem strange.'

'Doubly strange, because the damage done was trivial and quickly repaired. And Mr Coote, if he is familiar with the velocipede, would have known that. All of which suggests to me that whoever cut the spokes on Mr Ross-Fielder's bicycle it was not Mr Coote.'

'Who then?'

'I don't know. If we are looking for people who dislike bicyclists then there are too many to choose from. But no one suspicious was seen in the area. The club members are very efficient about guarding their property. The only people who could have damaged the machine are therefore the club members themselves, people who came to hire machines, the servants, and Jack Linnett. If the damage had been greater I would understand it, but something so quickly repaired is more surprising. Unless …'

'Yes?'

Frances shook her head. 'Let me think about it.'

'Oh dear!' sighed Sharrock. 'You're thinking again. That spells danger. I'll get the handcuffs ready, shall I?'

Frances declined to comment.

'I see that Pounder fellow has taken to the bicycle, being given lessons by your friend Mr Garton,' added Sharrock, nodding to where the professor was making his first attempts at the art, and doing rather well. 'And what a surprise, Miss Smith is there looking on and admiring him, and I seem to have spotted young Tom about the place, as well as Ratty. It's quite a little family excursion, isn't it?'

Frances said nothing.

'And something tells me you might prefer it if I didn't make those observations public.'

'Thank you, Inspector,' she said gratefully.

He made a salute and hurried away.

Although Frances and Sarah were keeping up the pretence of not being members of the same party, they took care to remain in each other's eyeline as far as possible. Frances saw that Sarah had noted Sharrock's presence, and sign messages passed between them to reassure both that all was well.

Mr Grove was busy giving lessons to beginners, and Frances decided on an experiment. She managed to catch his eye and sign to him that Inspector Sharrock was about. It was clear from his response that her message had been received and understood.

Cedric was soon back at her side carrying a paper. 'Well done young Ratty!' he said. 'That boy will go far! And did you see Pounder on the high-wheeler? What a man he is! I have the two-mile intermediate handicap later; this is the full list of entrants for the afternoon. Your friend Mr Grove is in the senior's contest. By the way, I thought I saw Sharrock and Mayberry here. Are they after Coote?'

'No, the Inspector is giving a talk on bicycling safety. But the Acton police have come to give out handbills about Coote, who has somehow managed to disappear.' Frances studied the list. 'How do they handicap?'

'It's a staggered start based on experience and wheel size. There are expert independent handicappers brought in to decide so there can be no suggestion of bias.'

'I see, so that does give a chance to the shorter man. Will Mr Toop race, do you think?'

'No, he might risk scratching his paint. He is very fastidious about that. Keeps his machine at the lodge so he needs to transport it as little as possible. He likes a slow decorous promenade, so people can admire the machine. One day we will see him parade himself about the carriage drive of Hyde Park with all the gentry.'

Frances had been thinking about Sir Hugo and his work. 'The next race is the novices' one mile and that isn't for another few minutes. If you don't mind accompanying me, I want to go and talk to Jack Linnett again. He works more closely with Sir Hugo than anyone, and I find it hard to believe that he has been left entirely in the dark. Perhaps he knows something but doesn't realise its importance.'

'My pleasure,' said Cedric. They linked arms and strolled over to the blacksmith's enclosure, where Jack was busy looking over bicycles for some of the racers. 'Going well?' asked Cedric. 'I might bring my steed over for a quick look before the race. Can't take any chances, eh?'

'That's true, sir.'

'Is there any word from Sir Hugo?'

'No sir, not that I know of.'

'All Toop said was that he was away on business and I know how long these things take. So how is the work going on with those side wheels? When I last saw you testing them, Sir Hugo said he wanted them made larger. Did that improve matters at all?'

Jack's grimace was all the information they needed on that point. 'Well, to be truthful, sir, it made it worse. I'm not at all sure we'll have any success with them.'

'Perhaps he would be better advised to try something else to improve the lot of wheelmen. How long are we to wait for Mr Rook's new saddle? Perhaps Sir Hugo could devise one of his own. I for one would welcome a more comfortable seat.'

'I've heard many a gent say so, sir.'

'Perhaps he might invent a bicycle for ladies,' said Frances, teasingly.

Jack smiled, though he made every effort to be polite. 'Oh, I don't know about that, Miss. That would be very hard for a lady to ride. And ladies already have tricycles.'

'But I think he should. The tricycle is all very well, but it is so much more cumbersome than the bicycle. Why should ladies, who weigh less than men, be expected to ride a heavier machine? That makes no sense to me at all. A bicycle that ladies can ride would be such a boon to the female sex. If Sir Hugo invented a ladies' bicycle, it would be very popular, but he should do it soon, before anyone else can steal the idea. That's the way things are done, isn't it?'

Jack blinked at this deluge of notions. 'So I understand, Miss. But that's all beyond what I know about. I just do what Sir Hugo asks of me.'

Frances had been lied to so many times she thought she could write a book about it. She had learned to notice the way some liars faced her with open-eyed expressions of childlike innocence, the way that others gave her a sideways glance with a twitch of the lip, unable to conceal a sense of mischief at what they had done, while others simply avoided her gaze with an evasive tilt of the head. Jack Linnett was the third kind.

'He's hiding something,' she said, as she and Cedric strolled away.

'Any idea as to what that might be?'

'Well this is just a theory, but it does look as if Sir Hugo has something of value, and Jack has been asked to keep quiet about it, in case anyone steals the idea. Supposing he had agreed to reward Jack if he makes a profit from his invention?'

'Ah, yes, he might well have done, with all the work the lad has done for him. Even a small share could make a big difference to his fortunes.'

'And his chances with Miss Hicks. But Jack has a great deal of respect, even affection for Sir Hugo. He wouldn't willingly reveal his secrets. So he pretends to know nothing.'

'If we only knew who stole Sir Hugo's red notebooks. Of course, if he recovers, as we hope very much he will, he might be able to recall someone acting suspiciously and that could lead us to the person who drugged him.'

'Morphine is an interesting choice,' Frances observed.

'Who can obtain it easily?' asked Cedric. 'Medical men, of course, medical students, chemists. Can it be purchased?'

'Morphine is extracted from opium, and sales of opium preparations can only be made by a qualified pharmacist and must be entered in a poisons register. In practice, members of the public without a medical qualification who ask to buy morphine will only draw attention to themselves.'

Cedric was thoughtful. 'I know you want to protect Sir Hugo's reputation, but don't you think, now that Sharrock is here, that we ought to tell him what has happened?'

'No. Not yet. Please trust me, Cedric. I can't. And I beg you not to. The main thing is that Sir Hugo is safe.'

As she said this, however, Frances couldn't help wondering if she or any of her party was truly safe.

CHAPTER TWENTY-ONE

The morning programme continued with four short races for senior riders, the first three finishers from each to go forward to a final champion of champions contest, which would end the day's programme. These sprints certainly showed who the best amateurs were. Spinning ahead of the field in magnificent style was Rufus Goring, who, enthused Cedric, had calves like a Greek statue, hard as marble and perfectly formed. Ross-Fielder was a lesser though proficient rider, and young Jepson also gained a place in the final twelve. Mr Grove was a highly competent bicyclist, and might have won his race, but on seeing another wheelman in difficulties, suffering from the heat and in danger of causing an accident, he stopped to assist him, and so lost any chance of competing that afternoon.

At the pavilion, preparations were in hand for the salad luncheons, although tea and coffee, which were being served throughout the day to thirsty visitors, were always available. While Cedric took a practice turn about the course, Frances decided to take a seat on the veranda, order refreshments, and see if she could have a word with Mrs Pirrie.

'Your cousin is a very courteous and well-spoken young gentleman,' said Mrs Pirrie, bringing Frances a pot of tea and a plate of biscuits.

'He is, I am very fond of him,' said Frances. 'I do hope he does well in his race this afternoon. What lovely prizes there are, and how generous of Sir Hugo to donate them.'

'Oh, generous to a fault, Sir Hugo,' said Mrs Pirrie, loading empty cups and plates onto a tray.

'There was one name I couldn't help noticing,' Frances added. 'The Morton Vance memorial cup. Cedric told me about what happened to poor Mr Vance. It must have been a terrible shock for all of you.'

Mrs Pirrie paused in her work and uttered a deep sigh. 'It was, that. A year ago, now, and it's all fresh in my mind like it was yesterday.' She shook her head. 'I shall never forget it.'

'Were there no witnesses to what happened?' Frances asked, careful to maintain the semblance of someone who had not spent the last two weeks making a detailed study of the evidence. She judged that Mrs Pirrie had probably told her tale many times during the last year and had quite extinguished her usual supply of those who had not heard it at least once. Now here was a new person she could tell. The temptation would be irresistible.

Mrs Pirrie wiped her hands on her apron and sat down at the table with Frances. 'No. None at all. The gentlemen had been out on their bicycles a bit before, but when it happened they were all back at the lodge having tea. Well, nearly all. But none of them saw anything. There was one funny thing, though,' she added thoughtfully.

Frances waited, hardly daring to interrupt, but adopted an expression of open-eyed anticipation that she knew was so rewarding to the storyteller.

'I was back and forth with the tea things and I remember looking out of the front parlour window because I thought I noticed something moving outside, and that was when I saw it.'

There was a pause for dramatic effect. 'Saw it?' Frances could not restrain herself from exclaiming.

'It was a sociable on the carriage drive with a lady and a gentleman in it.'

'Really? So they might have been witnesses. Was it coming in or going out?'

'Going out. I thought at first that it was Sir Hugo's, as he does have one he keeps for hire, but I was told later it wasn't.'

Frances nodded, reflecting that the ledger she had examined confirmed that there had been no hirings that day.

'And then it was a while after that when Mr Ross-Fielder came back with the news of what he had found. Oh, and what a state he was in!' She shook her head in sorrow. 'Quite beside himself, he was.'

'Mr Ross-Fielder didn't go out riding with the other club members?'

'No, he came along later.'

'And Mr Vance? Was he not with them?'

'No. He went out after the others had gone.' Mrs Pirrie looked grim. 'In fact, he was supposed to have gone out with the others but it was all down to his brother, Mr Phineas Vance, that he didn't. They worked in the same office but Mr Phineas is the senior man, and they had a bit of a falling out that day. Oh, nothing serious, only about something that ought to have been done and was forgotten about. It was a Saturday and they should have closed the office early, but he said that Mr Morton must stay behind and finish his work and that was what made him arrive late. If Mr Phineas hadn't insisted, they would both have gone out together and young Mr Morton would still be alive. When Mr Phineas found out what had happened and how it was partly his fault, he broke down and cried like a baby.'

'How small a thing, a little quarrel like that, and he will blame himself for the rest of his life,' said Frances sympathetically.

'He will, yes. He hasn't ridden a bicycle since, and today I think he is only here to award the cup in his brother's name, and see his memory honoured.' She looked wistful, and seemed about to rise and go about her business again.

'I expect the police must have asked you all a lot of questions,' Frances prompted.

'Yes, they came and talked to all of us to find out where we had been in the last hour. Not that anyone would have harmed Mr Vance, but they thought we might have seen something suspicious.'

'And had anyone?'

'No, well at the time of the murder we were almost all of us in the lodge having our tea. Mr Ross-Fielder was riding up from his home – he didn't see anyone near where he found poor Mr Vance – and Mr Toop had gone to see his mother.'

'Mr Toop didn't ride?'

'No, he looked after the coach house.'

'So after the riders came back, there was no one looking after the coach house?'

'Oh, there was, because Mr Iliffe very kindly volunteered to do it. I said to him, "But Mr Iliffe, you don't want to miss your tea," and he said I wasn't to worry about that as he would come in and have it later. But then I thought to myself, he will need some refreshment after the ride, so I asked Mr Waterfield to take a cup of tea and a sandwich plate out to him, and very grateful for it he was, too.'

'Did you tell the police about the sociable?'

'Oh yes. I think it must have been a lady and gent out for a ride on their own machine who decided to turn around and go back the way they had come, and the easiest way to do that is to come down the carriage drive and go out again. I've seen folks do that before, on tricycles, too. If they know Sir Hugo they'll know he won't object.'

'Did the couple ever come forward?'

Mrs Pirrie shook her head. 'I don't believe they did. I read about the trial in the newspapers of course, but there was no witness who'd been riding about in a sociable that day.'

'Do you remember how they were dressed? Was the man in a club uniform?'

'No, he was just in a gent's suit, and the lady wore a cape.'

'Would you recognise them again if you saw them?'

'I shouldn't think so; well, I only saw them from the back. I told the police everything I knew.'

'What a dreadful tragedy!' Frances exclaimed. 'And I heard there was a man hanged for it. A farmer, wasn't he?'

Mrs Pirrie wrinkled her nose. 'Pig-man. Nasty low sort. He got what he deserved.'

'There was no doubt that he was guilty? I mean, with there not being any witnesses?'

'Well who else could it have been? He'd threatened violence against all bicycling gentlemen again and again. That poor boy of his, you know young Jack Linnett who mends the bicycles, that's his son. The father led him a terrible life, and the lad is well rid of him. Chalk and cheese those two. The lad's a good lad and I won't hear a word against him.'

There was a cheer from the field as the last race of the morning, a two-mile for novices, laboured to a finish.

'They'll be wanting their lunches soon,' said Mrs Pirrie, standing up. 'I'd better get on.'

Frances studied the race list. The first events after luncheon were the short rides for seniors, then there were one- and two-mile handicaps in the second, of which Cedric was entered. After that was the much anticipated three-mile for professionals, and a break for tea, followed by the amateur champion of champions long-distance race. Frances knew that by rights she ought to have gone home immediately after Sir Hugo had been borne to safety. She wondered if the silver-haired gentleman would be angry with her for disobeying him. Mr Grove, however, who was present and nominally in control of the mission, had not ordered her away. Perhaps he had the authority to change the rules as events unfolded.

Inevitably she contrasted the attitudes of Cedric and Mr Grove. Cedric was so worried about her safety that she had been obliged to promise him she would go home as soon as he had raced. Mr Grove, on the other hand, accepted without complaint that she could remain in a place of potential danger, a position that she found both frightening and exciting. She began to wonder what Miss Dauntless would have done.

CHAPTER TWENTY-TWO

Mr Toop ascended the dais once more to announce that there would be an interval of one hour in which luncheon could be had. Refreshments, thought Frances, were for many an essential part of the day's entertainment, and sure enough, from her vantage point on the veranda she saw a drift of visitors approaching like a shoal of hungry fish coming to feed. Fortunately, there was an indoor tearoom for those who had not yet secured their table outside. Others had brought picnic baskets and were sitting on the benches laying out feasts of cold roast fowl, ham and bread and butter, or spreading blankets on the grass and opening bottles of aerated lemonade. The bright field resembled the green canvas of a painting, with summer dresses displayed like patches of flowers.

Frances studied the scene for familiar faces and unusual incidents. Cedric was having his bicycle checked over by Jack Linnett and Maud Jepson was being carefully squired by her brother. Frances wondered if those deadly rivals Iliffe and Babbit were likely to meet again, but neither was in plain sight. They were probably mingling with groups of other similarly uniformed bicyclists. She thought she saw Mr Grove on one occasion, but he was adept at hiding in a crowd and no sooner had she noticed him than he had vanished.

Mr Hopper was lurking by the scoreboard waiting for business. Every so often he delved into his pocket, removed something that he examined closely and then put it back. Frances thought it could be a roll of banknotes, or a betting book. The velocipede of his bulky assistant Peters was grinding about the field, although he occasionally paused to take a bite out of a large pie.

A flutter of yellow ribbons marked out the elaborate bonnet of Miss Hicks, the blacksmith's imprudent daughter. She paraded herself around the groups of bicyclists in the manner of a street vendor displaying a tray of confectionary and occasionally stopped to speak to them, but they appeared disinclined to engage her in any but the briefest of conversations. Some actually tipped their hats in dismissal, and turned away from her, and she was obliged to move on. She passed the blacksmith's enclosure, but did not pause in her walk to speak to her father's apprentices. Miss Hicks, thought Frances, was learning an important lesson. Flirting with young gentlemen above one's station was something to be conducted in private. Any attempt at coquettish behaviour in front of their friends and relations would meet with a very cold response.

Sarah and Professor Pounder took a table on the veranda nearby. Signs were exchanged to the effect that there was nothing new to report, but they kept strictly to their agreement not to converse without good reason to preserve the secrecy of the mission. Nevertheless, they spoke loudly enough for Frances to learn that the Professor had reported the suspicious behaviour of a youth who appeared to be planning to steal the trophies while an associate created a diversion, and Sarah had apprehended a pickpocket and handed him in to the police. Tom was moving about the tables offering handbills from bicycle manufacturers. He winked at Frances as he passed by but said nothing. She was beginning to suspect that he and Ratty had known all about Mr Grove's true identity for some time and had possibly even carried messages for him, but had been sworn to silence. She resolved to pay far more attention the next time the boys exchanged significant glances.

As Frances ate her salad lunch she realised how dreadfully she missed not being able to share her thoughts with Sarah. She was also obeying the strict orders of the silver-haired gentleman not to write anything down in a notebook, and she could see the good sense of this. She was obliged therefore to sit alone and revolve in her mind all that had occurred to date, and consider what mysteries remained unresolved.

The most important questions were who had drugged Sir Hugo and what precisely did they hope to gain by it? What had Sir Hugo intended to do in London and what was the subject of his proposed meeting with General Farrow? What was Jack Linnett hiding? And who had attacked Mr Grove? While it was obvious that these events were all part of a larger conspiracy, Frances wondered if there was any connection between them and the escaped convict Coote? Who had vandalised Ross-Fielder's bicycle? Who was EDW who had abandoned his velocipede in the old garden at Springfield Lodge? Who were the couple in the sociable who had failed to come forward after the murder of Morton Vance? In fact, who had actually killed Vance? The more Frances thought about it, the more she felt certain that Sam Linnett had been convicted simply because of his prior threats and his unsavoury demeanour and not because of any evidence that proved he was the murderer.

Regarding her mission, Frances' observation was that the opportunities to pass secret information were so numerous it was impossible for her to distinguish what was significant, what was normal commerce and what might be related to some other criminal activity. Mr Hopper, for example; was he simply operating an illegal betting business, or dipping his toes into something larger?

It was a very good luncheon but Frances hardly tasted it. She knew that once Cedric had raced, she must leave and all those questions would remain unanswered. Even if she stayed she was hardly likely to be able to answer them in a single afternoon.

Nearby, Rufus Goring was enjoying his luncheon in the company of Miss Farrow, her brother George and the General. It was a friendly enough gathering, and Mr Goring was in a cheerful mood discussing the races that had taken place so far and wishing young Farrow good luck in the two-mile. Miss Farrow said almost nothing, but simply smiled a great deal, which appeared to be all that was required of her. The General was not in the best of moods. He had the demeanour of a man who valued his time and did not like it wasted by the incompetence of others. Not only was Sir Hugo not there for the arranged meeting without leaving any message to say when he might return, but he had then been asked to make an impromptu speech. No amount of salad, however good, would compensate for that.

Miss Farrow was not a girl of exceptional attractions, but she had made the most of the portion she had been allotted. Her gown and bonnet were delicate and fashionable and she had manners to match. She liked to emphasise her charms by touching the glossy golden curls clustering at her temples, smoothing the soft silk of her skirt and inspecting the pristine lace of her gloves. Every so often she gazed at Mr Goring's face as if mesmerised by the beauty of his moustache. Curiously, she did not address him directly and he did not address her. Whatever their interest in each other it did not include conversation. Both, thought Frances, laid great store by appearances, and she wondered if there was any great character within either.

George Farrow, while accepting good wishes for the forthcoming race, looked a little nervous. He seemed unable to settle comfortably, and ate almost nothing. While he was making an effort to attend to the conversation it was clear that his thoughts were elsewhere. Occasionally he allowed his gaze to flicker across the field but whatever or whoever he was looking for was not at first apparent. Then he gave a more intense stare. Frances tried to follow his line of sight. Who was he looking at? Mr Grove was talking to Jack Linnett, Miss Hicks was fluttering her ribbons at Mr Toop, who appeared not to find them at all interesting, and Peters had just ridden past the veranda on his velocipede. Could it be one of these, or another person entirely who had so interested him?

'George!' snapped the General. 'Pay attention, won't you! If Sir Hugo doesn't appear, you must send him a letter first thing tomorrow, and this time make sure he knows when I expect to see him!'

'Yes, father,' said George. He hung his head over his plate and stirred its contents with his fork.

'I hope you are not taking any notice of that dreadful hussy,' said Miss Farrow. 'What a fright she is in that horrid dress!'

'I've never spoken to her,' said George.

Rufus Goring glanced at young Farrow and raised his eyebrows as if to imply that he detected a flaw in that statement.

'I should hope not!' barked the General.

'Her impudence is extraordinary,' continued Miss Farrow. 'Do you know the girl once spoke to me in a most familiar way and hinted that we might become better acquainted in the future. Whatever could she have meant? I would not have her as my laundry maid.'

There were some further words spoken, but unfortunately they were drowned by the efforts of the Acton Brass Ensemble, which burst vigorously into sound and performed mightily for about half an hour.

Cedric joined Frances at the table for luncheon and assured her that his bicycle was now at the very peak of its condition and beauty. He didn't expect to win the race – there were, he was forced to admit, younger men than he in the saddle – but he hoped to give a good account of himself. Cedric, Frances reflected, was always a little imprecise about his age. He occasionally admitted to being in the region of thirty, but never revealed whether the number was less or more. Since he took great care with his appearance he probably hoped to be in the region of thirty for many years to come.

There was another small gathering on the veranda, Henry Ross-Fielder, accompanied by a couple who were obviously his parents and a young man who, like the father, also wore a clerical collar. Frances recalled Cedric saying that Ross-Fielder's brother was in the Church, and presumed that this was he. She mused on the question of family resemblances since she could see that Henry Ross-Fielder was a younger version of his father in both face and form, while the non-bicycling clerical brother had the rounder face and more generously proportioned figure of his mother. They seemed like a close-knit and harmonious group, with deep sympathies existing between them. A leaflet was lying on the table they shared, one of those distributed by the Acton police regarding the missing Mr Coote. The reverend gentleman was shaking his head in dismay and Ross-Fielder clasped him sympathetically by the shoulder. The father glanced at him with a look of pain, and after some whispered words, sighed and nodded. Whatever comfort had been offered, it seemed to have little effect. While the sons looked concerned, Mrs Ross-Fielder maintained an enigmatic air and said almost nothing, but every so often the façade of dignity cracked and revealed that she too was troubled.

At last Mr Toop mounted the platform, speaking trumpet in one hand and a paper in the other. He waved the paper impatiently at the bandleader, who eventually understood that some reduction in sound was required if speeches were to be heard, and the ensemble ground to a stop.

'And now,' said Mr Toop, 'we have an exciting programme of events for this afternoon! We have a series of one-mile flat starts for those seniors who did not reach the final twelve for the champions race. Then there are the one- and two-mile intermediate handicaps, and of course the race for professional riders, which I know many of you are anticipating with keen interest. Our own Mr Paul Iliffe,' here there were cheers from the audience, 'will be challenged by men from four other clubs. After tea, the last race will of course be the Victor Ludorum! Finally, there will be the grand prize-giving, and that will include the very special award of the Morton Vance memorial cup for the most sporting bicyclist. And I have just been given to understand there will in addition be a very special surprise announcement. What that might be, I cannot of course divulge! You will also be favoured with an address to which I urge you all to pay great attention. Inspector Sharrock of Paddington

Green Police will be speaking to you on a very important subject – safety.'

Sharrock's speech was undoubtedly important but Frances thought it was not destined to hold the attention of his audience. As she saw it, the police were caught in the middle of two armies who, while not actually at war, were in a state of antagonism. On the one hand there were the carriage drivers whose presence on the road with their horses was a tradition as old as civilisation. Laws had been enacted to protect them and their horses, and also state what a carriage or a rider was permitted to do. Then along came the interloper, the bicycle, which was such a new means of locomotion that it was hard to see what it might be allowed to do or prohibited from doing, or even what it actually was. These two factions were vying for the same space, often the same business, and it was a situation fraught with danger. Frances hoped that in time they would come to some amicable arrangement.

'Cedric,' said Frances, cautiously.

'Ah, I think I know what you are about to ask,' he said.

'I know I promised you that I would leave once you have ridden, but I am sure you wouldn't want to miss the professionals' race, or the champions race or the prize giving. And neither would I.'

'And you want to stay on,' he said.

'I don't see any danger about, do you?'

'It's not visible danger that concerns me. Your friend Grove seems to know the risks and he was still caught out. He is a strong fellow and you are not.'

'But there comes a time when one must be allowed to take risks and make mistakes. You said that your man, Joseph, is horribly afraid for you when you go out on the bicycle, but he wouldn't try and dissuade you from doing it.'

Cedric sighed. 'Very well, this is what we will do. We will watch Iliffe and Babbit have their duel, then go for a nice cup of tea and one of Mrs Pirrie's lovely cakes, and then we go home. I insist.'

Unwillingly, Frances was obliged to agree.

CHAPTER TWENTY-THREE

The first events of the afternoon were merely to whet the appetite for the keenly anticipated final contests, the professionals' race and the race of champions.

Frances felt she would like to see the professionals ride from a closer position than the pavilion and moved to the barrier rope well before the intermediate handicaps started to secure a good view. Compared with the previous races there was some good humour and sportsmanship amongst the competitors, who saw their contests as amusing exercises rather than serious rivalry. The race marshal appointed the riders to their positions and they shook hands before they took their places.

It was clear from the outset of the two-mile race that Cedric was outclassed; however, he made a good attempt at it and bravely waved his hat to the crowds as he reached the finish in sixth place. Once he had taken his machine back to the members' enclosure he joined Frances at the boundary rope.

'Well that was a jolly run! Sorry I couldn't do better but I think I was a winner in the matter of style.' Cedric took a ribbon from his pocket. 'A gift from that foolish girl, saying that she wished I might have won. She is hoping to engage my heart, but I fear the colour yellow does not match my complexion.'

There was a growing sense of excitement as the professionals' race was announced. The crowds began to surge forward, some making their way across the grassy track while they could, and hurrying around the inner perimeter vying for the best position from which to view the contest. Others struggled to find the best places from the outside.

'This contest certainly attracts the biggest crowds,' said Frances.

'I suppose they believe that the professionals are the best riders, which is not always the case. It's an attraction for the spectators, mainly. Not all amateur wheelmen care for the professional races. Some think they are not truly sporting. If a man was to compete for money just once, he would be instantly damned as a professional and drummed out of the Bicycle Touring Club. A sad fate.'

'What do you think?' asked Frances.

Cedric shrugged. 'Oh, a man must make a living somehow, and if he can do it bicycling, why not?'

'All the same, I think some of the interest must be attributed to the enmity between Iliffe and Babbit.'

'That does add a little spice to the occasion, there is no doubt about that!'

The riders were taking their places. Apart from Iliffe and Babbit, there were three competitors from other clubs: the Chiswick club, in racing colours of chocolate brown with light blue hose; West Kensington, in dark blue with a blue helmet; and Mill Hill, in navy with a school cap. Paul Iliffe stood out by his height and broad shoulders, but Babbit was hardly less impressive in size.

The bicycles ridden by the professionals were of the most expensive variety, painted with hard shiny enamel colours, and highly polished. The riders displayed them proudly, making a great show of examining the machines to ensure that they were at the very peak of mechanical excellence. From time to time they also looked about to see if they were being admired and paused to stretch their arms and flex their leg muscles, which made the watching ladies giggle from behind their fingers.

Miss Jepson, a small, timid figure, approached the line of riders and offered a single flower to Iliffe, who accepted it with a smile and a bow, then tucked it into his pocket, so the flower head poked out at the top. Babbit, his face creased into a scowl, watched but did not interfere, and only polished his bicycle more savagely than before.

'What do you think of the other contestants?' Frances asked Cedric.

'Oh, it's a two-horse race,' he replied, 'the others won't be able to keep up the pace.'

Frances glanced at her schedule. 'I see this too is a handicap.'

'Yes, and it will be a hard one to decide,' said Cedric, as the bicyclists took up their positions. 'I can see they've brought in a man from the Hammersmith club to do it to ensure fairness. It's a specialised business when there is money at stake. He has to take into account the wheel size but also the experience and past wins of the competitor. The idea is to arrange things so that all the men have an equal chance. I expect that Babbit and Iliffe will go off last, but which one is ahead of the other is anyone's guess.'

'If the two are equal they could start together,' suggested Frances.

'They could, but that would lead to an early confrontation to get the best position. You might think that the man in the lead has the advantage but that is not necessarily the case. He has to ride into the wind and the man behind him gets the benefit of that. Also, the man ahead can't keep an eye on the man behind who can then choose his moment to overtake and surprise his rival.'

The handicapper, watch in hand, was speaking to the competitors and allocating them their places. The three more junior racers seemed content with his decision, but Iliffe and Babbit contested theirs loudly with much waving of arms, and had to be told to desist. The delay caused some unrest in the crowd, but not a little anticipation that it would be a hard-fought battle.

'Well now this is interestin',' said Tom, appearing by Frances' side. He gave her a handbill advertising enamel coatings and she pretended to read it. 'Don't suppose you've put a wager on the race?' he asked quietly.

Given the crush of people it seemed safe to hold a conversation unnoticed. 'I have not,' said Frances, 'but I expect many have.'

'See that lad, there?' said Tom. 'The one in the green cap?'

Frances looked up, to where a dishevelled reed-thin boy of about twelve was moving quickly about the field, threading his way through the crowds like an eel. 'Yes, I – oh he's slipped away. I think I know the one you mean.'

'That's Archie 'opper's best lad. 'E's a good 'un. Fast on 'is feet. You get that lad and you get 'opper.'

'Do you mean he's the one working the illegal betting business? Not Peters?'

'That's right. You see, everyone knows the big bully boy Peters, you can't miss 'im. Stands right out in the crowd, 'e does. But the police search 'im an' what do they find? Nothin'. An' all the time it's the little lad doin' the real business an' disappearin' like a puff o' smoke. An' I'll tell yer another thing what no one else 'ere 'as seen. 'E takes messages between Mr Iliffe and Mr Babbit. Blink an eye and yer won't know it's 'appened. I like that lad, I'd 'ave 'im workin' for me if I could.'

'Iliffe and Babbit?' said Frances in astonishment. 'Exchanging messages? Are you sure?'

'Oh yes.'

'What sort of messages? Threats, I suppose. Challenges. Insults.'

'Not a bit've it. I've seen 'ow they work. Notes back 'n forth an' some've 'em to 'opper 'n all.'

'Iliffe and Babbit and Hopper?' Frances was incredulous.

'Yes. Those two do a nice little act of 'atin' each other, but I don't think that's the truth've it. They're up ter summat, an' it's not what they might be proud of.'

'What do you think it is?'

'Well, from what I seen, I'd say they 'ad a tidy little bettin' cheat goin' on.'

Frances, concerned that they had spoken too long, pretended to write a message on the handbill. 'Tom, I want you find rider number 6 and tell him what you just told me.'

'Oh, the gent what useter 'ave the knife? 'E's a rum 'un.'

'And tell Sarah and Pounder as well.'

She gave him sixpence and he grinned and ran off.

'What was that about?' asked Cedric.

'Tom has just told me that Iliffe and Babbit have been exchanging messages using one of Mr Hopper's boys, and have sent messages to Hopper too.'

'Surely not!'

'If Tom can't spot that no one can. He thinks the men are not rivals after all, more like collaborators.'

'But —' Cedric lapsed into an astounded silence.

Love or money, Frances wondered? In this case, she felt sure that Tom was right and it was money. Poor Miss Jepson, she thought, to be nothing more than a pawn in their masquerade. 'I assume there is a great deal of betting on them?'

'Oh yes, large sums,' gasped Cedric when he had got his voice back. 'Both men have got legions of supporters. I myself put five guineas on Iliffe to win. Not with Hopper, I wouldn't trust him to pay out, but there are any number of private wagers amongst gentlemen.'

'Perhaps before you placed your bet you should have first asked Mr Iliffe which one of them they have agreed between themselves should be the victor today,' said Frances drily.

'But that's – oh no!'

'A gross betrayal of trust apart from anything else. If what they are up to could be proven they would probably find themselves in prison.' Frances did not say so but she thought that men who could cheat their own friends for money were just the kind who might sell their country's secrets to another nation.

'I suppose it's too late to warn people now,' said Cedric, unhappily.

'The wagers have been placed and the race is about to start,' said Frances. 'Far too late for today, I'm afraid. And all we have for now is Tom's observation and no actual proof. If we denounced them they would simply deny it. Once the meeting is over I shall ask Tom to tell Inspector Sharrock what he has seen, and leave it to the police to deal with.'

The handicapper raised his flag, pointed to the Chiswick man, then brought the flag down smartly. The Chiswick racer quickly mounted his bicycle and rode away. A few more seconds on the watch and it was time for the West Kensington man, and shortly after it was Mill Hill's turn. The handicapper stared at his watch for what seemed like a very long time, then he pointed to Babbit, flagged him away and almost immediately afterwards it was Iliffe's turn.

'I was looking forward to this race,' groaned Cedric. 'Now I can hardly bear to watch.'

'I'd rather you did,' said Frances. 'You know what to look out for. Signs of cheating, of some pre-arranged plan.'

'Yes, of course. If they are blackguards then I will be the first to expose them. One cannot have cheating in bicycling, whether amateur or professional, it's not to be tolerated.'

Frances, after watching the amateur races, was astonished to see the speed the professionals could bring to riding, even on a grass track, the vigour of their powerfully pumping legs moving like tireless machines. The three less experienced men in the lead were well matched, and she saw the determination on their faces not to be caught by the seniors, at least for as long as possible. Despite their best efforts, however, Iliffe and Babbit were gaining, and after the first three laps of the course were hard on the heels of their opponents. More importantly they made it clear from their manner that they were not taking the others seriously and were purely riding against each other. As they passed, the crowds roared, and there were eager supporters for both men, some of the ladies waving handkerchiefs at their favourites, like a little forest of lacy flags.

'Well you can't say they're not putting all they can into it,' said Cedric. 'No sign of either of them holding back.'

'Perhaps they'll wait for the last lap,' suggested Frances.

'Ah, yes, build up the maximum excitement. At least the crowds are having their value,' he added miserably.

The three junior racers were almost level with each other, and needed to take care at the turns, not daring to look behind them and see the danger creeping steadily up. Then one, the Chiswick man, made a sprint and moved inside the others, and began to draw away. In so doing he opened up a space that Iliffe and Babbit could take advantage of. The Kensington and Mill Hill men, almost nose to nose, laboured hard to catch up, but their efforts were fading. Mill Hill began to fall behind and now the three were in a single line.

It was halfway through the race, and Iliffe and Babbit could smell the scent of victory. With bared teeth and staring eyes, they focussed on the course ahead, Babbit just a little in front, but Iliffe waiting on his heels and far from beaten.

'I think Iliffe will take it,' said Cedric. 'He's looking for his chance and he's still fresh. He will keep up until the last lap and then pull ahead.'

With three laps to go, Babbit and Iliffe made their move. Babbit, doubling his efforts, began to overtake the junior riders, and Iliffe, too, found reserves of strength and kept up with his opponent. Before long, and to the rapturous roars of the crowds, the two jousting riders had swept past the three lesser men and were out in front. It was now, as Cedric had predicted, a two-man race. As Babbit and Iliffe passed by, roars turned to shrieks and several ladies fanned themselves briskly and appeared to be in danger of fainting away.

Two more laps and the rivals were almost level, with Babbit having a slight advantage on the turns and Iliffe threatening his position on the straight.

'Iliffe will take the inside position for the final run and pull ahead,' said Cedric, and, as predicted, on the last turn Iliffe made his bid for the lead. As he did so, however, he seemed to lose command of his bicycle, and it shifted away from his chosen line just for a moment. He managed to steady himself, but in so doing his front wheel collided with Babbit's back wheel and the two of them began to veer wildly off course. There were screams from the crowd as the riders fought for control of their machines. For a few horrible moments all was chaos. There was danger to both the riders, danger to the watching crowds and danger to the men following on behind. The three juniors had just enough time to adjust their direction and avoid a collision, but for Babbit and Iliffe it was too late. In a tangle of arms and legs and wheels and spinning cranks, they collapsed in the middle of the course and lay winded on the ground as the others sped past them, the Chiswick rider taking the victory.

There was an immediate rush of frantic persons who ducked under the roped-off barriers and ran to the fallen men in a wild hubbub.

'Well if they're not already dead they'll be trampled now,' said Cedric. He didn't sound too worried by either eventuality.

There were more screams and a sudden pulling back from the scene. Frances, standing on tiptoe, was able to see the two riders, now both on their feet, shouting incoherently at each other and starting to fight. In the middle of the melee members of both clubs were running forward, elbowing the teeming crowds aside. Reaching the furiously struggling rivals, they managed with an effort to pull them apart. Others took charge of the crowds and persuaded them to retire from the scene.

In the middle of the confusion, Mr Toop ran up, all of a sweat, and surveyed the mass of violent activity helplessly. He wisely avoided tackling the larger men, and instead decided to recover the tangled bicycles, trying to pick them up to see if they were damaged. He was lifting Babbit's machine when the owner gave a roar of fury and snatched it away so suddenly that Toop gave a little scream.

'I wonder how many people placed a wager on the Chiswick rider,' pondered Frances.

'Almost no one, I expect,' said Cedric.

'Mr Hopper will be very pleased with himself. How large a piece of his profits will he give to Babbit and Iliffe? Have they both made secret wagers against either of them winning?'

Frances looked about to see if Mr Hopper was in evidence, and at first was unable to see him, but at last he moved a little

cautiously out of the shadow of the scoreboard, stuffing something into his pocket. He was scanning the field with narrowed
eyes, and she wondered who he was looking for. Peters, his
strong-arm man on the velocipede, was not in sight, but the
boy in the green cap ran up and they ducked back into the
shelter of the scoreboard for a brief conversation before the
boy hurried away.

'Oh this is too awful!' exclaimed Cedric.

Frances realised that she had not seen Mr Grove for some
time. She was beginning to get concerned in case another
attempt had been made on him, then she chanced to see him
further away, talking to some of the Bayswater club members.

'Nice little earner,' said Ratty, skimming up on his bicycle.
''Opper ain't as 'appy, as 'e oughter be, though, dunno why.
Sent 'is boy all over an' aroun' the place, lookin' for summat.'
He rode away.

Eventually, Rufus Goring emerged from the crowds and
mounted the platform. Taking up the speaking trumpet, he
called out for calm, reassuring onlookers that neither of the
riders had been injured and announcing that there would be a
half-hour break for tea before the final race. It was several minutes before calm was more or less restored. The crowds went
to get refreshments, the handicapper had hard words with all
the riders, and the band struck up a popular dance melody.
Mr Toop, looking as if the cares of the world had all descended
upon him at once, sat on the steps of the podium, mopping his
brow with a handkerchief.

CHAPTER TWENTY-FOUR

'This day is the last day we can count ourselves happy,' said Cedric. 'Tomorrow the scandal will break and then the world of bicycling will never be the same again. Everywhere there will be nothing but distrust and suspicion.'

'Let us go and have tea,' said Frances.

'And after that, even I will want to go home,' said Cedric sadly.

They strolled towards the pavilion, arm-in-arm, and on the way Frances paused to look at the cups and medals. 'Who do you think will be awarded the most sporting rider?'

'Well it certainly won't be Iliffe or Babbit, not that either of them was eligible. No, we expect it will be Goring. Club captain, fine chap and all that.'

'Is there a cup for the best turned-out bicycle?'

'A medal. I'm sure Toop will get it. Expenditure always outshines taste, I am afraid.'

'He would do better to exercise a little restraint in that area. I can see that since he will never be a racer he must do what he can to make his mark, but I fear if he had one more attachment to his bicycle he would be unable to ride it at all.'

'Well we must allow him his little victories, I suppose. He has had many trials to bear what with his mother passing away, and that terrible business with his brother.'

'His brother?'

'Oh, I might not have mentioned it. A wild sort, apparently. Toop is the steady one of the family, but his brother could never settle to anything and joined the army for adventure. Went to war and was killed at Maiwand two years ago. The father has been bowed down with sorrow ever since and all the burden of management has fallen on Toop.'

'That must have been hard for him. Has the business suffered as a result?'

Cedric smiled. 'I see what you're hinting at, but as far as I can see Toop has risen to the challenge, and the wheels of industry have not slowed. It's curious how things turn out. I understand that the older brother was always the father's favourite, which is never a happy thing to know, but now that Toop has shown his true value I would hope that things have been rather mended.'

There was just a hint of chill in the air. The wind had started up blustery and James Jepson was having a struggle with some twisted bunting that had pulled loose from the podium and was threatening to fly away. 'I'll give him a helping hand,' said Cedric. 'You go on to the pavilion and order our tea. The largest pot they have. And make sure we have Bakewell tart, it's Mrs Pirrie's speciality.'

As Frances walked on she watched people still deep in debate about the last race, looking for who was speaking to whom. Miss Jepson and her lady friends were in earnest conversation with Iliffe, who seemed to be reassuring them that he was unharmed. Babbit had decided to keep his distance and was surrounded by members of his own club, who were commiserating with him for the unfortunate end to the race. Frances wondered how far the attraction between Iliffe and Miss Jepson had advanced. She hoped it was not too far so that the unfortunate lady would suffer the least possible sorrow when she learned of his disgrace.

Mrs Pirrie had emerged from the kitchen with her helpers, and they were standing on the veranda to view the proceedings. She was gazing about her anxiously and Frances realised that she must still be hoping for Sir Hugo's return. There was something in her expression and posture that suggested she was thinking that so much anger and chaos would never have happened had Sir Hugo been there to keep an eye on things.

As Frances was about to mount the steps she noticed something small fluttering in the grass at the side of the pavilion. A discarded handkerchief, perhaps, or a crumpled leaflet. Ordinarily she might not have taken a look, but today she was on the alert, bound to examine anything unusual. Moving closer she saw what it was, a yellow ribbon, possibly one dropped from the over-trimmed hat of Miss Hicks, the blacksmith's daughter. The ribbons, she recalled, had been plain yellow but this one unusually was patterned with spots of red. She picked it up and saw to her concern that the red was not a pattern but drops of what was probably blood. She also realised that the ribbon had not fallen because it was stitched badly; broken ends of thread and frayed material showed that it had been torn away from the hat. She looked around but Miss Hicks was nowhere in sight, and she could not remember having seen her at all during the race. Walking further along the side of the pavilion she saw the brim of the hat on the grass, protruding a little way from behind the building, its ribbons flapping fitfully in the breeze like the tentacles of a beached sea creature.

It was with a familiar sense of dread that Frances hurried to the corner and peered around it. Miss Hicks was lying on her back, stretched out on the grass, motionless, her arms flung wide. Several of her hat ribbons were tied tightly around her neck, cutting deeply into the tissue, compressing the throat beyond any possibility of drawing breath. There was no obvious knot, but that might have been at the back of the neck, suggesting that she had been strangled from behind. Her mouth was open as if in a final protest, and her eyes stared out blindly, the whites suffused with blood. Some drops of blood had oozed from her nostrils, and it might have been these that had stained the fallen ribbon that Frances had picked up. Apart from the open mouth and staring eyes the girl seemed calm. In the coarse silk dress, with hair piled in a series of rolls and curls, a flush on her cheeks like red paint, the body looked like a life-sized china doll.

Miss Hicks was undoubtedly dead. Even if Frances could have instantly cut the silk away, it would not have saved her. Frances had seen death before. She had seen it in those she cared for, and in strangers. She had seen bodies newly dead and others corrupted by time. Having never known the victim she nevertheless felt pity for youth so horribly cut short. Even if the girl had been all that was said of her, she might still have had a lifetime to mend her ways. Frances waited a moment to calm herself, then carefully surveyed the body and the scene.

Other than the marks of strangulation there was no obvious sign of injury and apart from the loss of the hat, the corpse's clothes were not disturbed. Even the hands were clean. The attack must have been sudden, unexpected, perhaps from someone she knew and trusted, who had impulsively used the long floating ribbons to commit murder, rendering the victim unconscious almost immediately before she had a chance to resist, and then tightening them with savage finality. She had obviously been killed exactly where she lay. There were no signs either in the grass or on her clothes that she had been dragged to the spot, and it defied belief that she had been carried there without anyone noticing.

Frances looked around, to see where there might have been a witness to the event, but the location was secluded and away from the eyes of the crowds. All that lay behind the pavilion was an expanse of fields and distant trees. Not far from where the body lay was a small back door into the pavilion. Either the girl had walked around the side of the pavilion or through it to the back door. Frances touched nothing, she did not even walk near to or around the body in case some clue lay in the grass for the police to find. She retraced her steps, returning to the front of the pavilion, where she saw Cedric standing looking around for her.

'Oh, there you are. I was beginning to worry. In fact —' he stared at her. 'What's wrong?'

'Where is Inspector Sharrock?'

'Over there, preparing to give his speech. Why?'

The Inspector was standing at the base of the podium staring at a sheet of paper, his lips moving as he perused the words, his expression showing no great anticipation that he was about to enjoy giving his talk.

Frances hurried to him. 'Inspector!'

'What is it now?' he said testily.

'There has been a murder.'

A number of emotions played across his features. At last he said, 'Where? When?'

Frances was still clasping the ribbon she had picked up. His eyes moved to it and he saw the spots of blood. 'This afternoon. There is a body behind the pavilion.'

He stuffed the paper into his pocket.

'Ah, Inspector,' said Toop running up with a smile, 'we'll be ready for your talk very soon.'

'Talk's cancelled,' said Sharrock. He took Frances by the arm and strode away. Toop stood and stared in helpless bewilderment, then made to hurry after them, but both he and Cedric were quietly dissuaded by Constable Mayberry before he joined his superior.

All was as it had been except that the fallen hat had been moved a little by the wind. Sharrock leaned over the body, and it was clear that he too knew from a glance that there was no hope. 'What have you touched?'

'Nothing. I picked up this ribbon before I found her. That was why I found her. It led me to the body.'

'Do you know who she is?'

'Yes, she is Miss Hicks, daughter of the local blacksmith. He isn't here but his wife and her sister are in the pavilion helping Mrs Pirrie with the tea.'

'Well, there's nothing we can do for her. Mayberry, you'd better get Sergeant Hambling here at once. It's a good thing he's brought constables with him because we're going to have to make sure that no one leaves the ground before we have everyone's name and address. I'll get the relatives taken aside and speak to them. One of them will have to formally identify her. Then we start asking questions. I want to look at everyone's hands. The killer might have marks from that ribbon if we're lucky.'

Mayberry nodded and hurried away.

'Most of the men here ride bicycles,' said Frances. 'I doubt there'll be one without some sort of graze on him.' She slipped her hands into her pockets as she said so, and fortunately Sharrock was so wrapt in thought he didn't notice the movement. 'Still, a cut from a silk ribbon and a scrape from a fall will look very different.'

Mayberry returned with Sergeant Hambling, who paused and shook his head as he saw the body.

'Who is the nearest doctor?' asked Sharrock.

'That would be Jepson. He ought to be here as his son is racing, but I've not seen him. I'll get my constables to look.'

'He — er —' began Frances.

Both Hambling and Sharrock turned and stared at her.

'He was here but then he was called away on an emergency. I don't think he has returned.'

Sharrock's eyes narrowed, but he made no comment. 'Barraclough, then,' said Hambling. 'He's at Church Road in Acton. I'll send a constable to fetch him.' He left quickly.

Sharrock turned to Frances. 'Miss Doughty, since you have already assured me that you are here purely for amusement and not business, might I suggest you re-join your friends and — now I know this might be hard for you — please take no further part in the investigation of this crime.' His tone indicted that this was less of a suggestion than a command.

Frances nodded. 'You are quite right, Inspector. It will be hard.'

CHAPTER TWENTY-FIVE

rances obediently withdrew, but not as far as Sharrock might have liked. She watched the development of events from a distance, and could even overhear some of the orders being given. Since she alone of all the civilians, apart from the murderer, knew what had occurred she was able to interpret what she saw and heard. Police actions progressed rapidly and as unobtrusively as possible. Sergeant Hambling and his men, under the direction of Inspector Sharrock, took charge of the area where the body lay, and formed a human barrier beyond which visitors were not permitted to go. One of the Acton constables was ordered to commandeer a bicycle to fetch Surgeon Barraclough, and in view of the large numbers present at the cricket ground, he was also to telegraph the Hammersmith police for further assistance. Sharrock deputised Mayberry to take Toop aside for a quiet conversation to put him in the picture, then prepared to break the terrible news to the family. Even though it was an unpleasant duty he had performed many times before, Frances could still see the Inspector taking a moment to steel himself before entering the pavilion.

'What's going on?' asked Cedric. 'It's not that convict is it? Has he been found?'

Frances drew him aside and spoke quietly. 'I'm sorry to say that I have just found a body. Miss Hicks. She was behind the pavilion, and she has been murdered.' Cedric stared at her in appalled silence. Moments later they heard cries of distress from within the pavilion. 'Inspector Sharrock has just informed her mother and aunt.'

Cedric put his arm around Frances' shoulders and gave her a cousinly hug. 'And now, of course, I really must take you home. No arguments this time.'

'I'm afraid that won't be possible. Inspector Sharrock has decreed that no one can leave until we have all been questioned, so I couldn't go home even if I wanted to, and neither can you, or indeed anyone here.'

'But that will take hours!' he gasped.

'They have summoned additional forces from Hammersmith.'

'Oh, what a tragedy! This has been the most horrible day imaginable. First the attempt on Sir Hugo, then the demise of honourable sport and now this. Is there nothing I can do? Any assistance at all — I am your man!'

Frances gave this some thought. 'The Inspector has told Miss Hicks's mother and aunt, and I am assuming that someone will be sent to the smithy to tell her father, but what about Jack Linnett? He will need a friend with him when he hears the news.'

Cedric nodded. 'Yes, of course. I'll stand by him. Prepare him for the worst.' He hurried to the repair enclosure, and Frances saw him take the youth gently by the arm and lead him aside. Although Frances did not suspect Jack Linnett of the murder any more than anyone else, she thought that in due course knowing how he had taken the news could be useful.

By now, the police activity had alerted most of those present that something unusual was happening. People began to gather in the area of the pavilion, and saw the human barrier of police preventing access to the back of the building, and a constable stationed at the door. Rumours were beginning to fly about, some suggesting that the convict Coote had been trapped inside and was about to be captured, others that there had been an outbreak of food poisoning in the kitchens, and no one was allowed to enter, still others that there had been a terrible accident and a doctor was on his way. Frances said nothing. She assumed that Mrs Hicks and her sister had been led to view the body by the back door as she did not see them.

Tom had been threading his way carefully through the crowd and quickly reached Frances. 'What's up?' he hissed. 'P'lice is all over. 'Oo's dead, then?'

'Miss Hicks, the blacksmith's daughter,' whispered Frances. 'She's been strangled. Make sure that Sarah and Professor Pounder and Ratty and Mr Grove all know.'

Tom nodded. 'Not sure I seen Mr Grove much this last 'alf 'our. Dunno what 'e's up to. Law to 'imself that one.' He hurried away.

As Frances waited for more news she tried to recall when it was that she had last seen the murdered girl. She had definitely seen her moving amongst the young gentlemen during the luncheon period, but had not noticed her particularly since. Then she recalled Cedric saying she had given him a ribbon after he had failed to win the two-mile race. That could only have been minutes before the professionals' race began. The crowds had then been numerous and pressing as Iliffe and Babbit had arrived for their duel, and all eyes had been on the bicyclists. All eyes including her own, Frances realised with a feeling of deep shame, as she recognised that she had been caught up in the enthusiasm of the moment and not continued her observations as carefully as she ought to have done. It was no matter that she had already promised Cedric that she would return home soon afterwards, there was no excuse for such a terrible lapse of attention.

It did mean, however, that Miss Hicks had most probably been killed during the race. Had her killer planned the murder? Frances thought not, since it seemed like an action taken in the heat of the moment, and not with any means the killer had brought in preparation, but by strangling the victim with her own ribbons. The meeting, on the other hand, could well have been planned, even if it had only been arranged that day. Miss Hicks had walked about the field and spoken to many of the young men there. In one of those conversations perhaps an interview had been arranged, and all by word of mouth with no evidence left to find. The ideal time for a meeting that was meant to be unobserved was when everyone's attention would be elsewhere. The professionals' race was the perfect opportunity. And the location was out of the way and out of sight. But what was the subject of the conversation? Whatever had been discussed, the encounter had erupted into murderous violence.

Frances next turned her thoughts to who could not possibly have committed the murder. There were of course the teeming crowds around the racetrack, but the only individuals she could be sure of were Cedric, who had been by her side throughout, the five men who had taken part in the race, and the handicapper who was continuously watching the proceedings. There were, on the other hand, two men who she did not think had been on the field at the time – Peters, Mr Hopper's brutish assistant, and Mr Grove. Now she thought about it, Hopper had been looking about for someone or something, and this could well have been the absent Peters. The other great unknown, however, was the convict Mr Coote. Could Miss Hicks have somehow been involved in that business?

The other thought engaging Frances was the behaviour of the people who were at the event. It was a cool individual who could commit a murder in the heat of the moment and then not look flustered. Now she considered it, there were a number of people who had seemed less than calm that day, even before the murder had taken place. Ross-Fielder and his family had appeared unhappy but that was almost certainly because of their concern about the escape of the convict Coote. George Farrow had also seemed anxious, although that could have been due to his bullying father who was angry at Sir Hugo's non-appearance. His worried scanning of the crowds could have been in the hope of seeing Sir Hugo's arrival, but what had he seen that had so caught his attention? Mrs Pirrie, even though she had been told where Sir Hugo was supposed to be, had revealed a growing concern about his continued absence. Mr Toop was flustered and nervous but that was understandable since he was trying to supervise an event in which the patron had unaccountably gone missing, and he was having to make some emergency decisions.

Frances glanced across the field to where Cedric had taken Jack Linnett aside, holding him firmly by the shoulder as he talked to him. Jack put his face in his hands and sobbed, and Cedric supplied a handkerchief.

At last, with the gathering crowds becoming increasingly restive, Inspector Sharrock emerged from the pavilion and made his way brusquely through the throng to the podium, where he mounted the platform, picked up the speaking trumpet and gestured for silence. The chatterers fell into an expectant hush.

'Ladies and gents, I'm sorry to have to tell you that no one is allowed to leave the cricket ground at present, except on police business.' A groan arose, but he quelled it with a gesture. 'There has been a very serious incident, and it may be necessary to ask questions of you all. I will be using the tearoom to conduct interviews. Please be patient and the better the co-operation you give to the police the sooner you'll be allowed home.'

He made to descend, but there was a torrent of shouted questions. Sharrock paused, held up his hands for silence once more, and spoke again. 'That is all I intend to say for now. I will make another announcement in due course.' This time he ignored the calls for answers, put down the speaking trumpet and returned indoors.

The curiosity of the assembled throng was freshly fuelled. The most devoted gossips divided their energies between inventing speculation that was almost as bad as the reality, and trying to extract information from those constables with whom they were acquainted. The constables stayed true to their duty and remained sternly impassive.

Some minutes later, a new sensation swept through the field as Surgeon Barraclough arrived in a fly and was conducted to the rear of the pavilion by constables who were under orders to ensure that none but the medical man should approach the scene of the crime. The crowd pressed after him with questions but he simply shook his head and waved them away with his top hat.

He was followed onto the field by a police van driven by a constable. The crowds rightly surmised that it was for the transport of a body to the mortuary, and groaned horribly as it passed them by, making a half circuit of the cricket pitch like a grim travesty of a fashionable carriage parading around the drive of Hyde Park, before drawing up at the side of the pavilion. The crowds pressed closer hoping to see something dreadful, and were pushed back by the line of police.

This vehicle was followed by a four-wheeler bringing an Inspector and three constables from Hammersmith, who descended and entered the pavilion. Soon afterwards, two ladies with shawls over their heads were conducted by a constable to the four-wheeler, which quickly drove away. The crowds sighed in sympathy, as it was obvious from the way they bore themselves that they were afflicted by grief, and some onlookers correctly guessed their identity. It was not until both Barraclough and the police van had left that Inspector Sharrock emerged from the pavilion, mounted the platform and took up the speaking trumpet once more. The crowd fell quiet.

'Ladies and gentlemen, it is my sad duty to inform you of the recent death under suspicious circumstances of Miss Clara Hicks.' He paused for the gasps and exclamations that he knew would follow, then spoke again. 'I would ask you all to have respect and consideration for the young lady's family at this terrible time. Police enquiries have already commenced. That is all I can tell you for now. Please remain where you are until you are told that you can leave.'

Not all of the visitors to the field that day were acquainted with Miss Hicks, and there were some whispered enquiries as to who she might be, but there were more than a few whose shock and grief were apparent. There were some, however, who failed to hide knowing expressions, implying that they had long anticipated that the victim would come to a bad end.

There was to be no more jollity that day. The bandsmen who had been waiting to play for the tea-drinkers, and deliver musical tributes for the prize giving, were struck silent and sat on the grass, clutching their cherished instruments. Bicyclists stood beside their machines, heads bowed low.

Mr Toop mounted the podium. 'Everyone,' he began, and paused to wipe his forehead. 'I am so sorry. We must, of course, out of respect and necessity abandon the proceedings.' A collective groan of dismay arose from the audience, but no one protested against the inevitable. 'There will be no more races today, and no prizegiving. The results of the contests held so far will be announced in the *Wheel World* in due course. Thank you.' He retired from the scene. There was a little gasp and a sob nearby, and Frances saw Rufus Goring standing by Miss Farrow trying to pat her hand, but the lady was petulantly determined not to be comforted.

Toop was busying himself gathering members of the club and discussing what was to be done next. The stallholders began to crowd around him, anxiously, demanding to know if they were to stop trading, and he was soon inundated with enquiries.

In the midst of all the confusion and uncertainty, Frances felt frustrated by a lack of purpose. Was her secret mission even to continue? Was she still bound by the rules she had been given? She didn't know.

Although Inspector Sharrock did not want her to take any part in the murder enquiry Frances still felt that she might have something of value to offer if she knew more of the facts, and in order to gather those facts she needed to enter the pavilion and learn what enquiries were being made. It occurred to her that while the police might not permit her to act as a detective, they might well approve of her taking on another role.

She glanced across at Sarah and signed for her to come nearer, then she walked up to Inspector Sharrock, who had just finished issuing orders to Mayberry.

CHAPTER TWENTY-SIX

S harrock did not look pleased to see Frances approach but she did not allow it to deter her. She took a strong fast stride, going past Mayberry so quickly that he did not have time to react before she reached her quarry. Mayberry knew Frances too well to attempt to do anything more than keep up with her. 'Now then, Miss, the Inspector is very busy,' he said gently.

Frances ignored him. 'I have a suggestion to make,' she said.

'I'm sure you do,' said Sharrock irritably. 'And my suggestion is that you wait until you are called to be interviewed. In fact, why don't I interview you first and then you can go home?'

'I think you should hear my suggestion, and once you have, I can guarantee you will not ask me to leave.'

He uttered a weary sigh. 'Very well, say what you have to, and then go and join your peculiar friend, wherever he is.'

'I was thinking, Inspector, that while people are waiting they might benefit from some tea. Since Mrs Hicks and her sister have departed, poor Mrs Pirrie has no one to assist her in the kitchen. Would you allow Sarah and me to go into the pavilion and help her? If you are interviewing witnesses it will be thirsty work for all, and you and your men might like some refreshment on a warm afternoon.'

Sharrock grunted and tapped his foot. 'All right,' he said at last, 'but,' he went on, shaking a warning finger at her, 'don't think I don't know what you're up to. Come on in, but don't interrupt any police work, or I'll have you escorted out again pretty quick.'

'Thank you, Inspector.'

'And if you should hear anything of interest, let me know,' he added reluctantly.

She smiled. 'I will.'

Sharrock indicated to the constable at the pavilion door that Frances should be allowed in, and when Sarah prudently held back, he beckoned her forward. 'Kitchen staff!' said Sharrock to the constable, who nodded and opened the door. Frances and Sarah hurried in together.

Mrs Pirrie was in the kitchen with another lady. Both looked shocked and drawn. They had been standing together in close conversation, and turned and stared at Sarah and Frances as they arrived.

'We have come to offer our assistance,' explained Frances. 'Tea is the best comfort at a time like this. The place is full of policemen and they do so like their tea.'

Mrs Pirrie nodded, and rubbed her palms on her apron. 'Thank you, it's been such a strange upsetting kind of day, what with Sir Hugo gone no one quite knows where, and then all that business with Mr Iliffe and Mr Babbit – I wish those two would make their peace, I really do. I didn't think it could get much worse, but …' she sighed. 'You know poor Mrs Hicks and her sister were here helping me out – the police came and asked them to look at the body. Such a dreadful thing.'

Frances and Sarah looked about the kitchen, which was a good size with a double sink, and ample space for the large numbers of cups, saucers, plates and teapots always required at a cricket match. A long central table was loaded with cakes, pies and tarts ready to be cut for afternoon tea, great hearty loaves of bread, a large crock of yellow butter and enormous pots of jam. At the rear of the kitchen was a door which had been left open, presumably to allow the circulation of fresh air, and Frances saw that it led to a short corridor and the back door she had observed from outside.

'You'll need clean cups,' said Sarah, spying a pile of used crockery waiting for attention. She rolled up her sleeves to reveal forearms that any pugilist would have been proud of. No one argued with her and she set to work.

'This is Miss Williamson,' explained Mrs Pirrie to the other lady, 'Mr Garton's cousin. And?' she glanced at Sarah.

'Miss Smith,' said Sarah, who had decided that her own surname was disguise enough.

'Well I'm very pleased to have your assistance,' said Mrs Pirrie. 'This is Mrs Easton, who very kindly stepped in when Mrs Hicks and her sister had to leave. Mr Easton is very important in these parts, as he manages the cricket ground.'

Frances refilled the kettle, took it to the range and set it heating. Mrs Pirrie looked on approvingly at how easily she handled the heavy container even when full. 'Is Sir Hugo returned yet?'

'I'm afraid not,' said Frances.

Mrs Pirrie seemed unsure what to do, but picked up a knife and began to slice up Bakewell tart. 'I hope people will want this. I expect there'll be many who'll find they have no appetite.'

'It looks delicious,' said Frances. 'My cousin Cedric recommended it to me.'

Mrs Pirrie did not seem to be cheered by the compliment. 'I wish someone would tell me what is happening,' she said hopefully.

'All I know is that no one is to be allowed home until they have spoken to the police and at least given a name and address. But I beg you not to worry. Inspector Sharrock appears to be quite rude, but I have the feeling that that is just his manner and he is actually quite kind underneath. In the meantime, I think there will be some demand for refreshments.'

Mrs Easton scowled as she picked up a long bread knife and started slicing bread with more energy than skill. She was younger and thinner than Mrs Pirrie, and rather sharp faced. She had donned an apron that was intended for a much wider person over a gown with some pretentions to fashion. Her hair was severely parted, scraped back tightly and held with pins that had been thrust through a hard little bonnet. Frances had the impression that Mrs Easton must have her own cook at home and regarded her presence in the pavilion's kitchen as an act of charity. 'I know it's a sad business, but I can't say I'm all that surprised,' she said.

'Oh, I wouldn't want to speak ill of her, she was not a bad soul,' Mrs Pirrie protested.

'I never said she was bad,' snapped Mrs Easton, pausing to scoop butter from the crock with a table knife. A blob of butter, softened in the heat of the afternoon, slid onto the table as she waved the knife for emphasis. 'Not as bad as some others I could name, but it was all those young men on bicycles that turned her head. I said to her once, don't you be fooled, you won't find one man among them who'll marry you; but no, she wouldn't listen.'

'Of course, we don't rightly know what went on,' said Mrs Pirrie, 'so I wouldn't like to judge.'

'I can tell you one thing that went on,' persisted Mrs Easton. 'I heard it from Mrs Hicks herself, so there's no mistake. That poor woman, what troubles she has had with that girl! It seems that young Clara has been giving away more than just saucy looks and kisses. Only last week she told her mother that there's a young man who will have to pay for his entertainment or better still, make her an honest wife. I said to her straight out, your Clara has been taken in by the oldest trick there is, and she's too young in the ways of the world to know it. And Mrs Hicks half agreed with me, although she did say the young man in question had promised to meet his obligations, though he didn't say how.'

'Oh, how terribly shocking!' Frances exclaimed, careful to give the impression that while she deplored salacious gossip she was still eager to hear it. 'Do you know the young man's name?'

Mrs Easton shook her head and applied butter to a bread slice as if she was trowelling mortar onto a brick. 'Either Clara wouldn't say or Mrs Hicks didn't ask. All she knew was that it was one of the bicycle men.'

'Not Jack Linnett, then,' said Mrs Pirrie, with some relief. 'Not that I would have thought it of him.' She left the Bakewell tarts and went to help Mrs Easton, whose bread slices would have done for an army of giants.

'No, not him!' said Mrs Easton. 'He was sweet on her, well we all knew that, but she wouldn't even look at him. Thought he wasn't good enough for her.' She gave a contemptuous snort. 'If you ask me, she wasn't good enough for him.'

'And this bicycle man was going to marry her?' asked Mrs Pirrie. 'I don't believe it!'

'Neither do I. But you can't be telling young girls that. They believe all the sweet promises.'

'So they do,' agreed Mrs Pirrie. 'And if a young woman has got a bad name then even if she points a finger at the man to blame, he can always say it was another man's fault, and how can she prove otherwise?'

'They say mud sticks,' said Mrs Easton. 'Some young men can just laugh it off or call the girl a liar, but there's some who can't or won't. She thought she could bring him to heel, but she was wrong, and I think that's what got her killed.'

'You're not saying it's a bicycling man who killed her to escape his obligations?' exclaimed Mrs Pirrie.

Mrs Easton shrugged. 'Who can tell? She might have had a dozen men all thinking they were responsible, and she just pushed the wrong one too far.'

'Poor Sir Hugo,' sighed Mrs Pirrie, 'he will be so upset when he finds out what has happened. He has a lot of respect for Mr Hicks, he always does for those who work hard, whatever their station in life.'

'Where is Sir Hugo?' asked Mrs Easton. 'I expected to see him running about and making speeches but he has been nowhere to be seen all day.'

'Business of some sort in London,' said Mrs Pirrie. 'Gentlemen and their meetings, they always take longer than they expect.'

The door of the kitchen opened and a constable peered in. 'Mrs Pirrie? The Inspector would like a word.'

Mrs Pirrie wiped her hands on a cloth. 'Of course, I'll tell him all I know.'

Frances had found fresh milk and extra butter stored in a cool larder. She prepared a tray, and loaded it with a large pot of tea, cups, milk and sugar, while Mrs Easton added a plate piled high with thickly buttered bread and a pot of jam, and Mrs Pirrie added a whole Bakewell tart. 'I'll take that,' said the constable, eagerly.

'Best put the kettle on again,' said Mrs Easton, and went to cut more bread and butter.

As Mrs Pirrie departed for questioning Frances glanced through the briefly open door of the kitchen and noticed young Mr Farrow on his way out of the pavilion. His expression was one of acute unhappiness, and he stared dispiritedly at the floor as he shuffled out. She set about making more tea, reflecting that it was a drink of which it was impossible for there ever to be too much.

'Wasn't it you found the body?' said Mrs Easton. 'Only I heard someone say it was Mr Garton's cousin.'

'Yes, it was.'

'You're calm enough about it, I'll say that. Some young ladies faint at the sight of a drop of blood.'

'They think the gentlemen expect them to,' said Frances.

Mrs Easton gave a humourless laugh. 'Well isn't that right! So, tell me, how was it done?'

'I beg your pardon?'

'The murder. How was she killed?'

'I didn't look closely enough,' said Frances, well aware that any information she revealed would be all over Middlesex before the day was out. 'I only saw that she was dead.'

'Stabbed?'

'I really couldn't say.'

'If there was a lot of blood the man would have it on him.'

'That is true,' said Frances, 'and I am sure the police will be looking for that.'

Sarah finished the last of the washing up, her burly arms reddened by the hot water, and Frances went to help her dry the chinaware and stack it ready for the next round of tea. As she did so, a thought struck her. There was one person who had been very upset at the death of Miss Hicks, and it was probably about the last individual she might have expected to be distressed at the news. She needed to know more.

CHAPTER TWENTY-SEVEN

'**M**rs Easton,' Frances asked, glad to be able to divert the conversation away from the method of Miss Hick's demise, 'do you know if Miss Farrow was a particular friend of Miss Hicks?'

Mrs Easton was amazed at the question. 'Miss Farrow? No, she'd have nothing to do with any of that sort. Nose in the air, that one.'

'I ask because I saw her very upset a little earlier, when the Inspector said that Miss Hicks had been killed. So I guessed that they might have been friends.'

'Well take my word for it; it wouldn't have been on account of Clara Hicks. If I had to guess, it was because the meeting was stopped. There was going to be a special announcement after the prize giving, and I feel sure I know what it was. I shouldn't think they'll do it at all now.'

'Oh yes, Mr Toop mentioned something of the sort.'

'It wouldn't sit well to be talking about betrothals and that young woman lying dead.'

'Miss Farrow and Mr Goring?' asked Frances.

'That's right. It's a good match. He has the looks and the prospects, and she has any amount of money to come. No love in it, of course, but then you don't expect that.'

'I had heard that he once showed an interest in Miss Vance.'

'So she liked to think, only he wouldn't agree. And even if there had been something, that all stopped when Miss Farrow came back from her school in Switzerland, just turned eighteen and finished off nicely, her hair newly curled, and a dowry that would buy half the county.'

'Young Mr Farrow must have prospects as well.'

'Oh him!' said Mrs Easton contemptuously. 'One of those idle young men – good for nothing.'

'Was he a special friend of Miss Hicks?'

'He's young with a rich father, so I expect she flirted with him same as the others. So she wasn't stabbed then?'

The great kettle was almost ready for the next supply of tea. 'I wonder if the ladies could do with some refreshment?' said Frances, changing the subject.

Sarah peered out of the window. 'They're out on the veranda sitting about fanning themselves and waiting to be questioned. They look thirsty to me.'

Frances hurried out before Mrs Easton could make any further attempts at prying information from her. There was a little cluster of ladies gathered about the tables in varying states of misery and impatience. Miss Farrow was being comforted by her brother. The prospective bridegroom was not in evidence, but presumably he was assisting Mr Toop with the arrangements for closing the meeting. 'I am making tea if anyone would like some,' said Frances brightly.

There were a few sighs and murmurs. Miss Farrow could hardly have looked unhappier if it had been a close relative whose murder had delayed her betrothal announcement. 'Please try something,' pleaded George, who was finding the duty of looking after his sister somewhat irksome. 'If only a little sip. It would do you good.'

Miss Farrow made a great deal of dramatic play over waving a lace handkerchief before her eyes. 'It is all just too terrible!'

'Adela, I know it is inconvenient, but really there will be time enough to make the announcement. It's not as if the wedding is next week. And it will be in the newspapers very soon.'

Miss Farrow refused to be comforted. 'But it was my dear Rufus's special day!' she wailed. 'The giving of the sportsmanship cup!'

'I know, I know,' said her brother, grimly, patting her hand rather roughly and without any enthusiasm for the process.

'I will fetch you a nice pot of tea,' said Frances.

'Please do,' said the gentleman, with the implication that sipping tea would at least quieten his sister's repeated protests.

When Frances returned to the kitchen, Mrs Easton was contemplating a tray of sliced cake for which no one seemed to have an appetite, and Sarah was filling teapots from the kettle. Mrs Pirrie returned, looking worried.

'I hope that wasn't too troublesome?' enquired Mrs Easton.

'Well it was in a way. The Inspector is a very coarse type, and makes all sorts of insinuations.'

'Who does he think did it?'

Mrs Pirrie seemed to be struggling to admit what she had learned. 'It's too bad, that's what it is! All they did was ask me about young Jack! Someone must have told them he was sweet on Clara Hicks and that she wouldn't give him the time of day. Jealousy, that's what they're thinking. Young man loves a woman and she don't love him back and he gets all hot-headed and angry and says well if he can't have her then no one will, and he kills her. That's what they're thinking. But they've never met Jack, and I said to them, he's a good boy. He'd never hurt anyone! I don't think they listened.'

'I'm sure Sir Hugo will put in a good word for him,' said Frances. 'That will count for a great deal.'

'Oh I know he will. I only wish he would come back. No, it's obvious who the murderer is, what with that convict about the place. He must have come here to try and steal food, and she saw him and was going to give the alarm. That's what happened!'

Frances was not convinced that Mr Coote had been anywhere near the cricket ground that day, but saw that the idea had convinced Mrs Pirrie. She wondered if she ought to speak to Jack again, concerning what Sir Hugo had been doing, but then considered that there was one other person who might just have some useful information. She put a pot of tea with cups and milk and sugar on a tray and took it outside. Not everyone wanted any but George Farrow poured a cup for his sister and tried to persuade her to drink it.

'Has Sir Hugo returned?' Frances asked, peering about looking for General Farrow.

'I haven't seen him,' said Farrow.

'Only I recall you saying that your father had a meeting with him this afternoon.'

'Yes, well, the man isn't here, is he?' said Farrow irritably. 'I mean, I sent him a note about the meeting as father asked, and he agreed to it, and then when he doesn't come it's supposed to be my fault!'

'That does seem a little strange. Do you know what the meeting was about?'

'No. He called to see father last week, but he made a mystery of it, apparently. Some invention, I suppose.'

'Not the side wheels he has been working on? My cousin told me about those. They sound very strange. But he hadn't perfected them yet.'

Farrow shrugged. 'I don't know. And why all the secrecy; I have no idea.'

Miss Farrow sniffled. 'He said he had to get a patent first.'

'When did he say that?' asked Farrow.

'When father was showing him out. I heard him say he was going to see about a patent and then they would talk about it.'

There was almost certainly more to learn but Frances was under orders to exercise caution, and the last thing she should do was behave as a detective when she was unable to disguise it as gossip. 'Well, enjoy your tea and let me know if you need anything more.'

Frances returned to the kitchen, where Mrs Pirrie was in full flood. 'And I said to them, before you start making any insinuations about young Jack, just remember there's an escaped convict you haven't found yet, and I wouldn't be surprised if he was your murderer, so you should go out and find him instead of bothering innocent folk, or we all might be murdered next.'

'That was telling them,' said Mrs Easton, approvingly. 'But I still say it was her fancy man who did it.'

'Well either way it wasn't Jack! People say "like father like son" but young Jack and his father couldn't be more different. Takes after his mother, poor woman. Old Linnett worked her to death; they say he knocked her about, too. He was a villain and no mistake! Up to all sorts. Drinking and brawling. I heard people say she could have got him hanged ten times over if she'd been allowed to speak out against him. But, of course, she couldn't, the law won't allow it, more's the pity, or the gaols would be full twice over.'

'At least Clara wasn't content just to be a fancy woman for the rest of her life,' Mrs Easton pointed out. 'She wanted a ring on her finger, all legal. She said she didn't want to end up like Mrs Cross.'

'Mrs Cross had a lot of difficulties in her life.'

'Mrs Cross only had one difficulty and that was Mr Cross.'

'Well wouldn't that always be the way,' said Sarah. 'So what did he do?'

Mrs Easton launched into her story with relish. 'Cross was a sneak thief and a burglar. And she knew it. But she didn't like to tell because she was fond of him. Poor woman. But then he got caught. And it dawned on her all of a sudden that she was better off without him. But he said she couldn't give evidence against him as they were married. And that was right. Then it turned out he had another wife and he'd married her beforehand so they weren't really married at all, so she stood up in court and told all she knew. Went to the Scrubs for five years. Good riddance. She got married properly to a better man the week after.'

The four ladies were kept busy serving tea and refreshments for the next hour, after which Sarah set to and cleaned everything in sight.

'That's done,' she said, and Mrs Pirrie and Mrs Easton stared admiringly at the spotless kitchen.

'I'll put away the last of these dishes,' said Frances. 'You have worked so hard, you deserve a rest.'

'Well,' said Mrs Pirrie, 'I have to thank you and you can come to the lodge for a nice tea any day you like. Once we're all done we'll close up the kitchen. Perhaps later on I'll put the last of the cakes out and people can help themselves. I won't have them go to waste. I'll take some back for Sir Hugo.' She shook her head. 'He'll be that upset when he finds out about all this. Last year Mr Vance and now it's Clara.'

'It's like a curse,' said Mrs Easton, frowning and shaking her head. 'A terrible curse.'

The kitchen was finally locked up and the keys hung on a board in the pavilion office.

Now that Sarah and Frances had shared a kitchen they could deem themselves to be friends, and they took a plate of cakes and found a place to sit in the shade of the veranda. The traders were still at their stalls, but the bicycle club members were dismantling the tents and enclosures and the racetrack had been reduced to a pile of poles and coiled rope. Miss Farrow, bereft of the comforting presence of both her brother and her intended, was taking the air with a group of fashionable ladies. 'Did you learn anything more?' asked Frances.

'Mrs Pirrie won't have it that Jack Linnett is to blame,' said Sarah. 'She said that Sir Hugo was never a truly happy man until he started working with Jack and then he was more cheerful, like he was a boy again; they even played games together.'

'Really? What kind of games?'

'Oh, you know, bowling hoops along, as boys do. Only they used to do it with bicycle tyres.'

'What, those big front tyres?'

'Yes, she saw them out on the path, running about, and the tyres bouncing about all over the place like they were on springs.'

Frances laughed at the thought of the two grown men playing like children.

CHAPTER TWENTY-EIGHT

'What will you do now? Sarah asked Frances.

'Inspector Sharrock has told me in no uncertain terms that I am not to look into the murder.'

'He always tells you that, and you never take any notice,' observed Sarah. 'So that won't stop you.'

'I also have orders regarding the mission that brought me here that I am to do nothing except observe. But that was before this murder. Maybe that has changed things; I don't know. I am supposed to go home at the first sign of danger, but the police are not letting anyone leave. If I have to stay I might as well be useful.'

Sarah nodded. It was the kind of nod Frances had seen before, when she had determined on a course of action and Sarah, realising she could not be deflected, accepted that all she could do was be on hand to help and make sure that Frances did not miss meals.

'What I am wondering is, suppose the murder is linked in some way to the reason we are here? Is there any connection with what Mr Iliffe and Mr Babbit are up to? Do we have three sets of crimes, or two, or only one? Is the man who killed Miss Hicks also the traitor?'

'You're not saying she was involved?'

'No, but it might come down to money. Was Miss Hicks asking for more than he could pay? Did he get involved in crime in order to meet her demands?'

'If a man can afford a bicycle and all the things that come with it, then he can afford to pay off the likes of Miss Hicks,' said Sarah matter of factly.

'Unless he has debts we don't know about. A gambling habit. Drink. Mistresses. All three? Perhaps he has some secret and is being blackmailed. On the other hand, it might have been subtler than that. Did the murderer fear an attack on his reputation, and killed Miss Hicks in order to maintain a semblance of a good name, and it had nothing to do with the other crimes?'

'The thing about Miss Hicks and her kind is that they only want one of two things. Money or a husband. Either will do, but both is better.'

Frances nodded. 'Whatever she was about it was something obvious and simple. Let us look at it from the man's viewpoint. If he gives her money he risks being asked for more over and over again, always with the threat that he might be exposed. If there is a child involved then he might have to pay for its keep until it reaches the age of sixteen. He hasn't, and never has had, any intention of marrying Clara Hicks. If he'd had any imagination he'd have found someone else to marry her, and he wouldn't have had to look far. A nice pay-off and a husband, that ought to have been enough. So why wasn't it? It shouldn't have been necessary to murder her. And it was no accidental killing, as so many men like to claim. They say they clasped a woman's throat to quiet her and suddenly find she is dead, and then they get away with manslaughter when it was really murder all along. This man meant to kill, there's no doubt about that. So why murder? Was that really the only way out?'

'Well, there's other suspects,' said Sarah. 'That escaped convict. Nasty type, kicking a reverend gentleman. Suppose Miss Hicks happened to see him lurking about and he had to stop her from reporting him to the police?'

'Perhaps, although I can't imagine why he would want to come here instead of getting as far away as possible.'

'Then there's your Mr Grove.'

'What do you mean? He isn't my Mr Grove.'

'He isn't anyone else's. Isn't he the one what used to be the Filleter?'

'Yes, but that's not who he really is.'

'He sneaks about, all secret like, disguising himself as who knows what.'

'Well of course he does – he's —'

'A spy. That what he is.'

'I suppose so.'

'Where is he now, then?'

'I don't know.'

'Exactly. And didn't he once tell you he'd killed people?'

'Well, yes, he has, but as a soldier might kill on the battlefield. Not an unarmed young woman. He works for the government. The British government. The Queen. I expect he has special permission.'

'Hmm,' said Sarah.

'I'd rather trust him than someone like Mr Hopper. Perhaps he is the killer? Or ordered his man to do it more likely. That Peters looks like someone who would kill a man – or a woman – without giving it a second thought.'

Sarah picked up the last of the cakes, took a big bite and munched thoughtfully.

'And Grove's the man who writes the Miss Dauntless stories?'

'Yes.'

'And he's the same man who saved you from being killed by the Face-slasher?'

'He is, yes.'

Sarah nodded and sniffed. 'Reckon he's all right, then.'

Frances was just contemplating this when there was a disturbance on the field occasioned by a group of ladies. Some of them were simply standing and giggling but the objects of their amusement were Miss Vance and Miss Farrow, who were having something of a contretemps, and it was not hard to guess the subject of their disagreement. There were shouts of 'It's not true!' and 'Yes it is!' as the two faced each other. Miss Vance's features were distorted in fury, and Miss Farrow looked about to crumple in fear.

Frances looked about, but Phineas Vance was not in the immediate vicinity and neither were the General or George Farrow; however, someone had pointed out what was happening to Rufus Goring and he began to hurry over to the scene.

Before he could reach the quarrelling pair, however, Miss Vance, with a cry of angry despair, launched herself at Miss Farrow and seized her bonnet. Miss Farrow shrieked and tried to clasp the article to her head, but Miss Vance was the larger, stronger woman and after a brief struggle the bonnet was wrenched away and flung to the ground. For one dreadful moment it looked as though Miss Vance in her rage had actually pulled Miss Farrow's head clean from her shoulders, but then it became apparent that she had actually removed the beautiful golden curls, which were now revealed to be a wig. Miss Farrow, who was as bald as a newborn baby, clasped her hands to her pink scalp and screamed. It was a high-pitched scream like a whistle, and it seemed as if it would never stop. Miss Vance who had been about to tread on the bonnet, stopped, and began to laugh, and the other ladies joined in.

Phineas Vance was now running over from across the field, but it was Rufus Goring who was closest. He stood quite still, gazing at his soon-to-be betrothed, thunderstruck with horror. After a moment or two of silent contemplation, he turned on his heel and walked away.

Sarah stood up, intent on action, and Frances did not attempt to dissuade her. She marched over to Miss Farrow and took her in charge, wrapping her huge arms protectively about her. A glare at the giggling girls ended their merriment and they backed away, although one of them had the good grace to pick up the bonnet and wig and hand it over. Sarah snatched it from her, then took Miss Farrow into the pavilion, away from the stares of the crowds.

Phineas Vance embraced his sister and succeeded in calming her, then led her aside to re-join their mother. This done, he hurried after Rufus Goring, who was still walking away. 'Goring!' he snapped. Goring stopped and turned around.

Vance, for all that he was the slighter of the two, looked more dangerous, his fists clenched in anger. For a moment the staring crowds thought that Vance might actually strike the popular captain of the Bayswater Bicycle Club, but instead he controlled his emotions. Goring did not speak but Vance did. He spoke too softly to be heard, but it was clear that his words were firm and to the point. By now, someone had alerted the General, who came striding purposefully across the field. Without a pause in his pace he marched into the pavilion as if he owned it, and no one tried to stop him. A few minutes later he emerged conducted his weeping and freshly bewigged daughter away. He took no notice of Rufus Goring, and once Vance had had his say, neither did anyone else.

Soon afterwards Sarah returned to sit with Frances. 'Well, that was interesting,' she said. 'Miss Vance had heard the rumours about Mr Goring and Miss Farrow, and if they had announced their betrothal this afternoon she was going to make a public accusation of breach of promise. I'd say that wedding was off.'

There was a thread of movement near the entrance to the field as a young constable, bicycling in at speed, circled around the cricket area before pausing in front of the pavilion. The constable standing guard at the front came down the steps and a note was passed from one to the other, then the messenger turned and rode away.

The note, which appeared to be a plain folded sheet of paper, was taken into the pavilion. The constable re-emerged without it and took up his duty again. Frances and Sarah waited to see what, if anything, would ensue.

After two or three minutes Inspector Sharrock re-appeared and mounted the platform, taking up the speaking trumpet.

'Ladies and gentlemen, your attention please. I have just received a message to inform me that the prisoner Coote who recently escaped from Wormwood Scrubs has been found. I know that many of you who live in the vicinity have been very worried to know that the man was at large, and I am happy to say that you can now put your minds at rest on that point.'

'Inspector,' called out a member of the crowd, 'does that mean we can all leave now?'

'No, it does not,' said Sharrock. 'Now I have heard some of you speculating that the prisoner Coote was the man responsible for the unfortunate death of Miss Hicks. We have good reason, however, to believe that he had nothing to do with it. Our enquiries on that matter are therefore continuing.'

'Well, I hope you won't let him go again,' said another voice. 'Even if he is in prison I'm sure I won't sleep at night.'

Sharrock smiled. 'I would like to reassure you all that he is no danger to the public at large,' he said, and stepped down from the platform.

There was a finality in the tone of his voice that Frances recognised, and she approached him as he made his way back to the pavilion. 'I gather that Mr Coote is in some way unable to constitute a danger?'

'You have a cynical view of the world, Miss – whatever it is you are calling yourself today.'

'But I am right?'

He paused then gave a curt nod. 'Mr Coote has been reduced to tweed, bones and buttons, and an indigestible scrap of prison issue underlinen. He made the mistake of hiding out in a pigsty to the north of Old Oak Common Lane. Hungry creatures, pigs. They'll eat almost anything. There was no evidence of him on the day he escaped, but the farmer has told us it appeared subsequently in the natural course of things.'

Frances was unsure if she ever wished to eat pork again. 'Then you believe he died very soon after his escape?'

'It looks that way, yes.'

'I suppose Reverend Ross-Fielder should be informed. He has been a very worried man, as he feared another attack. He will probably want to pray for the man's soul.'

'Oh, Ross-Fielder is all charity and light on the surface but the Hammersmith Inspector said it was hard to get him to even talk about the case. But if the reverend prays at all, I expect it will be to give thanks.'

'But he visited Coote in prison.'

'How do you know?'

'I heard Sergeant Hambling mention it. He said the reverend was Coote's only visitor. You had been wondering if a visitor had slipped Coote the funds he needed to bribe a guard to help him escape, but of course the reverend was the very last man who would have wanted him free.'

'That's true enough.'

'And there is something else,' said Frances. 'As you know, on the day Coote escaped from prison, someone entered the coach house at Springfield Lodge and cut the spokes on Mr Ross-Fielder's bicycle. When the members heard about Coote's escape they thought it might have been he who did it, but now it seems that it can't have been. I don't think he would have come to East Acton and then returned to the vicinity of the prison.'

'No, I doubt that he ever got as far as East Acton. We think that when all the hue and cry began he climbed into the pigsty to hide and learned more about pigs in five minutes than most men will ever know.'

'Poor man,' said Frances, since it seemed like a dreadful end for anybody. 'I hope he didn't suffer.'

'Let's hope not,' said Sharrock, although he didn't sound too troubled about it. 'So, if you don't mind, I will now continue to investigate the murder of Miss Hicks. I am content, however, to leave the mystery of the damaged bicycle to you.' He strode away before she could question him further.

Frances was thoughtful. With Mr Coote now no longer a suspect in that particular misdemeanour she wondered afresh who could possibly have been the saboteur. No one other than the club members and Jack Linnett had been seen in the vicinity, and all of them would have known that the damage was slight, easily corrected, and could not have caused an injury to the rider. Yet everyone was agreed that the spokes had been deliberately cut and not broken. In fact, the only result of the damage had been to prevent Ross-Fielder going out on the club ride and losing an afternoon's exercise. He might well have replaced the spokes and set out with very little delay, but had very sensibly decided to remain and check over the machine for any more dangerous and less obvious damage. Whoever had cut the spokes could not have anticipated that the rider would be held back by more than a few minutes. It was hard to understand why it had been done at all.

Frances doubted that the Inspector would have any further information, but glancing about the field, she soon spotted a man who might.

CHAPTER TWENTY-NINE

ergeant Hambling was a very busy man and also very hot and tired. He had been covering the field, directing his constables and reporting to Inspector Sharrock, and looked as if he had not had a rest or refreshment for some time.

'Sergeant Hambling,' said Frances, as he took a brief moment to get his breath. 'You have been working so very hard, I do hope you have been given tea and something to eat?'

'There hasn't been any time for that, Miss,' he said regretfully. 'A policeman's lot, as they say.'

'Oh, but you must keep your strength up,' she exclaimed. 'We can't have you fainting away, you know. Why don't I open up the kitchen again and make you some tea? There is some cake left, and bread and butter and Mrs Pirrie's home-made jam.'

He hesitated. 'Well that sounds very tempting, I must say.'

'It would take no time at all to prepare. Come to the kitchen in a few minutes and it will be ready for you.'

'That's very kind of you, Miss …?'

'Williamson. I am Mr Garton's cousin.'

'Right you are. I just need to speak to my men and I'll be right along.'

When Sergeant Hambling appeared in the kitchen there was a freshly made pot of tea and a feast of cake and bread waiting for him.

'Thank you, Miss Williamson, for going to all this trouble,' he said, as Frances poured tea into the largest cup she could find.

'Milk and sugar?'

'Yes please, plenty of milk and three spoonsful of sugar.'

Frances stirred the tea and handed him the cup. He gulped the almost boiling beverage gratefully. 'It's really no trouble at all,' she said. 'It is the least I can do, considering all that you have done today.' She proffered a plate of jam sandwiches and slices of cake. 'You must be so relieved that that nasty criminal has been caught at last. As we all are! The police have been so brave and so thorough. I am astonished that you could find someone like that. It must have been like searching for the proverbial needle in a haystack.'

'Well, we have our methods,' said the sergeant, munching on a sandwich. 'But in the end there's no substitute for hard work. We've been all over – gardens, orchards, sheds, stables. Everywhere a man can hide.'

'I do hope that the Reverend Ross-Fielder has been told the good news so that his mind can be at peace now. I saw him earlier today, and while he was bearing up well, I could see how anxious he was. And I believe that he actually visited his attacker in prison? What a kind and truly Christian act that was. Is the Reverend a frequent visitor to the prison?'

'Ah, no, I'm not aware that he has been there before. There is a prison chaplain, of course, who ministers to the inmates.'

'So it was a special visit, and to the very man who was so horribly violent to him. How extraordinary! But perhaps the Reverend Ross-Fielder thought that by extending a personal message of forgiveness, he might yet save the soul of his attacker and bring him to true holiness and peace.' Frances made a great show of passionate regret. 'Oh, how I wish he had succeeded! How ungrateful of the man to refuse the hand of salvation and commit yet another bad act!'

Hambling nodded and gratefully accepted the replenishment of his cup. 'You can never know what some of these types will do. Some will turn to the good if they are led, others will stay as they are.' He gulped more tea and helped himself to cake.

'Do you know if the Reverend offered Mr Coote any more practical assistance? Perhaps something to help him find honest employment after his release?'

Hambling smiled. 'No, just spiritual guidance. He gave him a prayer book, that's all. I'm not sure Coote even bothered to read it. He certainly didn't take it with him.'

'Perhaps I should feel sorry for Mr Coote, even though he was a criminal. I was told that he had no family to help him. Is that true? No friends? No one to take pity on him? No other visitors? How sad to be so alone in the world.'

Hambling dusted crumbs from his jacket. 'Yes, he was an odd one all right.' He took a deep breath of contentment. 'Well, thank you very kindly Miss Williamson, I certainly feel refreshed and ready to go about my duties!'

As Frances tidied the kitchen she could only wonder if the gift of a prayer book from a clergyman would be searched to see if there was anything hidden in its pages. But why, she thought, would the prisoner's victim help him escape? And was there any connection between that visit and the damage to Henry Ross-Fielder's bicycle?

During the course of the afternoon all those who had attended the race meeting were interviewed by the police, and after supplying their names and addresses were permitted to go home. The five men who had ridden in the professionals' race as well as the marshall were early departures, as were the men of the Acton Brass Ensemble, and after the contretemps between Miss Farrow and Miss Vance, Mr Goring had decided to leave.

A bicyclist had gone to Acton to hire cabs and these were arriving to convey the visitors home. The tricycles and sociables that had been drawn up on the field were being ridden away. The ropes and posts that belonged to the cricket club had been taken to the pavilion storeroom, while those that were the property of the club were waiting by the exit in readiness for when they could be replaced in the lodge coach house. With the departure of customers, the salesmen were dismantling their stalls and packing up their wares in preparation for leaving as soon as they were permitted. It was a quiet and mournful end to a day that had promised excitement and amusement.

Mr Toop, who had been interviewed early on and was therefore within his rights to leave, nevertheless insisted on remaining to oversee all the arrangements, which he did with the expression and manner of an usher at a funeral.

A miserable looking Henry Ross-Fielder, having helped with the dismantling of the track, had gone to sit on the veranda with his mother and brother. Frances assumed that Inspector Sharrock was currently questioning his father. She wondered when the family was going to be informed that Coote was dead. It was not, of course, her place to tell them. What would be their reaction when they found out? Relief? Sorrow? Had the Reverend really been the instrument of the convict's escape, and if so, why? Had Coote somehow persuaded him that he would be a better man if freed? That seemed doubtful. She wondered if Coote's death was really an accident. Had he been murdered and the body fed to the pigs? Had he only been freed in order to exact this horrible revenge? It was an extreme and unlikely action, but Frances reflected that there were probably many aspects of the meeting between the reverend gentleman and the prisoner that she knew nothing about.

Ratty called by, looking pleased with himself. "Spector says I 'ave ter be an extry pair 'uv eyes fer 'im. Y'know,' he added carefully, ''e ain't a bad old cove fer a copper.'

'That's true. I think you would make a fine policeman, and I expect he thinks so, too.'

Ratty shrugged. 'D'no about that.'

'Well since you have such sharp eyes, can you tell me if Mr Peters, the young man who has been riding about on a velocipede, is anywhere about? Has he been questioned yet?'

'Don' think so. An' I ain't seen 'im anywhere for quite a bit. Not since before the race where there was all that cuffuffle.'

'Really? As long ago as that?'

'Yeah.'

'Perhaps he has been interviewed and allowed home.'

'Nah, 'e ain't'. Cos 'is boss man, Mr 'opper, 'e's bin lookin' about for 'im. 'E wanted ter go off outside an' look but the p'lice stopped 'im.'

'What about Mr Grove, have you seen him anywhere?'

'Yeah, well 'e was gone for a bit an' all, but then 'e come back. 'E's bin up ter summat funny though. Dunno what. 'E's over at the smithy's place 'elpin' out young Mr Linnett 'o's a bit upset.'

Frances glanced over at the blacksmith's enclosure and saw that this was correct. Jack Linnett had his head down working on a bicycle, with Cedric and Mr Grove offering a helping hand.

'Ratty, I want you to keep a special watch on Henry Ross-Fielder and his family. I think the father is being questioned at the moment, but I would like to know what they say when he rejoins them. I think they have some sort of secret that they might only discuss between themselves. See if you can find it out.'

'Right y'are!' grinned Ratty and darted away.

Frances was all too aware that she was overstepping her instructions, and had been doing so for quite some time, but she suspected that everything had changed after the murder of Miss Hicks, and when the old rules no longer applied one had to make up new ones. In any case, she told herself, there was no harm in asking others to be vigilant and collect information. She had still not come to any conclusion about the identity of the traitor. Wherever there was the prospect of misuse of money that was where she was obliged to look.

The Reverend Ross-Fielder emerged from the pavilion, blinking into the declining sun. His family went at once to comfort him, urging him to sit down at a table. The gentleman had been a well set up man for his age but now he appeared shrunken and older. There was some agitated conversation before the father hid his face in his hands. Nearby, unnoticed, Tom and Ratty appeared to be playing a game of tag.

A constable approached the family group, his official manner not untinged by sympathy, and asked Henry Ross-Fielder to come inside to be questioned. He sighed, and pressed his father's hand before going in. The rest of the family drew close and there was more urgent conversation, which hushed whenever a policeman or other person drew near, but the playing boys went unregarded.

CHAPTER THIRTY

Frances sat down on a bench. Sarah and Pounder were walking about arm-in-arm, and, she felt sure, watching and listening as they went. In her opinion they made a fine couple. People had remarked upon them, usually with surprise, and often disparagingly, since Pounder was tall and well proportioned, with fine, manly features, while Sarah's many wonderful attributes did not include beauty. That was a shallow way of reckoning, thought Frances, since once one saw them together there was a comfortable unity about them, as sturdy and enduring as a rock.

Cedric walked over and sat on the bench beside her.

'How is Jack?' she asked.

'Taking it badly, as one might expect, trying to distract himself with work, but it's hard going when he keeps weeping.'

'There will be those who might accuse him of the murder, they will see it as a crime of jealousy, and think the son is like the father.'

'Then the sooner we call in Miss Frances Doughty to solve the case the better.'

'I agree, but I am not sure there is anything I can do today. Did Mr Grove say where he went during the professionals' race?'

'No, I didn't realise he had been missing then. You don't think he killed Miss Hicks?'

'I don't know; I doubt it, but he may have seen something important since everyone else, including myself I am ashamed to say, was watching the race.' Frances rose and, accompanied by Cedric, walked over to the blacksmith's enclosure, where Jack was showing Mr Grove how to replace a broken spoke.

Grove glanced up at her, and since they were not supposed to know each other, said nothing. Jack's face was grimy
with dust and sweat and there were dark puddles under his
eyes. He stood up and rubbed the back of his hand across
his face, which did nothing to improve the even distribution
of dirt and tears. Cedric patted him on the arm. 'Come,' he
said gently. 'You have worked all day without a rest. Sit down,
now.'

Jack sniffed and allowed himself to be led to a nearby bench,
where he sat dejectedly.

Frances pretended to make a close examination of one of
the bicycles, while Grove wiped his hands on a handkerchief.
Neither spoke to the other until Cedric returned.

'Allow me to introduce my cousin, Miss Williamson,' said
Cedric. 'Rose, this is Mr Grove, who has been assisting poor
Jack Linnett just now.'

Grove gave a polite salute. 'Delighted to make your acquaintance. Have you been interviewed by the Inspector yet?'

'Not yet, no, though I have spoken to both him and Sergeant
Hambling this afternoon.'

'Well, while we wait, shall we find some shade near the
pavilion?'

'Yes, why not?' He proffered his arm and she took it, and
together they turned to walk back to the pavilion. 'Will you
join us, Cedric?'

Cedric gazed at them and there was an expression on his
face which Frances was quite unable to decipher. 'I — er — if
you don't mind, I will sit with Jack.'

They walked on. Frances found herself unwilling to place
any more than the lightest touch on her companion's sleeve, as
if reluctant to sense the strength that lay beneath it. Once again
she felt the situation was part of a dream from which she would
soon awaken. Either that or they were players in one of Mr
Gilbert and Mr Sullivan's operas and they were about to step
onto the stage and burst into a comic song. She could not help
noticing that since she had last seen him Mr Grove's knuckles

had become bruised. 'Dangerous work, repairing bicycles,' she commented.

'Oh, this – no, that was done contacting something a lot harder.'

'What have you been doing?' she asked. 'You were not here during the last race.'

'I was attending to necessary business.'

'Oh?'

'By the name of Peters.'

She gave him a quizzical look and he smiled. It was a pleasant smile, quite unlike the sneer of the Filleter. 'Don't worry, he isn't dead, he is much more useful to us alive. I have him secure where he will be turned over to the police in due course.'

'Mr Hopper was worried by Peters' absence, I saw him looking about for him.'

'He will look in vain.' There were no places on the veranda, which was occupied by those waiting to be interviewed, but some tables and chairs had been placed on the grass in front of the pavilion to take advantage of the late afternoon shade spreading across the ground. They sat down. 'You see, one or two things started to come back to me about the unfortunate lapse from which you rescued me. First of all, a vague memory that when I entered Sir Hugo's workshop there was more than one man in there. And I also recalled that there was a velocipede leaning against the side of the building. I feel certain that one of the men inside was Peters, and quite possibly another was Hopper or one of his men. But there was at least one more, a man who was very careful to keep in the shadows. I anticipated that when I appeared on the field again someone would give himself away and sure enough, when Peters saw me free, he started to stalk me. I allowed him to think that I didn't see what he was up to, and so was able to draw him away. Peters must have thought I would be an easy target. But this time I was ready for him.'

'Do you think Hopper is the man behind it all? Or is he just a part of it?' Frances asked.

'I think he only provides the bullies and the messengers, for a fee, of course. Why should one engage a team of men and boys when there is already one to hand – and managed by an employer who disdains the law? Hopper knows his own business well, but he would be out of his depth with anything more subtle. I think if we can find Sir Hugo's notebooks we will find our man.'

'Can Peters be persuaded to talk?'

'I've tried, and believe me I have many ways of doing that, but I don't think he will. He is more afraid of his masters than he is of a spell in prison, and pain seems to mean very little to him.'

'So that means that Peters has an alibi for the murder of Miss Hicks.'

'He does.'

'And our other suspect, Mr Coote, is no longer available. Inspector Sharrock revealed to me that he died within a very short while of escaping, so he cannot have killed Miss Hicks and neither can he have damaged Mr Ross-Fielder's bicycle.'

'Do you think that is important?' Grove asked.

'I'm not sure, but it is one of those things – many things – that I can't explain. There is something altogether strange about Coote's escape, and I think the Reverend Ross-Fielder knows more than he is saying. Tom and Ratty are looking into that for me. Regarding Miss Hicks, I think she may have had a – shall we call it a dalliance with one of the men in the Bayswater or another bicycling club, who she met when he took his machine to be repaired by her father. She must have found herself in a difficult situation and demanded a meeting with the man, asking him for money, or possibly even marriage. There are men who are willing to meet their obligations and there are men who are prepared to commit murder to avoid them. Sometimes it is impossible for a woman to tell the difference until it is too late. The professionals' race was an ideal distraction – all eyes were on the riders, and the noise would have drowned any cries for help, if there had been any. There are at least seven men who we know could not have committed the crime: Cedric, who was by my side, the riders, and the marshal.'

'And they include Iliffe and Babbit, who you have informed me appear to have business of their own.'

'Yes. A betting fraud, we think. I suppose there is no further news of Sir Hugo?'

'None. I was intending to go and see Jepson but then the police secured the field.'

'Could you not have evaded them?'

'I could, and that was a hard choice to make, but I decided to remain.'

'I do hope Sir Hugo has recovered. He may very well hold the key to everything. And once we can reveal that he was drugged we can find out from Mrs Pirrie and Mr Waterfield the butler just who might have had access to the coffee.' She paused. 'I am sorry if I have done more than I was supposed to do, but so much has happened that I really couldn't help it. I have tried to be as discreet as possible.'

'You have been thoroughly disobedient and I shall have to say so in my report,' he said solemnly.

'It's my wretched curiosity, it always leads me astray.' She sighed. 'So, are you able to tell me more of what today's mission was really about?'

'I can tell you as much as I know. There are a number of foreign agents who operate in London and the immediate area, and there is one in particular who frequents the bicycle clubs and moves around faster than we can follow him. He has been here before and we received information that he would be here today, possibly for the exchange of information, but I believe that the stir over the escaped convict and the police presence made him cautious. I didn't see him, and I rather think he didn't come at all, or if he did he took one look at all the police about and changed his mind.'

'Do you know who he was supposed to be meeting?'

'I'm afraid not. But if we find him we will root out one small part of the system and he might be persuaded to talk and lead us to his masters.'

Ratty came down the steps of the pavilion. 'All I c'n say is, the rev is very upset. 'E says that 'e never went to see Coote in prison and someone else went wiv false papers pretendin' to be 'im. An' his missus and sons are very upset too, sayin' it's a terrible thing ter do ter a man's reputation.'

'Now that is interesting,' said Frances. 'I am obliged to assume that Reverend Ross-Fielder is telling the truth. In any case since he is a clergyman he is bound to be believed, whatever he says.' She thought back to the time she had visited Newgate to speak to a prisoner, and the fact that it had been necessary to seek written permission. It was probable that a similar rule applied in Wormwood Scrubs. 'I can see that many men might be able to impersonate a clergyman with the correct costume and manner, but surely they would have more difficulty in obtaining documents to prove who they are?'

She was lost in thought for a while, and Mr Grove allowed this to continue without interruption. The field was quiet and all around them was the soft whisper of conversations and the ripple of flags in the breeze.

'I don't know the answer,' said Frances at last, 'although I suspect what it might be, and I think I know how to get it. And if I am right, then I can also guess who damaged Mr Ross-Fielder's bicycle.' She gave a smile of triumph.

Mr Grove nodded, and very slowly slid his hand across the table until his fingertips were almost touching hers. 'Miss Doughty —' he began.

There was a sudden loud roar from the entrance of the cricket ground. They both leaped up and saw that a small carriage had just arrived, from which two men had descended. One of them was surgeon Jepson, and the other, his wild grey locks billowing in the breeze, was Sir Hugo Daffin.

CHAPTER THIRTY-ONE

As they watched, Daffin, waving his arms like windmills, began to run across the field towards the pavilion, making the lurching and unsteady progress of a dazed but highly determined man. Jepson gave pursuit and attempted to take him by the arm but Daffin shook him off angrily and plunged forward, his monocle dangling from its cord and his eyes glassy and staring.

'What in the name of all that is infernal is happening here?' bellowed Daffin. 'Jack! Where's Jack? Toop! Goring! Ross-Fielder! I want to talk to all of you! Why are the police here? Why does everyone look as if they have been to a funeral?' He staggered suddenly and would have fallen but two constables and Mr Jepson rushed to support him.

Sergeant Hambling and two more constables ran up. A crowd began to gather, but the onlookers were gently but firmly persuaded to stand back. 'I am so sorry,' exclaimed Jepson. 'But you know Sir Hugo; I told him to rest and he wouldn't have it. Insisted he came back here at once. I accompanied him for his own safety.'

Mrs Pirrie hurried across the field to her employer, uttering little wails of pleasure. 'Oh, Sir Hugo! I'm so glad you're here! Where have you been? We've all been so worried!'

Sir Hugo seemed not to hear her, he simply held his head in his hands and groaned.

'I'm sorry to say, Mrs Pirrie,' explained Jepson, 'that he doesn't know very much about the last few hours. But he might feel better for a nice cup of tea. Would you oblige?'

'Oh, of course, I'll go and make one right away!' Mrs Pirrie turned and trotted back to the pavilion.

Hambling and the constables now had full charge of Sir Hugo and guided him along. 'Where are you taking him?' asked Jepson.

'To see Inspector Sharrock. You'd better come, too.'

'But what has happened here?'

'The Inspector will explain everything, sir.'

As Frances watched the dazed Sir Hugo and his worried attendant being led across the field, Cedric appeared by her side.

'I suppose it's too much to hope that Dr Jepson won't mention us to the Inspector?' she said.

'Far too much. I suggest we wait here to be called.'

'He will be annoyed with me,' said Frances. 'But he so often is. Where is Jack?'

'He's still in a bad way. Jepson junior is looking after him.'

'I will join you later,' said Mr Grove, and hurried away.

'I wish I knew what that fellow was up to,' said Cedric.

'It is my belief that in time you will come to trust each other.'

'Perhaps, but the question is, can I trust him with you?'

They sat down and waited outside the pavilion for several minutes, then Constable Mayberry emerged and looked about him.

'I think,' said Cedric, rising to his feet, 'it might be myself and Miss Doughty you are looking for.'

'Yes it is,' said Mayberry. 'Inspector wants to speak to you.' He paused, awkwardly. 'He – er – he isn't very happy.'

'He is such a hard man to please,' commiserated Cedric. 'Don't worry, constable, we'll come quietly.'

Sharrock was alone in the tearoom when they arrived, sitting at a table with a large pot of tea and one of the bigger cups in front of him. He looked up with a surly expression. 'No trouble, Mayberry?'

'None at all, sir.'

'What a pity. I was hoping they'd make a run for it and be brought here under arrest.'

Frances and Cedric sat down and Mayberry took up a position by the door.

Inspector Sharrock fixed the new arrivals with an intense look from under bushy eyebrows. Frances was obliged to remind herself that she had taken tea with the Inspector and his family, and that his wife was a very pleasant woman who regarded him with great affection. The sight of his youngest child sitting on his lap smearing butter in his hair was not one she would readily forget. 'Now then, Miss Doughty, Mr Garton, I'd like you both to tell me what in the blazes is going on?'

'How is Sir Hugo?' asked Frances.

'Being looked after by Mr Jepson. He'll recover, but it was a close thing. Gent that age, you can't be too careful.'

'If it hadn't been for Miss Doughty we might not have found him and summoned a doctor in time,' said Cedric.

Sharrock leaned back in his chair and folded his arms. 'And where exactly did you find him? Because he seems to recall very little. One moment he's heating up some coffee for his breakfast and the next he's in Jepson's surgery.'

'We found him at home, lying on his bed,' said Frances. 'I saw at once that he was very ill and called Mr Jepson. I should explain that it was my experience of looking for missing persons that led me to feel concerned for him, which was why I decided to visit the lodge to see if there were any clues as to his whereabouts.'

'Well that's all very commendable, and you may very well have saved his life,' Sharrock suddenly leaned forward, and thumped his fists on the table, 'but then for the rest of the afternoon you deliberately failed to inform anyone of where he was, despite the fact that friends of his were beginning to worry. Why was that? Please take very great care with your reply.'

'Ah – well —' began Cedric and paused. 'That's a bit awkward, really.'

'If the man was ill, his friends and his housekeeper should have been told. If a crime had been committed the police should have been told. Miss Doughty, I want your answer. I am very curious to hear your reasons for this extraordinary behaviour. And while you're about it, I want you to explain how you entered a house which Mrs Pirrie assures me was locked up tight, and why I shouldn't arrest you both for that offence right now.'

Frances was considering her reply when there was a knock on the door. Sharrock scowled and muttered something under his breath. 'Come in!' he barked.

One of the Acton constables peered around the door. 'I'm sorry to interrupt you Inspector, but there's a gentleman here with an important message from the Home Office.'

'The Home Office?' exclaimed Sharrock, astounded. 'What has the infernal Home Office got to do with it? Oh all right, show me the message.'

The constable hesitated. 'He says he wants to speak with you personally sir. Shall I show him in?'

Sharrock gave Frances a very hard look. 'Why are things always more complicated when you're involved?' He sighed and turned to the constable again. 'Very well. Put these two in the kitchen and see they're well-guarded.'

The constable did his best to remain impassive. 'He said he wants to see you together with this lady and gentleman, sir.'

'Oh does he now? Well in that case show him in and make sure he has a roast dinner, a bottle of champagne and a slice of birthday cake while you're at it!'

The Acton constable ducked out quickly.

'Do you know this man?' demanded Sharrock.

'I believe we may have met,' said Frances.

Moments later the Acton constable returned and ushered in Mr Grove.

'And I wasn't joking about the cake,' bellowed Sharrock after the constable. 'There's enough uneaten cake round here to sink a battleship, and with the way things are going today I don't think I'm getting any supper.'

'Good afternoon, Inspector,' said Grove coolly, handing over a letter. He then sat down. Sharrock had hardly given him a glance, then he did a double-take and fixed him with a piercing stare.

'Wait a minute! I know you! Aren't you—?'

'It's all explained in the letter,' said Grove, who was clearly the only person in the room perfectly at his ease. Frances wondered where he had hidden the letter for this eventuality. It certainly wasn't something he would have kept in his pocket. If it had been found when he was captured he would probably have been killed at once.

Sharrock took his time reading the letter. The constable reappeared with a plate of cakes, which Sharrock began to devour as he read. When he had finished the letter and two of the cakes, he narrowed his eyes and stared at Grove very sharply. Finally he threw the paper down on the table and wiped crumbs from his mouth. 'And when exactly were you planning to tell the police about this?'

'To be frank with you, Inspector,' said Grove, 'we weren't planning to tell the police at all. It was intended to be a very quiet affair, mainly observation, so as not to frighten our unknown quarry into bolting. Unfortunately, the escape of Mr Coote from Wormwood Scrubs, the attack on Sir Hugo Daffin, the murder of Miss Hicks, and the uncovering of a betting fraud made things rather more complicated than we had anticipated. Any orders that were issued regarding the mission do not therefore continue to apply. We have been obliged to use our initiative.'

'Betting fraud?' Sharrock stared at Frances. 'Is that why you're here? I knew you were up to something! Well I'll need a full report on that before the end of the day.' He thought hard. 'Jepson said there was another man involved in finding Sir Hugo. Was that you, Mr —' he stared at the letter 'Grove?'

'It was. I accept full responsibility for all the decisions made and all actions taken.'

'So – and perhaps I can get an answer to this question at last – why didn't you tell Sir Hugo's friends where he was?'

'Because we were unsure of who his friends actually were. We had to remove him from immediate danger, and obtain urgent medical assistance. If his enemies had heard where he was, they might have made another attempt on him.'

'But the police should have been told,' exclaimed Sharrock, prodding the desk hard with his finger as if he would have liked to prod Mr Grove into compliance.

'I'm sorry. Orders from above. But I do have one suggestion to make.' Grove drew a bunch of keys from his pocket and handed them to the Inspector. 'The keys to Springfield Lodge. I took them from a man called Peters, who must have stolen them from Sir Hugo. You will find Mr Peters tied to Sir Hugo's bedstead, with a note pinned to him explaining why the police might like to interview him. He won't be able to escape even if he can untie himself, because he has a dislocated knee. He attempted to assault me when I confronted him about his illegal activities. There being no constable present, I took it upon myself to place him under arrest. He was unwise enough to resist.'

There was a short pause while the Inspector absorbed what he had been told. No one in the room was in any doubt as to the nature of the man confronting him. 'Right,' said Sharrock at last. 'Mayberry?'

'Yes, sir,' said Mayberry, who had gone a little pale under his pimples.

'Take these keys to Sergeant Hambling and let him know where to find Peters.'

'Yes sir!' Mayberry took the keys and hurried away.

'So,' said Sharrock, 'this Peters ...'

'A roughneck and a messenger. Works for Archie Hopper. Hopper runs a betting book but we think he also carries messages of another kind. Neither of them is the main man we are looking for, and we don't yet know who that is. I did question Peters but he refused to talk.'

Sharrock grunted. 'Perhaps you should have dislocated his other knee.'

'I was tempted.'

'Do you think,' asked Frances, carefully, 'that the men who work for Hopper are so dependable that they would be entrusted with anything of a confidential nature? I would have thought judging by Mr Peters that they are not that kind of man. After all, Coote used to work for him. And didn't Hopper have a messenger who simply ran off with the money he was entrusted with?'

'That's right,' said Sharrock. 'The Hammersmith police have had their eye on Mr Hopper and his crew for quite some time. I had a good briefing on them today. It's all very well picking them up for small matters and fining them, but Hopper always manages to wriggle out of any charges. They need to be shut down altogether. But this betting fraud – is Hopper involved? What evidence have you got?'

'Nothing definite as yet, only suspicion,' Frances admitted. 'It involves Mr Iliffe and Mr Babbit, who affect to be deadly rivals, and make a great show of it in public. There was heavy betting on the professionals' race, which had been built up to be an important confrontation, and I am guessing that virtually all of the money was either on Iliffe or Babbit to win. But you saw what transpired. It will be hard to prove but I believe their collision was no accident. Men of that skill and experience would be able to make it look convincing. Knowing the outcome, they would have had secret bets that neither of them would win, and perhaps they received a portion of Hopper's profits.'

'How do you know this?' asked Sharrock.

'Tom Smith saw one of Hopper's boy runners taking messages between Iliffe and Babbit. The boy in the green cap.'

'Hmm. Well, we'll look into it. But if they've been clever covering their tracks and no one will admit anything then it'll be hard to prove. Hopper's men won't talk because that would take away a nice income from their master and little gratuities for them.'

There was a knock at the door and Sergeant Hambling appeared. 'We have Mr Peters, sir, and he isn't a happy fellow right now, what with that nasty accident to his knee.'

'Is he willing to talk?'

'Not about his master, or his business, no. Says he just carries the messages and doesn't look inside them. One thing he did say, hoping we'd treat him more lenient for the information, he made an accusation against Mr Coote. Said that Coote hated one of Mr Hopper's men, Edward Cowdray, and reckons he killed him. Of course, he didn't know that Coote was dead.'

'Hopper dismissed Coote because he thought he was stealing from him,' said Frances. 'Then when Cowdray disappeared with some money he realised that Coote wasn't the culprit. So Coote did have reason to hate both Hopper and Cowdray.'

Hambling looked surprised.

'What the lady said,' said Sharrock. 'Anything more?'

'Well, according to Peters,' Hambling continued, 'Cowdray was doing some other business on the side that was bringing in money that Mr Hopper never saw, and Coote wanted part of it, but Cowdray wouldn't let him in. So he killed Cowdray. That's all he said. We'll never get to the bottom of it now.'

'Edward Cowdray,' said Frances, suddenly.

'Yes. Do you know him?' asked Sharrock.

'No, but I have had a thought. Hopper's boys are on foot but the young men ride velocipedes. Did the missing man, Cowdray, ride one?'

'I don't know – he could have done. Why is that important?'

'Because on an earlier visit to Springfield Lodge Cedric and I had a look at the old kitchen garden. It's very much overgrown, but in it we found an abandoned velocipede. It had some letters scratched on it, EDW. I thought they must be initials but Cowdray's name was Edward, which can be abbreviated to EDW. Perhaps it was his velocipede? Mr Hopper should be able to identify it. I thought when I was there that something had happened, but I wasn't sure what. Perhaps Cowdray was killed there?'

'You didn't happen to find a body you've not told me about yet?' asked Sharrock, his tone not entirely sarcastic.

'No, but I didn't search the whole area.'

'Full of surprises as ever, Miss Doughty,' said Sharrock. He nodded. 'Sergeant, I assume Mr Hopper has not left the field?'

'He has made a number of attempts to do so, sir, and we have had to place him under guard.'

'Right. You go along and ask him about Cowdray and his velocipede, and let us know.'

Sharrock stared at Frances. 'I don't know how you do it, but your fingers seem to be all over this business.'

'I was just keeping my eyes open,' said Frances. 'That was how I found Miss Hicks's body, by seeing her bonnet ribbon. I assume you have made no arrest yet?'

'No, but I don't think we have to look far.'

'It's an old story, I'm afraid,' sighed Cedric. 'I feel only pity for the girl. Men can be so cruel.'

Sharrock hesitated, tapping his fingers on the table. 'All right, I don't usually share information with civilians, but I know Miss Doughty has a certain way of looking at things, and you, Mr Garton, seem to be mixed up in it as well, and —' he waved a hand at Mr Grove as if unable to place him in any easily describable category, 'I want to keep my kneecaps where they are. So I'll tell you what we know so far, in strictest confidence, mind. I've had a full report from surgeon Barraclough, and it looks like it wasn't a fancy man who done it. There's been all those old women spreading the story that Miss Hicks was in the family way. Nasty tongues, they've got. Well according to the surgeon she was nothing of the sort, and —' here Sharrock looked a little awkward, 'well let's just say, she would have known it.' Frances didn't ask him to comment further. Barraclough, she thought, must have made an examination of the body to see if there was any disturbance of the garments, and found that the girl was in a situation incompatible with being an expectant mother. 'Of course,' Sharrock went on, 'she might have spun a story to get money out of a man, but any man with an ounce of common sense is not going to agree to anything unless he is sure of the truth of what she says and has a good idea that he is responsible. She had nothing to bargain with at all.'

'So what is your theory, Inspector?' asked Frances.

'Oh, it's still a crime of passion. Jealousy. All done on an impulse. Miss Hicks had any number of admirers she wouldn't give the time of day to because she had her sights set higher than was advisable. All we need to know is which of them was here today. And I can think of one name in particular. Someone with a father who had his neck stretched.'

'Mrs Pirrie would have words to say about that,' Frances observed.

'She already has,' said Sharrock drily. 'At some length.'

Sergeant Hambling returned. 'Mr Hopper said that Cowdray rode a velocipede and he also thought he had scratched some letters on the side. He didn't think Cowdray would have abandoned it willingly.'

'Right. I suggest we take him along to this garden and let him have a look at the machine. If he confirms that it does belong to this Cowdray then we will have to search the area. Might find a body if we're lucky.'

Frances was not so confident. The growth of the grass through the wheel spokes of the abandoned machine showed that it had been there for some considerable time. A body lying in the open air in the heat of summer, even behind that wall, would have attracted some attention within a few days. If the abandoned velocipede was Cowdray's and he was dead, then his body would be elsewhere.

Sharrock rose to his feet. 'Now there's no need for you to get involved, Miss Doughty.'

'I disagree,' said Grove. 'I think the lady's insights will be essential.'

'Home Office orders?'

'If you like.'

Sharrock knew when he was beaten. 'Very well. And you, Mr Garton? Will you join the merry throng? Another man to help the search wouldn't go amiss.'

'Of course,' said Cedric, graciously. 'How kind of you to invite me.'

'If you don't mind, Inspector,' said Frances, 'I would like to ask Sergeant Hambling a question about those people who wish to visit the prisoners at Wormwood Scrubs.'

Hambling looked at Sharrock.

'Just answer the question,' said the Inspector, wearily. 'Take my word for it, it will save time.'

'Very well, sir.' Hambling turned to Frances. 'What do you wish to know?'

'I assume all visitors must apply for permission and present some proof of who they are?'

'Yes, that is the case.'

'I happened to overhear' – at this statement Inspector Sharrock rolled his eyes but said nothing – 'the Reverend Ross-Fielder complaining that someone had visited Mr Coote in his name, but that he had never been to the prison at all.'

Hambling paused. 'Well, I don't know how you know that, but it is true. The prison records show that a Reverend Ross-Fielder paid a visit, but the gentleman denies it. He claimed that someone must have forged his papers, as he has none missing.'

'Might I suggest that a warder be sent for, who could settle the question? Someone who was present at the interview?'

Hambling nodded. 'I suppose we could ask the man to pay a visit to the Reverend and provide an opinion. I'm sure he will be pleased to have his name cleared.'

'If you don't mind,' said Frances, 'it is my belief that we would get more positive information if that warder was to come here this afternoon. And no member of the Ross-Fielder family should be allowed to depart until he has given his judgement.'

Hambling looked at Inspector Sharrock in astonishment.

'Do it,' said Sharrock. 'It shouldn't take long.' He hesitated. 'Send a man on a bicycle.'

CHAPTER THIRTY-TWO

Once a constable had been dispatched to Wormwood Scrubs, Hambling and Mayberry went to bring the unwilling Mr Hopper before Sharrock. Mr Hopper looked like a man who had only two moods, bad and worse. This one was worse. With his grim brown and grey thick suiting he looked like a travelling thundercloud. Frances was relieved to see that the prisoner was in handcuffs, although he wore them easily as if they were an accustomed item of embellishment.

'I don't know nothing about Cowdray except he was a right bad 'un!' he growled. 'Nasty little thief! Ran off with my money and not been seen since!'

'Describe him,' said Sharrock.

Hopper shrugged. 'Medium height. Bag o' bones, but strong. Finger missing off left hand. Got bit off by a dog.'

'It would be helpful if Mr Hopper could tell us when he last saw Mr Cowdray,' suggested Frances.

'True,' said Sharrock. 'What have you got to say about that, Hopper?'

'Last summer. When we had that hot spell.'

'Can you be more precise?' asked Frances.

Hopper scowled at Sharrock. 'What's this, you got women police now?'

'Just answer the question,' said Sharrock.

Hopper wriggled in his clothes as if they were itching him. 'Don't remember exactly do I? All I know is, the day after I last seen him, when he didn't come back from a job, I sent some of my boys out to look for him, in case he'd had an accident. The boys didn't find him, nor his machine, but they said the police were all over the place because there'd been a murder. I thought it might have been Cowdray who'd been killed, but it turned out it was one of the bicycle men.'

'Was that the Vance murder?' asked Sharrock.

'The one the pig-man did.'

'That means Cowdray was last seen the day before Morton Vance was killed,' said Hambling.

'Interesting,' said Sharrock. 'I don't suppose you reported him missing to the police?'

'No. If my boys couldn't find him, the police had no chance.'

'Perhaps Cowdray murdered Vance and ran away?' said Frances. 'Abandoned his velocipede and stole a different machine so he could move faster and not be so easily identified?'

'I feel I ought to remind you,' said Sharrock, heavily, 'that a man has been convicted of that crime and hanged.'

'Oh, the police don't care who they hang as long as they hang someone,' put in Hopper, with a noise that might have been mistaken for a laugh.

'Perhaps Cowdray saw or heard something that frightened him,' said Frances. She turned to Hopper. 'Was he easily frightened?'

'That one?' said Hopper derisively, 'No. Nothing frightened him. Always looking for a chance, he was, and didn't care much how he got it. Stealing, threatening, he was game for it all. I was glad to be rid of him.'

'Your man Peters said that he thought Coote killed Cowdray,' said Hambling.

'Coote? Might of done. Why?'

'Because we think we have found Mr Cowdray's velocipede,' said Sharrock.

'Oh yes? So that's what all the questions are about.'

'And we're going to take you to see it now. One word of warning; any attempt to escape custody will be dealt with very severely indeed.'

It was an unusual little party as they left the pavilion. Inspector Sharrock allowed Frances and Cedric to lead the way and Hambling and Mayberry took charge of the prisoner, with Sharrock and Mr Grove following.

'I assume I can trust you not to run off?' Sharrock murmured to Grove.

'I wouldn't miss this for anything,' Grove assured him.

It was inevitable that they attracted some attention from the crowds, and Frances realised that people were making the assumption that Hopper had been arrested for the murder of Miss Hicks. His habit of hiding behind the scoreboard did mean that it was hard to prove where he had been during the professionals' race.

They passed through the front gates, waved on their way by the constable on guard, then walked along the road to Springfield Lodge. Frances showed them the door to the kitchen garden. 'When I went in earlier today, the door was extremely stiff and had clearly not been opened in a long while,' she told them. 'The weeds were heavily overgrown, except for the area near the door, where they were still high but much less so. That means the door has been opened but not for some time. I found the velocipede by the remains of an old wooden shed, and the weeds were growing through the spokes, so it had clearly been there for some months.'

Hambling and Mayberry stayed in charge of the prisoner, while Sharrock, Cedric and Grove used their combined strength to force the door open, and they all entered the garden, Frances leading the way. As soon as she entered she saw that something was different. The debris around the shed had been disturbed as if someone had had a cursory look around and tumbled things about. Frances, with a feeling of foreboding, walked around the remains of the fallen shed. There was a patch of trampled weeds where the machine had been but the velocipede had gone.

Behind her, Frances heard Archie Hopper laughing.

The overgrown garden was thoroughly searched but there was no sign of a body. They returned to the cricket ground, where arrangements were made to take Archie Hopper to Hammersmith police station, and Frances gave the police as full a description as she could recall of the missing velocipede in case it should re-appear. 'It wasn't found by chance,' she told Sharrock, as he sat behind his desk in the tearoom once more. 'It has probably lain there for a year without being disturbed. But someone knew it was there and today they came and deliberately removed it.'

'Any idea why?'

'Yes, I think so. The police have been in the area looking for Coote. Sergeant Hambling told me they've been searching everywhere; stables, gardens, sheds. So whoever put the machine in the lodge garden must have feared that there was a chance that they would look there and find it.'

'That still doesn't tell us where it is now. Do you think you would recognise it if you saw it again?'

'Yes, I do.'

'Could have been sold on by now. It's worth a few shillings I expect. I'll send a constable to ask round the bicycle shops, they sell these velocipedes there, too, don't they?'

'I expect so. And quite probably parts to be used for repairs. It might have been broken up. The only thing that will tell us it is the one we are looking for is the letters scratched on the handlebars.'

Sharrock did not look confident of success.

Jepson arrived at that moment to report to Inspector Sharrock. He was somewhat taken aback to see Frances, Cedric and Grove in consultation with the Inspector. 'I'm sorry to have intruded on your interview, I will return shortly,' he said and made to depart.

'No, come in and take a seat. You can speak freely here.'

'Very well,' said Jepson, with a puzzled air.

'How is Sir Hugo now?'

'He is still very confused, but I have persuaded him to rest and Mrs Pirrie is caring for him until he can be taken home. I feel confident he will recover fully.'

'You have already said that you believe him to have been under the influence of morphine, most probably taken by mouth?'

'Yes, I could find no sign that it had been injected into him. It is my opinion that it was added to his coffee. I think I ought to say that I have never at any time prescribed morphine for Sir Hugo. Indeed, he was one of those gentlemen who are averse to taking medicines. He used a number of liniments and similar for the strains of bicycle riding but these were only ever for external application, and none of them contained morphine.'

'Do you keep morphine at your surgery and carry it in your medical bag?'

'I do, and I have checked everything very thoroughly and nothing is missing. All can be accounted for.'

'Has anyone come to you recently asking to be prescribed it? Have you been asked to sell any?'

'No, not at all. I don't believe it is something that should be in the hands of an unqualified person.'

'For what ailments would you prescribe it?'

'Those where the sufferer endures severe pain which cannot be ameliorated in any other way.'

'When did you last prescribe it?'

'I would have to look at my notes, but I believe it was about a month ago, for an elderly patient of mine in Acton who was dying. And before you ask me, I made sure when I certified his death that none of the medication remained. I always do.'

'Have you ever prescribed, given, sold or supplied in any manner any morphine to a member of the Bayswater Bicycle Club, or anyone working for or friends with Sir Hugo Daffin?'

Jepson bridled a little at the question but appeared to accept with some resignation that it was something he was bound to be asked. 'No, never. And I should say as well that I have questioned my son, who is engaged in the study of medicine, and he is adamant that he has never supplied morphine to anyone.'

After Jepson departed Sharrock shook his head. 'Barraclough said the same, more or less. We can check with the other surgeons in the area but it'll take time.'

'Do we know who had access to the lodge between the time the coffee was made and Sir Hugo drinking it?' asked Frances.

'I have asked Mrs Pirrie about it, but what with the race meeting there were any number of club members in and out asking about the arrangements, and then there were visitors from other clubs. I've been able to rule out Jepson, and Ross-Fielder, but that's all so far. All right, I must get on with the interviews.' He gave Mr Grove a hard stare. 'You're next.'

Frances was eager to leave the pavilion as she had determined to engage Tom and Ratty to look for any signs of the velocipede. She met Sarah and Professor Pounder outside, together with Cedric. It was a matter of moments before Tom and Ratty joined them, and all shared the information they had gleaned.

Frances supplied the description of the missing velocipede and suggested they have a good search for it once they were allowed to leave the field. ''Spector says we ain't to go till 'e tells us,' said Ratty. 'I fink 'e wants us 'ere for our special work.' He puffed out his chest. 'We're too important.'

'Ratty's goin' to be a p'liceman when 'e's old enough,' said Tom.

'I never said that!' argued Ratty.

'Din't need to,' said Tom, grinning.

'So this velocipede you're all looking for,' said Sarah. 'You reckon it's been taken away and either sold or broken up?'

'That seems the most likely explanation,' said Frances.

'I mean it's not the one that's been left behind the scoreboard?'

Everyone stared at her, then Tom and Ratty leaped up and made to run across the field.

'Tom, Ratty, not yet!' Frances exclaimed. 'Sarah, when did you notice it?'

'Just after they took Hopper away. I had a look around to see if he'd thrown away any evidence before they arrested him, but all I saw was this velocipede leaning against the back of the scoreboard. I knew his men used them so I guessed it was one of theirs.'

'You didn't notice if it had any letters scratched on the handlebars?

'No, I didn't think to look, but it was very dirty.'

Frances thought quickly. 'If it is the one we are looking for we shouldn't go and get it, we need to wait and watch and see who comes to collect it. Tom, Ratty, I want you to keep a lookout but take care not to be seen.'

Sarah and Pounder agreed to also be on hand if needed, and strolled away.

'I am a defeated man,' said Cedric. 'I acknowledge that there is now no possibility of my taking you home until you actually consent to go.'

'None at all,' said Frances. 'At present I am waiting for the arrival of the warder from Wormwood Scrubs, in the hope that he will be able to solve a mystery.'

'And this is?'

'The identity of the man who visited Mr Coote in prison. The Reverend Ross-Fielder has emphatically denied it was he, and I believe him – it would be a very foolish lie otherwise. He suggests that someone forged his papers and impersonated him, but I can think of a simpler solution. His papers weren't forged, they were borrowed and returned.'

Cedric glanced at the little family group on the veranda, two of whom were wearing clerical collars. 'Oh, I see,' he said. 'But why?'

'That is the question I would like to ask.'

Cedric smiled. 'Frances, my dear,' he began, turning towards her, 'about your Mr Grove …'

'He is not my Mr Grove.'

'Well, he certainly thinks he is. I have seen the way he looks at you. And I have seen the way you try not to look at him.'

'I really cannot talk about that,' said Frances dismissively. 'In any case, he has his own work to do. I may never see him again.'

Cedric recognised the finality in her voice and nodded. They sat in silence for some moments.

'These sunny evenings remind me so much of Italy,' he said at last. 'When I came to London to deal with my brother's estate I only expected to stay for a short time, and now here I am more than two years later. It has been a deuced complicated business, but I have just been told that it will be completed before Christmas.'

'What do you intend to do?'

'I am torn two ways. I have so many good friends in Bayswater, now, but my family has indicated that they expect me to return to Italy, and I fear that I will be obliged to obey them. They seem to think I have a head for business.'

'Will Joseph accompany you?'

'Of course; he is my gentleman, after all.' Cedric suddenly seized her hand. 'You know, if I was another kind of man I would marry you in an instant and take you with me.'

'But you are not,' she said gently.

'You can still come to Italy,' he pleaded. 'We could live together like brother and sister.'

'Oh Cedric, that is so very charming of you to ask me, but I think my place is here. I promise you I will visit whenever I can.'

'But I want to look after you – protect you. I can see that Sarah and Pounder are making a fine match, and you may find yourself alone before long. And that Grove – I am sorry to say it, but he is a dangerous fellow.' Cedric paused, and his eyes slowly opened wide in realisation. 'Oh, my word! That's what you like about him!'

Frances was just wondering how to reply when the policeman who had been sent to Wormwood Scrubs returned by bicycle, followed closely by a pony trap bringing the warder. The constable conducted the warder to the pavilion, and a few moments later Mr Grove emerged. 'I'm going to find out what the warder says,' said Frances. 'Cedric, I want you to talk to Mr Grove and try to be friends with him.'

'I wouldn't care to be his enemy,' said Cedric, but he remained seated while Frances hurried up the steps of the veranda and made herself busy brushing non-existent crumbs from the tables.

A minute or so later, Inspector Sharrock stepped outside together with the warder. 'Just look around,' he said. 'Careful, like. I don't want any fuss. But tell me, do you see the gentleman who visited the convict Coote, calling himself Reverend Ross-Fielder?'

The warder glanced about him, and his eyes settled on the family group of the Ross-Fielders. 'Yes, I do,' he said. 'Sitting at that table.'

'The older clerical gentleman?'

'No, he was a young man, only ...'

'Yes?'

'Well, he's not dressed the same today, he's wearing his bicycling uniform.'

'Ah,' said Sharrock. 'Well, thank you very much. I don't suppose you overheard what they said to each other?'

'I didn't, but I could guess some of it.'

'Oh?'

'Well, Coote always claimed that he had rich relatives who would help him make an appeal against his conviction. When I saw the two of them together I could see that there was a family resemblance. So I expect that was what they talked about.'

'And he just visited the once?'

'No, it was twice.'

'And I believe he handed over a gift?'

'Yes, the second time he came. A prayer book.'

There was nothing more to learn, but the new revelation set Frances thinking quickly. If Coote was related to the Ross-Fielders that would explain why he had felt entitled to demand money from the Reverend, and made him his target. The connection could well have been what he had been about to announce at his trial. Once he was convicted Coote must have threatened to expose the relationship and tried to blackmail the Reverend for funds to help him escape. If the unhappy clergyman had confessed to his sons that there was a family connection, it could well have prompted Henry Ross-Fielder's visit to the prisoner. Coote had made his demands at the first visit and they had been met at the second.

Frances thought further. It was a good theory, but did it explain everything? Would it really have been so scandalous if Ross-Fielder and Coote were related? Cousins perhaps? A connection of that order might have been surprising if revealed, but she doubted that it would have seriously harmed the reverend gentleman's reputation. It might even have earned him some pity.

Also, she asked herself, why had Coote not approached the Reverend before? He had been in financial difficulties since being dismissed by Hopper, but that was almost a year prior to the street assault. Why had he not asked for help then? Frances recalled something. At Coote's trial it had been said in mitigation that he had been distressed since the recent death of his mother. Had he perhaps been ignorant of the family connection up until then and only learned of it either because she had revealed it as she lay dying, or had left a note to be opened after her death? Mrs Coote had been said to be a widow. At any rate there was no Mr Coote. Frances found herself wondering what Coote's birth certificate might reveal about his parentage. A Miss Coote as the mother rather than Mrs? An unnamed father?

Inspector Sharrock had bid goodbye to the warder and was about to interview Henry Ross-Fielder when Frances intercepted him. 'Inspector?'

'I'm busy.'

'Please, this is very important.'

He curbed his irritation. 'All right, in as few words as possible.'

'I know that Mr Coote never worked for the Reverend Ross-Fielder, but I suggest that when you conduct your interviews you ask if Coote's mother ever worked for him.'

Sharrock looked appalled. 'Are you insinuating what I think you are insinuating?'

'I am afraid so, yes. The prison warder suggested just now that Coote was related to the Ross-Fielders. I doubt that they despised him as a family connection simply because he was poor and without employment. In fact, I can think of only one reason why he was able to blackmail them into helping him escape from prison.'

'They're a respectable family!' Sharrock protested.

'With a secret. One they will go to considerable lengths to hide.'

He paused. 'All right. I'll ask the question. I only hope you're wrong.' With that, Sharrock called Henry Ross-Fielder in for interview and with a pained look at Frances, ushered him into the pavilion.

Frances returned to her table where Cedric and Mr Grove were seated together in tentative conversation. They both looked at her as she sat down. 'I anticipate,' she said, 'that Mr Ross-Fielder is about to find himself in some trouble.'

'But he's a decent fellow,' protested Cedric.

'In a difficult situation, which forced him to make an unfortunate choice. It was he and not his father who visited Coote in prison, and he who supplied the money to bribe a guard to help him escape.'

'But why?'

'I suspect that they are related, and Coote was threatening to expose a scandal that would damage the family reputation.'

'Are you sure?' exclaimed Cedric.

'We will know very soon. Your friend is being interviewed now, and knowing the Inspector's methods I doubt that he will be able to dissemble for long. It does, of course, explain who damaged the bicycle.'

'A scurrilous act. Do tell,' said Grove.

Frances smiled as both men waited for her words with interest. 'Sometimes,' she said, 'it is necessary when solving a mystery to look at it from a different direction. We didn't know the identity of the perpetrator, and neither did we know the reason for the damage. What we did know, however, was the result of the damage. The result was that Henry Ross-Fielder, the vice-captain of the Bayswater Bicycle Club, did not take his bicycle out on the club ride on the day that Coote escaped from prison, and remained at the coach house all afternoon, checking over the machine in case there was some damage that was not immediately obvious. He had not necessarily needed to take that precaution, but he did so. The choice was his. This meant that by an apparent coincidence, he had not been any-where near the prison at the time the escape took place. The conclusion is irresistible. The only explanation for that slight, easily and cheaply repaired damage is that Ross-Fielder carried it out himself, in order to be far from the scene of the prison break, which he had known was about to happen.'

There was a brief silence.

'He might have simply made an excuse and not appeared for the club ride,' said Mr Grove.

'He might,' said Frances, 'but perhaps his original intention was to brave it out, and behave as if he knew nothing of the plans, but then he might have had second thoughts. He knew that the club ride took him in the vicinity of the prison and if he rode past he risked one of the searchers noticing the resem-blance, maybe thinking that he was Coote in disguise, and stopping him for questioning.'

Cedric nodded. 'Oh, how I wish you were wrong this time!'

Frances had deliberately not voiced the full extent of her suspicions in case she was mistaken, although she felt sure both gentlemen were well able to reach their own conclusions. Another and still worse thought had come to mind. To what lengths was Ross-Fielder prepared to go to protect the name of his family? There was only his word that Vance was already dead when found. Had Vance somehow learned the Reverend's secret and been silenced? No one could be beyond suspicion.

'And now, while we are waiting to see how the Inspector fares,' she continued, 'I would like to ask a question about bicycles.'

Cedric perked up. 'Of course. The finest invention of man!'

'Thus far. But I want to know this – supposing you could make just one improvement. Something that would make a bicycle more attractive for military use, what would it be? Gentlemen, I rely upon your ingenuity. We know that Sir Hugo has been working on improvements. We know that he arranged a meeting with General Farrow who is interested in the military capabilities of bicycles. We also know that he planned to visit the patent office. I really doubt that his work with the additional wheels was going to be of value. I have asked Jack Linnett about it and although I am sure he knows something, he remains silent out of loyalty to Sir Hugo.'

The next few minutes were spent in earnest discussion about the possibility of reducing the weight of the bicycle, making one that could be taken apart and put back together with ease, or devising one that could carry a weapon. 'Perhaps we ought to speak to Jack again?' said Cedric. 'His loyalty is highly commendable to a man he regarded better than family, but it does not help us.'

'Would it be an important improvement if a bicycle was more stable on rough terrain?' Frances asked.

'Very much so,' said Grove. 'But a bicycle needs a strong tyre, and a strong tyre is necessarily a hard one, which makes for a hard ride. That is something yet to be solved.'

Frances gave a little gasp. 'Perhaps,' she said in a moment of inspiration, 'Sir Hugo solved it?'

Inspector Sharrock emerged from the pavilion and had a word with a constable, who asked the remaining members of the Ross-Fielder family to go inside. Before returning, Sharrock gave Frances a stern look then came down the steps to speak to her. 'If you were my daughter, young lady, I would want to send you away and wash your mind of bad thoughts. I'm sure you were never brought up like that.'

'Did you ask the question?' she asked.

'I did. The man went white as a sheet.'

CHAPTER THIRTY-THREE

Before the Inspector could return to the pavilion, there was a rapid flash of movement on the other side of the field, and Frances saw Tom and Ratty break into a run. The object of their pursuit was the messenger boy in the green cap, who was now riding a velocipede. Alarmed by the sudden interest in his new prize he increased his pedalling. The machine was too large and heavy for him, and he was clearly not an experienced rider, but he had youth and energy and determination to assist him. Professor Pounder made chase in an extraordinary burst of pace for such a large man. The constable guarding the gate to the cricket ground left his post to try to intercept the rider but in so doing created a route of escape, and the boy put his head down and aimed for it. Pounder was nimble on his feet. He made the boy veer off course, but then the velocipede turned around and once again made for the roadway. Pounder, with his experience of the boxing ring, knew how to swerve with the best of them, how to feint and move and surprise his opponent, and his speed of attack was astonishing. At last he made a rapid dart and caught up with his quarry. Next moment he had lifted the struggling boy from the machine and tucked him under his arm. He then walked calmly back to the pavilion with his prize, wheeling the velocipede with his other hand. The boy yelled and struggled, but was helpless in Pounder's firm control, which both held him immobile and prevented him from injuring either himself or anyone around him.

'Oh, what an athlete!' exclaimed Cedric, who had jumped to his feet to enjoy the spectacle. 'What a man! I must say Miss Smith is a very fortunate lady.'

Sharrock gave him a hard look but said nothing and waited for Pounder to reach him.

Frances examined the captured velocipede, and there was no doubt in her mind that it was the one that had belonged to the missing messenger, Edward Cowdray. The letters EDW were scratched on the handlebars and dried weeds still stuck to the wheel rims. 'This is the machine that once belonged to Mr Hopper's messenger,' she confirmed. 'The one we were look-ing for earlier.'

'Is it now?' said Sharrock. 'Alright, Mr Pounder, bring the lad in, I'll get the sergeant to ask him some questions while I deal with that other business. I'm making you an assistant constable for the afternoon,' he added. 'Watch him or he'll be off again! Put him in the kitchen.'

Pounder obligingly handed the velocipede to a constable and carried the boy indoors.

'He is just a child,' said Frances to Sharrock. 'I really doubt that he has done anything wrong, but he may well have impor-tant information, and be too frightened to tell a policeman. He will certainly be less afraid if a woman is with him.'

'Oh, I can see where this is going,' groaned Sharrock. 'All right, I'll get Hambling to talk to him and you can make us all some more tea, but no interfering please.'

'I don't interfere, I help,' said Frances indignantly, and marched indoors.

Shorn of his steed, the boy huddled in a corner of the kitchen, looking frightened and pulling his green cap down about his ears. He was clad in a fraying shirt and rough trou-sers that were too long for him, rolled up at the hem to fit, exposing skinny ankles. Grubby feet were thrust into shoes that had broken open at the toe. He glanced about for a means of escape, but since the back-exit door had been locked and Pounder was between him and the entrance, there was little hope of that. Frances could not help thinking how well Tom looked after his 'men', even the humblest of them, and how his business had prospered since he had insisted that the boys were clean, decently clad and well fed. She filled the kettle and prepared a teapot.

'Now then, my lad,' said Hambling, producing a notebook and pencil. His manner was firm and official but not unkind, 'you can start by giving us your name. The sooner you tell us what you know the sooner you can go home.'

The boy wavered for a moment, then he said, 'Joe.'

'I see. Got a second name?'

'Stibson.'

'How old are you Joe?'

'Twelve.'

'And where do you live?'

He mumbled an address in Shepherds Bush.

'And what does your father do?'

'Ain't got no father. Ma takes in washing.'

Hambling made some notes and nodded. 'Now then, you were brought here to be questioned because you were riding a velocipede which we have good reason to believe once belonged to someone else. Can you say how you came to be in possession of it?'

'I was given it, wasn't I?' said Joe, a little too quickly.

'Oh yes, and who gave it to you?'

'I don't know. Just someone who didn't want it no more.'

'Very generous, I must say. Even for an old machine like that. Come on, you must know who you got it from. Speak up!'

There was a long pause, then the boy said, 'Well I didn't exactly get given it. It was more like I found it. It didn't belong to anyone, 'onest! I thought it had been thrown away, like rubbish, so I took it.'

'And how do you know it didn't belong to anyone?'

'It'd just been left lying about.'

'And where was that?'

'Just anywhere. I don't remember.'

'Come on, now Joe,' said Hambling, sternly. 'I think you know very well where you got it. And as it happens, we know too, because it was seen earlier today so you might just as well come out with it.'

Joe hung his head in misery. 'In the old garden by the lodge,' he muttered.

'I see, and you just happened to be looking in there? Why was that? Was it because you knew what you would find?'

Joe sniffled and there was a long pause.

'Come on now, lad, I want an answer!'

The tea wasn't ready yet, but Frances took some milk from the larder and offered the boy a cupful. He looked surprised, then drank it down thirstily. 'I heard someone say there was an old machine in there that didn't belong to anyone, and it was just there for the taking, so I thought I'd go and have a look and there it was. I haven't done anything wrong. It's not stealing if it don't belong to anyone.'

Hambling leant forward and looked very closely at the boy. 'Was it Mr Hopper who told you to get it?'

'No.'

'How long have you worked for Mr Hopper?'

'Don't know no Mr 'opper.'

'I think you do.'

'Don't.'

'You're lying,'

'No I ain't.'

'We know you work for him because you have been seen carrying messages.'

'I never.'

'Was it Mr Hopper who asked you to carry those messages?'

'I tole you, I never.'

'Sergeant,' said Frances, collecting the empty cup. 'Would you permit me to speak to Joe? I do have some experience in questioning children.'

Hambling looked dubious. 'Well you're welcome to try, but I don't think this one would know the truth if it bit him! We can hardly trust a word he says.'

'He is frightened, that's all. And he is far more afraid of Mr Hopper and bullies like Peters than he is of the police.'

Hambling grunted assent, and Joe stared up at her as if hopeful of more milk. His face was unwashed and there was a swollen bruise on one cheek. She could see that he was unused to kindness.

'Joe, did you ever meet a man called Cowdray?'

Joe shook his head.

'Well he used to own the velocipede you were riding. His first name was Edward. That was why the letters EDW were scratched on the side. Mr Cowdray was a messenger, and he worked for Mr Hopper, like you.'

'I never! I don't know no Mr 'opper!'

Frances smiled and spoke gently. 'Of course, we both know that isn't true. In fact, I am sure that you are doing some other business of your own that Mr Hopper knows nothing about. You carry messages for some of the bicycling men, don't you?'

'I'm not sayin' nothin'!' he fired back, but there was no doubt that the remark had hit home.

'You don't need to say anything about that, Joe, because there's nothing wrong in it, you may earn your money honestly in whatever way you please, only Mr Hopper is a hard man, a bad man, and he wouldn't agree. Now we think that Mr Cowdray did some of his own business, too, which meant that he was taking money that Mr Hopper might have thought should rightfully have come to him. If Mr Hopper had found out about that, he would have been very angry, especially as he also suspected that Mr Cowdray had been helping himself to some of his takings. That's why I think that Mr Hopper might have killed Mr Cowdray. I suspect he didn't do it himself, he must have got one of his men to do it. Either way, the body was hidden somewhere, and it still hasn't been found. No one thought to look for the velocipede, but today, with the police searching the area for the escaped convict, there was a danger that it would come to light. So the murderer became worried, and he told you to go and get it. He got you to do his work for him. Of course, you weren't to know the reason for it. Now that means that you must know who killed Mr Cowdray. All you need to do is give us the name of the person who told you where to find the velocipede. Then the murderer will be arrested and you won't have to be afraid of him.'

Joe frowned.

'I just want you to think about it.'

'I ain't done nothing.'

'I know. The police know it too. Joe, if you are afraid of Mr Hopper – and no one can blame you for that – I can help you get away from him. I have a respectable business in which I employ messengers – very good messengers – they work for me in Bayswater: "Tom Smith's Men". You might have heard of them. They are well paid and looked after. Tom himself told me that he thought you were good at what you do. I'm sure we could find you employment where you wouldn't have to worry about people like Mr Hopper or Mr Peters.'

Small tears glistened in the corners of the boy's eyes. 'I don't wanter get killed!'

'Of course not. Now then, why don't I get you another cup of milk and some bread and butter, and ask Tom to come and have a little talk with you and then we'll see what can be done?'

Joe chewed his lip, and then, after a while, he nodded.

CHAPTER THIRTY-FOUR

ergeant Hambling readily agreed to the plan and after supplying Joe with his supper, Frances went to fetch Tom. It took very little time for her to explain what was required and Tom went to talk to Joe.

Sharrock had completed his interview with the Ross–Fielder family, and came to speak to Frances. 'I have to say, that was neither easy nor pleasant,' he said. 'I don't often have to speak to persons of that class in such a way. In the end I had to promise the Ross-Fielders to keep the scandal quiet, and then they told it all. I'm saying this to you because you are not to breathe a word, either. If I hear a whisper of it in public I'll know where it came from.'

'Was I correct?' asked Frances.

'You were. The Reverend in his youth fell into temptation with their parlourmaid, a Miss Coote, who became Robert Coote's mother. I don't think Henry Ross-Fielder can avoid being charged with assisting a prisoner to escape, but it will have to be handled very carefully. As far as the public will be aware the Reverend, on discovering that Coote is a distant cousin of the family, felt guilty about not helping him when he was first approached, and the son foolishly decided to give him some money. I expect him to claim that his purpose was to make his relative's life in prison easier, and he had not a thought in the world that Coote intended to use the money to bribe a guard to help him escape.'

'I don't believe him,' said Frances. 'In fact, Henry Ross-Fielder's avoidance of the area on the day of the escape shows that he knew what was about to happen. He cut the spokes of his own bicycle as an excuse to stay away. A man who will damage his own bicycle is a truly desperate man.'

'Is that so?' said Sharrock, dubiously. 'Well I wouldn't know. The question is whether a court will believe him. Respectable family – they might give him the benefit of the doubt. He's going before the magistrates on Monday.'

'Did he say where he obtained the money?'

'The mother admits giving it to him, the other brother, the clerical one, claims to know nothing. I doubt we'll ever get to the truth of it. Still, that is one less thing to worry about. It only remains to determine who murdered Miss Hicks and locate Mr Cowdray's body and we can all go home and sleep soundly in our beds. Unless, of course, you have all the answers, in which case I would be much obliged if you told me.'

'That, I fear, may take a little longer,' Frances admitted. She looked around. 'Where is Jack Linnett? I hope you haven't arrested him.'

'Not yet, but he is under suspicion and for the moment I intend to keep him where I can find him again. He's in the storeroom, being watched.'

'I'd like to speak to him.'

'No doubt.'

'If, as you say, he isn't under arrest there's no reason why I can't.'

'I'm not sure if someone being under arrest has ever stopped you before. All right. If he wants to sign a confession, let me know.'

A constable was situated outside the storeroom, and after a brief word from Sharrock he allowed Frances in, where Jack had been given a chair, a cup of water and some bread.

He looked up hopefully as the door opened and Frances realised that he thought he was about to be freed, but he was surprised to see her. The constable stepped inside and the door closed.

'Can you leave us alone?' she asked the constable.

'Sorry, Miss, I can't do that.'

Jack stood up and offered Frances the chair. 'Thank you, I just wanted a word. We can both stand. It's nothing to do with police work, it's about bicycles.'

'Do you know how Sir Hugo is? No one will tell me anything.'

'I am pleased to say that he is very much better and Mrs Pirrie is looking after him. Mr Jepson says he will recover fully and can go home soon.'

Jack gave a sigh of relief. 'I was that worried! What happened to him?'

'We think someone gave him a drug so they could steal his work.'

'But who would do a thing like that?' gasped Jack. 'Sir Hugo is a fine and gentle man and has never hurt anyone. He wants to do good in the world!'

'I'm afraid that there are men who will do anything for money.' Frances beckoned him further into the storeroom where the constable could still see them but not overhear their conversation. 'I need to ask you about the new invention that Sir Hugo was working on. I don't mean the additional wheels, the other thing.'

Jack's eyes flickered. 'There isn't another thing.'

'Yes there is. The improved tyres. Something that would make it easier for a bicycle to move on rough terrain. You tested them out didn't you, the two of you, bowling them along like hoops. Mrs Pirrie saw you and thought that you were playing a game, but I think that you were testing the invention to see if it worked. And it must have worked very well. It's an important improvement, with possible military significance, and Sir Hugo meant to share the idea with General Farrow, but he was taking the precaution of securing a patent before he revealed what he had.'

'I don't know about that, Miss,' said Jack, stubbornly. 'He didn't tell me everything.'

'But you worked with him constantly. You were as close as family.'

'I do what I'm asked. He didn't always say why. I don't understand everything he does.'

'You must have seen his notebooks?'

'I don't read, Miss. I never learned. My father, he made sure of that, because he wanted me to stay a pig-man and work for him.' Jack turned his head aside as he said this.

Frances was stern. 'Well that was very remiss of Sir Hugo, who I know thinks highly of you and wants you to advance in life, not to teach you to read when it would be so useful to him if you could.'

Jack frowned, and she saw that she had hit home.

'You are probably the only person who knows what Sir Hugo was working on,' said Frances, 'and it is a big secret, not to be divulged to anyone except the proper authorities. I won't ask you for the details of the invention. I am not an engineer and would not be able to understand them. I just need to know that it existed.'

Jack frowned still harder.

'Tell me, has anyone asked you to give away Sir Hugo's secrets? Have you been offered any inducements to tell? Did you tell anyone that he was supposed to be going to the patent office this morning? I know about that because he was heard saying so to General Farrow.'

'No!' said Jack, angrily. 'I wouldn't tell on Sir Hugo, not for anything. Sir Hugo has been better than the best of fathers to me.'

'So, as far as you know the fact that he was going to the patent office was only known to him, and yourself, and General Farrow.'

'I don't know anything about General Farrow. He never said anything to me.'

'But someone did, didn't they? Who asked you? Not General Farrow, then. His son?' Frances recalled the snapped words between the General and his son, the orders to deal with correspondence and arrange a meeting. Had George Farrow, in return for the allowance from his father, been undertaking secretarial duties, and had access to the General's papers?

Jack Linnett hung his head. 'He said he only wanted to protect Sir Hugo. He knew he was working on something important because Sir Hugo had been to see his father, and he said there might be people wanting to steal it. He said I could help by telling him what I knew, and there were people very high up who would be grateful to me, and would help to keep Sir Hugo safe, and I could have money, more money than I had ever seen in my life, and if I had money then Miss Hicks would like me.' His lips trembled. 'I said I thought *he* was going to marry Miss Hicks.'

'Really? Is that what she told you?'

'Not in so many words, but I saw the two of them talking together and they seemed very friendly, and she told her mother she was going to marry someone whose father was a big man in the world.'

'What did Mr Farrow have to say about that?'

'Oh, he said she was a nice enough girl but he didn't want to marry her and he would be grateful if I did, and made her happy.'

'Did you tell him what he wanted to know?'

'I've told you, I would never tell on Sir Hugo. I said I didn't know anything,' he exclaimed angrily, wiping a grey hand across his face and leaving a long smear. 'It was all that talk of money. That was why I knew it wasn't right. I wanted Miss Hicks to like me, not go with me for what money I had. But he didn't understand that. He thought people could be bought. And it was cruel of him to lead her on like that, and make her think he would marry her and then say he could pass her on to me as he didn't want her. So I was never going to do what he asked. A man like that! I don't care about his grand family or his money! There's any number of humble folk better than him!'

'Sir Hugo had some red notebooks, didn't he, with details of his work? What happened to those?'

'I don't know. He kept them in the workshop. But there was nothing in them, only what materials he had, and a few ideas he made drawings of.'

'And the plans for the tyres?'

'There aren't any plans.'

'But he must have had some to apply for a patent.'

'Well then, the patent office has got them.'

'But he never went to the patent office. He was drugged before he could go.'

'Yes he did, he went a few weeks ago.'

'Oh! So he has already applied for a patent?'

'He must have done. Today was just for a meeting to talk about it.'

No wonder, Frances thought, that whoever wanted the plans had drugged Sir Hugo rather than killing him. There were some secrets that only he held.

'You said that Mr Farrow mentioned important people who would be grateful to you for giving away Sir Hugo's secrets. Did he say who they were?'

'No. Just that there were men higher up than him who would pay good money to know things.'

So, thought Frances, George Farrow was only a small link in the chain, the link that passed on information from the General to someone willing to pay for it.

'I don't suppose you know where Mr Farrow is now?' she asked.

'No, although I saw the General taking his daughter home.'

'And Mr Farrow wasn't with them?'

'No.'

'Thank you, Jack. You have been a good friend to Sir Hugo and I know he will appreciate it.'

Frances left the pavilion and sought out Cedric and Mr Grove to tell them of the possible involvement of George Farrow in the attack on Sir Hugo. The younger Farrow had been helping his fellow club members to clear the field, but when she looked about for him, he was no longer to be seen.

CHAPTER THIRTY-FIVE

'Where is George Farrow?' asked Frances.

'All the family have been given permission to depart,' said Grove. 'At least, I have not seen any of them for a while.' He glanced over at the entrance to the cricket ground where two constables, having discovered a ball, were amusing themselves with an impromptu game of football. 'I'll ask the constables if they have seen him. If they haven't he might still have slipped away during some of the distractions that have occurred. But I'll send Ratty with a message to the right quarters to ensure that young Mr Farrow will find himself being interviewed very soon.'

'I think it might have been Farrow who killed Miss Hicks,' said Frances. 'She was hoping to marry him, and he was trying to pass her on to Jack. If she was spending time with him she might have noticed something that suggested he was engaged in some underhand activity. She might not have known what it was, but she would have been aware it was something he didn't want revealed. And she knew from local gossip that a wife can't give evidence against her husband in a court of law. That was the bargain she wanted to make. Marriage to ensure her silence.'

'I feel you may be right. Poor young woman. If she had seen the true value of Jack Linnett she would be alive now.'

At that moment, to their surprise, Jack emerged from the pavilion, looking a little dazed. They hurried over to him. 'The Inspector says I'm free to go,' he said. 'There was a gentleman saw me watching the professionals' race and he told the Inspector I didn't move from the spot. So they know I couldn't have done it, now.' He was relieved but it was without any kind of pleasure at the situation.

'You should go home and rest,' said Cedric.

He shook his head. 'I've things to do first. To be truthful I ... I want to wait here awhile. I know it's cowardly, but I'm not sure I can face Mr and Mrs Hicks. I know I didn't do anything wrong but there's folks in East Acton will look at me in a strange way, as if they think that because of what my father did I am the same. And now with this, even if they catch the man and hang him, there'll still be people saying, "Oh Jack Linnett's father was a murderer, and the apple doesn't fall far from the tree. Maybe he did it after all."'

'There was no real evidence against your father,' said Frances. 'And although we know what he thought of bicyclists that's no reason to murder someone. He had no quarrel with Morton Vance.'

Jack looked surprised. 'Is that really what you think, Miss?'

'Yes, I do. I have read the inquest and the committal proceedings and the trial report.'

He gave an awkward shuffle on his twisted foot. 'Maybe they don't tell all the story.'

'Oh? Is there more?'

'There might be. These trials, when people stand up and are asked questions. Sometimes I think they aren't asked the right questions. And even if they are, then they don't tell all the truth. Not lying exactly, but just leaving things out and sometimes the things they don't say are as important as what they do.'

'Tell me, Jack, did your father have a quarrel with Morton Vance? Did anyone else? Was there someone Vance was afraid of?'

He shook his head. 'It wasn't like that. I know my father did and said some bad things after the accident to my leg. He always hated Mr Babbit for it, so much so that Mr Babbit always rode somewhere else after that. He didn't dare come near father. Then father went before the magistrates and was fined for putting things in the road and hitting out at the bicycling men, and after that, for a bit, all he used to do was grumble. And I thought we might have some peace at last. But then —'

Frances waited.

'If I tell you, you'll think it's nothing.'

'Tell me,' she said.

Jack looked about him to see if anyone else was in earshot, but they were far from being overheard.

'It was a few days before my father killed Mr Vance,' he said. 'We had taken the cart out, going down to the Vale, and one of the bicyclists went past us – I don't know which one – and the horse got all jittery and shied. No harm done in the end, but it was a bad moment, and it was a lot like the accident – the one where my leg was hurt. All of a sudden it felt like it had happened only the other day, not the year before. And father got real angry and some hard words were said and the bicyclist he made a sign with his hand, which wasn't called for. And father said that they were a menace to hardworking folk, and he swore by all that was holy and one or two things that weren't, which I won't repeat, that if he ever got the chance, he would do for one of them.'

'Did you believe him?' asked Frances.

'I thought it was just said in the heat of the moment. I didn't think he'd do it, but – he did. That day, the day of the murder, he'd taken the cart out, and he came back in, and told me that he'd just killed a bicyclist, stove his head in. Said it served him right, and he'd been wanting to do it for a long time, and, now he'd done it, he felt better for it. There was blood splashed all over his hands, and he washed it off at the pump. I wanted to go out to the lane and see for myself, see if the man could be saved, but father told me I mustn't have anything to do with it. Then he said that when he was arrested I had to be careful what I said. I mustn't say anything about him saying he wanted to kill a bicyclist. He was going to tell the police it was all done out of hot temper, and he didn't remember it. That way he might not get hanged. He promised me that if I did what he asked, then he'd let me go and get apprenticed to Mr Hicks as I'd been wanting to. So that was what happened, and I never said anything in court about that day, or what he'd threatened to do. Only it made no difference, and he was found guilty and hanged in any case.' He bit his lip. 'Will I get into trouble, now?'

'I don't know,' said Frances. 'But I am not about to report you for what you said or failed to say in court. I must admit that I had been wondering if your father was innocent of the crime, and wrongly executed, but from what you tell me now, it is clear that he was guilty and properly convicted. There has been no injustice done.'

Jack looked relieved. 'I weren't the only one who lied in court, anyhow.'

'Oh? Another witness lied?'

'Yes. There was a bicyclist there in the lane that day – the man who came after Mr Vance. He saw everything. Only at father's trial he said that he was back at the lodge at the time of the murder, and that wasn't true. Father said to me straight off that he was done for, as he'd been seen killing Mr Vance, and he thought he'd be arrested at once, but it took longer than he thought, and then our lawman told us that we had a chance as no one had seen the murder, but that was wrong. Then we thought maybe the man who saw it didn't want to let on that he was there. Anyhow he never told the truth of it.'

Frances was astonished. 'Jack – let me understand this. You say that there was another bicyclist who came on the scene just after Mr Vance had his accident, and this man actually saw your father commit the murder – but he denied ever having been there?'

'That's right. Father knew he'd have to pay the price, but he didn't care. He might have run off, but he had nowhere to run to, and he said he'd stay and whatever happened next would happen. That was father for you.'

'Did he say who the man was? The one who saw the murder?'

'Yes, he knew him all right. It was that champion racing man, Mr Iliffe. Father was standing over Mr Vance after he hit him, and then he looked up and saw the man stopped there with his machine, staring at what he had just seen. Father didn't say anything. Mr Iliffe didn't say anything. They both just looked at each other, and then Father threw the stave onto the ground and walked off.'

Frances was thoughtful. 'I suppose it might be understandable that Mr Iliffe wouldn't have confessed to being there. There was always the suggestion that Mr Vance was racing someone, another member of the BBC, which I had thought improbable, as Mr Vance himself had warned the other members of the dangers. If Iliffe and Vance had been going down the lane too fast, racing each other, then it was extremely foolish and negligent of them both. If Mr Iliffe had suggested the race then he would have felt guilty at getting his friend into danger. After all, as a professional bicyclist he does have a reputation to protect.'

'They weren't racing,' said Jack.

'Oh? How do you know?'

'Father said that when he was turning the cart into the farmyard he heard the sound of a bicycle coming around the corner, and looked up, and he saw Mr Vance riding towards him, and even before he saw the cart in the road and knew he would crash into it, the man was scared. He looked like all the creatures of – you know – the bad place – all them demons were after him.'

'Could it have been Mr Iliffe who was after him?' asked Frances. 'Was there no one else on the road?'

'Not that father saw.'

'If it was Iliffe he would have heard the collision before he saw it, and that would have given him enough warning of the danger to enable him to slow down so he didn't suffer the same fate. He's a strong rider, so it's possible. But why was he chasing after Mr Vance? Why was Vance afraid?'

'That I don't know,' said Jack, shaking his head.

'Do you know when Mr Ross-Fielder arrived? I know he found the body.'

'Father was in the farmyard when he saw another man come riding up from the south, so I suppose that must have been him.'

'And how long after the murder did that happen?'

Jack shrugged. 'Not long. Just a few minutes.'

Frances was puzzled. According to the trial evidence, Iliffe had been at the lodge looking after the bicycles in the coach house at the time of Vance's murder. And there was a witness to this, since Mrs Pirrie had sent the butler, Waterfield, out to him with tea and sandwiches. But according to Sam Linnett, who was not available to be questioned, at that very time Iliffe had been on Old Oak Common Lane, chasing after Morton Vance. Only minutes after the murder, Ross-Fielder had ridden up, found the body and headed back to the lodge to give the alarm, arriving at half past five, and had found Iliffe in the coach house drinking tea. How Frances would have liked to question Ross-Fielder and Waterfield about the times they had seen Iliffe, but Ross-Fielder was in police custody for his part in helping the convict Coote to escape, and Waterfield was not there to be questioned.

Although she did not carry the notes she had made about the timing of the activity on the day of Morton Vance's death, she had read them through so often that she could recall the salient times. The lady who lived in a cottage at the top of the lane and who had seen Morton Vance pass her house had been sure of her time because she had looked at her clock and had been adamant in court that it was correct. Ross-Fielder had been sure of the time he arrived in East Acton after discovering the body because he had heard the chiming of the church clock. Between Morton Vance passing the cottage and Ross-Fielder finding the body was about twenty minutes. From Vance passing the cottage to reaching Sam Linnett's pig farm was a matter of only about five minutes, but something had happened on the way, something that he had perhaps seen or heard which had transformed him from a cheerful man out on a pleasant ride to someone terrified of being pursued. He might have stopped briefly and then ridden away rapidly from what he perceived as a danger. And maybe, thought Frances, that explained why he had not turned back to East Acton. He must have thought that the danger he wanted to avoid was connected with the club and he might not find safety there. He was afraid, vulnerable, and he needed to get somewhere very fast where he would not be so isolated. Somewhere like busy, bustling Hammersmith, where he would be sure to find a constable.

But what could Vance possibly have seen? Was it feasible that he had seen Iliffe in his uniform, and his fellow club man had been doing something that had terrified and appalled him? He had raced off to report it and Iliffe had pursued him, only to come upon the scene of an accident, and witness Vance's murder at the hands of Sam Linnett. Iliffe had then returned to East Acton. Whatever he had been doing it was not something he wanted revealed. Far better that it should be assumed he was in the coach house all the time. It was Sam Linnett's insistence that his son say nothing about the day of Vance's murder that had prevented Iliffe's exposure in court, although any jury given the choice of believing a pig-man on trial for murder or a champion bicyclist would have had no difficulty in deciding whose story to accept. With what Frances now knew about Iliffe and Babbit, she thought it was possible that Vance had seen the two of them together, a secret meeting perhaps, something that neither of them would have wanted revealed, evidence of their criminal collaboration, perhaps even of a close friendship that went beyond the bounds of propriety. Both men made a great public show of being enamoured of Miss Jepson, but perhaps neither of them was. It was doubtful that either would be prepared to admit anything without proof.

To test this possibility, Frances returned to the story told to her by Mrs Pirrie. The men coming back from the run at five o'clock, Toop departing to see his mother, the tea being made and served at about ten past five, Waterfield taking some to Iliffe in the coach house, and having a conversation with him. That placed Iliffe in the coach house between about ten and fifteen minutes past five. The murder had most probably happened during or very close to that time. Ross-Fielder had found Vance's body at about twenty-five past. There was just not enough time for Iliffe to have ridden down the lane, witness the murder and travel back to the coach house. She was reminded of what Mrs Pirrie had said, that Iliffe had told her he would come indoors for tea later on, but then she had thought to send some out to him. This meant that Iliffe was not expecting Waterfield to bring him tea. If Iliffe's offer to look after the coach house had been a ruse to slip away for a secret meeting with Babbit, he would not have been there when Waterfield brought him tea, but he was.

CHAPTER THIRTY-SIX

rances wished she had her notes with her, or better still, her copies of the *Bayswater Chronicle*, the *Times* and the *Acton and Chiswick Gazette*, with reports of the inquest and court proceedings. Something was not quite right, but she would need to look at the details again. A tiny fact was buried deep inside her mind, and she was sure it was important, but she just couldn't recall what it was.

Inspector Sharrock, with a weary and jaded look, emerged from the pavilion and stood on the veranda. There were few people about now, and the dais had been dismantled and taken away, but he was still clutching the speaking trumpet, which he placed to his mouth. 'Ladies and gentlemen,' he announced. 'The police have now spoken to all those present at today's unfortunate events and I can now advise you that we will no longer be requiring anyone present to remain.' He handed the trumpet to Mr Toop, who had been waiting anxiously to hear that the club's remaining property could at least be cleared from the field. A small stream of visitors and the last few traders headed for the gate.

As Sharrock returned to the pavilion, beckoning his constables for a final word, an elderly gentleman wandered distractedly onto the field and stood looking about him, appearing to be very upset. A constable went to speak to him, and after a few moments, hurried to fetch Sergeant Hambling.

'Is that Mr Waterfield?' asked Frances.

'It is,' said Jack. 'Fancy coming back after a nice visit to find all this. It'll be a terrible shock.' He shook his head. 'At least Sir Hugo is better. I do hope they'll let him go home now.'

Sergeant Hambling strode across the field, exchanged a few words with the new arrival, then conducted Mr Waterfield to the pavilion.

'I'll go and clean the rest of the bicycles and then I can get them back to the lodge,' said Jack.

'You'll need help with the sociable,' said Frances. 'I'd like to try it myself. But we'll need another person, I expect.'

'It's not as hard as it looks as long as there's one strong rider. There's sisters go out on it, so it can be managed by two ladies as well as a lady and a gent. I've seen a gent and his son ride one, and the boy no more than eight years old, if that, and his feet could hardly reach down.'

'Well, if you need me to be a second for you, let me know.'

'I will Miss. Thank you. I'll get on, now.' He looked drained, with barely the energy to do his work.

'Is there anything you need? Have you had enough to eat and drink? I can fetch you something. Tea?'

'That's very kind, but I have a flask of water and that will be enough.' He trudged away.

Frances sighed. Tea was usually the answer to so many things. It refreshed and enlivened her and helped her to think. Sometimes the mere act of making a pot of tea, the sequence of those familiar actions, allowed her to meditate on the things that troubled her. She thought she could do with some tea now, but the last pot she had made would be cold by now and not palatable. She decided to return to the pavilion and see if she could make herself useful.

Mayberry was at the door, and knew better than to argue about letting her in. She found Sergeant Hambling and Inspector Sharrock in the corridor outside the tearoom. Through the partly open door, Frances saw Mr Waterfield sitting at a table looking frightened and confused.

'He's Mr Waterfield, Sir Hugo's gentleman,' Hambling was explaining. 'He was away visiting his sister and has just returned. I thought I'd better sit him down as he looked very unsteady on his legs. He went back to the lodge just now and found no one there, and then he came here.'

'I'll have a word,' said Sharrock. 'Once Sir Hugo is stronger on his feet we'll hand him over to Waterfield and Mrs Pirrie.' Sharrock noticed Frances. 'Kitchen is that way,' he said, pointedly.

'Inspector, I have just been speaking to Jack Linnett, and he has told me that there was a witness to his father's murder of Morton Vance. At the time the terrible shock of the event drove it from his mind, and it has only just now come back to him.'

'Has it now?' said Sharrock sarcastically. 'Well I can't say I'm surprised. That's exactly the sort of thing that happens all the time. Funny thing, memory. Does Mr Linnett say he saw it all?'

'No, he didn't see the murder, but someone else did.'

'So you're not claiming we hanged an innocent man? Well I'm very relieved about that. You had me quite worried there. It wasn't Mr Waterfield was it? He doesn't look like a bicycling man to me.'

'Jack Linnett says his father told him it was Mr Iliffe.'

Sharrock looked surprised.

'I know what you are about to say, Inspector. According to the evidence he gave at the inquest, and confirmed by Mrs Pirrie, Mr Iliffe was in the coach house at the lodge at the time of the murder. Mr Waterfield also confirms it, as he took a cup of tea to him. But Jack says his father told him that Mr Iliffe rode up and saw him commit the murder.'

'Mr Iliffe could not have been in two places at once.'

'Exactly.'

Sharrock shrugged. 'Well someone's made a mistake, that's all. And if Mr Iliffe really did see the murder, why didn't he say so?'

'Yes, why indeed?'

'I suppose I could ask him, but it was a year ago and our only witness is a dead man. In the meantime, I suggest you make a fresh pot of tea, as I think Mr Waterfield is currently enjoying the last of mine.'

Frances nodded, and then it came to her. 'Tea! Of course! Why didn't I see that before?'

'Dare I say it, because you were too busy looking into police business?'

'Inspector, if you would allow me to speak to Mr Waterfield, I might be able to find an answer to how Mr Iliffe was able to be in two places at once.'

Sharrock groaned. 'I suppose there's no putting you off, is there. Alright. Let me have a word with him first and then I'll ask him if he is happy for you to come in.'

Some minutes later Frances was called into the tearoom, where Mr Waterfield was being comforted by Mrs Pirrie. A wirily thin, slightly bent individual, his face was heavily lined and pouched under the eyes, but his hair, which was pure white, was perfectly cut and combed, and his cravat was fresh and neat. A fresh pot of tea was on the table in front of him and he was sipping at a cup, which he lifted to his lips with shaky hands.

'This is Miss Williamson, Mr Garton's cousin,' explained Mrs Pirrie. 'She was so much help in the kitchen just earlier. Makes the nicest cup of tea.'

'Oh, well, thank you, Miss,' said Mr Waterfield. 'Very obliged, I am sure.'

'I ought to say,' said Sharrock, reluctantly, 'that it is down to this lady that Sir Hugo is still alive. It's a long story and I'm sure you'll hear all of it in due course. But in the meantime, she would like to ask you some questions.'

Mrs Pirrie stared at Frances and gasped. 'You didn't tell me that!'

'Oh, it was nothing, really,' said Frances, modestly.

Waterfield put his cup down. 'Of course, we are so grateful that Sir Hugo is safe that it is really the least I can do.'

Frances sat down beside him. 'Mr Waterfield, I would like you to cast your mind back to that unfortunate day when Mr Morton Vance was killed.'

Waterfield sighed. 'That was a terrible thing, I shall never forget it.'

'Mrs Pirrie made tea for the young men when they returned from their ride and you took a cup out to Mr Iliffe, who was in the coach house.'

Waterfield nodded. 'Yes, I did.'

'Can you tell me what time that was?'

He frowned. 'Well, one tends not to look at one's watch at such an event.'

'No of course not, but was it at the same time that Mrs Pirrie was serving tea to the other members of the club?'

'Well it would have been,' said Mrs Pirrie, 'because all the tea was made at the same time, and I poured out a cup for Mr Iliffe.'

Waterfield nodded slowly. 'Yes. I do remember, now. Mrs Pirrie made the tea and took a tray with the pot and cups to the young men, and asked me to take an extra cup to Mr Iliffe.'

'And that would have been about ten minutes after five?'

'That's about right,' said Mrs Pirrie.

'I suppose it was,' said Waterfield.

'Only when Mr Ross-Fielder arrived at the coach house at half past five, he mentioned that he found Mr Iliffe there drinking his tea.'

Waterfield frowned.

'Mr Ross-Fielder was very certain of the time because he heard the church clock chiming the half hour. And that's strange because it suggests that Mr Iliffe, who was probably very thirsty after his ride, waited in the coach house for twenty minutes before he drank his tea.'

Waterfield pondered this for a moment. 'I did take the cup out to him as soon as the tea was poured. But – he wasn't there at first.'

'He wasn't there?' exclaimed Sharrock.

'No. The coach house was locked. It is always locked when there is no one in attendance. The gentlemen are very careful about that. I assumed, of course, quite naturally under the circumstances, that Mr Iliffe was absent in order to – well,' he said primly, 'for a personal purpose.'

'You didn't mention this at the inquest,' said Frances.

'It hardly seemed important. Mr Iliffe is not suspected of any wrongdoing.'

'Did you return to the coach house?' asked Frances.

'Of course. I had some duties to perform at the lodge, and then I thought I would go out again. It was about five minutes later, I think, but he was still not there. So eventually I made up some fresh tea, as the first cup was not really fit for drinking, and I took it to him and this time he was there.'

'When was this?'

'Just shortly before the half hour.'

'Mr Ross-Fielder had not yet arrived to give the alarm?'

'No, but that was very soon after.'

'I suppose you didn't ask Mr Iliffe where he had been?'

'Oh, my word, I wouldn't presume to do so, no.'

'How did he seem when you saw him?'

'As any gentlemen is after a long ride on a bicycle.'

'He looked warm?'

'Yes.'

'What was he doing when you arrived? Resting?'

Waterfield frowned again. 'No. He had a pan of water and was cleaning one of the rain capes.'

'A rain cape? But wasn't it a hot sunny day?'

'It was. I asked if I could help him but he said it wasn't necessary, it had just got some dirt on it.'

'Did you ask him to explain himself?'

'No – I would never dream of doing such a thing.'

'Is there anything else you can tell me?'

'I don't think so, Miss.'

Sharrock scratched his head. 'So that means?'

'It means,' said Frances, 'that instead of Mr Iliffe having almost no time to ride to the site of the murder and return he had twenty minutes or more.' She then recalled a previous mention of a cape, one worn on a hot sunny day. 'Mrs Pirrie? I remember you telling me that on the day of the tragedy you had seen a couple in a sociable on the carriage drive in front of the lodge.'

'Yes, that's right, I did.'

'A gentleman, not in the bicycle club uniform, and a lady wearing a cape?'

'Yes.'

'Was it a rain cape?'

Mrs Pirrie thought about it. 'Yes, it was, because I remember thinking it a bit strange as we weren't expecting any rain, but then I thought maybe the lady was being extra careful. Some ladies are.'

Frances rubbed her eyes. 'Oh dear!'

'What is it?' asked Sharrock.

'I think – I think I know. But I'm not sure I can prove it.'

'Prove what?'

'I think I know why Morton Vance was riding so fast down Old Oak Common Lane.'

There was a knock at the door and Tom peeped in. 'It's Joe,' he said ''e's talking. 'E says he'll only tell the police what he knows if 'e's kept safe, and also if the nice lady is there.' He grinned at Frances.

CHAPTER THIRTY-SEVEN

Joe's story, which he told very nervously, and with constant glances at Frances for reassurance, fitted with what she had already suspected. In addition to his work for Mr Hopper he had also taken messages between Iliffe and Babbit. Both of those gentlemen had communicated with Hopper. They had told him that they were pretending to be enemies for a joke, when they were really friends. It had to be kept a secret, and there would be a good reward for him if he did. Joe had also taken messages from the two bicyclists to other gentlemen who he knew liked to make private wagers, and he was paid well to be quick and discreet. One of the other boys who worked for Hopper had noticed who he was meeting, and said that a man called Cowdray used to carry messages for Iliffe and Babbit, but then he had run off with some of Mr Hopper's money. Joe claimed not to know anything about the content of the messages he carried and Sharrock smiled, patted him on the shoulder and said that he entirely believed him on that point.

Joe revealed that shortly before the professionals' race that afternoon, Mr Babbit had come up to him and asked if he would like to have a velocipede and it wouldn't cost a penny. It had been abandoned by someone who didn't want it any more. All he had to do was go and get it. The main condition for this bounty was that he had to keep quiet about how and where he had got it. Joe had naturally agreed with some enthusiasm, and Babbit told him about the overgrown garden. It had been hard work to move the stiff heavy door, but Joe had only needed to force it open a very little way to slip in and find his prize.

'I'll look after him,' said Tom, when Joe had told his story.

'Are you saying, Miss Doughty,' said Sharrock, once the two boys had left, 'that Mr Babbit killed Cowdray?'

'Not necessarily, but he was involved in disposing of the body. Logically I think the murderer must have been Mr Iliffe. Babbit, given his supposed enmity with Iliffe, would not normally have risked being seen around Springfield Lodge. Did Cowdray ask for a meeting with Iliffe? Perhaps Cowdray simply followed Iliffe back to the lodge on his velocipede and demanded to speak to him. If so, they might well have gone into the garden to talk because it was private and they knew they wouldn't be disturbed or seen by anyone as long as they stayed close to the wall. Mr Hopper told us about the kind of man Cowdray was. He knew that Iliffe and Babbit were making substantial winnings from their subterfuge, and must have been trying to blackmail them, threatening to reveal the betting fraud unless he received a share of the profits. I don't know how Cowdray died – either it was a fight or deliberate murder – but I think he must have been killed in that garden. There's a broken spade that could have been the murder weapon. Iliffe knew that no one ever went in there, so he had no qualms about leaving the velocipede behind. I suspect that neither he nor Babbit were aware that Cowdray had scratched some letters on the handlebars to mark it out as his; but in the heat of summer, he couldn't risk leaving the body there too long. Even on the other side of the wall, its presence would have been noticed soon.'

'So he got rid of it? How? Where?'

'I think he wrapped it in a rain cape and then got a message to his friend Babbit to come and help him dispose of it. They must have arranged to meet in secret the next day after the club ride was over and the other members, as well as Sir Hugo, Mrs Pirrie and Mr Waterfield, were all in the lodge. It was the only time they felt safe from being seen. They are both large men, and Cowdray, according to Hopper, was very slight, so it wouldn't have taken long. The body must have been put on one seat of the sociable and Babbit rode out with it, with Iliffe following on his bicycle. It is quite possible for a strong man to manage a sociable by himself if the other seat is not too laden. With two of them working together disposing of the body would only take a few minutes. They went north up the lane, and hid the body.'

'Of course it was a risk and it didn't quite come off. They weren't to anticipate that Mr Waterfield would come out to the coach house twice and see that Iliffe wasn't there but fortunately for Iliffe he didn't think anything of it or even mention it. Then when they were on Old Oak Common Lane, Morton Vance came riding past and saw two men, one of whom, even if he didn't immediately recognise him, was clearly in the uniform of the Bayswater Bicycle Club, and disposing of a corpse. He must have been appalled – terrified.'

'But no body has been found,' said Sharrock. 'Where is it – in a ditch? It can't be. It would have been found by now, and they didn't have time to bury it. The pig farm near Wormwood Scrubs? No one saw a sociable go up that far.'

'They didn't need to go so far. Barely two minutes' ride from Springfield Lodge is the Stamford Brook, the old river covered over and incorporated into the Metropolitan drainage system. It forms the parish boundary and runs down Old Oak Common Lane. All the riders knew about it because they had to take care when riding beside it. They must have slipped the body into the waterway through one of the access points, removing the rain cape first. Morton Vance must have seen the body being lowered into the drain. When he realised what was happening he rode off to report what he had seen. Iliffe raced after him and witnessed him being killed by Sam Linnett. But, of course, he dared not say anything about it, as he wasn't supposed to be there. In the meantime, Babbit returned the sociable to the coach house and Iliffe rode back. He was cleaning the rain cape when Waterfield arrived with his tea.'

Sharrock puffed out his cheeks. 'Well, with the evidence of the betting fraud from young Joe, I've good reason to take them both into custody. And then we'll see which one of them will give evidence against the other in return for being charged only as an accessory to murder.'

CHAPTER THIRTY-EIGHT

Out on the field, Jack was still helping Toop with the club bicycles, when Mr Grove entered the pavilion with a look of concern. 'Ratty delivered my message and agents were sent to Farrow's home to take him in for questioning, but I have just learned that he is not there and no one knows where he is. His father and sister are at home but they left the field without him, and when they departed he was still here. Has anyone seen him?'

'I have not seen him for some while,' said Frances.

'What is your interest in George Farrow?' asked Sharrock. 'I interviewed him this afternoon and there was no reason to detain him.'

'I have been told that he had been flirting with Miss Hicks,' said Frances.

'I don't think there's a man in the county who hasn't flirted with Miss Hicks,' said Sharrock. 'I'll ask the constables if he's been seen leaving the field.'

'Toop might know,' said Cedric.

'Let's see if his bicycle is still here,' said Grove.

They went to the club enclosure where Mr Toop, who seemed to trust no one with his prized machine, was polishing it carefully. He was hard at work, looking a little flustered, and the flower in his buttonhole was gone, leaving only a damp smear where it had once been.

'Mr Toop,' said Sharrock, 'have you seen Mr George Farrow about?'

'Not for about fifteen or twenty minutes, no.'

'Linnett, is his bicycle here?'

Jack obligingly searched, and nodded. 'Yes, it is. Mr Farrow is one of those gents who keeps his at home, so he must still be about, somewhere.'

'He has been assisting by taking the club machines back to the coach house,' said Toop.

'Is it open?' asked Frances. 'Is anyone in charge of it?'

'It should be kept locked unless there is a man there,' said Toop. 'Those members who have been allowed to leave the field and wanted to put their machines away borrowed the keys from me, and of course I trust them to leave everything secure and bring the keys back.'

'You haven't been there yourself?' asked Sharrock.

'Oh yes, Inspector, I've been back and forth quite a number of times. Your constables will tell you that. So much to do, and with Jack so long away being questioned I had more to do myself.'

'Did you lend the keys to Mr Farrow?'

'I did, but he hasn't returned them.' Toop paused and looked a little uncomfortable. 'To be truthful, Inspector, I am somewhat concerned about Farrow. I could see that he was a very troubled man today, even before that horrid incident with his poor sister, and Mr Goring's dreadful behaviour. In fact, he confided in me that he had done something very terrible that was weighing on his conscience.'

Sharrock folded his arms and stared at Toop. 'Now then, Mr Toop, there's no time for delicacy here. If there's something you know, just out with it.'

'I wish I could, but he said no more than that. I advised him that whatever it might be, he would be eased in his mind if he could only confess it. He said that he would consider it. In fact, when he took one of the club bicycles away he told me he would go riding for a short while so as to allow himself to think clearly.'

'Have you seen him since then, or looked in the coach house?' asked Sharrock.

'No, neither. He is probably still out on his ride. He will have to come back here in any case to collect his own machine. I hope he returns soon, as I was just about to take mine back.' Toop gave his elaborate steed an affectionate pat.

'I'll ask about in case anyone has seen him,' said Grove.

'I'll get the men to make a search,' said Sharrock, and bustled away with Mayberry by his side.

'Mr Toop,' asked Frances, 'if you are about to return your own bicycle, might I go with you to the coach house? I'd like to take a look at the lodge, in any case. And who knows, we might find Mr Farrow there, or see him on his way back?'

'Certainly. Jack, could you take one of the club machines?' They marched off towards the gates of the field, Toop and Jack both wheeling bicycles, and Frances striding along with them.

They saw no other riders as they walked the short way down East Acton Lane and passed through the gates of Springfield Lodge. No one was about, and Toop carefully leaned his bicycle against the wall of the coach house, but on approaching the doors he gave a sudden gasp. 'Oh! It's unlocked! Perhaps Farrow is here after all. Or —' he gave a little groan. 'I hope he has not been careless and left it unattended! Who knows, we might have had thieves! They could still be inside! Oh dear!' He turned to face Frances. 'Stand well back, Miss, you must allow me to deal with this. You too, Jack, you must take care of the lady if there is any danger.' Slowly and cautiously, Toop pushed the door open and peered inside. 'Farrow?' he called. 'Are you there?' Moments later he gave a sudden cry, a sound halfway between a sob and a squeal, almost like an animal in pain. 'Oh no! Oh how horrible!'

'What is it?' Frances demanded, running forward, but Toop had slammed the door shut and turned around with a stricken look.

'No! I beg of you! Don't look! This is not for the eyes of a lady. Oh this is too nasty for words! Stay there, both of you, and let me go in. If I call for help, Jack you can come in but on no account must the lady enter.' Before either of the others could say a word, Toop took a deep breath, pulled the doors open just enough to admit him, and slipped into the coach house.

Jack nodded, and leaned his bicycle against the wall, then stood ready to defend Frances should the need arise. 'What do you think, Miss?' he said.

'I don't know,' she replied. 'But if he has not returned in a few minutes you are to send for the police.'

There was a brief interval of quiet, in which they assumed that Toop was looking about the place, his eyes becoming accustomed to the change in light. Then there were more sounds from Toop, a gasp of effort followed by a convulsive gulp. Frances darted forward impatiently, determined to enter the coach house, but Jack took care to stand in her way, holding his arms out wide. 'Oh, Miss, please don't! Whatever's in there, it's not for a lady! Let me take you back to the field and we'll get the police.'

Frances could see that running into possible danger was not the wisest thing either of them could do, and had just decided to go and get help when Mr Toop emerged from the coach house. He was unhurt but he looked dreadfully shaken, and leaned against the doorjamb for support. 'Jack – go at once – get a doctor – a policeman, anyone!'

'What is it?' asked Frances.

Toop bent over, breathing hard, and for a moment she thought he was going to be violently ill. 'It's Farrow. George Farrow. He's gone and hanged himself.'

'Is he still hanging?' asked Frances.

'No, no, I untied the rope and brought him down, I thought – I hoped there might be a chance of saving him, but I'm sorry – the poor fellow is quite dead!'

'I know a little of medical matters,' said Frances. 'Jack, you go and fetch Inspector Sharrock, and Mr Jepson if he is still available, and I'll see what I can do here.' Jack nodded, and limped away as fast as he was able.

'Do you really think —?' asked Toop, but Frances ignored him, flung the doors open wide to admit as much light as possible and walked in. All was very much as it had been before. A few of the bicycles had been returned by club members, and she made a quick note of how many there were and where placed. In the middle of the floor lay George Farrow, the slackness of his crumpled body telling its own story. There was a noose about his neck, and a long tail of rope coiled by his side. An overturned chair lay beside him. Frances approached and felt for a pulse, looking carefully to see if there was any movement of the chest, but although the body was still warm it was clear that life was extinct. His neck was not distorted, he had not broken it as a man would have done if hanged from a long drop. Death had taken longer, by strangulation. She decided to touch nothing more, and retraced her steps. Outside, Toop was groaning.

'Mr Toop, I know this is upsetting, but can you describe how you found him? You say he was hanging.'

'Yes. He had put the rope over the beam, and then tied the end to one of the hooks in the wall. He must have stepped off the chair. Oh!' he wailed. 'That was my chair, the one I use when I am at my desk. I don't think I shall ever sit on it again.'

At that moment, Inspector Sharrock and Constable Mayberry arrived at a run with Jack limping behind them. Toop waved a hand weakly in the rough direction of the coach house and they hurried into the building.

'I hope they don't ask me to go in. I don't think I can look at it again,' said Toop.

'The Inspector will need to talk to you,' said Frances. 'Your evidence could be very important.'

Toop sighed and hid his face in his hands. 'Oh, what an abominable day this has been!'

Frances wondered about the terrible secret Farrow had been about to confess. Had he murdered Miss Hicks? Had he made away with himself through remorse, unable to live with his crime, or the shame of having sold government secrets, preferring death to the prospect of bringing disgrace to his family? People had taken their own lives for far lesser reasons.

Sharrock emerged. 'Well, he's gone, that's for sure. And it was you who found him Mr Toop?'

Toop nodded. 'Yes, just now. I had hoped to find Farrow here looking after the bicycles, and when I saw the door left open I was worried that he had been careless, and we had had thieves, so I went in.'

'That was very courageous of you, sir, you might have confronted some dangerous men.'

'I suppose I wasn't thinking,' admitted Toop.

'But there was no one else in there?'

'No.'

'Well we'll have to get the names of all the men who we know have been here this afternoon,' said Sharrock.

'Did you find my keys on the body? If so, I should like to have them back.'

'We did, and don't trouble yourself about them Mr Toop, the police will keep all secure. Now I know that Mr Farrow didn't say what it was he felt unhappy about but did you suspect anything? Did he hint at what troubled him?'

Toop uttered a sigh of abject misery. 'I'm sorry to say it, Inspector, but I did have my suspicions.'

'Yes?'

Toop glanced at Frances. 'It's not for the ears of a lady.'

'I think you'll find this lady has very strong ears,' said Sharrock.

'Well, if I must. It is my belief that Farrow was responsible for the murder of Miss Hicks. She had been insinuating that she expected him to marry her. Claimed that she was —' Toop glanced at Frances '— in a certain situation. I know that Mr Goring and Miss Farrow had been about to announce their engagement after the prize-giving, and Miss Hicks might have hoped that she and Farrow would do the same. Perhaps when she made her demands he suddenly lost control of himself and killed her.'

'But you've no proof of this?'

'None at all. But he seemed very contrite and whatever he had done I truly believed that he would make a full confession.'

Sharrock looked unconvinced. 'Why do you think Farrow confided in you?'

'He could hardly have told his father! I suppose I was his closest friend. He knew he could come to me if he had any worries. I try to be helpful to all the club members.'

The Inspector nodded. 'I'm sorry Mr Toop, but I am going to ask you to come into the coach house and show me how you found the body. We have covered it over, so you won't have to look at it.'

Toop groaned but complied, and Frances followed. Sharrock gave her a hard look. 'I have already seen it uncovered,' she said.

They re-entered the coach house where Mayberry had draped the body in a rain cape. 'So,' said Sharrock, 'where would Mr Farrow have got the rope?'

'We keep some in here,' said Toop. 'We use them to rope off areas where races are being held. They are kept on those hooks.'

'And all the members would have known there was rope here?'

'Well, yes.'

'And how was the body when you first found it?'

'Um – the rope had been thrown over the beam,' Toop indicated a thick wooden beam across the width of the coach house. 'And then it was tied to a hook in the wall. Of course I untied it and brought the body down in case there was hope, but it was too late.'

Frances glanced up at the beam, which was about three feet above her head. It was a roughly sawn piece with a square section, and was certainly robust enough to suspend a body. Studying the scene, she saw nothing of any note, and then it came to her mind how often that day she had berated herself, not for failing to observe what was actually there but for not appreciating what was not there and ought to be.

She stared up at the beam once more. 'Where was the rope? In the middle portion of the beam?'

'If I use one of the other ropes, I can show you how it was,' said Toop, helpfully, going to fetch one.

'Not yet,' said Frances. 'If you will allow me, I would like to take a closer look.' She took a large toolbox, placed it on the floor beside the desk, and using it as a step, nimbly mounted the desk, silently thanking the ingenuity of the dressmaker who had crafted her divided skirt. She glanced at Constable Mayberry whose lanky form was several inches taller than the Inspector's. 'Constable, would you be so kind as to join me up here. Inspector, please hand up the toolbox.'

'Oh well now we've had everything,' exclaimed Sharrock, but both the policemen complied with her request. Frances first examined the upper edge of the beam, and then climbed up onto the toolbox. After a few moments, she stepped back down onto the desk and asked Mayberry to take her place. 'Constable, look at the edge of the beam and also at its upper surface. What do you see?' she asked.

Mayberry peered as well as he could. 'I don't see anything, just some dust.'

'Precisely,' said Frances. 'If Mr Farrow really had hanged himself from the beam there would be the marks of a rope. But all we can see is dust, and it is quite undisturbed.'

'It might not have left a mark,' Toop protested. 'How can you know?'

Frances glanced down. 'And I can see one other thing – there, lying on the floor behind the desk. It's a flower.'

It was a little pale patch on the dark earth and Sharrock picked it up.

'I think it's one of the ones Miss Hicks was wearing in her hat,' said Toop. 'Farrow must have had it.'

'Miss Hicks's flowers were pink, this is cream colour,' said Frances. 'It's the flower you were wearing in your buttonhole earlier today.'

'It's been crushed as if torn off in a struggle,' said Sharrock. 'Perhaps you would like to explain that, Mr Toop?'

Toop clapped a hand to his buttonhole. 'I must have dropped it when I lifted the body down.'

'No,' said Frances, 'because I noticed that you were not wearing it earlier, before the body was found.'

'I – er …' said Toop, and then, abruptly, he turned and ran.

Sharrock charged after him while Mayberry and Frances got down from the desk as quickly as they could, only to see Toop disappearing around the side of the lodge on his bicycle and heading for the road.

CHAPTER THIRTY-NINE

Sharrock cursed. 'Mayberry – go after him!'

'Yes, sir!' said the constable, and began to run after Toop.

'Not on foot, you fool – take the other bicycle, man!'

'Oh! Yes sir!' gasped Mayberry and ran to get the machine that Jack had been wheeling.

Toop was not the speediest of riders, but he had youth, experience, weighty stability, and a good start. Mayberry looked understandably alarmed at the Inspector's orders, but seized the bicycle with grim determination.

Frances pulled the trouser fasteners from her reticule and held them out. 'Here – take these.'

Mayberry had already tried to climb onto the bicycle, but it now became obvious that he had never done so before. Not realising that there was a little step that would project him into the saddle, he had grasped the handlebars and tried to vault up from the side by putting his foot on the curved backbone. The result was that the bicycle tilted over and he was sent sprawling on the ground with the machine following. Jack limped up to offer assistance, picking up the bicycle. Mayberry, fortunately unhurt, scrambled to his feet.

'You get on from behind, sir, putting your foot just there,' said Jack, pointing out the step, 'and you hold onto the handlebars, like this, and push with the other foot and pull yourself up. Try again.'

'Right!' said Mayberry, adopting the position as demonstrated, one foot on the step, and hopping valiantly along on the other. This time he was almost able to make contact with the saddle, Jack hobbling along beside him with one steadying hand on the frame, but unable to establish control, he failed to reach the pedals. Once again the machine lurched over, but this time Jack was there to avoid possible injury.

'Don't worry, I think I can do it this time,' gasped Mayberry. With Jack's help he finally managed to mount the machine and got one foot on to a pedal, but steered a violently erratic path into the grass of the carriage drive, where he took a spectacular header.

There was really only one thing to do. Frances attached the trouser fasteners to her own skirts. They didn't enclose all the material, but they were good enough to hold the bulk of it away from the spokes. She ran up, seized the bicycle by the handlebars, pulled it upright, and began pushing it along.

'Miss Doughty, what in the name of blazes do you think you are doing?' shouted Sharrock, 'You shouldn't – you can't —'

Frances vaulted into the saddle and began pedalling harder than she had ever done before.

'Well blow me down!' exclaimed Sharrock.

Toop had by now left the lodge estate through the main gates, and after taking a left turn was heading in the direction of Old Oak Common Lane. When Frances made the turn she could see him well ahead of her, and about to go south. She gripped the handlebars hard, and got up a good rhythm. She had never ridden in the skirts before, but thankfully the fasteners avoided accident, and her long legs sent the machine, which had a much larger wheel than Toop's, bowling along faster than she could have imagined possible.

He was having to slow down to pass over the culvert onto the lane, and she was gaining on him. Behind her she heard the yells of the policemen, running along the street behind her. A fast running man might have been able to keep pace with Toop for a while, but she knew that only a bicyclist had the stamina to catch him.

Toop reached the junction with the lane and began to make the turn south. As he did so, he saw Frances' machine coming up behind him. He looked once and then twice, astonishment spreading over his features as he saw that his pursuer was a woman. Reaching the rougher track of Old Oak Common Lane, he wobbled violently and fought for control. The bicycle careered off the road, bumped over some stones and overturned, propelling its rider onto a thick grassy verge. Toop rolled over, gasping. He whimpered at the sight of his fallen bicycle, some of its more refined attachments having come away or bent out of shape. Frances soon reached the spot and dismounted, having no real idea how she might apprehend him and hoping that the running police would arrive soon.

He clutched at his shiny machine, panting, and Frances saw that one of the ebony handles had become detached, revealing a roll of papers hidden in the hollow steel beneath. 'Mr Toop,' she said, standing over him, 'be sensible, the police will be here soon. You must give yourself up!'

'Never!' he snarled with unexpected savagery. Toop reached into his coat and now it was Frances' turn to be astonished as she found herself facing a gun. There was no time to think, she kicked out as hard as she could, and luckily her boot met his hand, sending the gun flying out of his grasp.

She ran forward to where it had landed on the verge and made a grab for it, but before she could reach it, she felt a surprisingly powerful grip enclose her ankle and jerk her back, and she fell forward onto the grass. She looked around and saw that Toop, his face red, sweating and distorted with anger, had lunged forward and seized her with both hands, and was pulling her away from the weapon. She made a desperate snatch for the gun, but it was just out of her reach. Slowly, tugging fiercely on her ankle, he pulled her bodily towards him. She kicked out hard with her free foot, and felt the heel of her boot make contact with his face. He cried out, but did not let go, and she kicked again and again, each time finding a target, and hearing him scream with pain and rage. One more kick, as hard as she could, and this time there was a crack of breaking bone. To her relief, the grasp on her ankle loosened, and she was able to crawl forward, seize hold of the gun and stand up. Toop was clasping his mouth and nose, blood streaming down his chin. With a howl of desperation, he lunged forward again, his eyes on the gun. She levelled it at him and he paused, wide-eyed with amazement.

'One more move and I will shoot!' she exclaimed.

'Who *are* you?' he gasped. '*What* are you?'

Frances took a deep breath and straightened up to her full height, squaring her shoulders and holding the gun firmly so that he could be in no doubt that she would use it. 'I am Miss Dauntless,' she announced, 'and you, sir, are a prisoner of Her Majesty's Government.'

Behind her, running footsteps approached and there was the sound of a bicycle coming to a halt. Frances dared not take her eyes off the man before her, a man she now knew to be both a killer and a traitor.

'What a wonder you are!' said a familiar voice. It was Mr Grove, who had ridden up on his bicycle, closely followed by Mayberry on foot, with Sharrock bringing up the rear.

Sharrock, stooping to get his breath back, waved a pointing finger at Mayberry, who understood at once what was needed and pulled Toop to his feet and secured him in handcuffs.

'Aaron Toop,' said Sharrock, between gulps of air, 'I am arresting you for the murder of George Farrow.'

'I haven't done anything!' shouted Toop. 'You should be arresting her! She threatened me with a gun! And look what she did,' he added, pointing to his bloody face.

'With good reason,' said Grove. 'And that is my gun, as you well know, since you stole it when your associate Peters attacked me.' He held out his hand and Frances, with some relief, returned it to him.

'I think we may have found Sir Hugo's missing notebooks,' she said, removing the rolled documents from their place of concealment in Toop's bicycle.

'And possibly more than that,' said Grove, taking charge of the papers. He made a further search of the machine, which yielded still more hidden material.

Toop had given up the struggle, and Mayberry was able to march his dejected prisoner along the road to East Acton while Sharrock took possession of the damaged bicycle.

'Well done, Miss Dauntless,' said Grove, calmly. He and Frances retrieved their machines and rode back together as the summer sun began to set.

CHAPTER FORTY

'The thing about Mr Toop and his sort, I've met them before,' said Inspector Sharrock a few days later, as he discussed the events of the race meeting with Frances. There were times when he called her to his office at Paddington Green for an interview, but occasionally when their conversations were intended to be less formal, he came to see her and they enjoyed tea and some of Sarah's excellent pastries. This was the latter situation and they were seated in the parlour at the little round table where Frances interviewed her clients, making short work of a Bakewell tart, freshly made by Sarah from Mrs Pirrie's own recipe. 'They're cowards. I can tell them a mile away. Put them up against a young girl or a smooth-faced weakling like George Farrow, or put a gun in their hands, and they're as brave as you like. Take away the weapon or show them a hard time and all that courage just melts away.' He shook his head. 'Nasty business, though. I have a feeling that you know more about it than anyone will tell me.'

'Has he confessed his crimes?'

'Not yet, but he has been doing a lot of talking to try and save his life. Did you know he had a brother?'

'Yes, a soldier who was killed in Afghanistan.'

'Captain Joshua Toop, hero. It broke his parents' hearts to lose him. They put up a plaque to him in the local church. Toop had to look at it every Sunday. His mother passed away with the word "Joshua"' on her lips.'

'I could see that Mr Toop wanted to give an impression of wealth and success, and I had assumed that this was because of the deficiencies in his size, but now I understand it ran much deeper than that. What he really wanted was his parents' approval, but that all seems to have been directed at his brother. It is hard enough to compete with a living hero, impossible with a deceased one. That was why he turned to crime.' Frances was thoughtful. 'I know that Mrs Toop suffered a long illness before her death. Was she ever prescribed morphine?'

Sharrock smiled. 'Now you're not the only one round here who has bright ideas. We had a word with the Toop family doctor, and yes, she was.'

'Was I correct that the papers found in Mr Toop's bicycle included Sir Hugo Daffin's notebooks?'

'They did. The leather covers had been removed. We found them in the ash bin. And there was a lot of other material that Grove wouldn't let me see. All very secret. Toop claims he had them for safekeeping.'

Frances poured more tea. 'What do you think he will confess to?'

'I suspect that he will admit to killing Farrow, because we have the best evidence against him for that one, but he is hoping for a charge of manslaughter.'

'Really?'

'Yes. He'll most likely claim it all happened in a brainstorm when Farrow confessed to murdering Miss Hicks.' He gave a twist of the mouth. 'No, it doesn't convince me, either. I think they sneaked out one after the other, Toop saying he wanted a private talk, and then he strangled Farrow with the rope. Farrow was a weak link in his little scheme, and Toop must have thought he would talk, especially after Miss Hicks was killed. He had to leave the coach house unlocked, of course, to make the suicide idea convincing.'

'I don't think Farrow did murder Miss Hicks.'

'I'm sure he didn't. She liked to make eyes at him, but that didn't impress him any more than it might have impressed your friend Mr Garton.'

'Ah, I see. I think that she must have noticed something and thought she could make him marry her as the price of silence. Toop liked to say he was always willing to help a friend in trouble, but of course that was how he got people into his power. If Farrow went to Toop about Miss Hicks then Toop would most likely have told Farrow he would pay her to keep quiet, but he killed her instead. I remember that afternoon Farrow taking an interest in something or someone he saw on the field. Thinking about it now it was Miss Hicks speaking to Toop. That was when they made an appointment to meet in secret during the professionals' race. It was easy enough after that to try and put the blame on Jack Linnett. Did Toop have any marks on his hands from the silk ribbon?'

'He had some suspicious looking cuts but he said he got those wrestling with Mr Babbit's bicycle after the collision.'

'Before a large crowd of witnesses,' said Frances. 'How clever! Mr Toop is very adept at thinking fast and avoiding trouble.'

'Talking of fast thinkers, I had an interesting interview recently with Mr Grove. He has associates who seem to be very efficient at unearthing information that those who buried it thought would stay buried. Mr Farrow was sent down from University after a scandal, but left himself open to blackmail. There were compromising letters, I believe. If the General had got wind of it and seen what they contained, Farrow would have lost the allowance he depended on; in fact, his father might even have disowned him altogether. Military men do not forgive that kind of thing. Toop must have seen his chance when he saw that Farrow was upset about something, pretended sympathy for his friend, arranged to buy the letters back, and so got Farrow into his pocket. Farrow then found himself at the mercy of a different kind of blackmailer, and was obliged to pass on information from his father's papers. What Toop did with it after that we may never know. I know what the Home Office thinks.'

'Will Toop admit to getting information from George Farrow?'

'He might, but only if we can accept his story that he was motivated by a desire to advance his father's engineering business, and not the sale of government secrets to a foreign spy.

Still, early days. If we can agree the manslaughter charge the next step will be to hand him over to Mr Grove's men. Toop might deserve to die, but given the chance to live he will have a lot of interesting things to say, and a lot of names to name.'

'And he denies drugging Sir Hugo?'

'He does. I spoke to Sir Hugo yesterday and he remembers Toop coming to see him the evening before the race meeting, so that was probably when he slipped the morphine in the coffee. We're still trying to get information out of Hopper and Peters, who we reckon Toop got to do some of his more menial work. No luck there, but with what we have on the betting fraud it looks like we will get Hopper jailed at long last, not to mention Peters, as well as Babbit and Iliffe, who are in a class all of their own.'

'Fraud and murder?'

Sharrock helped himself to more cake. 'Babbit was the first to go to pieces. He claimed that Iliffe killed Cowdray and he only helped dispose of the body because he thought he would be killed as well. He'll turn Queen's evidence no doubt. Iliffe is saying it was done in self-defence. And the Hammersmith police found Cowdray's body in the drains. Very nasty after all that time, but we're fairly sure it's him. Skull crushed in from behind.'

Frances decided not to ask for further details. 'I read in the newspapers that Mr Ross-Fielder has been committed for trial.'

'Yes, with a very good counsel. He'll get off I reckon.'

'Is Sir Hugo quite well again? He must have been terribly distressed at how the race meeting went, and the loss of several club members.'

'He's well and full of plans to revive the club. But he's back on his bicycle, I'm sorry to say. It'll probably kill him one day.'

'I hope he managed to get to the patent office at last. I look forward to discovering more about his work.'

'Ah, well, that was a bit of a sore subject. He had the idea of improving bicycle tyres by blowing them up with air inside. But he has been told that someone else thought of doing it first and had already taken out a patent for it, so he didn't get one. It probably wouldn't have worked in any case, so he's gone back to fitting those extra wheels. If you ask me the sooner the fashion for bicycling is over the better. Which leads to my asking you how you managed to ride that infernal machine when young Mayberry couldn't? It was almost like you'd done it before.'

'Inspector, haven't you read *Miss Dauntless Rides to Victory*? It's all explained in there,' said Frances teasingly.

'Yes, well that woman is fast in more ways than one so I hope you don't go taking after her. I don't suppose you can tell me now what you were doing at the race meeting? I know you ended up poking your nose into everything but that's just your way. What were you really there for?'

'The sunshine, an excuse to wear a new bonnet, and watching Mr Garton ride in his race. Do I need any more reasons?'

Sharrock grunted. She could see that he was not convinced but accepted that this was the only reply he was likely to receive.

Once Sharrock had departed, Frances settled down to read the latest copy of the *Bayswater Chronicle*, which included the results of the bicycle competitions. Cedric, she noticed, had been awarded the prize for the best turned-out bicycle, and Mr Grove had won Most Sporting Wheelman for his action in giving up a chance of race victory in order to assist a fellow bicyclist. The betrothal was also announced of club captain Rufus Goring to Miss Sybil Vance.

Sarah arrived with the news that the date for her wedding with Professor Pounder had been set. It was to take place the following month. 'I'll be living downstairs to begin with, but we'll need to start looking for somewhere else.'

'Mr Garton will be returning to Italy before long,' said Frances. 'I'll be very sorry to see him go but his apartment will be available.'

'It's a bit fancy, if you know what I mean,' said Sarah. 'Anyhow, we'll find something. But whatever happens we won't be far away. I don't ever mean to be far from you.' She put a letter on the table. 'This just came. Don't know what it signifies, but I don't think it can be good.'

Frances picked up the envelope, which was addressed to her and was printed with the name 'Marsden and Wheelock, Solicitors'. 'Nothing that comes out of that office can ever be good,' she agreed, and opened it with some trepidation.

CHAPTER FORTY-ONE

'So we meet again,' said Timothy Wheelock, the new member of the infernal partnership of Bayswater solicitors Marsden and Wheelock. When he had been employed as Mr Rawsthorne's humble clerk, his small office had resembled a spider's lair, cluttered with cobwebbed papers and dusty bundles of juicy morsels waiting to be savoured. In his new incarnation he sat like a potentate at a brightly polished desk, surrounded by the steely glimmer of tall locked cabinets. He was immaculately dressed in a black suit and snowy white collar and his bronze locks had been shorn so they stood up like wires, but his fingers, with their array of knuckley gold rings, still bore the dark stains of his former occupation.

'I must congratulate you on your advancement,' said Frances, politely. 'Such things are not achieved without hard work. And your forthcoming nuptials – how happy you must be! I trust your betrothed is well?'

'Thank you, yes, she is as lovely as a picture. I can't wait for the wedding day, but then, what man can?' He grinned, showing the blackened inner lips and teeth of an inveterate consumer of ink. Mr Wheelock liked ink and that was one thing about him that would never change.

'I am not sure what business we can have,' said Frances, who had been astonished to receive the letter requesting her presence, a letter that had given no hint as to the reason for the interview.

'It's not personal,' said Wheelock. 'I'm not about to be hanged, and neither are you. Let us be grateful for that.'

'I take it Mr Marsden is not here,' said Frances, 'or I doubt that I would be given so much as the time of day. He wants nothing to do with me, not so much out of hatred as contempt.'

'No, he's a bit under the weather is my future pa-in-law; not been himself much lately, so he leaves a lot of the work to me.' Wheelock patted an envelope, the only item that sat on the desk in front of him. 'Now you might imagine that I would have had no communication of late with my former employer – your one-time solicitor and trusted confidante, Mr Rawsthorne, but there you would be mistaken. He is having a very unhappy time of it in prison, and I have agreed to look after his interests which are very – ah – complicated, shall we say, what with the bankruptcy hearings still in progress and all.'

'I would have thought you had little to gain from assisting him,' said Frances.

Wheelock chuckled, a noise like a bag of knives being rattled. 'Oh, but I know his business better than he does himself. There's always something secret put by, seeds planted, growing on the quiet, fruit to be taken when ripe.'

'I don't see what this has to do with me,' said Frances. 'Please come to the point.'

Wheelock leaned back in his chair and rubbed his inky fingertips together. 'The point is that fresh funds have recently come in. A will, made by a former client, an elderly widow who once had reason to be grateful to Mr Rawsthorne, and no family to inherit her fortune. He would have liked to have drawn on her while she was still alive, but her late brother put away everything safe for her long ago, where even Rawsthorne couldn't get his hands on it. Once he was disgraced she might have changed her will, but she was no longer competent to do so. It was tucked away nice and safe, waiting for her to die. And die she did, just last week, and that's when I stepped in. She left most of her fortune to charity but a nice little packet, rather bigger than anticipated, went to Rawsthorne. Not enough to meet all his debts, but the result is that there is money to be paid to his creditors, of whom you are one.'

Wheelock slid the envelope across the desk to Frances. 'You'll find a cheque and all the paperwork in there.'

Frances opened the envelope. When she saw the amount on the cheque she felt a little lightheaded. 'I – will consult my solicitor, Mr Bramley, to see that it is all in order,' she said.

'You do that. I ain't concerned.' He grinned again. 'Oh, and in case you was wondering – there won't be any more.'

It was not all the funds that Frances had lost, but it was more than enough.

'Don't spend it all at once,' said Wheelock.

Frances smiled. 'On the contrary, I think that is exactly what I will do.' She rose to her feet. 'I doubt that we will ever have business with each other again.'

'We never know what the future holds,' he said.

Frances could hardly rest until the cheque had been honoured. There were sufficient funds to settle all her concerns for the future, and to her delight, the owner of the house in Westbourne Park Road was still willing to sell. Her offer to purchase was accepted. Sarah and Professor Pounder made their wedding plans, the lady on the top floor moved away and Tom and Ratty took the apartment. The housekeeper, Mrs Embleton, and the maid, who had been concerned that the new ownership might mean a change in arrangements, were both pleased and relieved to learn that Frances wished them to remain. It would be a family home at last.

There was only one worry on her mind, and Frances at last broached the never-before-spoken-of subject of Tom Smith's father. To her surprise, Sarah was not offended by the question. 'I always wondered why you never asked me,' she said. 'He was one of my brother Jeb's boxing friends. I was thirteen, he was twenty-five. That's all there is to say, really.'

'Only, I wouldn't want you to spoil your present happiness, now that you have found a good man, by trying to find

Tom's father and making him pay for what he did,' said Frances anxiously.

Sarah chuckled. 'I might have done that long ago, but he was married with three children. Anyhow, he got a bad beating in the ring quite some years back. Addled his brain. He was good for nothing after that. The wife and children, they got looked after by the other boxing men, so they didn't want for anything. He died not long ago and the widow got married again. You met her once.'

'I did? When was that?'

'When you came with me and Pounder to see the family. She married my brother Jeb.'

'So who —?' Frances stopped. She had been about to ask the name of the man who had been the last opponent of Tom's father, and then she decided that she would rather not know.

CHAPTER FORTY-TWO

On a clear and bright summer morning, Miss Frances Doughty, lady detective and agent of Her Majesty's Government, was taking the air in Hyde Park when, as if by chance, she met a gentleman of respectable demeanour.

'Good morning Miss Doughty,' said the gentleman, as he sat beside her on the bench.

'Good morning, Mr Grove.'

'I have made a full report to my superiors on the events at the Bayswater Bicycle Club race meeting, and I am pleased to say that they have pronounced themselves very impressed by your contribution.'

Frances was both relieved and surprised. 'And this is despite the fact that I overstepped my instructions?'

He smiled. 'Not so much overstepped but bounded over them with great energy; however, I have assured my masters that what you did was both correct and necessary. Obeying orders is all very well, but sometimes one must use initiative. It is initiative that marks out the extraordinary from the ordinary. Importantly, from my point of view, I doubt that I would be alive now were it not for you.'

'You saved my life once – I was obliged to return the favour. But tell me, has Mr Toop now told you everything you needed to know?'

Mr Grove paused before he spoke again. 'He has told us all that he is going to. Once he was guaranteed his life he admitted to the killing of George Farrow. As you guessed, he lured him into the coach house on the pretext of a private conference, strangled him with a rope and then pretended that Farrow had hanged himself out of remorse. He did, however, continue to insist that Farrow confessed to the murder of Miss Hicks, since that provided him with a convenient excuse for his anger. We are sure that her killer was actually Toop, but I doubt that we can prove it. He also admitted that Farrow supplied him with information about government projects, which he gleaned from his father's papers. As we surmised, Toop initially earned Farrow's gratitude by dealing with a blackmailer after he was sent down from university, and then effectively became one himself. He would not admit to being a traitor, of course, but then we could never have arranged clemency for that.'

'So he would not name his masters?'

'No, and he never will. He was found hanged in his cell yesterday morning.'

'What – suicide?'

'It was hard to tell. Either his associates silenced him before he could betray them, or he realised that hanging would be a more merciful death than they would grant him if he did.'

'His poor father,' said Frances. 'I can hardly imagine what he must be suffering.'

'He will never know the full story. That is all we can do to soften his grief.' Grove rose to his feet and offered Frances his arm. 'Shall we walk?'

She rested her hand on his arm and they strolled in the direction of the Italian water gardens.

'I have been empowered to make you a formal proposition.'

'Oh?'

'Until now, your work as a government agent has been little more than the transmission of messages, and being watchful. You have carried out these tasks admirably well, and made an extremely favourable impression. This last mission, however, showed that you are capable of very much more. I myself have been certain of it for some time.'

'When you say, "much more" …?'

'There are missions which would be far more demanding of your energy, courage and resolve than the ones you have been given before. You would be expected to travel, take risks, and think quickly and decisively.'

This was both flattering and disconcerting at the same time. 'And you think I am equal to this?'

'You will be,' he assured her. 'There are new skills you will need to acquire, but I can teach you those, and I know you will be a fast learner. You are precisely the kind of individual we have always looked for; intelligent and brave, a free woman of good report. You are already highly competent with medicines, can ride a bicycle, speak in sign language and have no fear of guns, so that is a good start. There will be some dangers, but you wouldn't be on your own; in fact, I have requested that we should work together. I did have one idea – when the Filleter appears again he will be a broken man in need of support. He could have a sister, the Needlewoman. Of course, you would have to cover yourself in mud for the disguise.'

'Really?' said Frances, wondering what that would be like. 'Well – I suppose —'

'No, I'm sorry, that last part was my little joke,' he said quickly.

'Oh, that was very wicked of you,' she exclaimed. 'I was about to agree.'

They both laughed. 'But the rest I meant in all seriousness. Do you need time to consider it?'

Frances needed almost no time at all. A door was opening before her, and behind it was another world, one that only a few years ago she would never have dreamed existed. What lay in her future she could not know, but she wanted to find out. 'I would not like to abandon the detective agency, but I suppose that would serve as a means of concealing my other work.'

He smiled with relief. 'It would. So you agree? Please say you do.'

'I do,' she said.

'I am delighted to hear it.'

They reached the Italian gardens and watched the fountains throwing bright sprays of water into the air like showers of diamonds. For a long time nothing was said, and then, impulsively,

Grove took her hand. 'Shall I tell you a secret? This is not about the service, it is about me.'

'Please do.'

'I have admired you from the very first day we met. I appreciate that since I was then masquerading as the Filleter, I would have made an extremely poor impression. In fact, it was obvious that you found me repellent, as all right-thinking persons ought to have done. But I could not forget you. I could not stop myself thinking about you. And then came the day when you and Miss Smith arrested me because you thought that I was the Face-slasher and had murdered your friend. You pointed a gun at me, and there were tears of anger running down your face. I could see that you had never held a gun before, but it made no difference to my danger. You were unfaltering; determined; magnificent. I had no doubt that if I made the smallest error of judgement you would shoot me dead on the spot. But I also knew that if you allowed me to live, that I wanted us to have a future together; that you were the woman with whom I wished to spend the rest of my life.'

Frances hardly knew what to say. She knew that he was ruthless, but ruthless in doing the right thing. She knew that he was dangerous, but only to those with good reason to fear the law.

He seemed abashed by her hesitation. 'Perhaps it is too soon to expect an answer, but may I live in hope?'

She smiled. 'Yes, you may.'

No more words were needed. He slipped his arm about her waist and it was as if it had always been meant to be there, and then he kissed her. It was the first time Frances Doughty had ever been kissed, and she knew it would not be the last.

Author's Notes

I am greatly indebted to the online library of the Veteran Cycle Club (www.v-cc.org.uk), whose wealth of material has been both illuminating and invaluable. Any factual errors in this book are solely those of the author.

The dandy-horse, also known as the hobby-horse, invented by Karl Drais in 1817, was the first two-wheeled vehicle. It had no pedals and was powered by the rider's walking action.

The velocipede or boneshaker, first produced in the 1860s, had two wheels of similar size and was driven by pedals directly attached to the front wheel. The development of lighter frames and tensioned wire spokes enabled a substantial increase in the size of the front wheel and the evolution of the high-wheeler.

The vehicle we now call the 'penny-farthing' was in its heyday (c.1875 to 1885) known simply as a 'bicycle'. Following the introduction of the safety bicycle in 1885, the high-wheeler was often referred to as the 'ordinary'. The safety bicycle, with wheels of approximately equal size and a pedal-driven chain drive, revolutionised the cycling experience and opened up the activity for women. The emergence of cycling outfits for women meant that, unencumbered by long skirts, they were able to ride the high-wheeler. The 'penny-farthing' faded from popularity but retains its status as an iconic invention and symbol of Victorian adventurousness. It lives on in races and polo matches that can still be enjoyed today.

The machines displayed in the parade at the race meeting described in chapter nineteen all existed in 1882. For more information please visit the following websites:
www.unicycle.uk.com
www.pennyfarthingclub.com

The pneumatic tyre was invented by Robert William Thomson, who patented it in 1847, but it was never manufactured. It was developed and first produced by John Boyd Dunlop in 1888. Prior to that, attempts had been made to use the pneumatic principle to make more comfortable saddles. Bicycles were first used by the military in the 1890s.

Under the Stage Carriage Act of 1832, 'furious driving' became an offence punishable by a fine of £5, and applied to carriage drivers or horsemen riding in such as way as to endanger any passenger or person. In 1879 it was held that bicycles could be considered carriages in law, and cyclists were regularly fined for furious driving. (Reported in the *Times*, page 6, 26 March 1879) The law against furious driving remains in force today.

The *Wheel World* of August 1882 reported that the inventor Thomas Alva Edison was about to revolutionise bicycling after experimenting with electricity and a 60-inch wheel bicycle, the power source to be stored in the backbone, providing both driving power and light, and was about to patent the invention.

The *Volunteer Service Review* of 15 September 1882 reported the approval of the War Office for the formation of a Volunteer Bicycle Corps.

The Battle of Maiwand in the Anglo–Afghan War took place on 17 July 1880.

Although Frances wasn't able to visit the exhibition of ladies' hygienic wearing apparel, a report of the event can be found in the *Times* of 22 March 1882 on page 10. Amelia Bloomer did not invent the garment that bears her name – loose ankle-length trousers topped by a skirt – but she was a strong advocate of less restrictive clothing for women. Bloomers were briefly adopted in the 1850s but wearers were ridiculed, and the fashion was overtaken by the crinoline.

Police Sergeant Thomas Hambling and surgeon George Barraclough, both aged 40, are listed in the 1881 census for Acton.

The Bayswater and Oakwood Bicycle Clubs mentioned are fictional, but are typical of the many clubs in existence in the 1880s. The Mill Hill, West Kensington and Chiswick clubs did exist and I have described their uniforms as mentioned in the *Cyclist and Wheel World Annual* of 1882.

East Acton and the other locations mentioned are real; however, Springfield Lodge and Goldsmiths Cricket Ground are fictional. Acton Cricket Club was founded in 1908, renting land from the Goldsmith's Company. The Acton Brass Ensemble is not intended to represent the Acton Town Band of 1882.

The Italian water gardens with its marble basins and fountains is often said to have been a gift from the Prince Consort to Queen Victoria. It was constructed in the 1860s from an idea he proposed not long before his death.

The construction of Wormwood Scrubs Prison commenced in 1874 and continued, carried out by its prisoners, until its completion in 1891.

Cedric's friends, Miles and Fletcher, are probably not the same Miles and Fletcher who were living at 1 Tite Street in the 1881 census, where Oscar Wilde was boarding.

About The Author

LINDA STRATMANN is a freelance writer, and Vice Chair of the prestigious CWA. She has a degree in psychology and a life-long interest in true crime. She is the author of numerous fiction and non-fiction titles including seven Frances Doughty Mysteries and three Mina Scarletti Mysteries. She lives in Walthamstow, London.

Also By The Author

Chloroform: The Quest for Oblivion

*Cruel Deeds and Dreadful Calamities: The Illustrated Police News
1864–1938*

Essex Murders

Gloucestershire Murders

*Greater London Murders: 33 True Stories of Revenge, Jealousy,
Greed & Lust*

Kent Murders

Middlesex Murders

More Essex Murders

*Notorious Blasted Rascal: Colonel Charteris and the Servant Girl's
Revenge*

*Fraudsters and Charlatans: A Peek at Some of History's Greatest
Rogues*

Whiteley's Folly: The Life and Death of a Salesman

The Marquess of Queensberry: Wilde's Nemesis

The Secret Poisoner: A Century of Murder

In the Frances Doughty Mystery Series

The Poisonous Seed: A Frances Doughty Mystery
The Daughters of Gentlemen: A Frances Doughty Mystery
A Case of Doubtful Death: A Frances Doughty Mystery
An Appetite for Murder: A Frances Doughty Mystery
The Children of Silence: A Frances Doughty Mystery
Death in Bayswater: A Frances Doughty Mystery
A True and Faithful Brother: A Frances Doughty Mystery

In the Mina Scarletti Mystery Series

Mr Scarletti's Ghost: A Mina Scarletti Mystery
The Royal Ghost: A Mina Scarletti Mystery
An Unquiet Ghost: A Mina Scarletti Mystery